THE
FOREST HORSES

THE FOREST HORSES

a novel

Byrna Barclay

COTEAU BOOKS

© Byrna Barclay, 2010

All rights reserved. No part of this publication may be reproduced, stored in a retrieval system or transmitted, in any form or by any means, without the prior written consent of the publisher or a licence from The Canadian Copyright Licensing Agency (Access Copyright). For an Access Copyright licence, visit www.accesscopyright.ca or call toll free to 1-800-893-5777.

These stories are works of fiction. Names, characters, places, and incidents either are the product of the author's imagination or are used fictitiously. Any resemblance to actual persons, living or dead, is coincidental.

Edited by Jack Hodgins
Designed by Tania Craan
Printed and bound in Canada at Friesens

Library and Archives Canada Cataloguing in Publication

Barclay, Byrna
    The forest horses / Byrna Barclay.

ISBN 978-1-55050-447-7

    I. Title.

PS8553.A7618F67 2010   C813'.54   C2010-903839-8

10 9 8 7 6 5 4 3 2 1

2517 Victoria Avenue
Regina, Saskatchewan
Canada   S4P 0T2

AVAILABLE IN CANADA FROM:
Publishers Group Canada
9050 Shaughnessy Street
Vancouver, BC, Canada   V6P 6E5

Coteau Books gratefully acknowledges the financial support of its publishing program by: the Saskatchewan Arts Board, the Canada Council for the Arts, the Government of Canada through the Canada Book Fund, the Government of Saskatchewan through the Creative Economy Entrepreneurial Fund, the Association for the Export of Canadian Books and the City of Regina Arts Commission.

For Kostja and Sashenka
and
the memory of
Signe Maria Linnea Tares neé Bjonlin of Livelong.

Where are you flying, proud horse
And where will your hooves fall?
> – Pushkin, an ode to Peter
> the Great's bronze horse

It is not Leningrad which had been frightened by death. It was death which was frightened by Leningrad.
> – from Olga Berggolt's diary
> *The 900 Days*, by Harrison E. Salisbury

Bolsheviks must not go down the Jacobin path to self-destruction. We must never kill our own.
> – Lenin

Leningrad, Winter 1945

Under the creaking helm of winter soldiers circle the city, tanks gather speed in the dark.
 Inside, they lock their doors to troops certain to come, to boots bruising the snow. Racket of guns and doom of bombs blast their fear into the night. They build a fire of unforgettable books, tell old stories of love never on land. She wants wings and a voice, he, flying hooves and silence.
 A wick in a pool of oil, empty in a white light, their bowls.
 Her hair smells of snow, his of the smoke of sunrise.
 They wait for God to remember their names.

This is the Svetlov story, a tale of four journeys: Lena's and Pytor's, Maryushka's, and finally Signe's.

Pytor's and Maryushka's began with an escape from a brick factory for children.

Lena's story started on a Swedish island when she carelessly forgot to close a gate, and freed a herd of prehistoric ponies.

Half a century apart, Lena and her daughter Signe travelled to Russia, but for different reasons and with different endings.

Signe's flight from Canada to Russia was triggered by a bird, a robin fallen from its nest.

Signe

St. Petersburg, June 21, 2004

STILL UNSURE OF THE WISDOM OF RETURNING to the place of her birth – it was a hasty decision and unlike her – Signe deplanes in the early morning quiet of St. Petersburg, and follows grim-faced Russian business men and other flight-fatigued tourists to the oddly silent lines through Customs, and after having her passport stamped by a uniformed officer who barely glances at her travel agency name tag, she enters a small reception area where she is met by Intrav staff wearing red jackets and bearing red signs shaped like flags.

With ninety other passengers, she's hustled onto a bus that will take them to a riverboat, a kind of floating hotel that will, after four days in the city, tour the Russian river system. At the moment, she sees herself as the only Canadian woman travelling alone, judging by the couples bearing carry-on cases with stars and stripes identity tags. Signe's, of course, is a red maple leaf.

When the bus leaves the airport, a silence that has nothing to do with jet lag falls over the passengers and envelops Signe. No single-family dwellings. Mile after mile of slums. When the Intrav guide finally speaks, she says the post-war tenements each house at least one thousand families. She's a local blonde beauty with rouged cheeks and lips as bright as her red jacket. Though Signe has not heard them call one another by name, the tourists seem shocked by geographic and cultural distance into an instant coming together, in a sudden sadness laced with a collective notion of economic superiority. Leaning against each other, they stare through windows in need of a good scrubbing with vinegar and newspapers.

In a lovely but thick accent that reminds Signe of her Aunt Maryushka's struggle with English, the guide says that Russians hate conformity and resist it. Maybe that explains the failure of the Soviet governance. Cracked or broken apartment windows, warped panes, crumbling cement. Washing on lines strung across balconies. The guide points out the smaller, five-storey buildings built by Stalin after the War to house the survivors of the siege of Leningrad. They look worse than low-cost housing for welfare recipients and the mentally ill in Signe's home in Regina, Canada. Yet, if her parents had stayed in Russia after the Second World War, Signe might be living in a one-room flat right here. Maybe her daughter, Sasha, would still be alive, her son well and whole. Best not to dwell on impossibilities.

Only five years old when her mother and father and Aunt Maryushka left Russia for a homestead in Saskatchewan's northern bushland, Signe has few memories of her early home in Russia, the clearest of being hoisted onto a small pony by her father and led around a barnyard. He was angry when she fell off and landed in the dust. Her mother rushed from a large log house, dropped to her knees, and when Signe sat up, dizzy but not badly hurt, Mama said, *Thank the Lord*. Papa hauled her up, sat her roughly on the pony's bare back, thrust the reins into her hands and said, *She was born on the ice*, talking about Signe as if she were not there.

She didn't understand what he meant, and was afraid to ask because she suffered what she believed was an insult again and again later in Canada: when she was afraid to hike three miles down the tracks to Patchgrove School and cross the railway bridge – *You were born on the ice* –; when she was afraid to swim in the murky Turtle River or skate on it in winter lest the ice crack – *You were born on the ice* –; when she was terrified of storms – *You were born on the ice*. She thought it meant she was a cold person, one who could never make friends. A cowardly cur. Spoken in Russian, it sounded like the growl of a wolf ready to snap her head off with its sharp teeth. What could be expected of a child born on ice? It was all part of the mystery of the adult world and she feared punishment should she question the special meaning of the insult.

On streets veering beyond exits from the freeway, cars and trucks and vans look as if they were resurrected from junk yards. She feels as if she's weighted down with cinder blocks, the guide's memorized statistics about post-Soviet economy indecipherable, like neume notations, that musical alphabet found in her father's Orthodox songbooks.

Far removed from Regina built on a massive pile of buffalo bones, this is the city Peter the Great erected on the bones of Swedish prisoners after the Northern War, Signe's first known ancestor likely among those forced into labour, according to Aunt Maryushka, though her stories of the old country were so far-fetched and full of contradictions Signe often doubted the truth of many of them. If Maryushka and Pytor were orphans of the State who barely even knew their last name and went by the name of Svetlov because their father had, maybe, once owned land, how could Maryushka know anything about her ancestors?

Aunt Maryushka's one regret involved long lamentations late into too many nights to suit young Signe. She never returned to see her homeland healed after the siege of Leningrad. *Too old I am now to go so you do it, for me, yes,* she said the very morning before she wandered into the pasture looking for edible roots and flowers and stumbled onto a swarm of wasps burrowing underground to avoid the coming of a long cold winter. Her dying was long and slow, the angry swellings rendering her face unrecognizable. Her last words to Signe were: *Go home.* And she didn't mean return to Regina, or even to the Livelong homestead. That was on October 8, 1975.

SIGNE REMEMBERS THE DATE only too well. It was her mother's birthday and the farm and town folk who always travelled miles for the after-harvest celebration ended up at a funeral instead. Her father was inconsolable and when her mother sent him to the root cellar to fetch a sack of potatoes and he didn't return for two hours, Lena sent Signe to fetch him. Behind a barrel of salted jackfish he had found Maryushka's stash of potato peelings, corn husks, peapods, even shavings from carrots she had saved in a washtub instead of throwing the slop to the pigs. He held the tub on his lap as if it were a child needing comfort after a bad dream. Instead of trying to take it away from her father, Signe squatted on the dirt floor, leaned her head against her father's leg and wept too; and that is how Lena found them.

SIGNE

Signe is glad her Aunt Maryushka is no longer there to hear about Signe's first impression of her aunt's home, though she realizes that she won't be able to ask her what she thinks of the recent changing of the city's name from Leningrad back to St. Petersburg, a sign of the fall of communism. Maryushka let everyone know she had been a faithful Party member, which always caused her brother to go days without speaking to her.

Now, even the guide is silent, the only sounds the swish-whoosh of passing cars and the rattle of old trucks that look like their hubcabs are coming loose and tires will blow any moment.

These monstrous slums and dilapidated apartment dwellings would not have been here when Signe's family left Russia for Canada. Always her father's spoken hope and prayers before the Red Corner of the Livelong house in Saskatchewan was for a better life for Signe. He offered thanks for his small plot of rugged land so rock-bound it yielded little enough to keep his Russian wolf from the door of the homestead. He said he never looked back, yet the evening he left Signe, he spoke through his morphine-induced delirium and said, *I've been riding horseback all day across the ice.* Unlike Maryushka, he didn't tell Signe to go to Russia and find her icy self. When he left his homeland he was finished and done with it, yet he was a sentimental man with Signe's mother. In summer, every morning after milking the Herefords he picked wild roses in the pasture for Lena to find in the henhouse when she gathered eggs.

With no children of her own, Maryushka was like a second mother to Signe. She taught her how to make *blini* (a kind of pancake), *pryaniki* (gingerbread cake in the shape of animals, usually a bear or wolf), and *kulich* (plaited Easter bread frosted with the letters XB). She told Signe olden-day stories while picking Russian thistle encroaching into her rock garden. *Thistle cures disease and aching heart of love,* she would say. *Boil it, wax it, and wear it on trip to Russia!* She made a garland of the purple flowers for Signe to wear like the headdress of a fairy-tale princess, not just for everyday playtime, but also when Signe left the Livelong farm in northern Saskatchewan for university in Saskatoon, where she studied Russian literature and became so obsessed with the mysteries of those tales she ended up with two degrees, one in education and finally a masters that now enables her to teach at the university in Regina and so put bread and salt on Tapani's table.

The Russian thistle tiara now lies at the bottom of the old immigrant's steamer trunk in the attic of the homestead built by Pytor for Lena among other relics: Lena's green-glass apple; Pytor's fox-fur cap, with flaps; a violin wrapped in a mothy rabbit skin; and her father's cross, which her mother had taken from his neck when Pytor died after being kicked in the head by a stud horse while trying to help it mount a skitterish mare.

Finally, Maryushka's waxed thistle crumbled into dust in Lena's hands when she tried to retrieve it from the trunk. *Dushenka, vyso proidyot,* she always said in the comfort time, just before sleep. *My Little Soul, everything will pass.*

But Aunt Maryusnka had lied to the child. This pain of losing her own daughter, Alexandra, and living with her brain-damaged son, Tapani, never goes away, never leaves Signe, not even in her sleep.

Leaning her travel-weary head against the dusty and spotted window of the coach, Signe worries the maple leaf identity tag on her carry-on bag, flipping it until its plastic tie hurts her forefinger and its smacking sound irritates her raw nerves. Go to Russia? She doubts the wisdom of this foolish venture, and blames her son for driving her away, in search of a family myth with an ending that she fears will offer her little peace.

Two weeks ago, she tried to call someone – she can't even remember now if it was a friend or cousin or colleague. She dialed a wrong number, and a stranger answered, "Jesus loves you!"

Signe yelled, "He has a lousy way of showing it!" and slammed down the telephone so hard it hit the terrazzo tile with a crack that sounded like a bat hitting a baseball. When the receiver broke into two pieces the line was cut and with it the angry tone so like wasps disturbed in their nest. With fists pressed against her mouth, she looked through the glass patio doors: Tapani still on the deck sipping lemonade, his scarred face livid in profile, his brow heavy and bent with care, though he watched Pusskin leaping high, higher than the wooden fence. The cat caught a fledgling robin between its paws, stunning it. It fell onto the grass with a sickening plop, and Pusskin leapt upon it, while the adult robins swooped down and perched on a lawn chair, screeching in a futile attempt to distract the cat away from its prey. Pusskin wasn't hungry, and he lay on top of the bird, batting it with one paw each time it squawked. Sweat glistened on Tapani's forehead, and turning his head towards the kitchen, his eyes looked glassy, vacant, without eyelashes or eyebrows to soften the spectral stare. Grabbing her oven mitts, Signe rushed out to rescue the baby bird, pulled Pusskin up by the scruff of his neck, dropped him onto the deck, pushed him into the kitchen and slid shut the screen patio door. Then, returning to the stunned bird, she picked it up and set it on the highest branch of her flowering crab to recover its senses.

"Good going, Mum," Tapani said, then suddenly jumped out of the lawn chair with a warning cry that always reminded Signe of the shriek of a weasel in a woodpile when the trap snaps shut on its leg. Tapani cleared the deck with a single leap and put his fist through the screened patio door, the sound of wire mesh tearing her son's skin like a velcro tab on one of his running shoes. It ripped open her own frayed nerves.

He would retain no memory of the incident. While Signe tweezed bits of wire from her son's flesh before applying pressure with gauze to stop the bleeding, then dabbed antibiotic salve on the cuts, and finally wrapped the hand with a bandage, Tapani sobbed as if he were still a child of thirteen. Control, all choices of behaviour and consequences were lost to him so many years ago.

When Signe later told Tapani's doctor what she yelled to the stranger on the telephone, he strongly suggested she needed a rest. Why not take a trip? But where could she go, and how could she leave her son? He gave her the name of a woman who offered respite for families by taking people like Tapani into her home.

Go to Russia? It isn't as if it's something she always wanted to do for her career as an academic, though she had initially told her advisor that a grant or fellowship to enable her to see the places of the Russian literary masters she taught – Pushkin and Tolstoy – would enrich her lecture series. After the accident, leaving her son for any holiday seemed impossible. Leaving her bed in the middle of the afternoon when Tapani woke up from his nap was almost more than she could manage. Unable to taste food, not even the cardamon of her Swedish mother, winter and summer she huddled under the hood of her parka and brooded on the deck, the smoke from her chains of cigarettes blurring with the hoarfrost. And then, after the morning of the bird, when she was afraid she might collapse – and then who would look after Tapani? – she heard her father's voice mingling with the brushing of spruce boughs against the side of the house: *If you make yourself a canal, someone will pour water through you.* The words belonged to a wise man her father had been blessed to know in Russia from the time he escaped from the state orphanage. Father Viktor was a prophet of old, a *staret*, he said, and he helped Pytor survive life beneath the streets of Leningrad. Signe was unhappy at the time, it may have been boy trouble or the simple restlessness of a farm girl wanting to leave for the wider knowledge of the world that beckoned with the promise of studies in the city. Quoting Father Viktor, Papa Pytor said, *Your misfortune is in your own vegetable patch, now go weed it with your mama.*

Signe has forgotten the reason her father told her about Father Viktor, but she became obsessed quickly with the idea of going to Russia to find such an Old Believer to help her overcome her grief, something not even Tapani's psychiatrist has been able to accomplish. He would encourage her to stop day-dreaming about it and act on the impulse, but be open to a less simple answer or even another source of enlightenment.

And now, on this coach taking her through the concrete maze of highways and streets of St. Petersburg, she can imagine the Old Believer in the cloudless sky of the white night of Russia:

Carrying a staff, he emerges from the wilderness – perhaps on the island of Kizhi, a destination of the tour and once a refuge for Lena and Pytor. He wears patched clothes, old felt boots, a white kaftan. His flowing beard of Mozhik – just like her father's – and his long hair are the marks of honour, of a prophet. He wears chains and in a thunderous Groza voice he denounces injustices, indifferent to dead czars, old Soviet bosses, and new Russian capitalists. And then he speaks to Signe: *Let your hair grow long again. Plait it with red ribbons and wear a* kokusknik, *a high-peaked headdress made of river pearls to hide your hair from strangers. It will bring you good fortune.*

Blind, he senses her trouble, the stench of her grief as strong as algae-clogged Wascana Creek on a hot, windless day before the lake was dredged, deepened and refilled with fresh water. Without hearing her story, he says, *The truth has seven sides.*

Signe cannot complete the vision because she knows the homilies erupt from her past, spoken by her Aunt Maryushka. And that's why she's here, in the place of beginning for the Svetlovs. When she finds him, this imagined holy fool, he might not speak English, for he will only know the Language of Bells that in Russian literature sound the alarm of siege or revolution, but to her aunt and father church bells in their homeland merely warned of snowstorms.

She remembers a passage from the Bible worn thin by her father's work-blistered hands: *Peace I leave with you; my peace I give unto you.* Signe has yet to find any degree of peace, and she struggles to remember the part about fear. *Let not your heart be troubled, neither let it be afraid.*

The bus crosses a broad traffic bridge, with Victorian lamp-posts flickering out as if a lamplighter of old snuffs the candles. The four arms of the Neva river form a silver-grey marshy delta, an archipelago of islands and dark forests that Signe has read about but cannot see from the window of the coach. At the Gulf of Finland the Neva flows into the sea. She has no sense of direction yet, and this fills her old farm-girl self with unease, lest it prevent her from finding her way home again, a lesson hammered into her each day while hiking three miles down the railway track to Patchgrove School. She allows the coach to carry her towards docks where the tour will join a Russian riverboat that will remain docked for four days before leaving the city of Peter.

Over half a century ago – sixty-three years ago today – somewhere along this river, a coal barge bearing stolen ponies from the island of Gotland dropped anchor, and Signe's Swedish mother arrived in Leningrad.

She had come from the Swedish island of Gotland on Midsummer's Eve.

Lena always said: *After that day, nothing was ever the same again.*

Lena

Gotland, June 21, 1941

FOREVER AFTER, LENA WILL REMEMBER *Midsommarafton,* The Day That Never Ends, not so much as the holiday she should have spent in Visby, dancing around the maypole, but as the eternal white nights of Russia and the later starvation that seemed endless.

But here on the Lojsta moor of the Baltic island of Gotland, she believes that when the sun refuses to set and boys light bonfires, join hands with the farmers' daughters, and leap over the sparking embers, then promises made will never be broken; and her own story will have its true beginning – maybe with a Bertil from the mainland, or a Lars on holiday from studying archeology – not agriculture! – at the University of Stockholm, or even a handsome stranger from Malmö who will take her away from boring Gotland.

Ja, to be sure, Lena Maria Björnsson, only daughter of Gustaf and Carolina, owners of the Björnsson Stud-farm and caretakers of Gotland's forest horses for the Agricultural Society, wants her own story, not unlike her old mother's, just her very own, one that has nothing – and everything – to do with Gotland's forest horses, the prehistoric *russ* that have wandered the wooded Lojsta moors for longer than anyone can remember.

Maybe Tjelvar, the First Man, brought the horses to Gotland when it was bewitched. The island sank into the sea by day and rose again at night, but when Tjelvar brought fire it never sank again. Lena loves that story, and when her mother scoffs at it and says, *The Gotlänning believe there are lords above the hawk too,* Lena says, *It's true!* The story's told in the *Guta Saga.*

Her mother always says that for her it had all started with a rare, blue forest horse when the Björnsson brothers from Mölltorp in Västergotland descended on Carolina's home village of Hannas in Skåne, stole the hearts of the woodcarver's daughters and returned to their horse-trader father with nothing to show for it, except bruises inflicted by the local boys and the forest horse that Arvid sold for enough kroner for passage to Canada. Carolina's sister, Johanna, went after the heart of a hare, Arvid by name, ending up in the far north of Canada, leaving poor crack-brained Carolina in love with the youngest Björnsson, shy Gustaf, a soldier who, it was said by his brothers who didn't understand him, could never lie with a woman; yet he loved her in spite of her addled brain, and there was nothing for it but to follow him here to the Baltic island of Gotland when he, too, ran away from his horse-whip-wielding father.

Lena was born to them later in life, when Carolina should have had the Change. The trouble with Gustaf, Carolina explained, while blushing and whispering behind a hand chafed from soap boiling, was not the size of his staff, but the opening, which was on the side instead of the tip, and it finally took some doing to milk him into a bowl then collect his seed with a chicken baster and shoot it high enough into herself to penetrate her egg. After that story, Lena could never look at the baster without throwing a fit of giggles.

Carolina still suffers the home-longing, especially while boiling soap like her mother before her, and of an evening when she pens long letters to her sister Johanna in Canada, mostly about the new World War and the warring in her own besieged head, with Lena helping with the spelling of newsy words neither can truly imagine: *panzer, London's blitz, Luftwaffe*.

Lena's country remains neutral, though her father is chomping at the bit, hoping to be recalled into the Swedish army in spite of his age. Poland is now divided between Germany and Russia, Denmark and Norway were taken, France has fallen to the Germans. And last summer the Soviets took over the Baltic states, but left her island alone since it belongs to neutral Sweden. Her father says, *Not to worry, the Boss of the Russians, that Ivan the Terrible Reborn, will never break his 1939 Pact with Hitler; Stalin ships oil and wheat to the Third Reich – don't the Gotlänning see Russian barges and steamers passing their island almost every day?*

But Gustaf does fret every day, and fear of another world war permeates the Björnsson family, with Carolina throwing too many Mother Fits, and Lena hardly daring to raise her voice above a whisper, trying to keep her mother calm, to no avail. Her father brings home the scuttlebutt of foreign sailors carousing in Visby harbour. He says fights abound in the taverns over the truth of it, mostly out of fear of another war worse than the last. The news on Radio Gotland reports that German ports are now holding Soviet ships. Four hundred German tanks are only a few miles from the Soviet/Baltic border. The Germans have laid mines in the Gulf of Finland, and German engineers and business people and all ships have returned home from Russia and Soviet waters. Even the German Embassy personnel have sent their families home. Carolina says, *What's going to happen?* And throws her apron over her head, weeping.

TODAY, FOR EXCITED LENA, the War feels far away.

Up before the first cock's crow since Visby is a long way north and west, Lena is all ready to leave for the *Midsommarafton* celebrations; she wears her embroidered holiday costume, her fair hair braided with blue and yellow ribbons. Her folk-dancing team will perform on stage tonight, and she can hardly wait, her feet twitching to leap and twirl in her new dancing slippers.

She leaves the house with her mother, who takes the few stairs down from the stoop too slowly, Lena anxious to be off.

In the lane before the house, her father waits for his women. He's dressed in his medieval costume: the red Flanders cape with hood and liripipe that looks like a sausage, his black plumed hat. Behind the four-in-hand carriage, the good-tempered draft horses are hitched to their carts, ready to take children for rides, the proud show ponies and dressage horses groomed and beribboned; the skitterish jumpers and trotters chomping at the bit; all tied behind the carriage in a splendid equine showing; the best of the Society's herd of ponies, each one no larger than thirteen hands at the withers, yet true to its breed each bears the broad forehead, well-anchored shoulders and deep chest, clean forelegs with well-defined knees. Gustaf is the caretaker for the Society, an unpaid but highly honoured position.

Only five forest horses belong to the Björnssons: Thor, the black *Hingstföl,* his chestnut mares, Old Clara and three-year-old Cilka and her May-born foals, Frej and Freja. The rest of the herd was brought in from the wilds in 1932 during the last great hunt when two thousand were sent to Belgium, England and Germany to be used as pit ponies, leaving seventy-five in Gustaf's care.

Though Carolina wears her favourite broad-brimmed hat, she also carries an old-fashioned parasol since overly bright and direct sunlight hurts her weak eyes. In her pocket she holds the mistletoe to ward off the falling disease. Just as she is about to climb into the carriage, she bends over as if struck from behind, then her knees give way, and she collapses, jerking and kicking in the dust, spittle turning to foam at the corners of her Clara Bow mouth.

"The biting-stick!" Gustaf bellows. "Be quick about it!"

"Oh not today!" Lena says. Not another Mother Fit. She falls to her own knees, swiftly finding the golden-bough of the oak in her pocket, and wedges it between her mother's teeth. The cart ponies are used to it, and although Odin shivers and stamps one foot and Prins switches his tail and blows through his nose, neither pony shies or bolts.

When it's over, the seizure, Lena's father sweeps Carolina up in his arms and carries her back into the house, Lena following with the retrieved parasol. He lays her on her sleigh bed, and Lena removes her mother's hat, shoes, gloves, then hastens for a basin of cool water from the rain barrel and washes her mother's sweaty face, smoothing back strands of grey hair that escaped the plaits wound on top of her head. Carolina will sleep most of the day away, and Lena will have to stay with her. She's letting down her team and her partner for the dance.

"I'm sorry," her father says, twirling his medieval cap in heavy, work-worn hands. "There's nothing to be done for it. I'll bring you back a twist of *polkagrisar*." As if candy can make up for not going to Visby. "Mind your mother. Feed the foals."

And then he's gone.

From the bedroom window, Lena watches the caravan of ponies leaving the yard, the forty mares with foals left behind in the barnyard galloping alongside until they're stopped by the closed corner gate, and they turn back to the business of nursing their colts in the light of a young sun peeking over the top of the tree line like a shy *russ* Nanny for the first time watching a stallion let loose into the herd of heated-up mares. Thor grazes alone in his own pen, unmindful of the day's upset, content to wait for Lena to take him for a ride through the moor. He won't be released into the woods with the herd of mares because his three-year stint as stud is now done and he won't be used for another three. Good horsemen like Lena's father are careful to avoid inbreeding.

While Carolina sleeps, Lena checks to see if there is enough hay in the pens, puts out fresh salt licks, worrying already about the shortage of feed for next winter. For two summers running the harvest has been poor, often the straw was rotten, so everyone in Lojstahed with a cart loaded up pine needles,

LENA

juniper leaves and heather, and filled the haybarn in the winter pasture. Everyone prays for a good crop this year.

Lena gathers a bouquet of lilacs and places it on the dresser beside her mother's china basin and water pitcher so her bedroom will hold the fresh scent when she awakens, a kind of penance for feeling guilty for resenting her mother.

Everyone was too excited about going to Visby to eat much breakfast, and Lena's stomach growls like a small hare howling from the cold. After making an early lunch of leftover eel soup, ryebread and cheese, she carries the tray into her mother, sits beside her, while Carolina nibbles like an old mouse. Carolina says, "I'm sorry you had to stay home with me."

Lena ducks her head over her soup, knees shaking, and she almost upends the bowl, then covers her mouth with her hands to stop black words bubbling up from her throat hotter than the soup: *Because of you I never go anywhere!*

"Must you always do that? Stop fidgeting like a hedgehog stuck in a bush."

Lena's knees jerk, the bowl crashes onto the floor, cream pooling, bits of eel sliding on the slate. "Shit!"

"Whatever shall I do with you?"

"Nothing!" Lena jumps up, but bends to pick up the broken china.

"Not to worry. It might have been an eye. Be careful you don't cut yourself."

Lena mops up the soup, throws the rag in the clothes bag in the free-standing cupboard. Turns and faces her mother, hands on her hips.

"You spilled on your best skirt. Better change into your work clothes."

"I can't stand it any more." Lena feels as if she's an ugly

duckling, arms lifting and turning into wings; she could take flight – but where can she go?

"Go for a walk. It'll clear your head." Carolina moves to her rocker before the window and takes up her *Nya Psalmboken*.

"Will you be all right? Shall I fetch the mistletoe potion?"

Without looking up, Carolina reaches for her glasses, adjusts them on her long nose. "Get you gone." She'll likely have a nap and will sleep longer because of the Mother Fit.

"I'll check on the wild ones," Lena says. It must be done three times each day, though today her father reluctantly agreed to only an early morning and evening check on the horses when he returns from Visby. The Keeper of the Studhorse Book must worry about accidents or equinine tooth trouble, having never forgotten how, as a child in Hjo on the mainland, he had to wait until his father made a good trade in horses and there was money enough to take Gustaf to the dentist far on the other side of Lake Vattern, and then it was too late to save the decayed tooth. Gustaf is always tonguing his molars and stretching his mouth wide before the mirror over the washstand. He's as long in the tooth as his horses. Often he leaves it to Lena to make sure *russ* haven't broken through the fences, or someone has left open a gate. Accidents do happen. A roll in a muddy ditch or a too-deep hollow to soothe itching from insect bites and parasites could mean a mare has difficulty finding her legs again.

Lena is happy only when alone in the woods with the forest horses.

At last, free to leave the house, she fills her pockets with Stonechurch apples and pears for the ponies, raisin cookies for herself.

She can't get away fast enough, and doesn't bother to

change her clothes, the soup-stained skirt wants washing anyway. She runs from the house, but stops at the woodshed to fetch the book she's hidden from her father under a rusted bucket: *Wayfarers,* the latest by Knut Hamsun, ordered from Stockholm by the Visby Bibliotek for Carolina, but forbidden by her father since Hamsun is not only Norwegian, but, it's rumoured, is a Nazi sympathizer, not even his name allowed in the Björnsson house, never mind that he won the Nobel Prize. His words are so luscious Lena could eat them, *Growth of the Soil* about a harelipped woman finding love in Norway's far north, her favourite so far.

It's a bright, sunny day. Head down, scuffing her shoes on earth packed hard by hooves, she minds fresh horse buns on the lane, kicks pebbles out of her way. She feels sorry for herself, chubby and oh so ordinary Lena. Nothing ever happens to her on this boring island. She has few friends her own age, and eats for comfort: too much lifebread dunked in coffee slurped through sugar lumps, *russinkaka* and *havrekakar* cookies. Her mother tells her she'll never get a man unless she loses weight and if she does find a husband she'll eat him out of house and home. Her father says, *Nonsense, she's beautiful,* but more importantly, she has *fina tankär,* such fine thoughts, because she's kind to everyone, especially her mother – if he only knew what she really thinks! Her teeth are white and straight now, but she has ugly, gum-line fillings from too much sugar. She covers her mouth with her hands to hide her teeth when she speaks or smiles, for fear of teasing, having never forgotten the bullying at school, the noon-hour fights when she defended herself.

– *Metallmum! Metallmum!*
– *Metal-mouth! Metal-mouth!*

When other children wouldn't leave her alone, in spite of

heavy use of the principal's strap, the teacher let Lena stay in the classroom during the lunch break and at recess. Then, she lost herself in *Kristen Lavrensdötter,* or *The Wonderful Adventures of Nils* who flew on the back of a wild goose. For a while at least, she went somewhere else. Until she was caught reading too much, and chastised by her father for being lazy, for failing to clean out the pens, groom the ponies. What was she doing? Reading to horses! He accuses her of being worse than his brother Arvid, who always had his nose in a book; and look where he ended up: in a faraway land full of bush and rock and grasshoppers and rust in the grain.

    Half expecting her mother to call her back, she stops and turns to look at the house, as if, like the outlander Uncle Arvid she never knew, she's about to embark on a long journey and needs to memorize every detail lest she forget her home. The red farmhouse Gustaf built with his own hands, with its brick adornment around windows and gables, the dormer window high under the hip-roof, looks so small, so country, unlike the grand stepped-roof houses of medieval Visby. The wooden door is painted yellow. With the white lattice-work, the corner-jointed log house is not unlike his Molltorp home. Inside, Carolina has decorated the living-room with the few possessions she brought from Skåne: an ornate clock on the mantle of the sandstone fireplace, a three-tiered candlestick, many boxes made by her woodcarver father. Photos of sisters long ago gone to America and not seen for forty years hang on the drystone walls.

    In the wire-mesh chicken run, hens scratch and peck for scraps from Carolina's slop pail. Gustaf's red longjohns hang limply on the clothesline, like a medieval jester at the end of his rope. She should take them inside, in case it rains, but the sky is as clear as the first day of creation. She could take her book into the *punchveranda,* a kind of gazebo Gustaf built for Carolina beneath the added shelter of the oak, with latticework trim. He keeps promising to attach to the house a *bislag* for her, an open porch for benches, but the days are short for ageing Gustaf now and heavy with outside work.

The lace curtain parts in the kitchen window, and Carolina waggles her arthritic fingers, *yes yes yes, fine I am, get you gone.* Lena blows a farewell kiss to her mother, her last sight of Carolina: a bubble-brained woman in shawl and lace dustcap bent over her Bible. *Sing a new song unto the Lord.*

At the end of the lane, milkcans await pick up, the returned empties silver in the sun. Lena heads for her favourite place in the grove, where she can pick *kantareller,* yellow mushrooms to go with tonight's tenderloin of venison cured with Absolut Vodka and sugar.

She's hungry now, though she ate all her lunch and the soup her skinny mother left.

She wants to go to Paris and learn *joie de vivre,* ride an elephant in Nepal, discover the secret of the Sphinx in Egypt. Instead, she's stuck on her island, looking after her crackbrained mother. The most exciting thing that ever happens is going to a barn dance in Hemse on Saturday and maybe, but rarely, taking the train to Visby and staying long enough to see an American movie, starring Greer Garson, who is romanced out of her head by dashingly dark Walter Pigeon who doesn't have clumsy feet and a dumb smile and big cabbage-leaf ears and his hands aren't calloused and he sure doesn't smell of horse sweat or fish or home-brewed beer like Gotland's farm boys.

Eja, she stomps her new dancing shoes in the dust of manure. She should have brought a club with her to break up dung heaps left by the horses. Every task great or small brings its own kind of celebration. The Manure Bashing every spring when the farmers spread sun-dried fertilizer over the meadow and the raking of the forest hay meadow when wood anemone are in bloom, with the gathering and burning of last year's leaves and fallen twigs, are followed by singing and oldtime dancing to the hurdy gurdy and accordion and much imbibing of homemade beer; all of it just some small event to look forward to since nothing memorable or monumental ever happens here.

Biting her bottom lip against its trembling, she feels sorry for herself. So lost in her reverie of maypole ribbons and dancing – will anyone miss her? – she barely hears the soft padding of unshod hooves behind her. The Stonechurch apples and green pears from her mother's root cellar bobble in her apron pockets, an invitation to follow her into the dappled forest. Thor whinnies for his mares to follow, and their pace quickens to catch up to Lena. She looks behind her. Oh no, all *forty* of them following her. She forgot to lock the gate behind her! She'll be in big trouble with her father now, but she doesn't care. A bucket of oats and they'll follow him home, the mares will want to bed their babes down in the sweet newly cut hay in their pens. *Eja,* let them come with her. Better company than people, her ponies don't care if she's plump, if her teeth aren't perfect. And she doesn't fret about catching it good from her father for letting Thor out with his mares, he gets so lonely in the pen by himself, to be sure he does, and she must console him with kisses and carrots.

Thor. His birth was such an important event in her young life, whenever she thinks about it, it feels like it's happening again and now.

LENA

Gotland Moor, May 31, 1932

THE OLD MARE Isadora is due, and Gustaf has watched her with a hawk's eye for weeks. She is skitterish and shies away, refusing Lena's offering of carrot or apple. Then, one morning, on their tromp about the pasture, Isadora is not counted among the mares, and they set off looking for her, the darkening sky and building Gudrun clouds threatening the first thunderstorm of that spring. A cold wind from the sea sweeps over the moor, lashing the maples, while the pine sways as if in pre-mourning for the loss of Isadora. Underfoot, limestone whitened by the sun looks ashen, small waves on the waterholes turn up pale faces, lily pads tremble, and even ferns rustle warnings along the cartway. They duck through the underbrush, make their way deep into the woods, climbing the stiles, looking for a downed fence or gate left open, careful not to trip on exposed roots from the oak.

Gustaf finds a tuft of horsehair on a bared pine branch, a hoofprint soft in a muddy patch of moss. Lena knows he is worried since Isadora is twenty-five, the oldest mare ever to foal on the moor, at least since Gustaf became Keeper of the Studbook.

"Hushquick!" Gustaf says, stopping before a stone cairn. Lena listens as hard as she can, but all she hears is the sighing of the pine, the soft moan of the wind among the hawthorn, its hungry tearing of last autumn's berries. The warning of a storm soon upon them. Then the low grunting, a sharp whinny. A mare's warning: Don't come any closer.

They find Isadora on the other side of the stone pile, lying on her side, the black foal between her hindquarters still sheathed in its amniotic sac, only its wet head emerged, ears already alert to danger. Isadora lifts and swings her head, lips curled back, yellow teeth bared. Her hooves scrabble on the mossy limestone birthing bed, but she doesn't yet have the strength to stand. Blood seeps from her. "Don't move," Gustaf says, but Lena steps closer to her father's side.

Isadora swings her heavy head around, straining to reach her foal, shrilling at it, telling it to stay in the hiding position.

Then, from the roundabout side of the stone pile, the click of unshod hooves on limestone, and Isadora goes berserk, her body writhing, hooves scrabbling, and she shrills again, a long and haunting song of departure. As if sympathizing with Isadora and worrying about her newborn, the sky god rumbles, as if grinding his teeth in anger.

Clara, the old troublemaker, without foal, encroaches on Isadora's hiding place like a barren aunt trying to steal her sister's babe. Lena's father doesn't have to tell her that if Clara defeats Isadora and takes the foal away it will die without its mother's milk and her protection in the moor. Lena wants to chase her away, but must let her father deal with the danger.

"*Hej,*" Gustaf says. "*Kom, Töjs.*" Clara regards the caretaker with an odd mixture of recognition, curiosity, and threat. Gustaf takes three giant steps away from the foal, trying to distract Clara. He holds out his hand as if it conceals a small apple. "Come, Girl." Clara stamps one foot. She swings her head towards the sneezing foal, peering at it, lips curled. And Isadora lunges, kneels, then scrambles to her feet, while blood gushes from her. Lena gasps, her eyes suddenly stinging, a lump the size of a chestnut growing in her throat. Too weak to stand, Isadora sinks to her knees again, but comes down close enough to her foal to start licking away the waterbag. Gustaf picks up a stick, throws it into the bush, capturing Clara's attention for a moment.

LENA

Lena takes off her woollen cap, wanting to rub down the colt, but her father says, "No! You mustn't interfere with its scent. That's how Isadora knows it's hers."

"I know," Lena says, "but we have to do something!"

Isadora's rough tongue pierces the sac, and the watery membrane slides away from the foal. She smells it, nudges it with her nose, then cleans again. Lena kneels beside Isadora, strokes her sweat-soaked neck, velvety ears. "Good mother," she says. "Your baby is handsome." It's black, with tiger stripes. She looks up, wanting to ask her father if she can name the colt. He slaps Clara on the rump, something he never has done before, always gentling a cranky *russ,* coaxing it to do his bidding. A sudden crescendo of gathering thunder, and Clara takes off on a run, crashing through the woods. The thunder sounds like cymbals in the hands of the applauding Nordic god Thor. The lowering clouds release the rain.

There is nothing he can do to save Isadora, who grows weaker as the foal gathers its strength. Finding it's front legs only sends its back legs sprawling, then front hooves slipping again, it falls with a plop, all legs splayed. The wind knocks it down again and again. It whips the short hide into tufts. By the time it's dry, its bristly short mane curling, the foal is able to wobble to its mother, nudging her neck, then belly, searching for a teat. His short tail stands straight up like a bottle brush, and he wags it furiously.

A long, rasping breath, the large oval eyes entreating, as if asking Lena to look after her foal, and Isadora expires.

"She was too old." Gustaf says, cap held over his heart. "Such a thing never before have I seen." He turns away from Lena, his shoulders shuddering. How afraid he must have been for Carolina when she gave birth to Lena.

Every harvest, when farm wives gather to cook vats of *köttbullar* and mashed potatoes with lingonberry sauce for the threshers, the old ones always tell birthing stories to new mothers, each one trying to outdo the others in the telling, and no one can top Carolina's story of a long, protracted labour, how she refused the birthing bed and walked away her pain in the pasture, hour upon hour, with her man waving his arms and shouting at her, terrified she'd throw the Mother Fit and somehow prevent the babe from taking first breath. She knew what she was up to, the old wife, and finally hoisted her skirts and squatted beside a byre filled with fresh rainwater, and grunting four times, delivered of the girl-child as easy as dropping a foal. Gustaf fainted, so she bit the cord, then cleaned the infant's mouth and nose with her apron. She even buried the afterbirth. When Gustaf came to he spluttered and bundled Lena in his own shirt, with Carolina refusing so much as his arm to help her along, back to the house and midwife, who threw up her hands and said, *Serve you right if you fall down and don't get up again.*

Carolina always ends the story by turning to Lena and telling her she was the most comely babe ever born, with bright, already-seeing eyes, hair like spun gold, but never enough of the milk could she get, so Carolina had to give her cow's milk too, and cried all night Lena did, with the bellyache from drinking too much. Not bad enough that was, Lena was a projectile vomiter, but kept down the first bit of porridge spooned into her yowling mouth, so Carolina packed her bottle of cow's milk with porridge and cut a big hole in the nipple, and that's why such a fat baby she was, so chubby she couldn't sit up by herself.

Milk. "The colt!" Lena says. He can't survive even the summer without a mother. But she's afraid to say so to her weeping father. "He must have a strong name," she says. "I dub thee Thor," she says to the foal, "because you were born in a thunderstorm." He's so busy looking for his first meal, at first he pays no mind to Lena's patting and stroking, then in frustration he begins to bawl, more like a calf than a horse. "We have to help him!" Lena says. She struggles to her own feet, the wind fierce now, whipping her back, flapping her long skirts. Now, thunder sounds like the crash of shields in a war between sky gods of old. She fights her way to her father, tugs on his sleeve, but feels something touch her elbow. Thor has stumbled after her and nudges her. She half turns, and holds out her hand. He nips her fingers, licks them.

Lena is afraid of the slivers of rain, that the colt will catch cold. But then, her father jams his cap onto his head, turns up his collar, and stooping, lifts the foal. "Hang onto my coat," he says. "Stay close."

They struggle through wind and slanting rain, keeping to the pony trail though the woods, slipping on wet limestone, their boots squishing in muddy leaves and spongy moss. The woods are dark under the cover of clouds, not a squirrel or a hedgehog stirs, the flycatchers and tawny owls and starlings silent and sheltered in hollowed trunks. Lena clings to her father's coattail, head down, minding her steps and following her father's. She's chilled to the marrow, but afraid for the pony wrapped in her father's arms. "Is he cold?" she calls. "Is he shivering?" But the wind catches her words and breaks them into pieces as thin as slate and bears them away through the underbrush.

When her father finally stops she bumps into his back, and he shouts, "Let go! We're home." In the flung-open doorway, she feels a rush of heat on her face, then hears a shriek from her mother, and then she's before the blazing hearth, her mother's hands, shaking as much as her own, peel away her wet clothes, then wrap her in a blanket.

Gustaf lays Thor before the crackling fire, though Carolina fusses about getting wet and dirty her best rag rug. Before shedding his own sopping clothes, Gustaf rubs down Thor, giving orders: "Heat some milk. Put more wood on the fire."

"No baby bottles we have," Carolina says. "Pickling jars would do, but no nipples."

Gustav looks at Lena huddled beside the foal, a quizzical look on his face, then says: "Maybe a doll's bottle?"

Lena shrugs. All she wanted for Christmas this year was a rubber doll that you could feed with a bottle and it would wet its diaper, but instead her mother made her a new winter coat.

"Tomorrow, we get a bottle from a mother too vain to nurse, Mrs. Carlsson in Hemse. But for now, it can suck on a rag." Carolina takes the warmed milk from the woodstove, dips a twisted washcloth into it, and holds it out to the shivering *russ*. He sniffs, but doesn't know what to do.

"Let me," Lena says. She dips her forefinger into the milk, then touches Thor's lips. He licks it eagerly. "That's so good. Some more?" This time, he sucks her fingers.

"It will take a year to feed it that way," Carolina says, hands on her hips.

Lena soaks the rag in milk and just when Thor thinks he's going to suck her fingers again, she shoves the rag into his mouth. He snuffles, then slurps. "Again," Lena says. And it goes on all night, till finally the newborn is sated and they fall asleep curled together, Lena's head on his thick neck, his long head on her back, and the old parents find them that way in the morning.

From then on, Thor is Lena's pony, and they grow up

together, Thor pulling her to school in the cart in spring and fall, in the swan-shaped sleigh in winter.

NOW, PLODDING AWAY from their pasture, the new mothers are cleverly slow and stay behind Lena, in no hurry. Their skitterish foals, bounding along on spindly, stiltlike legs, never stray from their mothers' sides.

Here, not far from the farmstead long ago cleared by her father, the forest and other farms are intersected by fences so grazing ponies won't trample new shoots in the fields, creating the winter pasture that belongs to the co-op. Tomorrow, her father will move these twenty or more breeding mares, fifteen fillies and foals born last month to the summer grounds where the herd is free to roam with Odin until November when the foals will be separated from their mothers, a time of grieving for Lena, who bawls herself, head buried under a pillow that doesn't shut out the all day and all night calling of bereft mares whose foals have been sold. It takes two people to pull and push the babes, as stubborn as their mothers, into the horse vans. Usually, Gustaf moves them around the tenth of June, but he had a bad bout of bronchitis this winter past and wasn't well enough until now.

Breeding takes place in the moor, a dangerous time to be out in the woods with Thor and his mares. Though her mother protests, Gustaf says it's all only natural and lets Lena straddle the fence along the southwest pasture to watch the mares in heat fighting over Thor. Cilka, the light chestnut who had twins Frej and Freja this May, guards him jealously. Just when Thor finds footing, bracing his hind legs, front hooves scrambling on the rump of Bricenta, Cilka bites Bricenta's neck, then butts her belly hard so she side-leaps and poor unbalanced Thor loses his erection, hooves crashing on bared limestone, his long black dong swaying like a metronome. He utters a low moan, dashing after Bricenta again, mounts her, his moaning mingling with the higher scream of the mare in heat and the laughter and coarse shouts of encouragement from the farmers gathered to watch and cheer on their own mares.

It takes eleven months to grow a foal, and one month after foaling the mares are in season again! It all exhausts poor Thor. He's thinner by half at the end of the season, his eyes bloodshot and frenzied, forelock and hide streaked with sweat. All Lena knows is that she will never do that, no never. It must hurt terribly, otherwise why would the mares scream so much? At the very least, it must be like a bad horsefly bite, scratching it hurts more than the itch.

Her father doesn't like being asked questions when he's seeing to the business of mating. Yet, he brings flowers from the moor to Carolina, smoothing wisps of hair from her forehead and kissing it before taking his place at the head of the table. He winks at her when she asks him how was his day? and he must be tired. He's as subtle as a horny toad.

Birthing is the best time for Lena, when she's allowed to watch the colts find their footing, blindly rooting under their mothers' bellies for their first taste of milk. Her father says, *Don't get too attached,* but she has named each one born last month: Blacken; Frej and Freja the light chestnut twins; Thorsson for a male destined to be a good stud like his sire; Princesses Elizabeth and Margaret, both bays.

They have reached the wooded moor, not far from Gerem Crossing. Lena plods along, like one of her ponies with distemper. Yet, all is calm on the Lostja moor. After a long winter and dismal spring, with *snöblomma* breaking blue from the warming earth, the Baltic fogs have finally lifted, the *skogsstjärna* penetrate the woods and the moor flowers once again with forsythia and jasmine and priestcollar daisies, the air heady with their scent. If flowers could make music, theirs would be an orchestra of colour, resounding louder than the roar of German overflights on their way to Finland and Russia.

But, on this the longest day of the year, even the flycatchers and kites under the blue Baltic sky sing a dirge, sorry for poor Lena who couldn't go to Visby because of her mother.

At the end of the clearing, Lena halts, and the ponies crowd each other and bound around her, Freja quick to nudge her hand, looking for apples. "Naughty," Lena says. "You're supposed to stay in the pens." She stamps her foot, and points towards the farmstead. "Go back!" as if the ponies are large, obedient dogs. Of course they don't mind her. She doesn't have enough apples for all forty of them.

The *russ* are curious and affectionate by nature, yet independent and stubborn. They don't like to be told where to go, and will finally respond to direction if patience is exercised, so Lena gives in to their nudging, and offers them apples and pears secreted in her pockets. "*Lagom*," she says, "Not too much, not too little." The largest mare, a grulla-coloured Tarpan named Cilka, measures only twelve and a half hands high, and Lena bends so it can eat out of her hand. It nods its huge head, massive jaws working on the apple, and she strokes its thick neck.

"Who's next?" she says, and the twins bound forward, Thor backing up, with a small leap, to allow them to feed too. "You're such a good boy!" She gives Frej and Freja pears, they must have the same, or they'll squabble. While they munch, they swish their flaxen tails. Lena pats their necks, kisses moist noses, telling each one how handsome he or she is, how good, how strong. Soon all the treats are gone and the ponies amble away to graze in the grove, those who didn't get a bit of apple or pear shaking their massive heads as if grumbling to themselves and to each other.

Lena finds a patch of sunlight, settles herself in a mushroom bed beneath a stand of sleepy *björk,* not even bothering to pick cloud berries and *kantareller,* the apricot-smelling mushrooms her mother loves so much. She watches her charges, the mares rubbing each other's short and strong backs, their dorsal stripes itchy. Foals gambol in the long grass. She feels drowsy, the sun warm on her head, its light turning the pale strands to gold. Her book lies unopened in her lap. She hums the first lines of "The Everyday Song": *Every day the sun rises over the sea, bringing a new day/To some people's displeasure and others' joy.*

She hears a reverberating roar, and it startles her, for a moment afraid a predator will stampede her horses, and then she'll have difficulty rounding all of them up to take them home. But, it's only another overflight, nothing so new in that; for centuries the Germans controlled the Baltic Sea, first through their Teutonic knights and the cunning of the Hanseatic League, and now they have air power. Too many planes to count, squadron after squadron, maybe several hundred, like a great flock of Iron Age birds heading for Latvia only one hundred kilometres east of Gotland. Craning her neck to watch them causes a crook in her shoulder, and she rubs it, then gazes seaward. Somewhere, out there, some time in the fourteenth century, a great ship bearing gold sank during a storm. It belonged to Valdemar Aterdag, the King of Denmark. If she could find that treasure she could escape and see the world. She sings to herself: *One doesn't know where one has come from/or where one is going/One must kick oneself in the ass/and get up and keep on running.* But where could she go? From here, she can see the end of land in two directions, but no boat at anchor waits to transport her to the mainland. She's never even seen her mother's home in Skåne, much less visited Stockholm.

Thor begins to prance around his mares who seem to be heating up again, his ears pricked to another sound Lena cannot hear. He whinnies a warning, then stands his ground, while the small herd takes off in a V formation towards the shelter of the trees. The lazy and disobedient twins trot to Lena, paw at pebbles hidden in the grass, then kneeling, one on each side of her, take up sentinel posts, while their mother knickers from deeper in the grove. The smell of fresh horse sweat mingles with scents of sweet clover, the apricot smell of *kantareller*, and the muskier odour of priestcollars. Hides shivering, the soft breathing of many hot and shaggy ponies still shedding their winter coats. Thor's lips curl, he blows through his nose.

Above the treeline, the black spire of Lojsta Church rises like a spiked-helmeted Viking, an armoured knight on the lookout for enemies – Danes or Russians – or no, the steeple looks like hands pressed together for praying. Planes far in the distance soar northeast towards Latvia, motors beyond hearing.

It's so quiet now she can hear her own heartbeat. The songbirds cease their endless praise of spring, even the hysterical flycatchers that seem to laugh and cry and hiccup all at once. What has silenced them?

Something or someone is watching them. She can sense it too, as sure as the sun failing to set on this, the longest day. Thor sidles closer as if to protect her.

And then she sees something move, ever so slightly, in the

dappled underbrush, a new leaf falling, its underside full of aphids most likely, or a cocoon turning, opening with the squirm of new, sticky legs and wings. Thor blows again, pawing with one dark hoof. The leaves seem to be yellowing, look furry somehow, a dark patch the size of a gooseberry could be the nose of an animal. Yellow eyes, a blink. A slender trunk takes on the shape of a long snout. Thor's shaggy withers and shanks shiver.

The face of a man appears, but it's like looking at a wolf: the broad brow, tufted eyebrows, the slant of large oval eyes that appear yellow against the green of the foliage. The gaze is hypnotic. Her spine feels as if it's been struck by lightning, the pain so sudden, so sharp, right down to her tailbone; the nerve endings zinging. Thor's ears turn back, his short mane stiffening, erect. The left corner of the man's mouth turns up, the smallest of smiles softening his countenance, like a humble farmer having his photograph taken after his best pony won first prize in the dressage at the Agricultural Society's fair and he doesn't want to appear overly proud.

"Who's there?" The words crackle in her throat.

She jumps to her feet, the twins scrabbling to rise too, hind legs first, pushing with their front hooves. Thor's ears prick back, he bares his teeth. Lena's mouth is so dry she can't lick her lips or swallow.

And out of the underbrush steps – a Russian wearing a red star cap.

Signe

St. Petersburg, June 21, 2004

THE BUS TAKES A SHARP TURN off a boulevard Signe cannot read because the signpost is in Cyrillic. It grumbles down a gravelled lane lined with linden, beech and familiar poplar. And there: the *Novikov Priboy,* a five-storey riverboat. It's even larger than it appeared in the travel brochure; as big as an ocean liner. Not a yacht or motorboat that might capsize; solid and heavy, it could weather a storm at sea. Yet, when she steps out of the bus, her legs tremble, knees threaten to buckle. Afraid of water since the boating accident, she had trepidations about a river tour even before leaving Canada, but without knowledge of the Cyrillic alphabet she could never motor alone, unable to read a street sign, or a map. She had decided to chance it since the boat wouldn't actually leave the city until after the first four days of touring in St. Petersburg. Once the tour leaves for the country, if the boat, Lake Ladoga and the Volga prove too much she'll leave the river system, take a train and catch up with the tour in Moscow.

Water. Whatever possessed her? Has she lost her mind? Here, the Neva River is far wider and likely much deeper than the steep-banked North Saskatchewan.

She looks back at the buses. She wants to flee, but forces herself to join the other passengers making their way to the riverboat. Turn around. Lift your head. Look at it again. It's not going to explode or sink. She counts the storeys: yes, five. It's built to navigate rapids and the largest lake in Europe. Dockside, the all-Russian crew hold navy sea caps against tight-sweatered, muscular chests, and red-jacketed Intrav interpreters and guides wait at the end of the gangway as if a czar and his entourage are about to do a walk-about inspection instead of three busloads of American couples and one lonely Canadian who has no one except a brain-damaged son left at home to pine for his absent mother. She just hopes he doesn't bang his head against the care-home lady's wall and have to wear his helmet the whole two weeks she's away. She didn't dare tell him she would travel by boat.

Signe feels overly hot, the rush of heat causing sweat to trickle down her temples, like salty tears, though the weather is cool enough to warrant jackets and sweaters. Clutching her passport and letter of confirmation that states she has paid for the tour and will be housed in cabin #317 – three tiers above the waterline – she lowers her head and concentrates on her footfalls, the crunch of them on gravel. The man ahead of her wears rubber-soled deck shoes and steps on an aluminum foil gum wrapper. Gripping the rope, she takes the swaying gangplank slowly, the *Priboy* anchored so close to shore the river must be very deep here. One more step and she crosses the threshold, but is forced to stop and wait while the deck-shoed man ahead of her shows his documents and is directed – abaft?

SIGNE

The only nautical terms this prairie woman knows are fore and aft, and given the state of her nerves, the depth of her fear, she decides that since abaft rhymes with daft it means go crazy with anxiety. And then it's her turn.

The Intrav woman with the clipboard is tall enough to be a Swedish valkyrie and is just as blonde and buxom, and Signe wonders how many warriors drowned in the River Neva she has carried to the Scandinavian Valhalla. "Welcome aboard, Miss Svetlov," she says, with a smile that reveals a generous mouth and teeth perfect enough for a toothpaste commercial. How does she know Signe's name? Oh, the name tag slung around her neck. Since her divorce so many years ago, she has used her maiden name.

"You speak English," Signe blurts, unable to hide her surprise since she expected the crew of a Russian ship to speak only Russian. "I understand more Russian than I can speak properly, my father spoke at home, Russian, but my mother Swedish." When she's afraid, Signe always has an urgent need to talk, and fast, which causes problems when she goes to the dentist. Translation: *I'm afraid of water.* And she wants to shout: *Tell the Captain I can't swim and if the boat sinks he's to save me first.* Instead she says, "Where are you from? Do I detect a mid-western accent?" It's the flat vowels that give her away.

"Honey, I'm from Minneapolis, well actually a small town near it." She looks at her clipboard. "Svetlov. Cabin one twenty-three. Single accommodation." Does she have to emphasize the word: *single?* She probably thinks Signe is a spinster who crochets doilies and lives with seven cats. Wait a Minnesota minute. Signe's reservation is for a cabin on the third – level, tier, floor, whatever you call it. One twenty-three doesn't sound like a third-level room.

"Take the spiral staircase forward," she says, gesturing through the arch with her clipboard. "One flight down. Turn left at the bottom. Your luggage will be brought to you shortly. Intrav staff are here to help you, no request too small." She flashes her Crest smile. Apparently to get hired by Intrav one must be six feet tall, have gloriously long hair, and just love people, the paying public. She's too young and too beautiful to be a Walmart greeter. Too bad about her.

"Down?" Signe says. "But that must be below the waterline. Isn't it just for the crew?"

"Do you need help with the stairs?" Miss Minnesota beckons to a crew member wearing a white jacket, maybe a sous-chef or person in charge of laundry, but he's helping a tourist with a cane. He bends to pick up a dropped passport for him. In profile he looks like Ringo Starr, all nose and no chin.

"I'm more than ambulatory," Signe says. She lifts forty pounds at Curves, no sweat. She feels like flexing muscle for the beauty queen who puts up with fussy tourists in order to satisfy her own passion for world travel. "Look here." Signe opens her passport case, slides out the confirmation letter that encloses a drawing of the big boat. So carefully she studied it at home, deciding that she couldn't afford one of the suites on the top deck, but would feel safe on the third level, well above the waterline.

"I'm sorry, but I don't understand your problem. Your cabin is on the lower deck."

"No. It isn't." Signe speaks slowly, carefully, deliberately; it's her best teacher's voice, one that makes her students listen and then take notes quickly. "I purchased accommodation on the third floor."

"That's just for doubles. Singles are on the first level."

"I paid for a cabin with two bunks and that's what I expect to receive."

"Why don't you get settled and if there's a no-show we can move you up later."

"I'm not. Going. DOWN THERE."

"Would you mind getting a move-on?" Someone behind her pats Signe's shoulder. The voice is female, quavering. Signe turns to see a woman bundled tight in a fringed shawl she must have bought in the pre-tour trip to Finland. Her short, white hair is as curly as a poodle's, a style Signe hasn't seen since she visited her mother in the Livelong nursing home. She wears large black, wraparound sunglasses. She looks like a bug emerging from a cocoon.

'I'm sorry, but there's a problem." Signe says. "Do you mind?"

Miss Minnesota scribbles on her clipboad and says, "We can straighten this out shortly, once the passengers are all aboard. Please –"

"I'm not taking one step into the hold," Signe says. "Look for yourself." She holds out the letter of confirmation. "Cabin three seventeen."

The beautiful and efficient Intrav person taps the sheet with her red ballpoint pen. "There's been some mistake."

"You're darn tootin'!" says the mummified woman. "You get what you pay fer. I demand a suite!"

"I'll speak to the Tour Director. I'm sure something can be done. Now. Miss Svetlov, why don't you go to your cabin and I'll have Mary Lou straighten this out for you."

"I'm not moving," Signe says, hoping her voice sounds steadier than she feels. She won't cry. She takes a deep breath, swallows hard, and clenches her teeth.

"There are comfortable chairs in the lounge in front of the Gift Shop," says Beauty. "Why don't you wait there for Mary Lou."

The Cocoon says, "I talked to her on my cell before we left but it didn't help. She's from Chicago and you know what they're like, a bunch of gangsters."

"There's a ten hour time change from where I live, I didn't sleep on the plane out of Toronto or Frankfurt, and —"

"You said it, sister."

"You'll have to pick up your key when you drop off your passport at Reception. Regulation." Miss Minnesota folds the confirmation letter and hands it and the brochure to Signe, slapping it into her gloved hand.

"There has been a mistake, and I want it put right. Now." Signe considers what Intrav staff might do if she collapses from fear and fatigue. There must be a sick bay, but is it above or below the waterline? If she takes one step towards that spiral staircase she will fall flat on her face. Wait. The other alternative is to turn around and go home. "If you don't give me the cabin I paid for I will leave the tour and — and consult my lawyer." She's afraid she's going to be sick now. Fear rises from her belly to her throat, an acidic taste on her tongue.

At this point, the heavy man behind the chrysalis takes her by her shoulders and gently moves her aside so he can step forward and take charge. "My wife is right," he says. "We asked for a suite and we got a double." His confirmation letter has been scrolled into a weapon, as if ready to squash a bug. He taps one cheek with it.

Mrs. Cocoon says: "Give me 'n' Chuck a suite by the Panorama Bar and this here lady our room and everybody's happy."

"Well, I do believe there was one cancellation," the Crest

model says, smiling at the couple not from Chicago.

"What floor?" Signe blurts. "If it's a double I don't mind paying extra." *As long as I can't see water through the porthole.*

"Why didn't you tell us that before and save us all the trouble?" Chuckie says, but before the keeper of the gangplank can answer he guides his wife towards the spiral staircase – up. "See you later, no doubt," he says to Signe.

"No doubt." Signe follows them but at a distance, not wanting to chat with them.

SOON, SIGNE AND HER LUGGAGE are deposited in Cabin #317, which is the size of a monk's cell she once stayed in at a nineteenth-century Mexican monastery converted into a hotel; her husband called it a mockery of a monkery, this in the days of laughter and nights of love. The second berth has been closed into the wall, like a Murphy bed, its twin made up with a feather-thin duvet and rough blanket, red of course. She doesn't need a tour guide or interpreter to tell her that *krasnaya* means red and beautiful, not Soviet. A built-in closet, small cupboards and shelves to hold clothing and toiletries.

Here she is, on a boat, and she's afraid of water. She was also so worried about leaving Tapani she now can hardly believe she's about to try to sort out her ancestral past and what's left of her Canadian life by journeying into the old world.

Tapani isn't his real name, of course, but just before the boating accident, in grade eight, he played the smallest member of the Trapp family in *The Sound of Music* – a role created just for him by the drama teacher, the name an invention too. That was the year he also became the youngest student ever to receive the teaching certificate in violin. Later, blaming himself for his sister's death, he refused to answer to any other name, only Tapani.

She checks out the bathroom. Taking a shower would be an adventure, if she weren't alone. *I'll do you, then you do me.* But bathing is a necessity and done quickly.

The instructions on how to take a shower on this boat are framed and hung over the sink: FIRST PULL THE PLASTIC CURTAIN TO HIDE THE TOILET. TURN ON THE SINK'S TAP. ADJUST THE TEMPERATURE OF THE WATER TO YOUR LIKING. So far so good. She feels safe enough to shuck her travel-weary clothes, like a moulting; naked in the water closet, she lathers a weathered body betrayed more by grief than age. She's much too thin, her skin looks as shrivelled as a plucked chicken's. THEN LIFT THE TAP AND HANG IT ON THE HOOK BESIDE THE DOOR. The wire inside the rubber hose contracts as if she picks up a snake, and she sprays the ceiling, the mirror, the curtain. She drops it, and water streams into the hole between her feet, likely flushing its way though a maze of pipes into the river.

She retrieves the nozzle, receives a wet slap in the face, soap stinging her eyes, but it's the remembered glare of an exploding boat's gas tank that reopens unending pain, deeper than the Neva.

Stubbornly, she holds onto the Russian contraption – whoever invented it was a masochist – and holding a towel to her eyes, controls the shower head and manages to rinse her withering body. Gagging.

She turns off the tap, and stops shaking. Drying her body with a towel, she catches sight of her skinny torso in the bathroom mirror, then freezes, not sure who she sees since she no longer looks like her younger self. In her family a person's identity was revealed according to the right combination of inherited traits, and too often she was told she didn't look like anyone on either side of the family; it wasn't good enough to look like oneself. She's not tall and blonde and big-boned like Lena, not short and dumpy like Maryushka, though she has her aunt's wild hair, the colour of orange tiger lilies, white at the temples now; she's of average height, her nose ordinary, not long like Pytor's, not pronounced like Maryushka's; and her eyes are brown and oval, too big for her small face, not round and blue like Lena's. Her pupils look black, the sockets smudged with fatigue. She has never known who she takes after; as a child she needed a sense of belonging to feel secure, but never found it. Her mother and aunt always seemed upset and cross, as if somehow her looks betrayed them.

She was too different, they said.

She was born on the ice, they said.

And now, without family, except for brain-damaged Tapani, she's too much on her own.

She can't even enjoy bathing, dammit.

She dries her hair with the towel, ruffling it, bending so she can't see how sorrowful her face is in the mirror. *Sad.* It best describes Signe, just as *brain-damaged* is her constant way of thinking about her son now, a strange but necessary acceptance of the fact that he will always be different, never whole again, and that loss of his potential self is as great as that caused by the death of Sasha, who never grew up to become worthy of her full name: Alexandrà.

According to the schedule, there's time for a nap before the Captain's dinner. Maybe tonight she will meet some interesting people, who have read the wondrous *Firebird* history book recommended by Intrav, or even someone who loves the poetry of Pushkin.

She closes the curtains against casual strollers along the deck, and crawls into a folded duvet as if it's a cocoon. Don't think about Tapani. Don't be afraid. This is not a small pleasure craft. The riverboat isn't even moving. Listen to the waters of the Neva lapping the sides of the boat, to the lullaby hum of the motors.

Sleep, oh blessed sleep.

It takes her home:

A high wind rattles the shutters on Tapani's window. Thunder. Lights flicker. A gurgling and a rushing of water. The basement is filling rapidly. On the landing at the back door, Signe's children cling to her. Put the sewer cap on! she yells. In the basement: an explosion of water, pipes breaking. The house tilts like a listing ship, the upper floor about to collapse, beams creaking like masts. Turn off the water supply! *She receives no answer from below. The back door blows open, she's swept into a tidal wave, Tapani's legs now wrapped tight around her waist, his arms almost strangling Signe. She cannot see Sasha, if she's above or below or behind her. A river flooding, a fierce current. She kicks upward, her head and Tapani's breaking the surface. Gasp for air, submerge again, rise and sink, rise and sink, until they're flushed onto a street as if from a sewer. The wind calms, rain a mere spattering, then it ceases too. The street bereft of people, cars. No Sasha. Tornado. An empty lot, a hole where once stood a family home, its owners names already forgotten. Tapani squirms, flails his arms, trying to free himself from her hold on him. In her other arm, Pusskin, yellow eyes rolling back in its head, mouth open in a last gasp for air, its wet body stiff.*

Then she trudges on, arms wrapped around herself, the boy gone, cat too. Signe's lost, bereft of her senses, alone, unable to name streets, a house missing from every block, trees bared or uprooted and fallen, telephone lines down, water still gurgling beneath sewer grates.

Finally: a gas station, a few people lined up before a man in Esso overalls, a tractor cap. I need help. *The Esso man scowls, flaps his arms,*

SIGNE

smacking his pantlegs. You and a million others. *He doesn't understand. Signe doesn't know what kind of assistance he or anyone could offer, just that* I've lost my husband, daughter, son. And Pusskin.

SIGNE WAKES TO THE SOFT CHUGGING of the ship's motors, feeling relieved that it was only the recurring dream, but upset that she can never forget what really happened, not even while asleep.

It wasn't a tornado that took them, but it was just as bad, the boating accident.

Best to get up, dress, and move about, try to look at the skyline, meet some people, do something to make herself think about something besides her fear of water.

Half an hour later, wearing a long black skirt, her favourite red sweater, a black and red coral necklace, she finds herself in a reception room full of birdwatchers dressed in their best Tilley hats and Tilley pants, binoculars dangling from their necks. Some gather at the large windows, no doubt hoping for a sighting. Either they all know each other, or birds give them an instant bonding; they sound like robins chirruping in trees, welcoming a false dawn since there is no real night here. According to the schedule, the reading room is reserved for the birding group, and Signe belongs with the second group in the Panorama Bar on Deck 5, but the blonde, big-toothed tour director from Holland, says, "No time! The Captain is speaking now."

The tour director joins the Captain and his interpreter before the bar. She makes a short welcome speech, and points at a bushy-haired man beside Signe. She introduces him as an ornithologist from Moscow who was hired to escort and lecture to birders on their quest for blue throats, grebes, grouse, and rare species found in Russia. He bows, and everyone applauds.

And then Signe finds herself looking up at this Russian man with a long nose and close-set eyes like her father's, but his hair is so untamable it looks like the fur of a terrified grey cat. At once, she feels comfortable and strangely relaxed.

"How do you do? I speak English." His is the firm, warm handshake of a priest at the door of a church after mass. "My name is Konstantin, but I think better you should call me Kostja." A flash of gold incisor when he smiles.

This is my first sighting of the birdman. She almost laughs, but doesn't want him to think she might be laughing at him. Although he's dressed casually in jeans the colour of algae and a leaf-green shirt, as if for camouflage, he might as well wear breeches tucked in high boots, a kaftan and a blue fox *shapka*, he's so Russian: slightly slanted, close-set eyes as grey and watchful as a mountain cat's; high slavic cheekbones; the planes of his broad face narrowing to a pointy chin; skin as smooth as peeled birchbark. He has cut his steel-grey hair short, but unruly tufts spring up from his wide forehead like feathers, or no, a cat's fur brushed the wrong way.

"*Nemsti.*" The long-forgotten word erupts like a fresh spring from the earth.

"What is this?" he says.

"*Nemoy?*"

"Nooo! You are not dumb. What are you trying to say?" His furry eyebrows shoot up like a cat's when it first steps outside the door of its house and it's sensing: safety or danger?

"I'm a foreigner. I'm sorry I cannot speak well my father's tongue."

"You are not Russian."

"Canadian. But I was born here."
'Noooo! Where?"
"Do you know the expression *born on the ice?*"
Kostja looks confused. "Expression? No."
"I was born on Ladoga Lake." Signe doesn't like to think that her father delivered her, and always assumed the story was women's talk, Lena's and Maryushka's, just one more bit of evidence of her father's bravery, nothing more.

"Oh, I see. But not your fault, surely." He raises one bristly eyebrow, like a punctuation mark.

"My mother was Swedish. She met my father on the island of Gotland in the Baltic, my father a Russian horse trader, or so the story goes."

"Yessss. There is long history of warring between Russians and Swedish, but sometimes not too much fighting, no?" He almost smiles, just a slight lifting on one side of his mouth. Russians are so – serious. Her father refused to smile even while being photographed with his family at a picnic.

"They came to Canada after the Second World War when I was five years old."

It was January 27, 1945, Lena had said, a date to never forget. The battered battleships on the Neva River fired golden arrows, flaming streams of red, white and blue rockets and the salute from three hundred cannon, announced the liberation of Leningrad. It was the nine-hundreth day of the blockade. Pigeons, the first birds in four years, appeared in the cotes of Nikolsky Cathedral, and Lena said, the sight made her and her Pytor cry.

Finally, on May 7, Victory Day, when everyone in the city danced in the streets and toasted the Red Army, no patrols guarded the sea gates to Leningrad. Lena and Pytor and

Maryushka – and less than twenty surviving ponies stowed in the hold – stole away and escaped from Russia on a coal barge, their course set for the Gulf of Finland and the Swedish island of balmy Gotland where lived Lena's father and mother. She hadn't seen them since June 21, 1941, the longest day of the year, one that never ended for Lena, the date etched by her into Signe's mind as if it could conjure up the memory and make it real to her too.

Lena told Signe that her family reunion was a tearful one, for the Svetlovs were bound for Canada. The grandmother Signe never knew, Carolina Björnsson, threw a Mother Fit when she met the Russian poacher and Morfor Gustaf Björnsson went after him with a pitch fork for stealing his daughter – and his beloved Gotlandrussen. That part of the story made Signe laugh, and then her father chastised her, saying it was almost too true.

It was just another story from the old country, but now Signe wonders about the truth of it. Pitchfork, my sweet ass. Lena and Maryushka carried on, weeping when it rained and crying when there was drought; everything overly dramatic, even the sun rising over the faraway train trestle that seemed suspended above the forest. *Sing a new song unto the Lord,* Lena prayed every morning. And Maryushka would say, *A new day has dawned and we are still here.*

Signe says, "My mother told me there is a herd of prehistoric horses running wild on the island. She called them: *Russ.* But it might also mean red in Gutamål, the local dialect." *Rod* means red in Stockholm Swedish, Lena once told Signe.

"Noooo!" Taking a pen and small notebook from his shirt pocket, which he likely uses to record his sightings, the Russian birdman called Kostja scribbles on it. And Signe leans closer to read: *Russ.* "*Russ* was oarsman on small boat. He wore tall hat. That's how Russland became Russia." Signe already knows this from her academic studies, and she finds the similarities between the two languages fascinating. She also remembers how her mother always said Swedish was so close to English it was just a matter of pronunciation.

The tour director with the big teeth stretches her neck and claps her hands and announces that dinner is served, and together Kostja and Signe make their way to the dining room on Deck 3.

"How are you called?" he says.

"Signe, but my Aunt Maryushka, she called me *Ryzhiy* when she braided my hair."

"Nicknames are not a tradition any more, Rusty Hair."

"My father called me Lyba or Lybatsa." Even though it means Love and My Little Love, Signe hated it because it sounded so foreign. Her real name, Signe, wasn't much better when the other girls born in Canada were named Susan or Nancy or Betty and they tittered when the teacher had trouble pronouncing it, calling her Sig-knee instead of Sing-na. It wasn't much comfort that her Swedish cousins from Skåne were named Thora and Linnaea.

"What is your family name?"

"Svetlov."

"Ah, you are Svetlovnova, Daughter of Light."

"I don't think so." No one in her family ever indicated the name had any more meaning than Smith or Jones in English. Kostja turns it into poetry, and this pleases the student of Pushkin.

"Yesss! *Svet* means light." Of course it does. *Lift the spirit, like light.* In Russian, it was Maryushka's way of saying: *Cheer up, tomorrow is another day.*

They sit at a table with several other people, the couple from Chicago, the orthopoedic surgeon and his nurse wife, and a white-haired woman looking dreamy but alone and out of place in a Grecian gown. Signe pays them no mind, not caring if she appears to be rude, because she loses herself trying to crawl inside the Russian language, with Kostja writing words in Cyrillic then translating them into Roman letters and interpreting their meaning that will finally add up to the story of Signe's sojourn here. She's only interested in everything Russian, and the Americans pale into the mist of the white night. She even forgets she's on a boat, but not why she embarked on this journey.

She wants to, but lacks the courage to ask her new Russian friend to help her find her young mother and father and their child born on the ice.

Maybe tomorrow.

If only she knew where to begin the search for that small, insignificant Signe Svetlov.

She wants to remember, rather than just imagine her mother's first sight of her father and so make real the story until it becomes her own, an impossible task. And if she asks Kostja if such a thing is possible in the land of Pushkin where a peasant girl can turn into a firebird and live forever in the white nights he will shy away from her like a horse from a precipitous fall. Horse. And then it hits her like the iceberg ramming the Titanic: she should have gone to Gotland first to find the descendants of her mother's brave *russen*.

Never mind, when she feels she knows this man well enough she will ask him if there are any Old Believers left in Russia and if he knows where she might meet one. She'd ask now, except she's afraid he will ask why she wants to meet a wise man and she will have to tell him about Sasha and Tapani.

Instead, she dives back into the Cyrillic alphabet and her first lesson in recalling the Russian of her childhood, with Kostja's guiding her own fingers on the page.

"Three months with me," he says, "and your father's Russian tongue will be yours again." He closes one eye as if sighting a bird through a camera lens, and she can't know if he's serious or not; she'll settle for two weeks with this man leading her home.

Hesitatingly at first, Signe recalls for Kostja words and phrases from her childhood, and when he understands and no longer corrects her pronunciation or his face lights up and flushes with understanding, she becomes more confident, though she cannot think in Russian and must translate her own words from English into Russian.

And then, walking arm in arm along the corridor from the Panorama Bar to the upper deck, she realizes she has forgotten she's on board a ship and afraid of the grey water. Its silver caps glint beneath lights cast from street lamps. She turns her back on the river.

They take deck chairs beneath the shelter of an awning, and she folds her arms against the chill, thinking she must buy the red shawl displayed in the gift shop window and wear it tomorrow night. *Krasnaya* certainly does mean red and beautiful. Red army. How is it possible, ever, to think of an army as *beautiful?* Maybe it has something to do with the way the word is pronounced.

Across from her, Kostja looks at her through his camera eye, then without taking the photograph, he looks at her sideways, squinting as if she's a bird that refuses to take notice of him and he must wait to capture it, eye to camera eye. "You look like a cat," he says, "wary but not unfriendly." That was how her father often described her mother: a feline licking good cow's milk from its whiskers after he squeezed old Bessie's teat and sprayed milk into the mouser's mouth.

Kostja doesn't look like her father, yet there's something about that long nose, the close-set eyes and wolfish grin that prompts her to say, "Were you a Soviet in your youth? Did you ever own a red star cap?"

Lena

Gotland, June 21, 1941

HIS CAP GIVES HIM AWAY: a peakless leather, with a red star. When he removes it and folds it between his hands, his wild yellow hair tumbles to his shoulders, all raggedly as if it was cut by blunt sheep shears. Just the hint of a smile. A flurry of consonants pours from his mouth, like bees swarming, and then he says in poor Swedish: "Well, well, what have we here? Someone nice and cute." What does *L'apachka* mean? It sounds like a name, or maybe it's a term of endearment spoken with sarcasm. "What shall I do with you, Pony-girl?" In the bombardment of consonants that follows she understands only one Swedish word: *flicka* instead of *töjs*. Girl. "Why you no in town?"

"My mother is sick so my father and I stayed home with her," Lena says. She points back, towards the farmstead. "Papa, he's coming now, I think."

But the Russian looks confused. "*Dadya,* no I see him."

"What brings you to Gotland?" she says, trying to act casual, as if it isn't unusual to find a stranger in the pasture. There used to be many Russians wandering about the medieval city of Visby, four Swedish miles away, but now it's rare to see Russians in the only town on her small island. For centuries they traded vodka and horses with the Gotlanders, drinking them under the table, sometimes making off with an innkeeper's daughters, something Lena has only heard about when neighbouring farmers gather around her mother's table, downing home-brewed beer and telling tales of the olden days when the Russians even had three churches in Visby, the Ryss Garden now a shop that sells Gotland-made furniture. But this Russian doesn't look like a trader: no fur hat with flaps, no astrakhan coat. He's no Russian bear. Too thin. He's not much taller than Lena, who takes after the Björnssons, all tall northlanders, unlike her mother's short and dark family from Skåne – too much Danish in her mother's Lundahl blood, according to her northlander father, since the Danes ruled the south of Sweden for three hundred and fifty years. He never lets her mother forget that Scanians even speak a different dialect from Gutamål, both so guttural to her father's northern ear.

Maybe the Russian's growth was stunted as a child. He has the look of a salt too long at sea and suffering from scurvy. She almost mistook him for a wolf, not just because of the eyes; his face is so lean, his cheekbones push against his sallow skin, and his long jaw narrows to a point, like a blunt knife. Head cocked, a glint in his eyes, he circles her, with small steps, legs turned out in a swagger, his boxcalf boots bruising the smooth capped *kantareller*. "Something bad you do? Naughty girl you are?"

She doesn't understand him. Is he trying to tease her? There's something dangerous yet appealing about him. He wears dark blue, trousers tucked into boots, the tops folded down, blouse under his waistcoat left hanging out. The small cross around his neck swings, and the sight of it gives her hope, if only she could speak his language and appeal to his Christian heart. One thing she's sure of now: he's not a Soviet. No Party member would dare wear a cross. Maybe he's a thief – or worse: a bandit. Not used to meeting strangers – anywhere – and never told to beware of one, Lena isn't sure if she should trust this man who makes her face hot and her heart leap into her throat.

"Horses," he says in heavily accented Stolkholm Swedish, then tries in Gutamål: "*Skogsruss, skogsbaggar, skogshästar?*"

"To be sure that's what they're called," she says, deciding that he wants the horses, not Lena. Now that she thinks of it, her father is always on the lookout for poachers, and still talks about the great loss of the First World War when food shortages led poachers to hunt the Gotland ponies, and they suffered near extinction until the Society fenced off two hundred acres for the last eight horses, the ancestors of the herd that roams the wooded moors today. Well, no one is starving anywhere now. Just let him try and steal her ponies! Not to worry, there are far too many for one man to herd alone. And, where could he take them?

If it's horse-trading he's after, this Russian, he must be a breeder. Her father told Lena that the last Tarpan in Russia died in a game preserve at Askania Nova in 1876, but who cares anyway? The Skogsruss are living proof that the prehistoric horse is not extinct, and the Gotlanders/Gotlänning harbour its value unto themselves. She must protect them.

"I have nothing to trade," she says. "My ponies are not for sale either. Goodbye!" Thor is grazing, and she chucks him under the chin to make him lift his head so she can wrap an arm around his neck. Thumb and forefinger between her teeth, she whistles for her horses. They lift or swing their heads, but don't come running; they're happier loose on the wooded moor than cooped up in barn or pens. "Time to go home," she says. "Thor, call them!" Before she can round many up, the cunning and quick-footed Ryss blocks her way.

"No do that."

"Let me pass."

"You not going."

"What do you want?" she says, hiding her shaking hands behind her back. She mustn't let him see how afraid she is. No use hollering for help. Every islander for miles around has gone to Visby or Hemse to celebrate *Midsommarafton,* The Day That Never Ends.

Hemse. Then she remembers: oh yes, she's seen this Russian rake before, lurking around the Wednesday market stalls at Hemse, making eyes with the sweet-seller's daughter. He doffed his cap at Lena as if she were an old friend, and her scolding mother pushed her towards the ponycart, recognizing a wolf in dark glasses if ever she saw one, never mind her own weak eyes. *Never talk to him,* she warned, *or you'll end up like the girl from Unghanse farm.* Lena groaned and rolled her eyes. The farm girl had fallen for Valdemar the Dane and sheltered him until Visby was vanquished – in 1361! Then the girl was walled up alive in the Maiden Tower in Visby. It is said her cries can still be heard at night wafting towards the sea though Lena doesn't know anyone who claims to have heard them.

Lena brooded the rest of that day, and brushed her teeth ten times.

The Ryss must have scouted out the whole island, the moors and forests, the stud-farm, then waited until the longest day when everyone went to Visby or Hemse and no one would see him stealing the forest rams. What he obviously didn't figure into his plan was Björnsson's daughter left behind to guard the herd. If the starving poacher steals her horses the Gotlanning will be sorry, all of them, especially her father for leaving her alone with her crack-brained mother.

She doesn't like the glint in his eye. She crosses her arms over her chest, which only makes her breasts bulge out of her peasant blouse. If she runs he'll catch her for sure. What to do? She wishes she had the Manure Bashing club.

She drops one arm, feels for the biting-stick deep in her skirt pocket. She lifts it and points it at him, hoping he will think she's concealing a knife. "One step closer and I'll poke your eyes out!" That halts him in his tracks, but he just laughs, the sight of a farm girl all decked out in traditional Mayday costume hardly threatening, though she's strong; she has milkmaid arms, well-muscled from milking cows, hauling buckets of water and winter feed for the ponies, chopping kindling and carrying armloads of logs for her mother's fire. She just bets she could take him in an arm-wrestle, to be sure.

Then he turns on his heel, melting back into the foliage, and quickly she takes hold of Thor's halter and begins to lead him away. But before they have taken more than a few steps, the Russian emerges out of the bush, star cap back on his shaggy-haired head, with coils of rope slung round his shoulder, the ends in his thin hands. Now. Now she should run, but fear and the need to keep an eye on him stops her. Like her *russ* she's rooted in curiosity and the need to out-think the thief.

She watches while the absurdly attractive Ryss carefully stalks Thor, who lifts his head, wary but not unfriendly. Then this poacher squats a few yards away from the smallest horse in all her world, sets his ropes beside him, and from the inside pocket of his waistcoat produces a box of sugar lumps. He pops one in his mouth, grinning like a farm hand caught with his pants down in the bushes with a milkmaid. Thor swings his head, lips quivering. The poacher tosses three or four cubes like a juggler at the fair, then holds out one hand in offering. Of course, the friendly Tarpan performs, bounding from side to side, tossing his head, but slowly moving forward – "No, Thor, don't!" Until he's eating out of the Russian's hand. This young man knows horses, but not forest rams. If you want to catch a wild horse on open ground you need to spread hay over a noose, with the rope secured to a pine tree, and when the horse steps into the noose you pull the rope tight, immobilizing its front legs, and it falls to the ground. Then it's easy to put a halter on it. She certainly won't help the thief by telling him how to manage Thor!

The Ryss strokes Thor's neck, murmuring thick words into his twitching ear – *"L'apachka, S'olnishka, Dushenka"* – while fastening the end of the rope around Thor's neck. Stop him! But three mares want sugar too, and they bound forward, almost knocking Lena down, their sturdy bodies a barrier between her and the Russian thief. They encircle the poacher, nudging the pockets of his waistcoat, his scrawny arms, the backs of his tapering fingers while he strings them together, leaving free the foals who will follow the mares to the end of the earth. The poacher smoothes Thor's long fetlock, brushing it out of his eyes.

Feeling helpless and confused and desperate, she yells, "Oh no you don't!" She pushes Frej and Freja aside, lunges, and tackles him, flinging herself onto his back, smacking his head, this side, the other, till he's turning in circles, gripping her calves and trying to throw her off. "Steal my horses, will you?" Thor rears, then races in circles around them, trying to distract the poacher away from Lena. The poacher is down on his knees, rolling over, she with him, and then he's got her at his advantage, she's flat on her back, with one arm pinned behind her neck; he straddles her. She kicks and tosses her head from side to side, baring her teeth, trying to lunge upward, bite his neck. He says: "I no hurt you." He lets go of her left wrist so she smacks him one, right on the cheek, good. It sends his red star cap flying. Her skirts are bunched up, baring her legs, and all her wiggling and writhing arouses him, he's so hard on her belly, but he shouts: "Girl, be good. Let you go, I will."

She doesn't trust him, but she stops kicking, still ready to spit in his face, scratch or bite. A short silence reigns between them, both tense and apt to spring, one upon the other, till he releases her left wrist, then the right so she wrenches her aching arm free; and he stands up, over her. "Don't run."

She sits up, rubs her right wrist, then pulls down and smooths her skirts, all grass-stained. Thor bumps her head with his blunt nose. "Yes, I'm fine."

"Stay!" Pytor says, as if he's training a wolfhound. She glowers at him.

Then he takes the dangling rope and tries to lead Thor and his train of ponies out of the wooded moor, but more stubborn than a mule, Thor balks, pushing back with his front legs, bending his hind legs; and they're locked in a tug-of-war. Forest horses decide where they want to go, and resorting to force instead of love will doom an impatient rider or pony-cart driver.

The Russian probably wonders why the horses followed Lena, but won't be led by him, in spite of further offers of sugar. Thor and his mares calmly hold their ground, staring at the intruder with an intelligence he can't decipher. He smacks Thor's rump and shouts, "Move!" Thor does take a few steps, but backwards, not seaward.

Lena chortles. "*Torksdbodd!*" she says. Knucklehead. To get Thor and his charges to follow him all the poacher has to do is walk away, glance back at them and whistle, then keep on walking. She holds her own ground, a signal to Thor, who nods his head and slowly blinks his long-lashed eyes.

Hands on her hips, and shading her eyes against the high sun, Lena tries to out-think, outwit the Russian. She can just imagine him trying to lead the herd of *skogsbaggar* out of Lojstahed all the way to Visby harbour in broad daylight since night will not fall. He must be mad. Nowhere to hide the horses, except in the forest. He wouldn't kill them, then cart the meat to town for trade at the market – would he? There might be other poachers, waiting with a getaway boat or barge. But how does he think he will not be caught? The harbour master checks the cargo of every vessel before it leaves Gotland. Her fear abates enough to allow her to decide to outlast this thief, and in its place she gathers enough anger to give her strength to take action; she bides her time.

The Russian runs to the end of the long train of horses and smacks the rumps of the last three mares, trying to make them push Thor forward, to no avail. The free foals stay close to their mothers.

"*Dumskalle!*" she shouts at the poacher. Idiot. The mares stamp their feet, and Thor whinnies a message to them. They hold their ground.

After grazing, they all will want saltlicks and long drinks at a water hollow. If the mares heat up and start fighting each other over Thor the poacher will find himself in a fine bed of nettles. Most of them have been quiet and gentle today so they must be pregnant by Odin.

Now the poacher hops and leaps and jumps, waving his arms, like a Russian dancer she once saw in a newsreel while waiting to see a movie. "*Hopp! Hopp!*" He could be singing, but out of tune. "*Hussa! Juch!*" To make them obey all he has to do is make kissing sounds. Thor sneezes. The mares nicker, as if laughing, but none of them move out of their moor. Lena needn't be afraid he'll steal them after all. It's really just too funny, and what a story she'll have to tell her father tonight. Imagine, all forty of them and only one stupid Russian! Even her mother will laugh so hard she'll have to wipe her eyes on her apron.

He retrieves his red star cap, plunks in on top of his wooly mess of hair, then doffs it as if to say, *After you.*

Calmly, head held high, Lena strides over to Thor, picks up the dangling lead rope, and says, "Let's go home." Obediently, he follows. And this makes the poacher go berserk. Huffing and chuffing, face flaming, he takes the end of the rope, wraps it around Lena's neck, and roughly takes her arm, the grip iron-strong; and he yanks her around and forward so abruptly she stumbles, but finds sure footing; and they're off, Thor and the string of mares following Lena, the Russian grim-faced, Lena kicking his ankles sideways, only the pain in her neck and arm stopping her from squatting and refusing to move, more stubborn than a *russ.*

"I'll get you good for this," she says. Her face and neck burn, but not from the sun.

"*Kak vas zav'ut?*" he says. "*Meen'ya zav'ut* Pytor," patting his chest. "Pytor."

"*Ja*, to be sure," she says. "And I'm Catherine the Great."

"You?" he says. "Me. Pytor, how you say in Svenska, Piter?"

"I don't speak Swedish," she says. "I speak Gutamål!" He doesn't understand what she says, much less her pride in being counted among the Gotlänning. "Lena Björnsson," she says. "My father is the caretaker for the Society – a very important man – and just wait till he catches you. He'll cut off your balls!"

She thinks she has a safe way out of this mess. It's four Swedish miles to Visby by road, and they're sure to meet farmers returning from the celebrations. It's less than ten kilometres to the west coast from here. Thor could run the distance and not even be winded, and if they follow the old waymarkers by the sea, they will be sighted by the skippers of any number of steamers or ferries or fishing boats. If nothing else, the sea patrol will spot them and wonder why so many ponies are roaming free. No need to panic.

They're leaving an easy trail for her father to follow after he returns home and finds Lena and the ponies gone. They leave behind a sweeping, easy-to-follow trail of hoofprints and piles of steaming horse buns. To be sure, every few metres she leaves a clue, snaps a dead branch from a pine, catches her skirt on a hawthorn bush and leaves a bit of lace, stomps down hard to leave a footprint in a patch of dried dung.

The sun is at its zenith, sweat stings the rope burns on her neck. "Take it off," she says. "I'll lead the horses." She bats his shoulder with her free hand, and says, "Please?"

He says, "*Izvin'iti.*" She thinks it might mean he's sorry. He grabs her by the waist, she kicks of course, but he sits her on Thor's broad back. "Lena, you ride." Smart. Thor loves to be ridden.

She winds the thick mane around her fingers, hanging on, heels Thor's sides; the long caravan is moving seaward again.

She could take off and outrun him, but the horses behind might stampede. Best to slow him down, and hope someone too old to make the trip to town will spot them and ring a church bell since power lines and telephones haven't yet reached Lojstahed. "*Saktare,*" she says to Thor. "Slow, go slow."

"*Izvin'iti,*" Pytor says again. "Better yes?"

"You're not half as sorry as you will be when they catch you. Do you know what they do to poachers? Tar and feathers, a stockade, hanging from the rafters of my father's barn would be too good for you." She wishes she knew a really bad word in Russian so she could hurl it at him. All Russian nouns seem to end with *nik*. "You – you – *Nik-nik!*" She means it as an insult. "*Dau kan sparka dej själv i röven!*" she says: "You can kick yourself in the ass."

She's expending too much energy. Better to calm down, save her strength for later, not knowing what will happen next, but wanting to be ready for anything.

Without a watch, she can only tell time by the sun, its movement across the Baltic sky. It must be early evening, but the unclouded sky remains as pale as the promise of frost in autumn.

Much too quickly to suit Lena, they reach the Gerem Crossroad and the clearing where the Evaluation Day always takes place during the last week in July. When the hooting and shouting of farmers driving the herd to the Traps resounds over the moors, Gustaf is the moor-rider who leads the way to the open fences that meet in a wedge to hold the ponies. Trapped, the horses mill, whinnying for the freedom of the woods, then try to break out, but quickly find a noose around their necks and a bit in their mouths, their ears tagged.

When it's Thor's turn for his evaluation, he stands tall, showing off his well-balanced proportions: elongated shoulders, spacious chest cavity, prominent withers making for good saddle position, his strong back and flanks. Lena bursts with pride when the judge remarks on how clean his forelegs, how well-defined his knees, the delineation of the cannon; then the hind legs of good conformation, how muscular his gaskin, a good angle to the haunches. Then she takes Thor through his walking and trotting paces, and he performs with perfection, his step springy; how lively and rhythmic his movement. He always wins first prize.

Because the fields are so soft their hooves don't wear down as fast as they grow out, and Lena always holds Thor's head, comforting him with soothing words, the smell of fear rank in his flared nostrils, while another farmer holds a hoof so Gustaf can work the pincers. Good handling calms a *russ,* and Thor quietly gives in to the sound of bone cutting, the quick click of the pincer, the snap of bone.

But it isn't the memory of Evaluation Day that sets off the mares now, making them skitterish and balky, refusing to take one step closer to the Gerum clearing. They must remember the November separation of foals from mares, when the colts' necks are freeze-marked with their birth dates. Perhaps they still feel the scrape of the straight-razor when the neck is shaved, smell singed hide, blue-grey smoke stinging the eyes and nostrils when the neck-hide is branded, and how the braying and bawling foals must be pushed and pulled into the horse trailers by their new owners. Forest horses are so good-tempered they never have to be broken in, and don't even buck when saddled and mounted. They just don't like to be told when and where they must go, and Lena is counting on this trait and the time it takes to move them forward to save her. It comforts her to remember her horse days with Thor.

Now, the mares mill, side-stepping and bumping each other, and not one reaches for wood anemone, the raking flower they like so much. Lena decides to do nothing. Let Pytor the Poacher figure out what to do now. The ponies number too many for him to manage well without her help. She will leave it to Thor and his mares to get her out of this escapade.

The poacher lifts his arms, shrugs, then slaps his sides, in bewilderment. Then he points westward, towards the sea. Lena crosses her arms, and smirks. Then she says to Thor, "What do you want to do, Boy?" He has to keep his mares in check, Bricenta and Cilka rubbing rumps, ready for a kicking fight again. They want Thor to cover them, and will remain rivals until both are with foal. Lena lets the rope go slack, and Thor trots off, skirting the pens and leaving the cartway, heading for the woods, with the chain of forty mares following, their ears pricked up, as if to say, *What's doing?*

The herd trots through the woods, following a path beaten hard by thousands of unshod hooves through the centuries.

Once they're out of the forest, it's slow going westward, towards the sea. Pytor the Poacher lopes along, one hand gripping the rope, the other rubbing his chin as if pondering a great philisophical question. When they cross the cartway at a Visby waymarker that looks like a stone house for a hedgehog, or an ancient gravemarker, Lena hopes for but does not see one motorcar or truck in either direction. As if sensing her dashed feelings, on the other side of the cartway, the horses stall, reaching for grass and daisies. Pytor chases a few back on track. Thor nickers and stamps one foot impatiently, and Lena strokes and pats his neck, reassuring herself as much as Thor that the ever-present danger is not as great as the threat of the constant overflights.

They cover more ground, more kilometres than Lena feels is wise, given the fact that she has rarely been this far west. The going is slow, and she leans down to whisper in Thor's twitching ear: "Remember when we fell into the sea? I need you to save me again."

Once yes, she rode Thor as far as the seacoast, trying and failing to run away, the memory triggered by the smell of sea and salt. It comes to her as brilliant and as eternal as the milky way but happens as fast as the flick and swish of Thor's tail.

ONCE AGAIN IT'S AUGUST 18, the day of her tenth Name Day in the Haying Month, when the seeds are so ripe they rattle, and the farmers spread hay in the sun and turn it each day for a month, then stack it in the evening to protect it from dew and rain.

She had asked her mother to invite her classmates to a party, and Carolina made a three-tiered cake decorated with whipping cream and blue *salmbär* berries Lena had gathered in a basket. Now, the table in the *punchveranda* is set with a lace cloth, Carolina's best blue dishes, pewter bowls from Skåne for the ice cream – Lena spent all morning cranking the handle of the wooden ice cream maker – and Gustaf has hung paper streamers and lanterns all around the lattice-work.

But no one comes to her party.

Gustaf says everyone is haying and either forgot or are afraid of rain – look how grey the sky, though its wispy clouds promise nothing more than a sun shower.

Carolina asks Lena if she gave out the invitations at school — as if she's as bubble-brained as her mother and could forget something so important. Lena spent three nights drawing a picture of the *punchveranda* and girls eating cake on each invitation. And then, Carolina washes her hands in the basin, her back turned to Lena so she can't tell by her mother's face whether or not it's a white lie in the making when she says Heather Graham, the daughter of the Scottish lumber baron, has a birthday party planned this very day, and who can say no to the wealthy Grimms? That's what everyone calls them behind their backs: the Grimms. According to Gustaf, Graham is a hard-driving, purse-proud man, heartily disliked by those employed to cut the lumber and work in the sawmill.

Lena waits, perched on the swing Gustaf hung from a sturdy branch of a maple. She waits, scuffing her shiny Sunday shoes in soft dust. She waits, twirling till she's dizzy, then turning the opposite way. She skip-hops to the end of the lane, shades her eyes from the high sun, but not one cart or bicycle or pony or schoolgirl swinging a beribboned gift appears on the cartway. Lena bawls like a foal separated from its mother.

And there is Thor, on the other side of the Bandfast tun fence separating the farmstead from the woods. He paws one hoof in the soft moss, tosses his head, as if chomping at the bit. She climbs the fence, unmindful of slivers, and throws herself onto his back. He swings around, and she grips his bristly mane, her legs tight around his belly. "Let's go!" she shouts, heeling his sides. Thor loves to run. He takes off, and she lets him have his head since he isn't even haltered. He leaves the ponypath, bounding among sun-burnished ferns, finding his way between Em trees used for brewing beer and tying fence posts, their feathery leaves brushing her wet cheeks.

And then, a clearing, and he leaps into a gallop, his powerful legs beating a rhythm, Lena moving with it, trusting him to carry her away from her shame, the pain in her tight chest. The wind of his rushing dries the tears on her cheeks, leaving salty streaks that begin to itch.

His last harness race on ice at Bogeviken was one thousand metres long, Thor was clocked at two minutes per kilometre and declared the fastest *russ* in the world. So fast their speed, she feels exhilarated now, girl and pony in full flight.

They pass a windmill of old, which only reminds her of cross-eyed, thumb-sucking Heather Graham, the sawdust on her patent-leather Mary Janes. "*Snabbare! Snabbare!*" she hollers at Thor. "Faster! Faster!"

They leave behind the familiar summer pasture, the cartway north to Visby, the ancient stone waymarker offering directions and distances she cannot decipher for overgrown lichen. They splash through a *brye,* the water brackish in the hollow, the hawthorns around it heavy with red berries. Moor frogs croak warnings. The ground is spongy here, Thor's hoofs softly thudding on moss, clicking on bared limestone, avoiding the rarely-seen, black grass snakes warming on sun-heated rocks as if they too are celebrating Midsommeraften. "*Snabbare! Snabbare!*" she cries again. Thor sweats, his fetlock flying. Far off a fox howls. He doesn't stop, though the heather must tempt him, the rich unmowed grass. The forest thins, the heather and grass thicken, but she doesn't look where she's going, not caring, as long as Thor takes her away, away.

In another water hollow, the carcass of a stray horse that must have rolled in the mud but couldn't regain its footing or broke a leg. Its hide is shredded, covered with maggots, the huge teeth bared in a death grin, eyes pecked out by birds.

The sight terrifies Thor, who emits a long, low and haunting moan, and leaps forward with a burst of speed that almost unseats Lena.

Thor could compete against the largest cold-blood and win any marathon. He's so strong he bests them all in logging and ploughing competitions. The Society would never let her run a marathon, not until she's twelve, but oh if they could see her now, racing for land's end, the taste of salt on her tongue, the wind's breath cold and clear in her chest.

The maple and oak give way to dwarf Arctic birch and pine, the sovereign rulers over planed, inland rock. Here the bedrock is full of fossils, shells, skeletons of snails, catskulls. She could gather some to take to school and show up that mean and mousy Heather Graham, but Thor won't slow down, not even when she calls, "*Saktare, saktare.*" His flying hooves unearth nests of guillemot, bits of white and green and black feathers puffing up as if blown by a troll's breath.

Finally, Thor slows, though he's far from winded, and takes sideways the slopes blue and pink with anemone and butterbur, disturbing goosanders and long-tailed ducks fluttering up from their nests. He picks his way among woad springing up among shingles on the beach, along a carpet of alpine bearberry. Here, long seaweed banks infested with flies and spiders. Above the high water mark, birds feed on sandwort, parsnip and meadow sweet. They come upon a small landing stage for fishermen's boats and the huts where they spend the night when the catch is good. A stock dove pokes its head out of a decayed, hollow trunk, then ducks down again. Overhead, the persistent song of a flock of flycatchers, luring Thor ever closer to the sea. She pulls on his mane, trying to halt him before he steps into the water. Her mouth is as dry as the sand. She's immediately hypnotized by the surge of white-crested waves hitting the broad beach ridges. Yes, they'll cool down in the water. She urges Thor forward, and he bounds into the sea, the water sloshing around her ankles, her best shoes will be ruined, but she doesn't care, she's in hotter water for running off without permission anyway. If you misbehave, her cross-patch teacher always says, you'll be sent to Klintska Huset in Visby, the house of correction for the old, the infirm and orphans taken from their parents, failing to mention that the Huset was built in 1815 and closed twenty-seven years later.

She leans down, scoops water onto her hot face, her sun-burned arms. Thor turns, and angles away from the shore, up to his shoulders now, and suddenly he's swimming, heavy head and long jaw resting on the water, ears pricked up, his powerful legs churning the water. They aren't that far from shore. His back is wet and slippery now, and instead of righting herself, she suddenly slips sideways from his back and plunges head-first into the water. She tries to stand, but sinks, kicking. She opens her eyes. Thor stepped from an underwater ledge, a flat rock stretching out to sea and cut out of the cliff by water erosion. She tries to climb onto it, but the rock is soft and gives way, opening into a sea cave hidden until now.

She surfaces, sputtering, her braids slapping her neck and back. "Thor!" she screams. He's found footing on solid rock, and plunges upward, trying to scale the rockface. "Wait for me!" She strikes out, with the breast stroke so she can keep her head above water, her breath so short her throat aches, salt stinging her eyes. Thor makes it safely to the rocky incline of the beach, shakes himself, snorting. "Thor!" she calls. "Help me!" Her hands touch the edge of the flat rock ledge, and she hangs onto it, though its so soft she's afraid it will break. The undertow pulls at her legs, feet, she's slipping away. Wildly, she scans the shoreline, but no boats, no fishermen. It isn't far to the landing stage, but the current is so strong, the wind so high, she will flounder. Thor regards her, the white hair around his eyes making them seem even larger, widened with fear. He huffs and chuffs, then arching his neck, he throws back his head and whinnies as if she's a foal trapped in a water hollow. She sticks her free fingers into her mouth and whistles. And he leaps from the rock ledge into the water, with a great splash, causing her to lose her grip on the ledge.

He begins to swim back towards the landing stage, throwing his massive head back and sideways, whinnying her to follow him. Turning, she lets go of the rock, kicks off, and shoots towards him, but her outstretched hands cannot grab onto his tail fanned out in the water. Kicking, she surges forward again, misses again. He's swimming as slowly as he can without sinking. Again. Her legs ache, a cascading wave blinds her, and she takes in a mouthful of water, spluttering. And then: panic. The undertow is pulling her down, down. She kicks and beats the water, trying to call Thor, and submerges, everything grey and green-blue before her eyes. Thrashing, three times she sinks before she falls into a black cave.

When she sees light again, she's floating on her back, her wet blouse so tight around her neck she can't breathe. She coughs and spews water like a whale. Her first breath stabs her waterlogged lungs. The Baltic sky wheels above her, a flycatcher bouncing on updrafts beneath a murderous sun. She undulates in the heave-ho of the sea, bumping against something cool and heavy. She touches it: sleek and wet horsehide. Thor has the collar of her blouse between his teeth, and he's pulling her alongside him towards the landing stage. She reaches up and grabs the forelock and mane streaming over her own left shoulder. "Let go, Thor!" she says, and her tugging makes him pull harder. Buttons press sharply into her throat. Now, she can't breath at all again. Holding tight to the mane, she manages to throw her left leg up, but can't reach his back and it slides down his heaving side. But he feels her effort, and the next time she tries, he lets go of her blouse; she's got her ankle on his back, pulling on the mane with all her might; and she flops onto his back, her arms sliding around his neck, her face pressed between his ears. It still hurts to breathe.

Then, they break through, he's on solid ground again, she feels as if she weighs a trillion tons, seawater cascading from their bodies, and he plods up the beach, wheezing.

Bedraggled, exhausted and contrite, they trudge home to take their just punishment: a separation of girl from pony for an unbearable month.

IN THIS VERY PLACE where Thor saved Lena's life so long ago, Lena and Pytor the poacher and the ponies move slowly along the shore through the heat of the day that won't fall into night this time of year.

From time to time, she tries to trick the poacher, directing Thor towards a cartway or close to a farm or church where they might be sighted, but he's too smart to be outwitted and turns Thor's head back on track. Until today, she didn't realize how thinly populated her island, the villages nothing more than a few scattered farmsteads near a church, with the woods stretching seemingly endless between them. In the clearings here, the curly-horned *hanlamm* graze on wood-meadow grass and bearded couch.

To the northwest, the horizon glows over Visby's harbour and medieval towers and wall built around the city. The bonfires have been struck, accordions and fiddles play ancient Gotlandska songs of summer, barrels and barrels of beer and shot glasses of aquavit are downed by young men gathering their courage to ask the Gotlandska girls to leap over their fires in troth, while the old ones indulge in story contests, speaking Gutamål. And here she is, stuck with a horse thief who doesn't even know how to steal a friendly *russ* properly. She's mad all over again. Better to try and stall him, rather than put up too much of a fight now. She tries to reassure herself: The closer to the sea the greater chance of rescue by a passing ship or someone returning home early from the celebrations, maybe even her father. Better stall the thief some more, and try and find out where he's taking her and the ponies.

"I'm hot and tired and thirsty." She tugs on Thor's rope, swings her feet away from his belly. "*Ptro,*" she says to Thor, and he halts. "We're not taking another step!" she says to Pytor. She wipes sweat from her face with her apron. She lets her tongue hang out, and pants. Pytor understands, stops, looking around for people who might be returning home from Visby, perhaps. They're far from the road, south of Visby and its harbour, but much closer to the sea. There's salt in the air, the smell of seaweed and fish.

"*Ja,*" he says. "Here we rest." He takes the rope, ties it to a hawthorn bush, then lifts her from Thor's back.

"I can get down myself," she says, pushing against his chest.

The horses bunch, resting their heads on each other's backs, while the foals nurse, the twins butting each other out of the way until each one has a teat. Two bays, back to back, engage in a kicking fight; they're heating up again, and seem to be showing off for Thor, who stands by, swishing his tail, his dong hanging down past his withers.

LENA

She plunks down in the middle of a patch of priestcollars, removes her apron and holds it over her head for shade, wishing she'd brought her sunhat. Now she feels like crying, but won't give him that satisfaction, that feeling of power.

The next thing she sees beneath the apron is a pair of sun-warmed hands holding a soldier's wide-mouthed canteen and something wrapped in red cloth. She takes the canteen, unstops it, and eagerly takes a drink. It tastes like beets. She unwraps the cloth and finds sausage, cheese, a half loaf of bread. He did come prepared after all, but where did he get the food? Did he bring it all the way from Russia? The stale bread is hard as a stone, the cheese soft and curdsy, the sausage spicier than she's used to, but she eats her fill. And another Russian word pops out of her mouth: "*S'pasiba.*" Besides please and thank you, the only other Russian words she can remember from her history lessons at school are good morning and goodbye.

"*Nichiv'o*" he says. "Enough rest. Now we go," he says in Swedish.

But the earth trembles, a sudden landward wind whips the apron from her head, and the horses mill, Thor rearing and calling an alert. A flash of light from the sea, as if a giant gaslamp has just been lit. The ponies shrill, panic, then stampede back towards the woods, Thor pulling the rope and with it the bush and its roots, then dragging it behind him. Black smoke, flashes of fire igniting within it. Towers of water rising, and then flames blind her. Screams. One of them her own. Pytor pulls her down to the ground, one arm shielding her head.

When her vision returns and the ground no longer shakes, she dares to rise up, support herself with her elbows, and look down at the coast. Off shore, the hull of a steamer burns, its Latvian flag torn but bravely still borne far above the blackened smoke stack. The boat lists, beginning to sink. Her eyes water, stench of burning oil and metal searing the inside of her nose. She hears faint shouts from sailors floundering, while an iron whale rises out of the sea, the first German submarine Lena has ever seen, except in newsreels, moving too fast towards shore, the high rattle of guns and smaller flashes of red and yellow lights, like giant fireflies, so swiftly lit, so swiftly burnt out; the survivors of the steamer clinging to wreckage or flailing in the water, machine-gunned. She doesn't need to understand the Latvian language to know they call for help, beg for mercy. Screams of fleeing seabirds.

Finally, only humps of backs bob in water running red, and her hopes of being rescued from the Russian are dashed.

Pytor helps her to her feet. "Are you fine?"

"No."

"You hurt?"

"I'll be all right."

She almost doesn't even feel the sting of salt in her eyes, how wet her cheeks. Beside the cursing poacher, she watches the German U-boat slowly return to the depths, leaving dead men floating amid mangled iron, burning wood.

It all happened so fast, and all she could do was watch it.

Pytor makes the sign of the cross, bows his head, and seems to be praying – another surprise.

It's still a long walk north to Visby. But wait, maybe the Latvian steamer's hold was meant to transport a herd of Gotlandrussen to some zoo or scientific institute that would pay good money to breed a whole new race of Tarpans. And now the way out has been destroyed by trigger-happy Nazis. Why would they attack a Latvian boat? Oh, because Latvia is part of Russia.

Stunned, she barely feels Pytor take her hand, and lead her back to the now obedient ponies. They rush Lena as if they want her to explain what happened, and take them safely home. Frej rubs his nose against her left leg, Freja crowding close behind him. Pytor frees Thor from the bramble bush, takes Lena by the hand again, and they retrace their steps seaward, heading across the limestone plateau, then struggle down the bank towards the coastline, angling away from the burning wreckage, the corpses. She can't think now. She feels weak from the shock, almost faint, just minding her steps, watching for loose rocks that could trip her and send her flying down the embankment, the inside of her nose burning from the stench of woodsmoke, burning oil.

Where is everyone? Surely someone must have heard the explosion. Can't they see the smoke? She wants to hear sirens. Firetrucks. Ambulances.

They pick their way down to the beach where soon city-slick Stockholmers will once again sunbathe in the nude. They come in droves, every summer, and now she'd cheer the sight of them, of anyone who might help her.

Here, long banks of seaweed, bits of broken wood, a water barrel, a sailor's cap. Her slippers are wet, feet chilled. Surely, soon, a patrol boat will round the bend, a skipper will holler Ahoy! She avoids stepping on dead turbot and eels. Salt stings her eyes. Her nose runs and she wipes it on the sleeve of her blouse. Pytor's hand tightens over hers. They've reached the bend in the shoreline, and there, at the end of a small landing stage belonging to the farmstead on the plateau above, a coal barge at anchor – flying the yellow and blue flag of neutral Sweden. No wonder the U-boat didn't torpedo it too. His hand tightens over hers and he almost drags her towards the barge. No skipper at the helm. No crew lowering a gangplank. The barge is full of coal, a small black pyramid. It can't possibly hold Thor, forty of his mares and their foals.

"*Nyet!* I am not going on that boat. Not me. Not my horses."

Pytor looks at her gravely, as if deciding what to do with her. Let her go or take her with him?

She wagers he's got the flags of Latvia, Estonia, Finland, and of course Russia ready to hoist, depending on where he docks next. She prays it will be Oland or even Stockholm in the north – not Leningrad.

"I won't tell anyone, I promise. I won't send anyone after you." But no, she can't abandon her ponies. She must save them. They're her responsibility, her family's livelihood.

"I need you," he says. "For horses."

"*Nyet, nyet,*" she says. "This is as far as we go – you – you Communist!"

That does it. Bending, he thrusts his shoulder into her belly, so she flops onto it, and he holds her legs tight so she can't kick, and straightening, he totes her towards the barge, while she pounds his back, hollering at Thor: "Go back! Home! Go home!" But he follows her faithfully, and with him the mares and the foals.

The Skogsbaggar trip down the dock, their unshod hooves clicking on planks, heads swaying from side to side. At the end, Pytor sets her down, and before she can make a break for it, he ties the rope around his own waist, letting out enough length to enable him to leap onto the barge, turn a crank and lower a gangplank that thuds onto the landing stage. At least there's no quayside lifting gear to terrify her ponies.

She turns in circles, like a dog chasing its tail, trying to reach the knot of rope at her back. If she weren't tied to him she could dive into the water, hide under the dock until he sets out for – wherever he's going – and run all the way to Visby and send the sea patrol after him.

Too quickly to suit Lena, he jumps back onto the dock, rewinds the rope into a heavy coil and hoists it over one shoulder, throws her over the other, making kissing sounds at Thor; and the ponies make their way up the gangplank then down a ramp into the surprisingly empty hold of the coal barge. "Help! Help!" she yells, but there's only a few gulls to hear her.

In the hold it's dark, so dark she can't see Pytor's wiry head, just feel the tickle of his hair on her bared thigh, one of her garters has unsnapped, her best white cotton stocking slipping down to her knees, her full skirt and petticoat uncomfortably bunched and likely exposing her drawers.

He sets her down, she feels dizzy, the barge rocking against the aftershock of the explosion further down the inlet since the sea is calm. Unmoored, it drifts. The ponies mill, rumps bumping, hooves pawing against the unfamiliar planking. Dirty, coal-dusted portholes above the waterline filter the light, turning it into shafts of grey filled with black motes. Too high to reach to see out, call for help, breathe fresh air. Pytor lights a kerosene lantern, hangs it on a beam. It's light reveals a false ceiling above, and over it enough coal to fool any sea patrol or landing officer at a border crossing. Sacks and sacks of feed. Water barrels. Buckets. Signs of a long journey ahead.

What should she do? Beg? Bribe him with kroner her father could raise only if he sells the herd left behind and taken to Visby for the celebration? Without language, how can she make him understand? Best to bide her time, hit him over the head with a shovel when he least expects it.

He hands her the rope. "Tie," he says. "Horses." He gestures towards the sweating walls, but she can't see clearly enough yet, so he guides her, until her hands touch railings the height of a forest horse's back. Makeshift stalls, mangers. "Feed," he says. "Water," he says. "You."

"Don't leave me here," she says. "Don't leave me alone."

"I am sorry."

And then he's out the doors. They close with a penal clang. She hears an iron bar falling into place; and she's locked in a hole, like a prisoner in the Gulag.

Signe

Novikov Priboy, June 21, 2004

HERE THEY ARE, Signe and Kostja, a bird man.

Some jet-lagged tourists have flown the coop of the dining room and gone to their cabins and the birders have taken over the uppermost deck looking for night fliers, leaving Signe and Kostja alone in the Panorama Bar, warming their chilled hands with glasses of coffee and snifters of brandy. The bartender clears tables with the help of two stunningly beautiful identical twins in red jumpers, embroidered blouses and headdresses with trailing ribbons along with other young Russians the tour director had earlier introduced as students of history from Moscow University. The twins give each other fish eyes, likely wanting to scram to their own rendezvous below deck. Chatting to each other in Russian, they push the lounge chairs closer to the windows and set up rows of metal chairs in the centre of the bar before a platform that will serve as a stage for the concert scheduled here in one hour. A soundman in tight black jeans and muscle shirt plugs in and tests two microphones.

Signe doesn't want to go to her cabin. She doesn't want to

be alone, though sleep is needed if she's to adjust to the time change. It feels like late afternoon, there's a hazy tone to the light as if the earth is too lazy to revolve and show its other side to the sun. Across that vast ocean Tapani will be wanting to sleep in, but may be lured to the kitchen by the smell of freshly baked cinnamon buns that Sylvia, the carehome lady, promised to bake for him.

"Where is your home?" Signe asks Kostja.

"I live in wilderness outside Moscow. I can't take the city, the consumer war against naturalists and romantics – like you I am beginning to think. But best, I like to live in a tree. I build – how do you say? – a platform."

"Tree house? Like Peter the Great, in a large linden, so he could smoke and look at the sea flowing westward."

Imagine the climb, taking a sleeping bag, a lantern or flashlight, binoculars of course, scalding tea or blackberry vodka, and then falling asleep under the white night listening to the birds talk with each other.

"The trees are their corridors of communication. They hear each other above the forest. Their songs hold musical dialogue, reciprocal questions and answers."

"What do they say to each other?"

"Look out, there's a Canadian with rusty hair eating your supper."

"What is bird in Russian?" There were birds, many of them, and a pond, but Signe can't remember where or when –

"*Ptitsa.*"

Of course. *Ptitsa, ptitsa, listen how it sings: Good Morning – dobra outre!* Signe still can't find a place for the remembered voice, the morning she first heard that word: *ptitsa. Say good morning to the robin.*

"They sing like many bells. Robin is *zaryanka* from *zarya* meaning sunrise. Over dark forests, across the steppes and lakes and rivers, bells once pealed, and peasants crossed themselves. The saints were near. In Moscow, when all bells ring, it's like thunder. Deafening. You will hear it, yes."

"Tell me about the changes in your country."

"It is very hard. Very hard." Kostja's voice seems to fall down, like a wounded bird from its nest. "We don't yet know what this new order means, what will replace the old idealism, principles, tenets of one's youth. Everything bred into us is bad now. You won't see statues of Stalin, only two of Lenin left, no hammer and sickle. So we go to church. Everybody." Suddenly, Kostja looks through his binoculars, catching a gull on the wing port side. He's like a cat that can hear beyond the range of the human ear. He lowers the binoculars, but fiddles with the strap around his neck.

"What my mother told me about Russian history – as tragic as it was – gives me hope. Look at Peter the Great. Since his reign, Russians have taken an idea or concept from the West, Russianized it, and created something new the rest of the world never dreamed of, with astonishing speed. When they are done with their new governance their democracy will go too far beyond constitutional monarchy or the American model."

This is no time for a dissertation from a professor of Russian literature. The history of politics does not fit with the poetics of Pushkin, not on this boat, with this man who, given his white hair and lined face, was likely raised as a Soviet. Her father and Aunt Maryushka never talked about the Revolution, afraid of being called communists in their new world. Signe didn't know how they voted, if they were old CCFers or if they had turned against socialism entirely, until one day a sharp-nosed, local candidate, who looked like a weasel poking its head out of a woodpile, showed up and asked her father what he thought about the possibility of government owning all the land and leasing it back to the farmers. Pytor chased him out of the garage with a hammer, yelling: *I left Russia to get away from your kind, get the hell off my land and don't ever come back!* Politics was never an easy subject around their kitchen table.

Kostja says: "We have old saying: What Russia can't resist she swallows up." Yes, the armies of Napoleon and then Hitler. Pytor always said: *Russians are not afraid of fatigue or suffering.* Then, the implication was that Signe was half Swedish and therefore not worthy.

"When you are forced to think one way but need to behave in another way, soul cannot rise," Kostja says. He describes Tapani, perfectly. Even before the accident he was too much like Pytor. Tell him something now and it goes in one ear, twists around, and comes out the other backwards. He's a rebellious boy in a broken man's body.

In his notebook, Kostja draws a fortified tower, arrows shooting towards the sky. "Once the sun was hidden by black arrows of our enemies, but Prince Igor saved the people."

Signe doesn't know what to say now. *Only in suffering does the spirit grow.* Pytor. He drove her away from his kind of faith with his incessant preaching.

There was no Orthodox church for miles from their farm, and while Pytor knelt before an icon of the Madonna and child in his Red Corner, Lena hustled Signe and Maryushka to the decrepit '46 Fargo truck, with its peeling red paint and running board, heading five miles down the washboard road to the small Livelong church, not caring which itinerant pastor was visiting, God wouldn't care whether or not the service was liturgical. Lena was a wild driver, holding to the middle of the road, the red Fargo straddling dried ruts, and backfiring, while Maryushka shrieked, *Gunshots! The Nazis are coming.* Because her mother didn't laugh or scold, Signe understood that her aunt was serious and had been so traumatized by the war that sudden noise from any source frightened her.

Too much she lives in the past, Lena said, *so our Little Mary can't tell it from the future or the present.*

Everyone turned and stared when they entered the church, every single Sunday, Lena commanding and bold, her straw hat tilted on her head, gripping protesting Little Mary by the hand, determined her Soviet sister-in-law would find religion in the new land; they resembled a stork leading a fat little sparrow. Signe trailed far behind, trying to look like she didn't belong to them and had come to church on her own, cursing her domineering dad, bossy mum and loony-toons aunt. Then feeling guilty, together with the Lutheran congregation she silently confessed her sin in thought and word and deed, of not honouring them, something she must somehow do on this trip.

In the large Panorama Bar, large windows on each side are meant for cruising, for sightseeing, but all she can see to her left is another riverboat at anchor beside the *Priboy*. To board the other ship from shore, passengers must walk up the gangway of the *Priboy,* through the reception area, and exit through another door to a gangway that connects to the sister ship. But looking ahead she sees Kostja's reflection in the opposite viewing window, his white hair with its twin cowlicks making his head look like the back of a mountain cat suspended in the foliage surrounding the shore and the short clearing that leads to the major artery of the city. Was it only this morning that the bus brought her down that road to this boat, to this moment of peace? At this time of night the traffic has diminished, the hum of it softened and more distant, so the real world of St. Petersburg and her Canadian home drift away with the gentle surge of the Neva retreating from the land.

With Kostja she may find herself lost in her past.

He doesn't ask if Signe is married, has children, and if he does she'll evade his questions, the Russian remnants in her are tattered curtains closed to strangers. Yet, she notices the plain gold band on his left ring finger. As if reading her mind, he leans forward, places one hand on her shoulder, and whispers: "I have baby coming – in July!" So that's why he's on the boat without his wife. Or no, she wouldn't be able to go to work with him; he's hired to take the members of the Birdwatcher Society looking for birds after the boat leaves the city. His cat-eyes turn to slits, gold incisor glinting. "A girl, yes. But no name yet. Not until forty days after the birth when childbirth women are cleaned up and can go to church. A son I have too, nineteen." The smile is forced now, and he leans back in his chair. "Not a good pupil."

Be glad he's healthy and doesn't bash holes in walls. Yet, she understands and has sympathy for Kostja. Education is as important to a Russian as are the arts, and a child who doesn't promise to be a good student will be a great disappointment. At least Signe didn't shame her father by bringing home poor grades. Pytor lighted the coal oil lamp and sat by Signe every night while she did her homework, then checked it against her textbooks again and again until he was satisfied that she got it right. Her mother chastised him for being too hard on her.

"Your wife –?" Surely, she's too old to have another child. Kostja must be close to Signe's age, unless his hair is prematurely white and the deep lines around his eyes are from squinting into the sun while photographing birds on the wing. The lines look like scars, as if a cat scratched him. They deepen when he smiles.

"A botanist."

Flowers, of course. To go with the birds. "My Aunt Maryushka believed that flax flowers are blue because they swallowed the sky." She was always raiding Lena's flower garden, eating mignonettes, daisies, wild rose petals with sugar, until Lena declared war, and then Maryushka began to cook edible wild plants she picked in the pasture: nettles, dandelions, burdock, and goosefoot. It made Lena cry. *It's not just because of the Siege,* she told Signe. *Never in her life did she have enough to eat, our Little Mary.* Nothing must go to waste, and Maryushka hoarded leftovers from the table in her bedroom. While Maryushka napped, Lena made Signe steal into her room and riffle through the closet and dresser, looking for anything that had gone bad: mouldy bread, a cup of sour milk, an end of Danish blue cheese though it smelled rank anyway.

The stillness of the night that is not night is broken by heavy footfalls and high-pitched small talk, while tourists stomp down the stairs from the uppermost deck, exclaiming over the white light, the size of the boat, the pain in knee or hip. They file into the Panorama Bar for the concert. At the other end of the barroom a fleet of bartenders and waiters hustle after-dinner liqueurs and coffee for the crowd streaming in the opposite doors.

Soon the other bucket chairs by the windows are taken, and everyone else has seats on the metal chairs before the stage. Signe and Kostja remain seated at a table by the portside windows.

The riverboat idles, not even rocking; it's so heavy and securely anchored, tied up to the dock.

Intrav staff hand out song sheets.

On stage now, a trio dressed like gypsies: a heavily rouged, middle-aged woman at the keyboard of a synthesizer in a swishy skirt, red blouse, a fake rose in her crow-black hair; the balding tenor with long hair pulled back into a ponytail in brown striped trousers tucked into black army boots; the fat violinist in a purple satin kaftan.

In halting English, the tenor introduces their first song "about a very long way and only a good song can help to stand it." The melody is familiar, and snatches of lyrics in English filter through to Signe: *Those were the days, my friend/ we thought they'd never end.*

The Americans whoop and holler, a resounding applause. Kostja looks glum.

The fake gypsies launch into *Dark Eyes*. Signe follows the English translation on the song sheet. *Kiss me, you won't get poisoned. And I fear you. Perhaps meeting you was bad luck.* Everyone is rapt, so Signe stifles her laughter.

Leaning against her shoulder, Kostja whispers in her ear: "If you heard real gypsy violin it would make you cry."

If he could hear Tapani play, it would bring on a downpour. Signe makes her son practise in the back yard — or soundproof basement in winter — where she can't hear his compositions. Long and haunting, they make her think of waterfalls, rapids, water dripping on stone. Sometimes she wishes he'd have one of his fits and smash the violin, a final dashing of her hope for any degree of recovery.

The violin belonged to Pytor. After he died and was laid to rest in the graveyard outside the hamlet of Livelong, Signe put the violin in the storage area of her basement and forgot about it until Tapani turned thirteen – and found the case. Then, she was afraid to open the dusty box. Shelved for decades against night noises. Hinges creaking. The case might open like jaws. Snapping. Shrieks like a fingernail on a blackboard. Freed, the violin might float over her bed, bow drawn by her angry papa's disembodied hand.

After all these years, dare she open it? She peeled away the rabbit skin. Hinges broken on the box. Inside, the smell of old resin. Coil and spring of snapped cat's gut. Wood warped. Neck broken. No wonder the violin might have wailed nightly for oily palms and the sweat of a musician's brow. Pytor would never forgive such neglect.

She took the violin to a gruff, mustachioed Hungarian who repaired instruments for the Regina Symphony Orchestra. He told her to try and bring it back in the old country way of restoring wood, then he would see about its refinishing.

In the dead of night, she dug a hole in her flower bed big enough to bury a box the size of a child's coffin. She covered the violin with rich damp loam. She watered it every morning, just as the sun rose at the call of early robins. She tended the small cairn until the wood absorbed the moisture, and Tapani could play a new song of forgiveness.

How could Tapani not blame himself for his sister's death when even Signe harboured such great resentment? Why didn't she see that before?

Now, the fake gypsy's violin weeps. Kostja turns away, gazing out the large windows. He looks like a cat, snoozing, then jerks suddenly, ears pricked to a sound humans cannot hear. He leaps out of his seat, dashes for the doors. And the song becomes a dirge, even the rose in the false gypsy's hair droops:

Of the more than two hundred people on this boat, why did she have to meet a bird man? Right now, he's likely on the uppermost deck, photographing thrushes. Communing with the birds! Calling them to St. Petersburg.

WANTING BED, SIGNE CANNOT FIND the night. It's still light at midnight, this sky an immense grey-blue shadow. She misses the brilliance of the sun setting over the river near her childhood home in Canada, refusing to dwell on the fact that her son will be rising for the day, might refuse breakfast if he's too sad to eat without his mother.

In her cabin, she closes the curtains across the large window in case someone on deck strolls by the window.

Curling into the duvet, she still feels hard boards under the thin mattress. Small prickles of guilt crawl up her arms like bites of invisible insects. For the first time in twenty-odd years, ever alert even in sleep, she won't be called by her son, or startled awake by a too-heavy silence emanating down the hallway. What if he sleepwalks, stumbles outside without his helmet and wanders away, in search of his dead sister and, unable to find her, is seized with one of his fits and bashes his head against a cinder block wall, or an iron street light?

Since the boating accident, this is the first time she has dared leave him, having found a respite bed for him in a care home. As impressed as she was with Sylvia, a no-nonsense, bosomy woman, with flour dusting her ruddy cheeks, it was hard to leave Tapani, who stood at the picture window watching Signe depart, his pale forehead pressed against the pane. She turned the corner, parked her Land Rover, snuck back and hid behind a Dutch elm, hands folded, although she wasn't praying. Then, she saw Sylvia beside Tapani, offering him a plate of cookies hot from the oven, and he followed her back to the kitchen.

En route, after arriving in Toronto and before she boarded the plane bound for Frankfurt, Signe called Sylvia from Pearson airport and telephoned again from Frankfurt after landing, but each time Sylvia assured her that Tapani was fine, he hadn't banged his head on the floor once, or put his fist through a wall, don't worry, he even slept the night without calling for his mother. If he ends up doing well with Sylvia, Signe may have found a solution for her chronic worry about what will happen to Tapani when she's gone and will never return, not that she's not in good health now, never mind her long-standing aquaphobia.

Now, the sun will be rising on his second day without his mother.

Here, on the other side of the world, it isn't even dark yet, the white night refusing closure. Her weary head sinks into the feathery pillow, this her last thought: *I'm allergic to feathers – what am I doing here?*

SHE SLEEPS FITFULLY, the mattress so hard, she wakes every time she turns over, and the bedframe seems to be attached to the bunk in the next cabin because the end jerks, with a thump, and she imagines a man as huge as a bear tossing in his sleep on the other side of the wall. When he gets up his feet hit the floor with a reverberating thump, and he seems to be opening and shutting his cupboard doors, probably in search of Gravol or sleeping pills.

Then, she finds herself in a boreal forest, but silence reigns in that green cathedral. No birds. Even the squirrels absent their midden. Sasha and Tapani – no older than six and four – gather bunchberries and Indian pipes, poke pitcher plants with sticks to see if they're eating insects. They find a trembling aspen, scarred by bear's claws. High above the tamarack, a lonely loon sweeps the sky, this land a last sanctuary. They move on, towards the Eye of the Bog, bare feet slipping on a boardwalk raised over the muskeg. Water seeps over the planks. A Canada Parks sign warns of an endless depth, and the boardwalk becomes a maze, like the criss-cross crust on a pie. It shifts beneath their feet, Tapani slips, and Signe catches him up, onto her hip, lifts Sasha onto her other hip; and turning, she tries to retrace their path, but the boardwalk tilts, turns, like a chessboard on a turntable. It begins to rain, long and slanting, like shafts of silver light. And she's running and slipping on moss and encroaching lake water; running from her own shadow, cloaked and hooded, all in white.

IN THE MIDDLE OF THIS NIGHT that is not dark, Signe wakes with a start, feeling the thrum of the idling ship's motors, and believing it's a morning light filtering through the curtains, she hopes she hasn't missed breakfast. She looks at her watch: 4:00 A.M. She parts the curtain above her bed, only to discover the other riverboat still anchored beside the *Novikov Priboy*. The only sound is the slapping of the Neva's waters against the ship's sides, a spectral chant. The summer nights really are white here, making up for the long siege of winter when there are only four hours of daylight.

Since today is the first of four days touring St. Petersburg before the boat leaves for the lake country where Signe was born, she can face her fear of water after seeing the sights of Peter's City. She's glad the boat isn't moving yet.

Her eyelids itch from the feather pillow. Reaching for her carry-on bag on the small table beside the bed, she digs out her antihistamine pills, gulps one down like a squab, throws the pillow on the floor, then nestles into the hard bunk bed, dropping off to dream again of memories, played to the music of the motors.

SIGNE

Lena's hothouse is made from old windows. Her hair is fair and long again, braided, and she wears Maryushka's red-flowered babushka, a peasant blouse, many petticoats under her skirt. Lena lies on an old sheepskin coat, her feet are bare, they're always hot at night, and she keeps one exposed, it will feel the Frost Giant's breath, and she will rise and cover her tomato plants with sheets.

SHE CAN'T STOP CRYING in her sleep.

Awake now, Signe thinks that when she was born Lena should have put her in a sack with kittens and dropped it into a hole in the ice.

She wishes her mother had never left Gotland, or more precisely had never been taken away from Gotland against her will. How different her life could have been. Lena might have married someone else and Signe would be a different person, someone who didn't have to leave her own home for Russia where she now finds herself tossing in a hard bunk in an anchored boat during a night without dark.

Lena

Off the coast of Gotland, June 21, 1941

LENA HAS NEVER SET FOOT OFF the island of Gotland before — not counting the bird paradise island of Beg Karlso.

Her mother has promised her often enough to take her to Hannas, Skåne on the Swedish mainland to see where she was born, where she met Lena's father, and the *kyrka* where all her family forever were christened. Gustaf said he never wants to see Molltorp – or even Stockholm – ever again. Like his brothers, he ran away from home without saying goodbye to his horse-trader father after the old man beat the brothers with a barbed-wire whip for chasing after Skåne women instead of trading horses.

But, Lena didn't have a chance to say goodbye to her mother or father. Soon, they will rouse the neighbours and search the wooded moor for her, her father leading the way with the Manure Bashing club. They will find hoofprints and horse droppings all the way to the sea. They will send out patrol boats. Her mother will wail so loudly they will hear her one hundred miles away in Latvia. Don't despair. Don't think about the wreck of the Latvian steamer, how they might believe she and her horses went down with it – until no traces of horses can be found washed up on the shore, and then it might be too late to find her. Lena and her horses will be long gone from Gotland.

At least she's not afraid of the dark. Quickly, she grows accustomed to the grey light filtering through the portholes, the yellow light of the lamp enough to give her her bearings.

The barge's motors begin to grind and hum and rumble, halting its drift, and she leans against the damp wall, hoping to feel the barge turn and begin to move west toward the Swedish island of Oland and the mainland where she speaks the language, where she might find someone to help her find her way home, but slowly it chugs south, the direction it was pointing when she boarded it. Where can her kidnapper be taking her? To be sure, he's avoiding Visby in the north. Maybe he's going around the southern end of the island. Will

Pytor then angle north until he passes the tip of Faro and Ryssudden, the Russian Cape? After that, his way will be clear towards Latvia and Estonia, may God help her.

Although the sea is calm, she feels unbalanced; she'll have to find her sea legs fast. She has to be able to – run! – when the poacher opens the door. Yet, she's as afraid of getting lost so far from home as she is afraid of the Russian.

Thor lifts his tail and dumps the first load, while Freja relieves herself; the stench instant, and though Lena is used to horse smells, this will never do; within a few hours the barge will be rolling in urine and manure. No straw. The stupid *Ryss* didn't think of that – or did he? That's what the coal shovels and mops are for, but where to put it if she can't heave it overboard? Ah ha, an empty coal scuttle. With trembling arms and shaking hands, she shovels the horse buns into it, finds the wooden lid from an empty barrel and covers the mess. Then, swabbing down the floor as best she can, she wonders where she's supposed to eliminate her own wastes. It seems that the poacher didn't plan on having a guest on board.

Now her horses. There aren't enough stalls for all forty ponies, but they can double up, they're so much smaller and shorter than work horses or thoroughbreds. Anyway, they like to be together. First she tethers Thor to one of the makeshift mangers – without straw, damn the Russian's hide! – then begins to work at the knots on the long string attached to each mare, breaking already short fingernails to the quick, cursing the poacher; until they're all separated and nicely in their stalls, stamping hooves, tossing heads, the foals nursing again.

Then she takes a pail, turns the spigot on a water barrel, and begins to water the ponies, one by one; they're so thirsty after the long trek through the woods and moor. She's afraid to drink some herself in case the water isn't pure; who knows where Pytor the Poacher filled the barrels.

Too many ponies, not enough coal pails, she can't keep up with their dumps. At least the going is smooth and not one feels seasick, though horses can't throw up, which makes them bloat and become ill faster, oh dear God, don't let them get sick.

Much later, she's hot, tired, hungry, and wants to lay down her head – and bawl. Instead, she takes a shovel and bangs it against the iron door. "Open the door. I'm going to suffocate. I can't breathe!" Oh, the stench. Even though she's used to the smell of manure, it's strong enough here to make her gag. This time she screams, holding her head.

The only response is the sound of the motor, Thor's snuffling, the sucking of hungry foals. Didn't her kidnapper up there in the wheelhouse hear her scream? If he did, he obviously doesn't care if she suffocates or dies from fear and loathing.

She has no idea how long she's been at sea, how long it took her to water the horses and clean up after them. She's about to give up all hope of survival for herself and her forest horses; she sinks down to the floor, leans against the cold steel wall, shivering. She wraps her arms around herself, lays her head on her knees, listening to rats scurrying about the feed sacks, gnawing on them. She's afraid to sleep lest they bite her. If the poacher is headed for Latvia, only one hundred miles away, at least she won't be shut up overnight.

Frej and Freja duck out from under their mother's belly, wriggle under the lowest rung of the makeshift stall, trot over to her and plop down, one on either side of her; their small bodies emanating heat. Soon, she's curled safely between them, and falls into an uncomfortable sleep on the hard floor.

Some time later, Thor makes a racket, banging his front hoofs against the manger as if pawing to get out, and instead of heeding his warning, she mumbles, "Go back to sleep."

SHE WAKES UP TO FIND HER HEAD on the long curve of Frej's thick neck. The left side of her face is hot, sweating. She smells horse sweat, manure, mould. She's covered with a coarse horse blanket that scratches her neck.

She sits up, momentarily unsure of where she is, perhaps in the middle of a strange dream. Above her head, the kerosene lantern swings, casting a half halo of light on sacks of feed, the water barrels, stacks of horse blankets. Horseshit. She stretches out her cramped legs and her slippered feet hit something hard. Throwing off the blanket, she lunges forward, onto her knees, and discovers a tray has been set there for her to find. A tin cup of steaming coffee; a wooden bowl full of hot mush, buckwheat likely a poor Russian's version of porridge; an opened can of condensed milk; a half loaf of rye bread; and a small saucer of strawberry preserves. At least he doesn't plan to starve her.

Cool, salty air on her neck, and she looks up to discover the portholes open. That's why the light is so much better now. The smell is still unbearable. But how could she have slept so soundly she didn't hear the raising of the bar, the clang when it fell back into place on the doors? Thor tried and failed to warn her that the man who calls himself Pytor had returned with food. She won't ignore Thor again. She'll be ready for the horse thief the next time he checks on her.

Wolfing down the food – unmindful of the taste she's so ravenous – she plots her escape. Demand fresh air, exercise, and when he lets her up on deck, she'll jump overboard. She's a strong swimmer, and barges usually stay close to shore – don't they? To be sure, that's why tramp steamers and motor barges are called coasters. But she could never escape without Thor. Don't think about how bad it would have to get to make her abandon him.

She needs a chamber pot, but settles for a bucket. She isn't a horse! Furiously, she rips the hem of her petticoat to use for a wipe, and discovers blood. Cramps, but not caused by the food, thank the Lord. What rotten luck. No clean rags. She tears another strip from her slip, folds it, tucks it inside her underpants, the stretch forces a loose button to pop and clatter onto the floor, and here she is with no needle and thread. She ties a small knot in the waistband. What she wouldn't give for a bath, clean clothes. Instead, she wets a square of her petticoat, rubs her teeth, rinses with water and spits it out, then swabs her face and neck.

The horses are restless, farting. Maybe she gave them too much water, though none look bloated. Thor bucks, his head appearing above the highest railing of his manger, then disappearing again, his unshod hooves banging on the planks. He's had it with being confined. She fills a bucket with oats. "I'm coming, I know you're hungry, good boy." She climbs the railing and jumps into the manger beside him, careful to avoid his hind legs. "Breakfast." Her familiar voice calms him, he smells oats, and almost upsets the pail in his haste to get his nose into it. "We need a feedbag. There, there. Good. That's right, but not too fast, you'll get a bellyache." She sets the pail down. "Now don't upset it. I've got your entire family to feed, don't you know." Her mother always says males are impatient, always chomping at the bit. She clenches her own teeth, refusing to take out her anger at the Russian thief on her ponies.

There aren't enough pails for the whole herd, but feeding them fills the empty hours, their company a comfort. She's given up cleaning the floor.

When all are munching, she finds a leather satchel beside the wooden tray. She was so hungry she didn't notice it before. It might make a good feedbag. The thongs are tied so tight it takes some tugging and pulling with her teeth to loosen them, but finally she dumps the contents onto her blanket-bed and gasps with surprise. Books! All are very old, leather-bound, with gilded Cyrillic lettering. She leafs through them. Photographs of the authors and illustrations help her identify some: the Brothers Grimm, Hans Christian Andersen, children's tales by Tolstoy, Chekhov and Gorky. She has no idea of their value, though her mother hoards all books, each one a collector's item because it means something very important to her: knowledge and proof she's not crack-brained. Why would this Pytor bring books from his childhood on a voyage of ill intent? Does he always live on this boat? She suddenly has a strange, sad image of a young man without a home.

If she can understand him, maybe she can outwit him and escape. She knows enough about Soviet life from her social studies classes at school to know that no Soviet worker is allowed to display initiative or act independently of the good of the collective, and this Pytor – she can't finish the thought, but it has to do with the cross around his neck, with this awful independent act – unless he doesn't plan to sell them and the ponies are bound for a collective farm or – what did the teacher call them? Exile villages. The object of the lesson was how much better socialism works in Sweden because they avoided a revolution by keeping their constitutional monarchy, while the Russians always go overboard with everything they do, and murdered Czar Nicholas and Czarina Alexandra and all their children. She wishes she'd paid more attention, studied harder, then she could figure out this Nik-nik, but school is a faraway place in what feels like a long ago time.

If the horse thief gets caught with forty Gotlandruss will she be implicated? A clean jail would be better than this stinking hole.

Best to be nice to the young man called Pytor, and when he least expects it, make a break for freedom. A plan will devise itself, or may not be needed. With the war – and who knows what's happening in the Baltic states now – surely there will be checkpoints, Russian patrols, and the horse thief won't have a bill of sale or trade. Oh. Forgery. He could have false papers. She knows from the news on her father's short-wave radio that special visas are needed to enter Baltic states, but they're hard to get, and reports from travellers and traders tell of Soviet secret police in Baltic cities arresting members of non-communist parties: farmers, businessmen, even priests and ministers. They're looking for secret members of the Latvian underground.

But maybe he's not bound for Latvia or Estonia.

In Visby, they say a person can get into Russia, but once there you can never get out again.

If the barge stops, she'll excite the horses, holler her head off, bang on the walls with the shovel. Then some customs inspector will hear the racket and find her and send her home because, after all, Sweden is neutral.

She wishes she knew what day it is, the time. Without watching the sun rise and set she has no structure. Wait now, she slept, she ate breakfast, so it must be June 22, Sunday, yes. Quickly, she takes the biting-stick from her pocket, and scratches a line on the coal-blackened wall. Day 1.

She's afraid she will never make another mark because this Day will never end.

SOME TIME DURING THE SECOND NIGHT without darkness – her best guess is well after midnight – she's wakened by planes droning, so many squadrons, it seems the overflight will go on forever.

The windows are too small and too high for her to see out and jumping only wastes energy best spent – or saved – to deal with too many ponies eliminating their wastes. She decides to ration their feed and water.

The air grows warm and smells smoky as if many brush fires burn on a field far away, but one smell can never completely hide another. Thor's eyes roll with fright, and she lets him out of his stall so he can stand guard beside her and she feels less alone. Safer.

Later, she's again wakened by the roaring of planes overhead, explosions on land – or sea? – and the feeble racket of answering AA guns above the banging of hooves against mangers. Thor's high and steady shrilling sounds like a politician with false promises of peace or a pastor warning of the Second Coming but drowned out by static on a radio. She burrows her head under the blankets but they don't even dim the sounds of war echoing from the first Nazi air attacks, likely from the Gulf of Finland to the Black Sea, judging by the length and distance of the explosive booms and racket of answering guns. All she knows is that a sea battle rages somewhere that feels like north and east, though she can't be sure of her directions now.

She kicks over a bucket of water, which only makes the floor even more slippery and mucky.

She crouches there, for what feels like hours, until the going becomes rough, and she hears foghorns and whistles of – other ships? – and the barge seems to be weaving, as if through a watery maze. She guesses that Pytor raised the hammer and sickle flag when they left the northern tip of Gotland, and she's afraid a German bomb or a torpedo will hit the barge. She smells cordite, the stench of heavy gasoline and something else burning sweetly, as if her mother has taken a fit while standing at the stove and scorches beefsteak. It reminds her of the attack on the Latvian steamer.

Then, merciful silence.

She's soaking wet with sweat. Rising, she moves among the ponies, soothing erect manes, stroking arched necks, patting noses. It calms her too.

Then she hears – music! Above, on the bridge, Pytor has likely turned on a short-wave radio, which makes her think of her father, and a lump grows large as a mushroom, thick in her throat. She hears the Spassky chimes from Moscow playing a tune she recognizes, *The Internationale,* and thunderous male voices – *Vstavay, strana ogromn*aya – a choir or a troop of Russian soldiers? *Vstavay, na smertnyi boy*. She doesn't need to understand the language to know it's a patriotic call to fight for the motherland. *S fashistkoy siloy temnouy/S proklyatoya ordoy!* The voices rise in a crescendo, and with them all her suppressed, pent up fury makes her afraid her face might explode. *Pust yarost blagorodnya!* She bangs the shovel against the wall. *Vskipast kak volna!* Thor rears and shrills. *Idyot voyna narodnaya/Svyashennaya voyna!* The clang and bang and ring of the shovel cannot diminish the song of Russian patriots. Her shoulders and upper arms ache, but she whams the shovel against the wall of the barge again, throwing all her weight behind the impact, puffs of coal dust like black breath on her sweating brow and cheeks. The music and singing soften, followed by static, then changes to jazz and a male voice singing in English: *We'll meet again in Lvov, My love and I.* She understands the words, but has no idea where in Russia Lvov might be. She collapses against the coal-dust-blackened wall, slips down, exhausted, the shovel clanging at her side. Sudden silence, except for the slurp and suck of the nursing twins.

Then: the click of a lock opening, the doors slide back, and there's the thief looking like he just had a bath, hair all wet and slicked back, his cheeks freshly shaved. He grins like a boy asking to take her to a barn dance and expecting no rejection. Pytor brings her supper on a tray: good pickled herring and rye bread, a small tin of condensed milk. He grunts some kind of approval at her care and feeding of the horses, or it may be disgust at the slimy floor.

"Straw," she says. "You didn't think of that, you stupid Russian horse thief!" Not waiting for an answer she says, "What's happening up there?" She points, but he doesn't understand her question. She shouts, "Boom! Boom!" then tries to imitate the sound of droning engines, of explosions.

Of course he answers in dreadful Swedish: "No! You not afraid." He extends his arm, pointing. "Mine sweeper, how you say? We follow, yes. Is safe."

"Whatever that means, it makes me feel much better, Niknik. If I ever reach a safe harbour I'm going to bury you in horseshit!"

He leaves her alone again. A small wave before he shuts and locks the doors.

After she has eaten her supper her strength returns, but with nothing to do except look at the pictures in his books, she curries the ponies, even braids the foals' short manes, wishing she had cheerful ribbons.

Much later, wondering if Nik-nik ever sleeps, her lids droop and, thinking about Visby's two-thousand-year-old wall of defence, she drifts to the strains of a popular Soviet song: *Dalenko, dalenko;* Far away, far away...

THIS MORNING – IS IT THE SECOND or third? – she's convinced they're headed for Leningrad, likely well past Estonia, maybe even well into the Gulf of Finland, unless he made a detour and set a course for northern Sweden, a small and foolish hope. Waiting for her food and wishing she had a map, she tries to figure out distances and travel times from memory. Let's say it's over nine hundred kilometres from Visby to Leningrad. How fast is the coaster travelling? Nine or ten knots per hour? Come come, you're an islander, you should be able to figure this out. One knot equals 1.85 kilometres. That means about 18.5 kilometres per hour. Impossible to divide 980 kilometres by 18.5 without paper and pencil. After almost three days, she must be close to Leningrad, smack dab in the middle of the Gulf for sure.

When Pytor appears, she's ready for him. She must get him to trust her, maybe even like her, so she can make a break for it whenever he docks. She thanks him for the food, invites him to join her in the meal, patting the blankets beside her, but he just hauls the stinking slop buckets out the door, heaves their contents overboard, them returns with the empties. A curt nod, the imperceptible hint of a smile in the left corner of his mouth.

"I can't stand it any longer! I'm stir-crazy!" This draws a blank look from him. She ruffles her hair. "It's filthy!" Spreading her arms, she looks down at her coal-dusted dress, the manure-stained hem, then sniffs under her armpits. "I stink!" She lifts one foot, then the other: never dry now, her dancing slippers are rotting, the seams unravelling. She shows him her hands: blistered, red and raw, fingernails ragged and broken from shovelling shit, mopping up horse piss.

He points at the water barrels, the buckets. "Wash," he says. Then he takes a length of rope and strings a makeshift clothes line for her from one manger to another.

"That's very nice of you," she says. But starts to bawl. It has been a long time coming, this despair, and her shoulders shake, chest heaves, with the sobbing. She sinks down, onto the blanket-bed, throws her now ragged apron over her head like her mother before her when she misses her Skåne family, and just howls. Even in her own ears, it's more chilling than the bay of a lone wolf; surely, he'll understand her plight now.

"*Nyet, nyet,*" Pytor says. And then she can hear him breathing heavily, smell rank Russian tobacco. He's gripping her shoulders, lifting her to her feet, shaking her; and she goes limp, like a rag doll, the apron falling away from her face. But she can't stop wailing, she wants to go home, she wants her father's strong arms to lift her and carry her away from this stinking dark hole. She even wants to hear him chastising her, roughly, for leaving her mother, for wandering alone in the moor.

Pytor lets go of her. She mewls and hiccoughs, unsteady on her feet, still trembling like an aspen leaf after the rain. It would appear that he feels no sympathy for her, at best doesn't know what to do with her so he leaves her alone to feel sorry for herself.

Hoping he won't come back, but just in case he does, she quickly strips off her clothes, dumps them in a pail of lukewarm water to soak, except for her petticoat and apron she needs to make rags. Wash now, but be quick about it. She lets down her hair, then takes another bucket of water and pours it over her head. The shock drives away her tears, and she's standing there, licking water from her lips and chin, without a towel, dripping, in all her misery when Pytor does return, the sight of her nakedness obviously stunning him for a moment, and he drops a duffle bag. She throws him a defiant, don't-you-dare look, but crouches, shaking with fear, trying to hide her breasts.

Sheepishly, he hands her a bar of hard soap, the kind her mother flakes with a knife to use for scrubbing floors. "A knife," she says, pantomiming shaving the soap, and pointing to the bucket of sopping clothes. From the pocket of his baggy pants he produces a switchblade. Instead of giving it to her, he shaves soap into the clothes bucket, while she shivers there, crouched, arms over her breasts, her hair plastered to her face, strands over her eyes. If she can't see him clearly in the dim light maybe he can't see more of her than is safe. Then he gives her the remains of the soap. She points at the doors: "Go!"

After the door clangs shut again, she soaps her hair, body, sniffing, but the soap has no perfume. Blood trickles between her legs. She's sore from the rags rubbing. She dabs herself dry with what's left of her petticoat, then folds a new rag — but no clean underwear – or clothes – unless, yes, the dufflebag holds two pair of men's trousers, a purple undershirt, and three white chemises with blowsy sleeves. The white drawers are long in the leg, with a button-up fly, and they fit to perfection. The trousers are too big in the waist, tight in the thighs. She digs deeper into the bag and retrieves: woollen socks! And a pair of soft Russian boots – *valenki?* – that fit well enough with extra stockings. The peasant shirt is baggy, the sleeves too long, but she rolls them up to her elbows. Now, if only she had a brush. She combs her hair with her fingers, plaits it, and ties the braids on top of her head; the ends will loosen when dry, so she covers them with another soft cap, without the red star. She could pass as a boy, a disguise she just may need once they reach their destination. Lena is a neutral Swede, a Gotlandska, but who knows what enemies Pytor may be hiding from besides Germans, now they've attacked the Baltic states. She wishes she knew where she is and where this wretched! stinking! rat-hole of a barge will anchor.

Feeling clean at least, she carefully folds strips of her petticoat and apron and stuffs them into her jacket pocket to keep them clean. She has one Stonechurch apple left in the apron pocket and she tucks that into her jacket too. Then she begins to wash her own clothes, hanging them on the line Pytor strung between two manger railings.

The iron doors open, and blessed sunlight bursts into the hold.

The Nik-nik wolf whistles when he sees her wearing his clothes. "How Russian of you!" she says.

He bows, like a courtier. "After you, brave lady."

She doesn't wait for a second invitation. She dashes ahead of him, then is blinded by the sun.

Signe

St. Petersburg, June 22, 2004

DISAPPOINTED THAT SHE DIDN'T EVEN DREAM of a *staret*, Signe wakes up in the real morning hardly able to see, and blames her swollen eyelids on the duvet feathers, surely not from a bout of weeping in her sleep.

In the bathroom, she dabs cortisone cream on the lids, takes another antihistamine, and dresses hastily in jeans and heavy sweater, throwing her slicker over her shoulder in case it rains.

She hastens to the dining room, hoping to have breakfast with Kostja and ask him if it would be possible for him to take her to a church or cathedral to ask a priest where she might find an Old Believer, a *staret*.

Having been raised in the Anglican church in Livelong, christened and later confirmed in her mother's faith by an itinerant Lutheran pastor, as an adult in Regina she'd found and attended an Orthodox church, at first drawn to it simply by the traditional onion dome. After the boating accident, her priest, Father Sergei, told her about a *poustina* in Combermere, Ontario, but then she was unable to even think about leaving Tapani for more than a few hours each day when she had to go to the university for lectures and meetings with her students. Of course, she had read about holy fools in Russian literature, those wanderers with healing powers, who often spoke in tongues. Aunt Maryushka had said that when a holy man returned from the wilderness his wisdom was meant for everyone in the village, and all who listened to him achieved a profound interior silence. Peace. And that was what Father Sergei had offered her, a place where a person could meet God through solitude, prayer and fasting. In Christian doctrine, he said, *poustina* was interpreted to mean *something to be changed,* and in Judaism it was a *place of liberation.* In Canada, a devout Russian noble woman who had escaped the revolution created a retreat in Combermere, but even Ontario was much too close to home for Signe who needed to run away from grief to an Old Believer, someone who would make real the words once spoken by Aunt Maryushka: *Dushenka, vyso proidyot.* Only then would it be possible for *everything to pass.*

She joins the chirpy and overly cheerful birders, but Kostja isn't among them. He must be eating with the riverboat staff in their dining room, or maybe he slept in. She does enjoy the hearty breakfast of porridge, *blini* with butter and syrup, but declines the traditional caviar. She never acquired a taste for it because Lena couldn't afford to have it shipped from Eastern Canada to the northern bushland. The glass of coffee is strong enough to choke a horse or please a babushka.

Then the passengers are divided into two groups: the birders and the tourists, Signe with the latter group herded onto a touring bus. She has no idea where the birders are going, and assumes that Kostja has gone with them, though she didn't see him board that bus.

She really doesn't care for birds, especially the raucous crows that overrun her Regina neighbourhood, the mountain ash and cottonwood shaking like old women trying to stave them off, and the boulevard in front of her house blanketed thick with them after a good rain when earthworms writhe to the surface of the loam. At Wascana Park, it's impossible to lay a picnic blanket without encountering goose shit scattered like brown pebbles.

She's ready for any discovery in this, the land of her father, but this morning's city tour begins with the battleship *Aurora* whose guns heralded the beginning of the revolution. It also played a minor role in the Second World War, but that has nothing to do with her mother and father and Aunt Maryushka. Nor does the cabin built by Peter the Great himself – in one day, according to legend – although it looks like the first rough-hewn house built by her father on the Livelong farm and now settling into the earth. She still feels guilty for its neglect. In Senate Square, while admiring the magnificent statue of Peter the Great on a rearing horse carved from rhodonite stone found only in Russia and the simple inscription – TO PETER I FROM CATHERINE II – Signe remembers that Aunt Maryushka told her that people planted cabbages and potatoes in the Summer Gardens during the Siege. They raided parks for marigolds, violets, dandelions and especially pine needles to make a brew to combat scurvy. Maryushka traded her worker's padded jacket for a glass of *klukva,* which sounds exotic but is only cranberry juice. That was when Maryushka's teeth were decaying and loosening. The idea that Lena and Pytor and Maryushka may have walked these very avenues sends prickles up her spine. But then, inside the magnificent and awe-inspiring Hermitage known as the Palace of Loneliness, among the hundreds of great works of art, Signe feels the pain of recognition in Reuben's portrait of Clara Serena, his daughter who died at age twelve – one year younger than Sasha when she left Signe – but rendered as he imagined she might have looked had she lived to see age thirty. If Sasha hadn't been taken so early, she would be taller than Signe, big-boned like her grandmother, her freckles faded on her nose, the birthmark at the base of her neck likely hidden by long honey-coloured hair highlighted, no doubt, with some shocking blue or violent red vegetable dye.

Then, during a short bus ride, a fragile woman all in white, with hair as soft as a cloud, comes out of a reverie as if she's been submerged in a pool and has broken to the surface. She moves to the seat beside Signe and tells her in too much detail the story of her favourite horse disappearing from her ranch in California, and then being hit by a truck on a highway. While telling the tale, she weeps into a white handkerchief embroidered with the letter J in the reddest of threads.

Signe manages to escape from Jean and her mourning in the imposing Cathedral of St. Peter and St. Paul where the czars are buried, Catherine the Great beside the husband she murdered – something Signe should have done to the father of her children before he left her for a Vietnamese waitress young enough to be his daughter. Without warning she thinks of her ex-husband Durwood and how there's nothing like exotic love to lift a depressed spirit.

How they fought. Signe blamed Durwood for not being home when the accident happened, and he accused her of neglect, of being too permissive – how could she let Tapani and Sasha go alone in the boat?

The last time Signe saw Durwood was in the office of Tapani's psychiatrist, a bald and bearded man with such a long face he looked like he needed an antidepressant – and fast! Durwood slouched on the sofa, held his head between his hands and wouldn't talk to anyone. Tapani tried to cut the vinyl on a chair with plastic scissors he found on a children's tea table. The doctor said he wanted to tranquilize Tapani. Signe took a sheet of construction paper, put it before Tapani, and told him to cut it in the shape of a bird instead of stabbing the furniture – as if he were five years old.

The sad doctor told Signe he believed that Durwood blamed himself for being at a conference in Montreal instead of at the lake with his family and driving the motorboat. Moreover, Durwood couldn't bear the sight of his disfigured son, missing one ear, the right side of his face a purple blotch, and worse, he couldn't live with a bereft mother who had no comfort of her own to offer her husband. No reaction from Durwood to the psychiatrist's summation. He'd already gone somewhere beyond boats and flames. *Your husband has been stolen from you,* the doctor said. *Taken away by pain.*

And then, at the tomb that held the recently discovered and unearthed bones of Nicholas II and Alexandra and their children, Signe feels like kneeling before it. It does look like an altar. When was the last time she visited Sasha's grave? She never erected a headstone. What could be engraved upon it? Like those royal children, Sasha died too young.

Tapani suffers another kind of loss.

He never had a job.

He never had a girlfriend.

The last book he read was a grade eight history text about Romulous and Remus.

In a daze and heavy of heart, Signe merely follows the guide and other tourists back to the bus that takes them to a restaurant in Pushkin's village that looks like an ancient wooden church mated with a fortress.

SIGNE

After an exquisite dinner of traditional Zakuski borsch, grouse roasted in sour cream and Volga sterlet with white asparagus in a restaurant the bus takes the tourists to the Markinsky, the intimate theatre of the czars and the home of Nijinsky and Pavolva.

IN THE LOBBY, WHILE WAITING for the theatre doors to open, Signe reflects on the fact that the second day of touring St. Petersburg has not gone well for her. Not only has she not seen Kostja all day, she has made no progress in searching out a wise man of old to help her come to terms with her grief and fear of water. She shifts her weight from one blistered foot to the other, keeping her head lowered and hoping no one will notice her distress, not all of it caused by her swollen eyelids. Why don't they open the doors?

Once again Signe refuses the tears threatening to carry her away to a watery bog so deep her feet will never touch ground again. Between her palms, Signe warms the antique locket that holds miniature portraits of her children, and then touches it to her swollen eyelids. Aunt Maryushka used to say that the gold rim of a wedding band would cure a sty, so maybe the locket will take away the pain of her allergy.

Oh no, Jean is coming at Signe, wanting to talk about her horse again. She approaches as if she's emerging from a dream. If Signe were to write a poem about her she'd title it "The Woman in White." Jean wears white jeans and embroidered cowboy shirt. Even her boots are white. Her tightly permed hair looks like a cloud floating above her dreamy eyes. At lunch at the Astoria Hotel she told Signe that she was the first woman to cross the Grand Canyon on horseback in one day. Sure enough, she's still clutching her scrapbook, it lightens her spirit, and she pauses before Signe, opens the book and says, "Here's the photo. He was seventeen hands high."

Signe says, "Is that the one you told us about at lunch?"

Jean says, "He was killed on the road. After he mysteriously escaped – or was let out of the corral."

Signe says, "Maybe your horse was stolen." If she tells Jean about her mother's Gotland ponies, about crossing the Ice Road, she'd never believe her. Just once she'd like to hear a story about how well someone lives, or about how someone found something – extraordinary. It's no comfort to realize that no one's life remains untouched by loss. Lena would have loved Jean's story, this horsewoman, though she might have felt shy in her homemade housedress and perpetually red, workworn hands before this classy woman with a white cashmere shawl topping white shirt and designer jeans.

"Excuse me," Signe says. "My eyes." She flees to the washroom where she looks in the mirror and discovers that her right eyelid has shrunk almost back to normal, but the left one droops, fluid still there. Her feet hurt, and looking down she realizes that her feet are beginning to swell. Too much salt in the Volga sterlet.

With only five minutes until the curtain rises, Signe avoids Jean by pretending to study the photographs and posters of the great Nijinsky. He was only five feet, four inches, no taller than Tapani before the accident, and he weighed one hundred and thirty pounds, same as her son now. He created frenetic twists, asymmetrical, angular movements, perhaps in imitation of his brain-damaged brother who fell from a second storey window and was never right in the head again. Tapani. Does everything in this formerly God-abandoned country have to remind her of her son?

At twenty-nine in 1917, Nijinsky went mad, but no reference is made in the guidebook to the revolution as a cause of his paranoia. He was afraid of imaginary glass scattered on stage. Like Tapani, he never looked at anyone he spoke to; surrounded by people he was always alone, which is exactly how Signe feels while teaching at the university, while touring now. Except with Kostja.

She reads on: Nijinsky lost his memory. She suspects shock treatments. She told the doctors they'd have to tie her down and zap her before she'd let them tamper with the electricity in her son's already damaged brain. There is epilepsy in her family — Carolina, Lena's mother, had it — and Signe is still afraid that shocks might trigger an otherwise latent disease. How often she stood rock-hard, as unmoving as the deepest boulder in her father's wheat field, refusing to sign the necessary permission papers that absolved all psychiatrists of responsibility. She said, "You'll have to shock me first."

She looks up, moves on to the next poster of Nijinsky, and is transfixed before it. Remove the tightly curled golden wig with tiny horns, the ears elongated and pointed with wax, and behold: the face of her boy, the purpled half in shadow, faun-like eyes. How arrestingly and impossibly beautiful.

Refusing to be harnessed further by this pain, at least while attending a Russian ballet, she shifts her feet on the plush, red carpet. Ahead, Jean has seated herself on a portable tripod that she uses as a walking stick when the legs are folded and the seat becomes a handle. Signe can imagine her on a saddle, commanding the Grand Canyon to make way for her horse. Perhaps she should tell Jean about the crossing of the Ice, about heroic *russen*. Signe has no doubt that Jean loved her lost horse as much as Lena loved her Thor, but Lena's gratitude to and pride in the forest horse outshone her loss. Still, Signe would like to yell at both women: *They were only horses!* And what would old Lena answer to that? Something in Swedish, a raunchy drinking song about jumping up and kicking oneself in the ass in order to keep on going. She sang it while weeding her garden, while churning butter, while lifting stooks of wheat, each one too heavy for most women. Signe can never be as strong as her mother, and that resentment once made her kick over the milk separator when she couldn't make it to the woodbox and dropped an armload of poplar. But that anger can never match the fierce undertow of resentment that she now feels towards a great dancer because, in only one of many balletic roles, he happens to look like her son. If it weren't for Tapani she wouldn't be drawn to objects of art that represent or express loss, just as at home in Regina what she notices is always determined by her mood of the eternal moment of accident. When she's sad the willows beside Wascana Lake lean towards the water, and when she's happier the light lifts or breaks through that dark foliage.

Oh where is the Believer who will make all this disappear? Who could she talk to now? Not Jean, shifting on her tripod seat, and fanning her pale face with a programme. Kostja. She'd just like to see him, to hear him speak only to her. Where is he? Well, yes, she supposes that the touring company wouldn't purchase tickets to the ballet for those in their employ, and even if he bought his own they likely frown on staff accompanying clients to events ashore. Maybe he's in his cabin writing a postcard to his botanist wife, telling her what glorious flowers she missed seeing in the Winter Palace gardens. Apart from Tapani, Signe has no one to send a card to, and she certainly doesn't wish her son were here now.

Doors opened, the crowd moves slowly into the intimate theatre of the czars, where the State symphony orchestra conducted by Gorkovenko warms up. But for the accident, her son might have gone on to a conservatory and played first violin in a Canadian orchestra. If only he were well enough to attend a concert – anywhere. Would this small but magnificent theater thrill him too? Instead of gowned and medalled aristocracy or even the limousine socialists and Party bosses of the last century, the velvet seats are filling up with American women in sneakers and windbreakers, their men removing Tilley hats and wraparound sunglasses. With no air conditioning, it's already heating up and programmes are used to fan flushed faces and beefy necks. At least there are no American hotdog and popcorn vendors. And there: the czar's box with its private dining room that she read about, and now she can see it in all its gilded magnificence for herself.

She feels like lifting and spreading her arms and embracing the ornately embossed prosidium arch, the very stage where Nijinsky changed the role of the male dancer forever with his flights of the Russian soul.

Signe finds her seat just at the curtain rises on the "White Adagio" of *Swan Lake.* The swan, an old symbol in Russian folklore for faithfulness in love, sheds its wings at night to become a maiden. After the *pas-de-deux,* Signe still has not seen a new Nijinsky, no great leaps into the rafters, though each and every dancer is precise and poetic in his or her execution of *La Danse.* And, it's the music from "The Dying Swan" that moves her finally, as if she just emerged, steamed to exhaustion from a sauna, leapt into the heart-stopping-cold of a northern river, then risen from the water energized, light of spirit and – not afraid! The performer, listed as A. Lineva in the programme, becomes the swan dying for the love of a human, her arms metamorphosed into wings, her neck elongated, her fingers the tips of feathers.

On her feet for the standing ovation, Signe applauds till her hands burn, crying, "Bravo! Bravo!" And then the Russian word from her childhood erupts from the pain in her throat: "*Bis! Bis!*" That's what her father shouted from the back row of the school auditorium when she read a Pushkin poem at a talent night. She was mortified in front of the English speaking parents of her friends, but now salt stings her raw eyelids.

She wishes Kostja were beside her. After all, a swan *is* a bird. She could never tell him she missed him. He might get the wrong idea and think she's smitten, just because after oh such a long time, a kind man shows interest in her. She feels foolish. Yet, she hopes he's waiting for her on the uppermost deck of the *Novikov Priboy*.

LATER, SHE HIKES UP HER SKIRT, and rushes up the carpeted stairs two at a time, then halts at the entrance to the Panorama Bar, but doesn't go inside. There, outside on the uppermost deck, Kostja, camera and binoculars slung over his neck, leans on the railing, one foot crossed over the other; he does seem to be waiting for her. Backlit by a sun refusing to set, his face shines when he sees her.

She wants to tell him about the dying swan, how the music moved her, a kind of momentary liberation from grief, but her tongue freezes as if stuck on the rim of her mother's rain barrel in winter; she doesn't want to cry again.

"Take lots of pictures?" She tosses one end of her shawl over her shoulder, it's always falling loose, but she forgot to pack a brooch. She shivers. It's too cold for June, that's all. She is *not* trembling with excitement, no never.

"I was preparing my lecture for tomorrow," he says.

Suddenly, out of nowhere, the wail of a tenor sax, but no person in sight.

"One of the crew," Kostja says. She leans on the railing beside him. Below the lifeboats, on the lower deck, a sailor fills the night with *Birth of the Blues*. Signe takes his photograph, then they nestle on the deck chairs, Kostja brushing away mosquitoes. He crosses his legs, leans back, taking a good look at Signe as if he wants to photograph her in Russia's everlasting light.

"What?"

"You look like a tabby curled on the sleeping platform of a stove, warming its back."

Kostja looks like a cat too, grey, the way he curls in his chair, arms raised, claws hidden in paws as velvet-soft as the undersides of mushrooms. When he sleeps, third eye open, his cat-spirit must slink into the white shadows of the eternal night here.

If Signe doesn't take care she'll become entangled with Kostja, be unable to leave, and will end up like Pasternak's Lara during the civil war, hidden in a dacha, waiting for her lover to save her – from what? From that wild child who is still trying to run away forever.

She will try to be as evasive as the birds he out-waits, outlasts.

And yet to her they have begun: nightly trysts under the eternal, white Russian night.

BYRNA BARCLAY

Lena

On the coal barge deck, June 23, 1941

UP ON DECK, Lena takes her first deep breath of fresh sea air, closes her eyes, a true Swede, worshiping the sun on her face, neck, arms.

Then she takes in the sea-battered deck, the boxy wheelhouse with its sooty stovepipe chimney and black whistle, the single lifeboat with a loose tarpaulin flapping like a fish out of water. She rushes around the planked perimeter of the hold to the side, clutching the sun-hot iron railing. The barge idles, its anchor dropped beside the first of many buoys, and she takes in green forests to the north. Here, the broken hull of a passenger-freight with a tattered Estonia flag. The *Pukhno or Rukhno?* – she can just barely make out the lettering of the steamer that almost blocks the centre of the channel. Sailboats still intact in the harbour, as if it's a holiday and they're waiting to take their owners for a pleasurable sail. Did any of them pick up survivors – or corpses – yesterday? So the sinking of the Latvian ship wasn't an isolated incident.

She leans against the railing, breathing deeply, swallowing hard. Refuse from the Estonian steamer floats in the brackish water. A barrel. A bottle. If she could fish it out of the sea she could stuff a message in it.

Then she hears the cry of a bird, turns her head to the left, and there on the railing a wounded seagull. It hops on one leg, balancing with one out-stretched wing, the other dragging, held loosely at its side. Wingbones rattle, the feathers scorched. The gull screams, but inches closer. The bird must have been shot out of the air, burned feathers suggest a bullet graze, the friction of metal on feathers causing them to ignite and burn. She finds the last of her Stonechurch apples in her jacket pocket, takes a small bite, places bits on the railing. "Come," she says. "Eat." The gull hops forward, pecks the first apple bit, its throat working. "That's it, now another one." She sidles closer to the bird. It eats another piece of apple.

The coal barge lies at anchor now, seawater lapping at its sides as if it wants to wash away streaks of charcoal that look like upside down first efforts of a child trying to write Cyrillic letters. She turns away from the railing, pretending to ignore the bird and not notice Pytor who has just left the wheelhouse and slowly makes his way towards her, minding the roll of the barge with every careful step, a quizzical look on his face. Then he takes a chunk of coal and hurls it at the bird, just missing it. "Don't!" she says. The bird lifts off, screeching, but it can't fly with one wing. It lands on the railing again, toppling, but not falling. Pytor picks up another piece of coal, but before he can throw it, Lena moves even closer to the bird. "Don't scare it away!" she says, holding up her hand, palm turned toward Pytor.

He stares at her, and lowers his arm.

"The wing isn't broken," she says. "Just burned." She fishes into her jacket pocket for the strips of petticoat, a perfect bandage. "If only I had some healing salve." Straightening, she waits for the gull to take one more hop towards her, but the gap between apple bits is too big, it flaps its wing, and before it falls, Lena catches it. She slides down, onto the deck. The bird flaps its wing, screeching. She smooths its ruffled neck feathers. "Don't be afraid. I won't hurt you." Its claws dig into her thighs, she strokes its head with one finger. "There, there." She places the strip of petticoat across her knees. Its legs buckle, and it wiggles down, on top of the bandage; it nestles in her lap. She feeds it another bite of apple. "Help me, Pytor. Hold the bird while I tie its wing to its body. It won't hurt so much if the air can't get at it and that way it has a chance of healing."

Not a word from Pytor. She lifts her head. He's leaning against the railing further down, looking as if he might jump overboard, his eyes widened as if he's just seen another steamer blow up in his face. "Come here, please," she says. "Help me with the bird." He seems not to understand what she says, what she wants him to do. "Now," she says. "While it's settled and not so terrified. Come here, Pytor." What's the matter with the man? Surely, he's not afraid of a little bird. His face flushes, and his jaw knots.

The gull closes its eyes, chirping, throat working. It rests, but the pain must be almost enough to knock it out. She coos, head bent over the bird.

A shadow falls before her, Pytor's. He kneels before her, his wild hair falling over his face as if he wants to hide how he feels, his lips pursed as if he's trying mightily not to cry. "Don't touch it," she says, "not yet." She lays one hand over his to still it. The wounded wing lies flat against the side of the bird's breast. "Easy," she says. She begins to wrap the makeshift bandage around the bird's belly, easing it under the good wing, then over the burned wing. "Hold it," she says, lifting the bird by its belly and handing it to Pytor. The bird screams, but it can't flap either wing, its legs working like scissors, its claws splayed and talons curved for scratching, but Pytor holds it firmly, while Lena wraps the wing tight to the body, splits the end of the bandage into two strips and ties a knot. Pytor gently lays the bird back in her lap. She strokes its head with one finger. Its eyes dart with fear. It refuses another bit of apple.

"You do this?" Pytor says. "For bird going to die?"

"What do we do with it now?" she says. "I can't take it down to the stinking hold!" It will take weeks for the burn to heal and feathers to grow back, before it can exercise its wing and take flight again.

Pytor holds one hand over his chest, as if it hurts. He tries to stand, but he's trembling so much he slips on the deck, landing on his backside. He curses in Russian, finds footing, and pushes himself up, his face redder than the burned flesh of the bird. He dashes into the wheelhouse and returns with a box, a cushion, and a tin can filled with fresh water – and an ice pick. He squats, punching holes in the top of the box with the ice pick, then lifts the lid, places the cushion and water inside the box. "Is good, yes?" he says in Swedish, like a boy looking for praise.

"Yes, very good." Lena puts the bird in the box, and before Pytor can put the lid on it, Lena stops his hands with her own. "It can't fly," she says, "so no need to imprison it." She looks at him hard, throwing the meanest and most threatening look she can muster, as if she's trying to lift the back hoof and leg of the stubbornest *russ* on the Lostja moor.

They look at each other, and Pytor's gaze is so intense she has to look away. What has come over him? What a strange, complicated man, this horse thief.

She points at the wheelhouse. "Take the bird out of the sun."

Pytor leaves her there, taking the bird inside, and within minutes he has raised the anchor and the boat moves east again, passing another barge, this one loaded with sand.

WITH PYTOR IN THE WHEELHOUSE, Lena is free to lean on the railing and try to figure out where she is now and where Pytor is taking her. The barge moves easily through invisible sea gates into the Neva inlet, traversing the estuary into a sea canal, the banks reinforced with rocks on either side, with fortress and lighthouse. At the lee, it leaves the open Gulf and its German mines. It passes an island and a naval fortress that looks like a battleship. A grim garrison. Sharp-edged traps made of concrete look like giant teeth. And Lena realizes that the barge is now on the edge of the city, moving swiftly towards it. Pytor calls her name from the window of the wheelhouse, gesturing at what looks like miles and miles of workers. "*Blockadniki,*" he shouts, and she understands they are People of the Blockade. Women in pants and padded jackets as well as old men, even older children, dig trenches, concrete gun pits, creating a bastion of fortifications, airfields for new, fast fighters and bombers she has seen in newsreels and flying over her island. They're building an iron ring around the city. While they work, they – sing! *Vstavay, strana ogromnaya. Vstavy, na smartnyi boy.* The song has the rhythm of a march, like a national anthem, though no one holds a hand or cap over the heart. When they lift their heads in pride their solemn and serious faces shine through dust and grit. A call to arms or a dirge? *S fashistkoy siloy temnouy. S proklyatoyu ordoy!*

Lena feels stunned, as if someone has struck her on the top of her head. She's being taken into a war zone.

On hills near a village, piles of small objects that could be rocks – or crude explosives? Maybe to throw at panzers if they break through the front. Soldiers in khaki and blue uniforms everywhere. What would her father think of all these preparations for war? He clams up whenever anyone mentions the Great War and the lack of Sweden's part in it. He must have needed to fight to prove himself a man to his father. The Soft-hearted Soldier, Carolina calls him. If she were here she'd say, Out of the frying pan into the fire. Lena wanted to get away, but not into the middle of a war. Now she feels as if someone is smacking one side of her head, then the other. She fights to keep her wits about her, not wanting to miss a single sight, no matter how frightening or strange.

There: Leningrad! A skyline of spires and onion domes, brilliant and gilded in the sun. Blimps over the city, like white whales under scattered clouds. Shabbily dressed people pour onto one bank of the river from the west and south, lugging carts full of belongings, crates of chickens, leading goats, even a few cows. They must be evacuees. Where the river narrows she can see houses on either side, so close together they seem to huddle for protection. Boards and paper strips hammered onto windows – for reinforcement? Some have crosses for divine protection, another surprise to Lena. Entrances to buildings and courtyards full of new lumber and bricks, garrets emptied, instructions shouted through loud-hailers, bursts of military song: *Pust yarost blagorodnaya*. Boys play soldiers – perhaps White Russian vs. Red – among barricades made from rusty springs, bedsteads, barbed wire. Bulky chemises and undershirts hang on clotheslines, which makes Lena long for a bath in a real tub before a hearth, her own clean clothes.

She's moving into a strange and frightening place, so far from peaceful Gotland with its walnut and mulberry and maple trees, bird sanctuaries, and oh, the orchids in the balmy south. There, the greatest tension involves the farm wives' scraps over the price of eggs and butter and bread offered in their market stalls.

Might she find people who could help her find a way home? Likely no Swedish embassy, of course, the Northern War so sharp in the collective memory it might have happened yesterday. When she makes her escape she'll search for the British embassy. First thing, she'll send a telegram home, her parents must be mad with worry, Carolina throwing a different kind of mother fit. They looked after each other, Lena and her mother. What she wouldn't give for a hot water bottle to ease her cramps now. Even her head hurts.

Far ahead: a needle spire, surrounded by scaffolds and netting. The barge chugs into a basin, and before her rises a breathtaking vision of golden cupolas and a dome of a huge cathedral, the needle spire drawing ever closer. The barge yields the right of way to a ship flying the colours of the Danish flag. Pytor's in the wheelhouse, his back to her, so he can't see her wave frantically at the passenger steamer, but a sailor merely doffs his cap. So many ships in this anchorage. Surely, one could take her home. If only some official would halt their passage. She feels as if she's a buoy in a harbour known for rough weather, constantly rising and falling with the tide of her own emotions. No need to panic; she can withstand the knock-about storm-driven waves, the surprise of shifting winds, even the drifting when it's calm.

Then the barge passes a stunningly ornate, Baltic-coloured palace, like something out of a fairy tale. But another officious looking building spattered with brown, green, and grey paint pulls her back to the grim reality of war. More nets. On roofs of neighbouring buildings huge guns aimed at the sky make her feel like crying. A maze of trenches and machine gun nests. Four tanks at the entrance. Gunboats on the river's embankment. Troop trucks. Searchlights. Armoured cars. She can hear the distant blare of military music from loudspeakers mingled with more singing: *Pust yarost blagorodnaya/Vskipaet kak volna* – It's all too much, the strange sights and sounds bombarding her senses as if she's been transported to another planet. She feels slightly sick to her stomach.

Another cathedral now looks like a fortress covered with rigging. More of those nets. Gotland boasts ninety sandstone churches from the thirteenth century, but none so grand, so monumental as these. And oh, the colours! Gold and silver and precious gems glint in the sun. Yet, grey-green sandbags protect buildings and sculptures on bridges.

Then: a shipping dock. Grain elevators. The barge stops suddenly and she's thrown sideways, allowing herself to drift with the barge until the anchor is dropped.

Before she can think of jumping onto the dock, Pytor leaves the wheelhouse, takes her by the arm, leads her back into the hold, ignoring her frantic protests – "I promise I won't run away! Let me stay on deck." But, once again she's in the dark hold, with only her ponies for comfort, their need for oats and water, the day's shit-shovelling and deck swabbing awaiting her too.

She's glad to hide from the sights of war, but is angry with herself for not trying to escape, for forgetting too about her forest horses and how they need her.

She hears them before her eyes adjust to the dark of the hold: flies.

FLIES. HUNDREDS OF THEM swarming about the ponies, hovering over dung and urine. Her food tray looks as if it's covered with black lace netting. The irritated *russ* swish their tails, swing heavy heads, stamp hooves. Furious at being put back in the hold, she takes one of Pytor's books in each hand and wages war, trying to smack the flies dead with a resounding clap, a hopeless task. Then, the barge merely rocks, its motor shut down, and she listens for but cannot hear Pytor leaving the boat, his soft boots soundless on the wharf. He must have horse business to attend to, finally. But no transfer of ponies onto land can be done without Lena, or at least not without someone discovering her imprisonment: this her last shred of hope.

She's still cramping, has passed far more gas than normal, and too often today she's had to empty her bowels. If she were home her mother would make her a concoction of herbs to clean out her system, to take away the cramps. The memory of Carolina sitting on the edge of Lena's bed, pretending to taste a spoonful of foul medicine to show Lena it's not so bad after all springs tears to her eyes but doesn't stop their burning. Suddenly, she feels as if she's been hit in the belly by a medicine ball, and she hunches over, with a cry not unlike the seagull's. Nausea rises like a hot iron in her throat, and she throws up before she can reach a bucket. This is not seasickness. The cramps unceasing, she eliminates only burning water.

Weak and dizzy, she feels hot, and curls onto her blanket, holding her belly.

She needs a doctor. A hospital. Her mother. But she never was a bawl-baby and isn't about to feel that sorry for herself now.

Minutes or hours or days later, someone's shadow falls across the grimy floor. She thinks it's her father come to take her home.

BUT IT'S ONLY THE NIK-NIK bending over her, swabbing her hot head with a cool cloth. She lifts her head, and bile rises like boiling acid in her throat. While she retches, he holds her forehead, rubs her back. When she's done, she collapses back onto her blanket-bed. He looks frightened, and says in Swedish: " You drink – water?" He tries to help her to her feet, and when her legs give way, he swoops her up, grunting, adjusts the heft of her – "You weight a ton!" – and carries her out of the hold, down the gangplank, onto a wharf. There he deposits her – "Stay! Help, I get you." He races through a linden-lined lane, but she's too weak to stand unaided, much less make a run for it. She squats on the dock.

Soon he returns, again lifts her, and staggering, manages to carry her to a street where a truck waits, and before he helps her into its cab, he whispers: "Shhh! Don't say. Word." He gives directions to the driver, who looks like a worker – he's wearing overalls. The only vaguely familiar word is *prospekt,* which may mean street. If she could speak Russian she could tell the driver she's been kidnapped, ask him to help her, but her instincts tell her to trust Pytor and hold tight to silence. She hopes they're taking her to a doctor, but that might be too risky for Pytor. Maybe he's taking her to his home. If so, once she's better she'll find a way to escape, find a foreign embassy, at least wire her parents.

The worker puffs one of those vile Russian cigarettes, the smoke makes her gag and choke, so he tosses it out the window.

Inside the truck's cab, she leans back, holding her belly against the cramps, and Pytor wraps an arm around her, pulls her closer so her head lies on his shoulder, and she stares out the front window, praying she won't mess in her clothes.

At first everything is blurry: leafy trees, likely aspen, and flowering lilacs. Then she sees a detachment of shabby, emaciated men marching like defeated soldiers. Why would guards hold machine guns at their backs? Lena doesn't know who the men are, perhaps criminals moved from one prison to another, or they could be political prisoners being forced to go to war. Against her temple, Lena can feel Pytor's jaw working in anger, grinding his teeth. The men look too weak to fight. How sad.

Here, she wonders about cement blocks, if they are intended to bar the passage of German tanks. Railroad iron criss-crossed where Nazi troops might break through look like dragons' teeth.

The truck passes a heavily walled and sprawling cement structure, with smoking chimneys that must be a steelworks. The driver of the truck says something and she catches one word: Kirov. And then another: tanks. Hundreds of workers file through its gates, and she wonders if the driver works there and will be late for his shift. What if he's stopped by police and she's discovered? Would it get the kind man in trouble – and what about Pytor?

A network of canals. They cross a bridge and drive along a long promenade of palaces beside the Neva. Red Army soldiers clamber down to the river with buckets and pans – to drink the water? Water! That's what's made her sick. She didn't drink it, but did try to clean her teeth with it.

An officious building with bare flagpole, broken windows and two signs, one in unreadable Cyrillic, the other in German, and she recognizes one word: embassy. The driver spits out the window.

So many automobiles and horse-drawn carts and electric streetcars with machine guns mounted on their fronts, and the traffic becomes so heavy, finally, the truck slows, and she can make out crying children on the trams, amid bundles and boxes and valises; they must be going to an evacuation point. If she wasn't so sick she'd jump out of the truck and try to hide among them, make her way to – where?

Every street sign seems to read the same, so it must mean street or avenue. How strange to see numbers 3 and 6 mixed in with letters, a backwards R. If she escapes, how impossible to find her way when she can't read street signs or even signs above stores. Windows of shops sandbagged and criss-crossed with newspaper strips. Long queues of mostly kerchiefed or shawled women, waiting their turn, with cards in their hands. Food rationed so soon in a war that, as far as Lena can tell, is only one or two days old? Surely, not. Maybe there's always a shortage of food.

Posters with pictures of soldiers, strange-shaped letters and words she can't read on lamp posts, likely calling men to war. A blind beggar plays an accordion, the song, *Katyuska,* that she's heard often enough on her father's short-wave radio when he dials into different foreign bands late at night. How she wishes she were home, eating her mother's homemade ice cream and listening to the song far away. Having also heard it sung in Swedish and English on the network from Stockholm, she knows the lyrics. Pytor sings softly, likely in an attempt to make her forget how her head throbs: *Katyuska came to the shore/To the very highest bank. She came to sing a song/For the one she loved/For the one whose letter she kept.* It sounds as soft as a lullaby, as sad as a love song. Maybe she can trust him just a little bit now, not that she ever was afraid of him, oh no. Never mind, he'd never let her escape.

He whispers in her ear: "Feel better? No far too much we go now." His Swedish is so bad she almost laughs, wondering where he learned to speak.

"*Katushka!*" the worker says, then in English: "Rockets! Secret weapon!" He's talking with his hands now and she wishes she dare shout at him to keep them on the wheel. Her father and the other farmers have heard from Latvian friends about these new weapons that shoot long arrows of flame, like meteors shaking the earth, their screaming and fiery trails so terrifying they were supposed to stop the Germans if they attacked Russia.

Seamen and soldiers everywhere. The driver seems to be telling Pytor a story, still waving one arm, but Pytor holds tight to his secrets, the first being that the sick boy beside him is really a Swedish girl he kidnapped. They seem to be humming instead of talking, a cello to a bass fiddle.

Loudspeakers on every corner lamppost, blatting what she suspects is news of the war, the metallic voice like a machine gun rattling.

Daffodils and cherry blossom twigs on sale at kiosks. The smell of meat pies. Bile rises in her throat again. Pytor rolls down his window. The air is warm and smoky. She looks up, between buildings, and sees a false sunrise – something burning far away. A beam of light slashes the sky. Then leaflets falling. The truck stops, the driver curses and shakes his fist so the messages must be from the Germans, not the Russians. At a great distance, the racket of guns, a feeble answer to whatever propaganda is written on the papers falling from the sky. Now she sees firefighters on roofs, at the ready with sand pails, water buckets, shovels and axes. What if the Germans start bombing? Where could they hide? Fear shoots up her spine like an electric shock from a cattle prod. Then English words slam into her aching head: *Bomb Shelter*. In newspapers from the mainland she read about Londoners spending whole nights in the underground *subway,* no word for that in Gutamål, the old language, or even in Gotlandska, the new. When the first bombs hit Leningrad the people must have been taken by surprise, with no shelter to be found. She covers her mouth with both hands so she won't scream at Pytor for stealing her away, for placing her in such danger.

She retches so hard her chest aches, and Pytor offers her a clean, white handkerchief to hold over her mouth. She has the shakes now. He whispers, "Almost there." Where? She needs a doctor, but wants her mother's cool hands on her forehead. She's so hot his breath on her ear makes her shiver.

Then she smells – evergreen or pine? They're stopped beside a cart, wreathed with flowers. Oh. It's a coffin covered with red cloth and pulled by white horses with funeral draperies. Behind it a band plays a dirge, followed by weeping relatives. There must be a priestyard nearby. She hopes the person died from natural causes, not from the first bombs to hit the city. She wants to go home where it's safe. Her belly cramps again. She can barely hold her head up, and she rests it on Pytor's shoulder again. She needs water but doubts she could keep any down.

They overtake and pass the procession, turn down a street only to discover it's barricaded with a wall of sandbags that don't fully hide machine guns and soldiers smoking those vile cigarettes. The truck retreats, turns back the way it came, then makes a detour down a street where children with pails of whitewash paint over street signs and house numbers. So much bouncing and jouncing makes her feel dizzy, nausea burning her throat. At the other end, another barricade, a jungle of paving blocks and timbers, railroad iron, steel tubing. The truck stops at a large corner house. She hopes it belongs to a doctor.

Pytor offers rubles to the worker, but the rough man shakes his bristly head. Pytor helps Lena out of the truck. The pains in her belly force her to bend over, clutching. Sweat streaks down her cheeks, yet she shivers with cold. Pytor helps her up a short walk, through a portal into a courtyard piled with those strange rock-sized explosives. He takes her through the gated entrance where a steel-framed box holds those big guns – anti-tank or anti-aircraft? – and flintlocks and muzzleloaders she's only seen before in a museum. Clearly, Russia was not prepared for Germany's attack, and now arms its citizens with guns from antiquity. She'll worry about that later, when she's well again, to be sure.

Is this a military or citizen's command post? She doesn't care, as long as there is a doctor to make her better.

Inside, a single blue lightbulb hangs from the ceiling. Another set of doors, a long hallway, a staircase. Pytor helps her, one step at a time, up two flights of stairs, their boxcalf boots crunching on dirt. They take a short rest at each landing, Lena panting and gagging.

Finally, they stop before a door, which he bangs with his elbow. No answer. He shoves with his rear end, the door opens, he swivels around, and sits her down on a Victorian stocking-chair, then kneels and removes her boots, she falling forward and clutching his shoulders so she won't faint from pain in her belly, her head.

A small, red-headed woman dressed in a loosely tied robe holds a rifle, cocked and aimed, but lowers it when she says, "Pytor!"

The woman disappears and the room fades into black.

Maryushka

St. Petersburg, June 23, 1941

IN THE LIGHT FROM THE WINDOWS LOOKING onto the street Maryushka has been reading today's issue of *Leningradskaya Pravada*. The news circulated by Moscow is grim. German troops have arrived in Finland, leaving only twenty miles between Leningrad and the Finnish border. The Germans close in on Leningrad from the south and west. Blitzkrieg, the Lightning War, has begun without warning, and the Soviet air force was all but destroyed during the first hours of the war.

It's all the fault of NKVD Police Chief Beria, everyone knows that, and it's the topic of conversation during every lunch break at the Kirov factory. They say that under Stalin's command, Beria had wiped out the Red Army during *Yezhovshchina,* The Purge of Purges in 1937–38, when every commander of an army corps had been shot and every division commander was shot or sent to Siberia. Class enemies had numbered in tens of thousands, and not one worker Maryushka knows can claim a family untouched by the purges; they cower in fear, but whisper among themselves: How can the army fight without leaders? Everyone is frightened but also afraid to talk about the purges lest the NKVD arrest them too; disloyalty is equal to treason. At the Kirov, Maryushka keeps her head down, and focuses on her work.

Her hands shake while she reads, and twice she has to wipe sweat from her eyelids with one of her husband's handkerchiefs she keeps tucked in her bosom.

But of all the articles, the one about Tamerlane's Gur Emir mausoleum confirms Maryushka's worst fears. On the very first day of the war, at The Hermitage, a slab of green nephrite was lifted from the sarcophagus and under the great stone lay the skeleton, with one leg shorter than the other. The legend that Tamerlane was lame and that if the tomb was ever opened it would release an horrific war has been fulfilled; and now Maryushka fears for her people, for her brother Pytor and beloved Mikhail as never before, not even when she was imprisoned in the Children's Brick Factory.

Already the bombing has left sections of the city without water and functioning drains. When radio broadcasts warned of cholera, typhus and dystrophy caused by starvation and the lines increased at *Gastronom* grocery stores, Maryushka withdrew her small savings from the state bank, and has begun to hoard nonperishable food: canned goods, sugar, flour, groats, sausages, salt. Maryushka has little to trade for food or extra ration cards. She receives the eight hundred grams of bread a day allotted for workers, ample amounts of cereals, fats and sugar. So far, she has lugged home a bushel of turnips, slivers of compressed meat, a sack of potatoes, another of dried beans, jars of pickled herring, sheepgut jelly and tins of condensed milk. She still needs flour and powdered eggs, and plans to sell or trade the Victorian stocking chair she sits upon for an extra ration card. This afternoon she will take part in the trading that has begun at the steel factory.

Food. That's all the women at work ever talk about now: what's for supper tonight, how hungry they still are, till it turns Maryushka's stomach, and she wishes she could lose interest in food. Yet, she loses sleep at night and sometimes can't concentrate on her welding for fear there won't be enough rations. Panic spreads within her like a swarm of angry bees.

She holds the newspaper to her thin chest, rocking it as if it were a child, unable to rise and rinse out her glass of tea before she leaves for the Kirov where she is one of thousands building tanks for Stalin. A knock on the door causes her to jump with fright, and her heart leaps into her throat like a grasshopper. She's not expecting anyone, with Mikhail called to the newly created Front with the People's Volunteers on the very first day of the war. Quickly, she looks out the second-storey window for a Beria's Black Crow – one of the wagons of his secret police that take people away to Leningrad's Shpalerny Prison or the Kretsti. There's only a rickety worker's lorry beetling far down the road. The hammering on the door doesn't stop. With shaking hands, Maryushka folds the newspaper, rises from her rocker, hastens to place the paper on top of the kindling box for tonight's fire. Banging on the door makes it rattle on its hinges, but Maryushka doesn't call out to let the person frightening her know that yes, she will answer it. She has to fetch her rifle still on the table beside her bed. Now the pounding on her door changes her fear to anger. She grabs her rifle and releases the safety catch, ready for thieves. She opens the door.

And there he is, Pytor, on her threshold, holding a sick boy in his arms. No wonder the banging on the door was so loud, he would have had to kick it. The small face beneath the cap is flushed with fever, and he's so listless his eyes droop. Pytor says, "Help."

She hasn't seen her rascal of a brother in months.

Pytor is not entirely welcome in her home since he has never been one to be told what to do and what to think, and is not a Party member. It's always dangerous to give him shelter, and usually she sends him packing with a parcel of whatever food she can spare, telling him to be careful, to stay hidden in the hills with other homeless wretches – many of them bandits and gypsies – and not come back to the city. It does no good to remind him he's the son of a traitor to the State. Unlike obedient and rehabilitated Maryushka, Pytor has no identity papers, no honest employment, and has never been accepted into the KOMSOMOL. Worrying about him is a never-ending rollercoaster ride for Maryushka. Lowering the rifle, Maryushka says, "I'd hoped that you had seen the error of your ways and joined the army of workers fortifying the city."

So here she is, prepared to give a parcel of food to her brother – he's always so hungry – but quite unprepared to deal with this sick bird he's brought to her doorstep.

The boy's head flops forward and his cap falls off, exposing yellow hair braided on top of his head. A girl!

Maryushka yells, "Don't bring one of your *urki* here!" Before he can answer she adds: "What have you done now?"

"Help me," Pytor says, his arms obviously tiring. He almost drops the unconscious girl. "She's sick. I think she must have drunk the horses' water."

"What horses?" Maryushka catches up the girl's legs, and together they lug the dead weight into her foyer.

"*Po muzike khodit,*" he says, lapsing into slang, *move to the music* a thief's way of saying commit a crime.

"Don't give me any of your *Blatnoe Slovo!*" she says. "No thieves' talk in my house!"

They carry the girl through the short hallway. Pytor stumbles, and his left foot knocks over the umbrella stand.

"*Blatnaya muzyka.* It's a perfectly legal deal – only the horse trader went back on his word because of the damn war – and now insists I owe him for the boat and feed."

Maryushka doesn't want to know the name of the trader, for fear such knowledge will implicate her in the theft. "And I suppose you stole the girl too." It's always the same for Maryushka. She's constantly afraid for her brother and how his actions might impact on her status with the Party, yet he makes her so angry sometimes she could just disown him. He always makes her feel like she's a child again, when he used to push her on the playground swing: feet up and head dropped back, she's swinging upside down, dizzied by the downswing, the sudden pitch and toss in the pit of her stomach, yet unable to make herself drop her feet and drag them in the hollow before she's sailing backwards and up and up; and on the descent again, from behind he pushes her even harder.

"*Idti na shalynuyu,*" he says, shrugging. Unplanned theft. "The horses will make us rich!"

"Not me," Maryushka says. She doesn't want to know any more, for fear of being implicated in the theft – and maybe kidnapping. She has to get him out of her apartment as quickly as possible. "Take her into the bedroom," she orders. "But she can't stay here long – understand?"

Pytor lifts and carries the girl like a bride who has fainted.

In the bedroom, he lays her on Maryushka's bed. She smacks the girl's cheeks, trying to wake her up, her skin hot with fever. Her chemise is stained yellow with bile. She smells rank of horse, sweat, vomit. Together, they strip her of her filthy clothing, which Maryushka dumps in the laundry tub. "Slap her wrists while I get a basin of water."

Shortly, she returns to find Pytor seated beside the bed, stroking the girl's hands, calling her *Dushenka,* My Little Dove, as if she's a child, then Lena, begging her to wake up, she's going to be well, if she'll just talk to him he'll take her home. Where did he learn such tenderness? Kindness is a foreign word to her brother. The only love he has known was given him by Maryushka herself, long ago when they were children in the brick factory. Already, this girl has taught him something more than just how to survive? That it's safe to let down his guard? Ah, the man has fallen in love, likely for the first time for all Maryushka knows, but he's too dim-witted to know it yet.

"And where might home be?" Maryushka says.

"Gotland."

A Swede! There are patrols all over the city, looking for foreigners, any person who looks suspicious. Anyone without a Party pass is shot on the spot, no more questions asked. Any violation – the taking of photographs – will be punished under the new military law. "You never learn, do you? Have you lost your mind?"

Maryushka pushes her brother out of the way, and begins to bathe the Swede with cold water, to cool her down, as well as clean her up – she smells worse than the dairy barns near the Kirov works.

"I'll get papers for her. I know someone."

"I'm sure you do! But if she's stopped, what then? Can she speak Russian? Even if she does, she looks German enough to be shot on sight. There are spies – everywhere – building up a fifth column." Maryushka points a finger at her brother. "You know the NKVD!"

"Stupid cops."

"I could just shake you! If they decide she's a German disguised as a Swede they'll torture her until she confesses to espionage. I'll have to report her – or get arrested myself if she's discovered. A neighbour might have seen you bringing her here." Maryushka's arms and chest feel prickly as if she's suddenly been stricken with a painfully itchy heat rash.

The girl's hands are work-worn, fingernails ragged, grime embedded in the lines of her palms, like a field worker's or a farmer's. Maryushka washes them.

Her brother looks frightened. Like Maryushka, he must remember their earliest childhood years on the prison island for women and children of State traitors. "Is she going to die?" Pytor's voice cracks, as if he's still a boy coming-of-age in the orphanage. He acts tough, and no one could tame him, not Gulag guards or rehabilitators in the Children's Brick Factory, not even the kind farmer who caught him stealing eggs and put him to work in a collective until Pytor ran away again because only *Khozyain,* The Boss, was allowed a chicken for his family. It's a wonder he's survived this long.

When he fingers their mother's cross around his neck Maryushka can't help but soften her feelings towards him. She has seen his tattoos: on his left shoulder, *I'll Never Forget My Mother* scrolled beneath a seagull to remind him of the island of his birth; on his chest, the head of a wolf baying at the moon.

With the back of her hand, Maryushka tests the Swedish girl's forehead and neck: much too hot, the sponge bath having failed to bring down the fever. "She better not die on you! Hold her up while I put a nightgown on her."

When they sit her up, the girl opens her Nordic-blue eyes, the lids flutter, then she looks at Pytor as if he's her guardian angel come to take her home. "*Russen,*" she says.

"I'll take care of them," he says, gently lowering her back on the pillows. "Don't worry."

"Bird," the girl says. Her pronunciation is poor, as if she's just learning to speak Russian.

"I won't forget to feed the bird," Pytor says.

"Is she delirious?" Maryushka says. "What's she talking about?" But she can't wait for an answer. "It wasn't enough to steal horses," she says, stomping off to the water closet to fetch some medicine. "You had to steal a girl too!" He's never done an honest day's work in his life; he began his career as Thief-in-law at age five when he stole bread from the orphanage kitchen.

"She got in the way," he says, raising his voice.

Returning with a bottle of milk of magnesia and a spoon, Maryushka says, "I've got nothing to do with this." She raps his knuckles with the spoon.

Pytor covers the Swedish girl with a blanket, tucks the ends around her neck. "I have business to attend to," he says, rising. "My sister will look after you. Open your mouth. It will make you better."

Maryushka spoons the medicine into the girl's mouth. Then she opens the tall window shutters to let in cool air, and with it the scent of lilacs blooming in the courtyard below. She takes a deep breath, then turns and faces her brother. He dips a cloth in the cold water in the washbasin, and places it on the girl's forehead. Her eyes are glazed, yet overly bright, a bad sign. What if she dies? How will Maryushka explain to the authorities that she really isn't harbouring a spy? "You can't leave her here! I've got to go to work."

"Call in sick."

"I'm not irresponsible like you!"

"Small sister, come away with me. I'll take care of you."

Maryushka says, "The people will stay and fight to death for our city. It seems that you are not one of them." She advances on her skinny brother as if he's a chicken that has wandered into the house on a hot summer day when the door is left open. And the sudden memory flashes before her of her mother chasing one out of a summer kitchen with a broom. It makes tears spring to her eyes. She has so few memories of their mother before they landed on the island of Anza in the Gulag, and too rarely do they launch themselves into her mind like an unexpected but welcome guest.

Maryushka raises an arm as if to hit him. "Maybe you are no longer my brother." Then she drops her arm and her voice breaks. "Don't you need to be useful to the war effort – to help our people?"

"Just now, Lena needs me, I think."

"Who?" Oh, the Swedish girl.

"I won't be long." And Pytor brushes by Maryushka, plunks his orphan's cap on his head – he should have thrown away that old hat and the past with it years ago. He's muttering to himself and picking at scabs on his neck, something he always did when frightened as a child. She hears his mumbled curses directed at some vague circus people and then something about zoo animals being evacuated. And he's out the door, their mother's saints only know where he's going and what he's up to now.

She just hopes he doesn't get caught by a patrol. Then whatever would she do with this foreign girl?

Lena

Leningrad, June 25, 1941

ALL DAY AND ALL NIGHT, while German JU-88's fly over Leningrad, dropping their deadly loads near and far and shaking the ceiling and the strange bed she lies on, fever-ridden Lena has been flying over the blue-green Baltic, homeward bound for the Lojsta moor.

She isn't asleep.

She isn't awake.

Thor has sprouted great white wings, with the broad expanse of a swan's. His strong body plunges through the misty air. His thick and silky mane is twined about her fingers. Her own hair is wet, crusted with salt and slaps her bare and sweating back. The wind is behind them, pushing them forward, through a blue maze of snow petals the colour of lilacs. Far away, the sounds of many pounding hooves, a wild, invisible army overrunning the northland. She presses her knees against his soughing belly, lays her head against his neck, looking down at the greening earth rising to meet them, like a billowing patchwork quilt airing on a clothesline. Foam at the pony's mouth, like the crest of a roiling wave. And there, at the bottom of the garden, her mother shades her eyes with one hand and waves her green apron with the other. Then her knees buckle, and she collapses with another Mother Fit.

The forest horse rears, pawing the air, shrilling with fear. His wings melt under the burning sun.

They fall.

LENA

Into silence.
Into the scent of lilacs.

THE SCENT WAFTS THROUGH and penetrates a smoky haze from an open window, lilacs must be flowering far below it. The sky is heavy with smoke, a haze no sun can burn away by noon. Lace curtains billow, a chill in the air.

She sees a rifle propped up in a shadowed corner. In the doorway, the likely owner of the gun pauses, as if waiting for an invitation to enter what must be her own room. She's dressed in blue overalls and boots, a padded vest. She ties back her wildly red hair with a paisley kerchief.

Lena says, "I'm sorry if I've caused you trouble." She throws off the feather tick, swings her legs over the bed. "I'll be leaving now." Her stomach growls, but no longer hurts. "First I need a chamber pot." She finds footing, feels a little dizzy, and although her head clears and she clings to the bedpost, she's unable to bend down to look under the bed. Realizing that the flannel nightgown she wears is so short it doesn't cover her knees, she balances with one foot pressing on top of the other.

The woman dressed like a man beckons for Lena to follow her, and Lena takes her first hesitant steps in – how many days? She shows Lena a closet that holds an indoor toilet, with a water tank halfway up to the ceiling and a long chain to pull when she wants to flush it. Of course, Lena has seen such a wonder before, when her parents took her to a dentist in Visby and, when she didn't cry or even complain while he drilled, they rewarded her with an ice cream sandwich at a chocolate shop where she went to the ladies' room and pulled the chain seven times just to watch the water swirl down the hole in the toilet.

The woman Lena believes is Pytor's wife gives her an unused toothbrush in a clear glass box and a packet of tooth powder. How wonderful, and the Russian words she utters astonishes her more than the kindness: *"Tak korosho!"* And then: *"S'pasibo."*

The small but tough looking woman says something that must mean, Come out when you're ready.

"What is your name? I'm Lena." She pats her chest, trying out what she hopes is universal language of gestures.

"Maryushka Elizavitanova Pytoranova." Little Mary, daughter of Elizabeth and Peter. She points to the red dressing gown hanging from a peg on the door. She leaves Lena alone in the water closet.

Grazhdane I grazhdanki Sovetskogo Souza! The tin voice makes Lena jump out of her skin. *Sovetskoe pravitelstvo I ego glva tovarish Stalin prouchill mne vystupit so sleduyshim zayavleniem.* She doesn't know where the voice is coming from, an outside loud-hailer or an inside radio, maybe even from a microphone hidden in the toilet tank. *Bez ob'yavlenia voyny I bez preduprezhdeniya Germanskie voiska napall na nashu strtnu, takovali nashi granitsy vo mnoqih mestah I podvergli bombezhke so svoikh samoletov nashi goroda.* Lena feels as if someone is watching her go to the bathroom, wash her face and hands, clean her teeth. *Napadenie na nashu stranu proizvedeno nesmotrya na to, chto mezhdu USSR I Germaniey zaklyuchen. Dogovor o nenapadenii. I Sovetskoe pravitelstvo so vsei dobrosovest*nost*'yu vypolnyalo vse usloviyha etogo dogovora.* A person cannot even pee in peace. Lena is glad she lives in Gotland, on a farm where the only morning sound is the crow of the cock, or the first call of the robin greeting her mate returning with a worm to the nest. Do Russians have to listen to this awful racket every day?

LENA

Trying on Maryushka's red chenille bathrobe, she discovers it is too short in the sleeves and barely reaches her knees, but she ties it tight, the collar turned up as if she's going out into a wintery day.

When Lena comes out of the water closet the metallic voice seems to follow her. *Pravitelstvo prizyvaet vas, grazhdane I grazhdanki Sovetskogo Soyuza, eshe bolee splotitsya vokrug slavnoi bolshevistskoy partii, vokrug Sovetskogo Pravitelstva I vokrug nshego lidra tovarisha Stalina.* The jackhammer voice is leading her on too. How can it be behind her and ahead of her at the same time? She's glad she can't understand Russian, the words might be terrifying if they were spoken in Swedish. Ignorance may not be bliss, but it does provide a certain comforting protection. Having understood three words – Stalin, Bolsheviks and Germans – she does gather that Stalin and the communists don't like the Germans who attacked their country.

She finds the woman named Maryushka in the other room at a huge wood-burning stove made of blue tile, complete with a sleeping platform Lena had read about in novels but had been unable to imagine. Maryushka must have slept on the stove, giving Lena her bed. The samovar is very old, made of copper and brass, with embossed firebirds strutting around its round belly. Maryushka scoops small doughy pancakes onto a plate, and the aroma makes Lena's stomach growl again. "I'm so hungry I could eat a whole *hanlamm,"* she says.

She prays Pytor has fed her ponies properly, brushed their coats, and – oh please God, don't let him sell them.

Maryushka gestures towards the food and says something in Russian that must be an equivalent of *Var så god,* the Swedish Be-so-good invitation to the table, this one small and set for two, covered with a lace tablecloth, a vase of tulips in its centre beside a Bakelite wireless blatting in Russian: *Nashe delo pravoe, My podemim, Pobeda budet za nami!* "Molotov," Maryushka says, and Lena has a vague idea of who he is, a bigwig close to Stalin.

"What's he saying?" Lena takes a seat, carefully folding the robe over her knees, though the stove warms the corner.

Maryushka takes the other chair, and offers the plate of pancakes to Lena. "*Blini,*" she says. Though Lena knows what blini are, these pancakes are the size of a kroner, pleated around the edges, reminding homesick Lena of her mother's thin pancakes, each one rolled around a fried sausage, then heaped with whipped cream and strawberries.

Somehow, she must talk this small Mary into letting her go home. It's not her fault that stupid horse-thieving Pytor stole her away from her island.

Lena folds her hands, bows her head and begins to say the Blessing, "In Jesus name, to the table we go."

Maryushka's hands fly to her cheeks, she jumps up so quickly she knocks her chair over backwards. "*Nyet! Nyet!*" She rushes to the window and slams it shut, closing the shutters with a click. She returns to the table, uprights her chair, sits down, and places a trembling finger to her lips. "Shhh."

Not knowing if it's the Swedish language or the saying of a prayer that is forbidden and frightening Maryushka, Lena squeezes her eyes shut and says the rest of the Grace in her head, remembering how her mother smacked her hand if she took one bite before her father finished saying the Blessing. Then she tries one small blini, butter melting in her mouth, the blackberry jam sweet and tart. It stays down, and she eats another. The coffee is as black and strong as Carolina's boiled in a saucepan, but it's served in a glass instead of a cup. "Home," she says. "You have been very kind, and I thank you, but I must go home."

Maryushka turns off the wireless, leaving Molotov hanging in the air outside, the same tinny voice crackling from a loudspeaker on a telephone pole she can see through the window without shutters.

Just as Lena is about to try and find a way to communicate to Maryushka her need for help in finding passage home to Gotland, the door opens, which gives Maryushka such a fright she leaps up, her chair crashes over, and she grabs her rifle, raising it, ready to shoot – Pytor!

There he is, Pytor Petrovich, arms bearing gifts, an impish grin on his face, the troll! And there goes Lena's chance to escape. She promises herself that if she gets another opportunity she'll bolt and run, but before that she must be ready with a plan.

"*Valenki!*" Maryushka shrieks, and Pytor lifts one muddy boot, then the other, trying to shrug his shoulders, but his arms are too full of daffodils and packages wrapped in brown paper.

He says something that Lena guesses might be: "Don't shoot me."

Maryushka puts the rifle back in its corner, within easy reach if someone else intrudes upon her home, privacy an apparent impossibility in Russia. Why didn't Maryushka bolt her door? In Gotland, farm folk have no need to lock their doors. What could be worth stealing? Her mother's foot-operated sewing machine?

Pytor tracks in manure and bits of – straw! He has seen to the horses. Lena hopes he fed and watered the bird too, but doesn't know how to ask him.

"You are well!" he says to Lena in Swedish. And he offers the bouquet. "Here. Take. *Tsveti, tsveti.*"

Wrapping the folds of the robe tighter around her knees

and trying to hide her bare legs deeper under the table, Lena doesn't know what to do now so she repeats the Russian word: "*Tsveti*." She accepts the flowers, then gives them to Maryushka to put in a vase.

"Little Mary," Pytor says, offering her a single rose, with gold and orange tints at the edge of its petals. "Glory of Peace," he says in English. "Flower is new. Slow-blooming." he says in Swedish.

"Haymarket —!" Maryushka says. Lena understands the word market but not the derisive tone Maryushka uses to express it.

"— is Hungry Market now," Pytor says. "Bread is common currency. A smart man can make a fortune." He continues to speak Swedish and beams, a proud boy who has just brought home good marks from a teacher he doesn't like very much.

Maryushka turns to Lena and says something Lena cannot understand.

Lena says, "Pytor, translate!"

Pytor says, " Money, I have money, and so much more where this came from, once I —" He looks at Lena, ponders something, then says, "A meeting I have, with a horse man today, ah but I need to resolve now the problem where to hide *russen.*" Pytor unwraps the largest parcel, whips out a flowery, flouncy skirt, and whirls about the room with it. "Life is like horse ride. You always think to finish with deal and have some good time, without the fuss in doings, but always each next day you have more to do than in previous one." Though he mixes the Stockholm and Gutamål dialects, Lena understands that he's trying to impress her with the skirt and horse talk.

"Berserk," Maryushka says, twirling one finger about her ear. Lena isn't sure if she's talking to her or to Pytor, but the gesture makes her laugh, and that spurs Pytor on: he waltzes the skirt about the room.

"Berserk," Lena repeats in Russian.

"What's crazy is staying here when bombs fall," he says in Swedish, returning to the package and flourishing a red silk blouse, with padded shoulders, the latest style. Soft calfskin boots. A scarf for her head. A fringed shawl.

"This is far too much," Lena says. "I can't accept these expensive gifts." Trying to hide her confusion and unbidden pleasure, she bends her head over and opens another parcel containing a silk slip, a garter belt, white cotton stockings, and lacy underpants, the pushup brassiere she's only seen in European magazines. Heat spreads from her neck to the roots of her hair.

Pytor peels paper from a Red October chocolate bar, and Lena recognizes the wrapper from gypsy sellers at Visby fairs. He pops a square into his mouth, smirking, so bloody pleased with himself.

Maryushka takes a bit of skirt fabric between her fingers and rubs it as if testing its quality, then sneers. She says something derisive and Pytor translates for Lena, all this obviously for her benefit. "Very practical. No one will notice you dressed up bright as fire cracker." He laughs, and Maryushka snorts.

"Disguise," Pytor says in Swedish. "Put on, put on. I wait." He plunks down on an intricately carved rocking chair, crosses his arms over his chest, still happy with himself, but a bit on the defensive. "We go to country," he says. "Dacha we find, very nice." Then he switches to Russian again, and Lena thinks he may be inviting Maryushka to go too. The more he smiles and winks, the redder Maryushka gets in the face, until her skin looks sunburned and even her freckles look so angry they might jump up and down on her wolfish nose.

Maryushka yells something, picks up the red blouse and slaps it back on the wrapping paper. Why doesn't she like it? Or maybe she wishes he'd bought the clothes for her.

Lena says firmly, "Translate everything or I go home." Of course, she has no idea how to find her way to a train station or even to the docks and a steamer heading west. Although dim, the city sounds of cars and trucks and streetcars careening along their tracks with electric sparks shooting like stars just below the windows infiltrate the high-ceilinged room like unwanted pests. She stamps her foot. "Home. It's time for me to go."

Pytor doesn't fall for her bluff, or even laugh at her. He seems intent on his own plan, perhaps. He takes a leather folder from his inside jacket pocket, unwinds the strap, then spills many greasy passbooks on the table. "Worth more than gold!" He smacks them with his palm. "With these I can feed army!" So he isn't just a thief, then. He's into forgery or selling passports. Lena doesn't know what to think now. She wishes he didn't make her laugh. It's getting harder to hate him.

Maryushka gasps and covers her mouth with her work-blistered hands.

Pytor says, "Maryushka, she thinks I go to Gulag for stealing – or forging books to trade for food – when poor workers go hungry."

"*Blaton!*" Maryushka shouts.

"She call me, *Blaton,* professional criminal now, and proud I am of it. *Vor v zakon.* I am Thief-in-law. Is better than starving." Pytor jumps out of his chair and spreads his hands. He seems to be begging Maryushka for something. Lena only understands three words: mother and father and safe.

Though she hears her own name, and Pytor looks at her with cow eyes, Lena cannot know what they are arguing about, and such confrontation makes her uncomfortable; she doesn't know what it is to fight, and has never heard her father and mother so much as raise their voices to each other. She's determined to learn Russian as quickly as she can so she can begin to understand this strange man who steals horses, has kidnapped her, yet treats her with respect and seems to care that she fell ill. The clothes. She will need them to make her escape, to disappear into city crowds, but will Russian clothes alone make her look Slavic enough? She hasn't the high cheekbones and long wolf nose, her eyes are wide apart, not close together.

She just hopes he's not a slave trader intending to sell her and the horses to – wild Turks or infidels she read about in novels from the nineteenth century. And what about her forest horses? Her plan to escape must include them; she can't take the risk that he might trade them. What to do? She must act fast. The pressure weighs as heavy as a wheat stook the size of a man.

First, she'll go along with the disguise.

"Excuse me," she says, and takes the clothes into the bedroom to try them on, while Pytor and Maryushka argue loudly, maybe about Lena, what to do with her, the horses.

IN THE OTHER ROOM, quickly she takes off Maryushka's robe and gown. First, the underwear and stockings so silky on her skin. Her breasts are embarrassingly large, so she doesn't put on the push-up brassiere, it's too French anyway. Then the skirt and blouse and jacket. She looks at herself in the mirror, straightens her shoulders and lifts her head higher, then turns to view her back: not too wide in the beam as she always believed, the straight line slimming, her own full skirt with its bunches of pleats at the waist always had made her feel so fat. She's surprised at her reflected image: tall, yes, but statuesque –

a delicious word she once found in a romance novel and thereafter tossed at other farm girls like so much chicken feed when they teased her about being taller than her folk dancing partner. Her waist is nipped in by the close-fitting jacket, the skirt slitted to reveal nicely proportioned calves and well-turned ankles. Now the boots. How did Pytor know what size to buy, or was he just lucky to pick clothes that would fit so – beautifully? The colour is outrageous, of course: so red! *Krasnaya* means beautiful and red. How does she know that word? Oh, from the old Russian vendors at the market at Hemse, who fled their homeland during the revolution.

She leans forward, stretches her mouth and opens it to look at her teeth. Nice and straight. White. Then she smiles at herself, normally, and behold the gum line fillings don't show at all. Until this day of her transformation into a woman of the world – is that possible? – she always performed her morning toilet in haste, avoiding her face in the mirror when she brushed her teeth, never looking at herself in the long, free-standing mirror in her mother's bedroom, not wanting to see how tall she'd grown, how fat she must be now, just like her mother's sisters, Carolina always said. She wanted to keep Lena down on the farm. And hadn't Lena promised often enough never to leave her crack-brained mother, to look after her always?

"Here I come!" she calls, and leaves the bedroom.

WHEN SHE RETURNS ALL DOLLED UP, as stars like Bogart and Bacall say in the American movies, Pytor wolf whistles. Maryushka bangs the frying pan on the iron stovetop.

"I'm sorry. I didn't mean to cause trouble between man and wife." This draws a blank, and she struggles for a word: "*Femka?*"

Pytor laughs, a kind of grumbling in his throat. *"Nyet, nyet,*

LENA

brother and sister, we are." He leans in, shoulder to shoulder with Maryushka, touching her long nose, then his, "See, the same," a finger to her lips, "just like mine." He ruffles Maryushka's wild red hair. "But is different colour, no?"

Maryushka pushes him away, but she isn't too displeased after all. She picks up new, clean sheets from the top of the packet of greasy papers on the table. She raises one eyebrow as if to say: Well, Mr. Smarty-pants, how are you going to tell her about these?

Pytor says, "Sit," and when Lena takes her chair at the table, he pulls another chair closer to hers and seats himself, showing her a ration card with a picture of a loaf of bread printed on it, and identification papers not unlike Swedish papers, but they have the hammer-and-sickle stamp, in red instead of yellow and blue, her own homeland colours. The letters are all Cyrillic.

And then begins a pantomime, involving much pointing and stabbing at lines on the pages, more waving of arms and shaking or nodding of his head and finally, drawing of pictures on the dull side of butcher paper. Slowly, Lena begins to learn who she is now, in this strange land, the details of an invented Russian life, her protection.

Her name is now Lena Ivanovna Svetlova, daughter of Ivan, married to Pytor Petrovich Svetlov.

"Marry you? Never!"

Pytor taps the fake papers.

Oh, a paper marriage only. Yes, for her protection and survival, though Maryushka's posturing before a photo of Stalin with expressions of fear help Lena understand that being the wife of Pytor makes her, Lena, an enemy of the State too, what a dullard is her brother; Maryushka demonstrates this by letting her tongue hang out of an open mouth and rolling her eyes upward.

Then, it takes more than half an hour for Pytor to explain that the new Lena was born on October 8, 1920 near Uglich – Pytor guesses her age as older than her eighteen years, which pleases her – the daughter of Ivan Ivanovitch, a watchmaker in the factory there and his wife, Olga Konstantinovna, both members of the KOMOSOL. "Papa," he says. "Make the watch," and he toys with the pocketwatch and fob dangling from his vest pocket.

So much to remember. Can she do it? She worries the fringes on the Russian shawl she now wears, while Pytor and Maryushka argue some more, the sister's gutteral Russian words sounding as hot as the water she pours from samovar into the teapot. The more she steams the harder Pytor works to convince her. Lena has never seen such a nervous, fearful person, sometimes sounding like a screech-throat nag, yet other times as hard and as tough as a one-eyed gypsy haggling over the price of flour sacking.

Finally, Pytor pretends he is deaf, and then he can't even talk. He's walking on his knees, just a child, and then he flops over, sick as a colt; all the while pointing at Lena and saying, "You. You. You." So now Lena understands: she is a deaf mute, caused by a sickness as a child, which is important if she's stopped by a patrol or the NKVD. Pytor holds one finger to his lips, then mimes zippering them shut. She must never utter a word! She must learn to turn her head, look away when Pytor says her name, as if she hasn't heard him, and is distracted by a sight elsewhere. To make her understand, Pytor says, "Lena Ivanovna," and Maryushka, pretending to be Lena, looks away and chews a fingernail.

She is employed as a seamstress, making overalls and padded jackets for factory workers. Pytor mimes sewing, using the hem of Marushka's jacket, his finger for a needle.

Because of her inability to hear and speak she is excused from voluntary *subotniks* and factory meetings. Pytor puffs up his chest, waves his arms, as if he's an important man making a big speech.

If she's to stay here she must try to master this difficult language, the impossible alphabet with thirty-three letters, one letter alone indicating not just a sound from deep in the throat but a whole word, according to her history teacher now so far away in Gotland. Until then, she is deaf to him and everyone in Leningrad. Mute.

The theatrics have tired her and she wants to sleep, but Pytor says, "Now. We go!" He points at the door.

But Maryushka stops Pytor, with a hand on his shoulder. From a line strung above the stove, she unpegs the trousers and chemise Lena had worn when she arrived, stuffs them in a string bag, then adds a few tins of meat she takes from a free-standing cupboard, a loaf of black bread, the bottle of peppermint-tasting medicine, just in case. "*Vsego samogo khoroshego,*" Maryushka says. "*Obnimayu.*" And she hugs Lena, kissing her on both cheeks, nearly knocking her backwards with surprise.

"What is this?" Pytor says. "Lots of food we have on boat." He says this in Swedish, likely to impress upon Lena that he not only looks after his sister, he's a generous man.

Lena hopes and prays he's decided to take her back home. Her mother will be shocked by Lena's clothes, *shame on you!*

She can't help it, she feels worldly and wicked, tromping out the door, down the stairs. Yet, having rarely visited even the small and isolated city of Visby, she trembles with trepidation. The City of Peter is besieged.

Signe

Novikov Priboy, June 24, 2004

ON THE FOURTH MORNING, seeking a quiet place to read an English translation of Pushkin's poetry, Signe wanders from the crowded and noisy games room up to the Panorama Bar, and finds she is just in time for Kostja's slide show on – birds, what else?

She takes one of the deep leather swivel chairs against the large picture window, wishing for the first time that the riverboat was already on its way to Lake Ladoga so she could look out and watch for dachas and villages in case she gets bored by too much talk about birds. She's anxious to begin her search to find her young mother and father and the child born to them on the Ice. There hasn't been enough free time even to shop for souvenirs much less seek out a church and Old Believer who might help her overcome her fear and grief. It's not enough just to breathe Russian air, to feel at home simply because the thicket on the shore boasts the same fir and poplar, and know that the river system she's about to experience is much longer, wider and more expansive than the great Saskatchewan that rises in Alberta and divides into two forks that surge north and south, over half her province. She wants to see her place of birth and see what memories are conjured there.

Once again, chairs have been set up in the middle of the Panorama Bar, the tourists have taken seats, and this time Kostja waits beside a projector, pointer in hand. The Dutch tour director introduces Konstantin as writer, biologist, explorer and wildlife photographer, on loan to Intrav from DERSU UZALA, an ecotourism company. Kostja actually bows, so old world, and although he must be used to a dais and giving lectures, he appears – prickly – his ears and neck reddening and moisture gathering on his upper lip. She hopes he impresses the audience and the tour director. He told her that the Russian staff only make four hundred dollars per month, but he and the historian make six hundred, their food and lodging inclusive; he needs the extra work to supplement his meagre income as a writer for Russian *National Geographic*. Wages and fee scales are not private topics in Russia; the waiters and local tour guides and maids and bus drivers all seem to make a point of telling the American tourists that they have university degrees and subsist on terribly low incomes even for post-Soviet Russia. Then on the bus, the local guide always thanks the passengers in advance for their generous tips at the end of the tour.

This is Kostja's first tour for the company. Signe is nervous for him now.

With a pointer, Kostja outlines on a map projected on the screen, a forest of spruce and fir, where to find waterfalls frozen like beards of hermits. His enlarged photographs are iconoclastic, for the eye of the camera captures the eye of the bird or animal he photographs. Red deer. Bison that remind Signe of her own prairie. His forest in autumn looks like an impressionistic painting, with branches like forks of swift rivers. People are cast in shadow, their black silhouettes might have been cut with scissors by a caricaturist at a fair.

Along the great belt of the steppes, he has captured ridges and spurs, ancient pathways, the Churya river system joining Russia to Mongolia. "Kurum," he says, "are the mountain passes with stony fields that lead to Alpine meadows." Here, furry paws of cedars. Foaming rapids.

The girl running the projector for him is usually at the reception desk. She looks like Lisa Minnelli in *Cabaret,* with ebony-black pixie cut and long false eyelashes, upper and lower, accentuating overly large, star-struck eyes. When he wants her to change a slide, Kostja bows, and the girl bats her lashes at him, a flirtatious gesture right out of a Russian novel, but in this twenty-first century it's too reminiscent of Lucille Ball. All she needs is a fan, a low-cut dress in the Empire fashion and corset to shove her boobs into his face.

"Where the northern and southern steppes meet," he says, "you can see tiger and brown bear together." In the subtropical forests, he hiked into the mountains of Siberia looking for birds that breed in Cold Russia: blue and pine flycatchers, the Chinese sparrow hawk, green-backed tern.

Years ago, when Signe was first learning to live with wounded Tapani, his doctor asked her to keep a record – a kind of journal – for him, but it was as hard to write about the head banging and wall punching and sleepwalking as it was to stop Tapani from hurting himself since he was too big to hold down, and each episode remembered on paper always arrived in a kind of shorthand: *fell to his knees, like a Muslim on a prayer carpet. Spread his arms, palms pressed against tile as cold as my fear. Arched his back, swung head to one side, and banged it on floor.* The rhythm of his head knocking sounded to Signe like an indecipherable code.

There's a message for Signe in Kostja's lecture, a riverboat song or found poem. In her notebook she begins to record phrases, the meaning gathering, as if the lecture is intended only for her. She writes: *Kostja's Lecture.* No, make that: *Kostja's Riverboat Song.* As he speaks, she listens for hidden meaning and skips phrases that don't suit the interpretation she wants, so he becomes her guide through the wilderness of her grief.

Where you will find only bears & tiger trails to follow
   & it's easy to get lost

Where waterfalls are frozen beards in winter
   & Heracleum plants burn the skin

Where red-crowned cranes disappear
   & poachers kill tigers for skins

Where the Siberian grouse
   allows you to touch

Where northern & southern steppes meet
   & it's easy to find each other

Where always the eyes,
   the eyes turn on you

When once again the sun is hidden by black arrows
   & you meet a man who casts no shadow

There in a field of stones
   come to me.

EVENTUALLY, HE PAUSES, bows again to the projectionist, deeply from the waist, his thick unruly hair flops over his forehead and he brushes it back, but it only falls into his eyes again.

The last slide takes away Signe's breath. Wolf in the snow of southern Siberia. A magnificent beast, just emerged from a forest of frost-lightened, glistening poplar and beech. It has just swung its head to look at the photographer, its gaze steady and explorative – friend or foe? Unsure of the scent upwind, it has halted in mid decision: run or pounce? Its yellow eyes constant against a field of white.

The snowbanks make Signe think of the field near the airport where one winter long ago city trucks dumped snow cleared from the streets until the walls of snow created a giant igloo, with the night sky its roof. When Durwood insisted on a carefully turned-down bed, lights off, and practically timed their lovemaking – *I have to be up by six* – she lured him to the snow dump and made love to him under the stars.

It was always good for her outside, the phallic birch and poplar a turn-on in the bush country holidays. She kept a blanket on the back seat of the Land Rover. On the road between cities, she heated up, and halfway, when she unzipped his trousers, he was so afraid of an accident, he had to turn off, onto a farmer's field and park the car behind abandoned outbuildings. Signe always returned home with bits of leaf or twig or hay in her wild hair.

Lena told Signe that she was conceived in a hammock on a coal barge in the wilderness of Russia, at a small place called Mandrogi. Maybe that explains her wild impulses.

Kostja is most definitely an outdoor cat too. She hopes his new baby was conceived in a flower bed.

Now, the birders applaud wildly, and Kostja bows stiffly.

While the birders meander to their cabins, likely for naps, Signe waits, her back still to the windows, and sure enough Kostja hastens to join her.

She says, "The birders loved it."

"And you?"

"The wolf in the snow might have just come out of my own bush country."

Placing one hand on her shoulder and leaning over her, he says, "What is this you are reading?"

"Pushkin, who else?" Quickly she hides her notebook and the poem under the book of poetry read so many times its spine is worn, the pages raggled-tagged.

A true Russian, Kostja quotes in Russian from memory, and knowing the words for people and poet and love, Signe recognizes the poem: *He loved as in our age / People already do no longer; as only / The wild soul of the poet / Is still condemned to love.*

Kostja gives her his book, which he says is on conservation, on the preservation of the species.

"I just went to the reading room, but CNN is blatting so loudly I couldn't think, much less read."

"Maybe we should find an unused cabin," Kostja says.

Signe would prefer a blanket in the woods. Or his lookout platform.

"You could ask in Russian."

"Yes, I could."

The man is married. Signe's too old and too burdened for romantic nonsense. She didn't embark on this voyage looking for a shipboard romance. What has come over her? Still, she thought she'd never feel this way again, like quicksilver, or iron shavings swooshing up from a blank page to meet the pull of a magnet.

How fortunate Lena was, to have been captured young by her Russian horse trader, that noble thief. She told Signe: *I have never loved another.*

Lena

Leningrad, June 24, 1941

SHE'S STEPPING OUT WITH A BEAU for the first time, this pony-girl from isolated Gotland, but the man who offers her his arm is no farm boy with bangs cut by his mother, using a small mixing bowl on his head to get them straight across his pale brow. He's absurdly attractive, is decent enough, with a kind sister, but he's still the man who stole her away. Signe's instincts remain as keen as a lighthouse at land's end that tell her to watch for tide pools and undertow in false inlets that contain capsizing shoals and rocks. She must step carefully.

Two flights of stairs later, Lena feels weak in the knees, light-headed, and at the gate of the courtyard lilacs and bird-cherry welcome her into the bright sunshine of an uncertain future in a land where she cannot communicate her needs, not even if she becomes lost.

A soldier sits on a bench between a mound of grenades and a peasant cart. He smokes, using a tin can for an ashtray. He jumps up when he sees Pytor, and Lena is afraid he will ask to see her identification papers, but Pytor crosses his palm with kopecks, and seems to thank him for minding his *telegi,* which must mean cart. Then Pytor gestures so she understands she is to ride on top of a heap of belongings covered with canvas. He boosts her up, then jumps between the poles, picks them up, pulls backwards, then pushes the cart forward; and they're out the gate.

Once they leave the barricade and move into early morning traffic, Lena looks about her. In spite of the hideous signs of war — barricades, blimps, gas masks dangling around necks of citizens, a brigade of ragged soldiers returning from the front — spring has overtaken Leningrad, so beautiful yet brooding in the heat, waiting for and dreading the enemy at its gates. Great lindens glow greenly along the wide avenue; beneath them, mushrooms sprouting after the rain, which remind her of *kantareller* at home. Oh, an ill omen, yes, her bookish mother told her that Russians believe many mushrooms are a sign of many deaths, a belief nurtured by babushki long before Napoleon, for all Lena knows, perhaps back to the time of Ghengis Khan.

Fresh flowers at the base of statues, in kiosks, in a lover's arms.

A crew washes down a huge square with pails of water, brooms. In the adjoining palatial gardens, volunteers dig trenches, uprooting shrubs and flowerbeds. Women old and young build — shelters? Lena has never witnessed an air raid, but doubts that anything above ground would offer much protection from exploding bombs. With shovels, others bury marble stallions on a bridge. Youth bearing long-bladed, Finnish hunting knives are being trained to fight.

At the portals of a grand building crates are loaded onto trucks, likely for evacuation, but Signe has no idea where they might be hidden safely. Peter calls to her, "Hermitage!" Workmen lug *papier-mâché* guns and tanks and seem to be placing them in strategic positions, so they must be intended as decoys.

Pytor points to an immense statue of a horseman in a great sandbox. A czar? The horse makes her wonder about

Thor and the ponies. Has Pytor fed them? Maybe he took them to the country and let them loose. If so, how will she ever find them? Her face feels so prickly she rubs her cheeks with her fingertips.

At another bridge she cannot name, statues of military heroes – maybe conquerors of Napoleon – are sandbagged, but Lena's history lessons give her hope: Russians invented the Scorched Earth Policy; their fierce winter defeated Napoleon too.

"Where are we going?" she calls to Pytor, who turns and frowns fiercely, placing one finger to his lips.

Women and children carrying hoes and spades are dressed in white – but why? So they will be recognized and not shot by German troops when they advance on the city? Or to make them disappear against a white landscape when winter comes? Surely this war will end before winter, and long before *that* she and her Gotlandruss will be safely home again.

Machine gun nests and anti-tank traps everywhere. Big boats with guns on the Neva embankment, guarded by stone sphinxes.

On a large canal, sunlight turns the gold and tatterdemalion enamel of a great church into a shrine, its domes and cupolas and turrets now seeming to reach for a sign from God, a divine promise that Leningradski will not perish. Loudspeakers on every corner, the message the same and she thinks it means: *Victory will be ours.* She has yet to declare war on Pytor. If only she could speak Russian or his Swedish was better. Then she could ask him what he intends to do with her, with her ponies. Thor could pull this cart so easily. When they stop she'll tell him so, make him take her to her favourite horse.

She doesn't know where Pytor is taking her now, perhaps back to the boat and her ponies. He's very strong, his head bobbing left and right, like a good draft pony's. His face and neck are red, knuckles turning white on the poles.

She could jump off easily, disappear into the crowd of citizens hastening to work, to shops. But where could she go? To the docks to find a passenger steamer to take her to Estonia? She has no money for a ticket. She couldn't leave without her horses.

A billboard advertises sewing machines, which makes her think of her mother and how she would work the treadle furiously, sewing crooked seams in a summer frock for a daughter who isn't there and may never come home again. But this is no time for self-pity, not even for sympathy for her worried mamma.

When Lena does return – and she's determined that she will – how will she ever describe these preparations for war? Sentry posts at every intersection and every bridge, at the entrance of buildings. Yet, no one so far has stopped them. Maybe they're mistaken for evacuees from the western front, or simple peddlers.

Rubbish in gutters. They move into poorer quarters again, away from the avenue of grand palaces. She wishes she could read Cyrillic, name the boulevards turning into streets, but remembers that the history of Russia may be found in its place names: Third of July Street, Trotsky Street, Proletarian Street, Twenty-fifth of October Street. If she ever reaches a quiet and peaceful place she will ask Pytor to teach her the alphabet so she can read street and shop signs; she will need to be able to identify landmarks when she escapes from him.

Red flags hang limply from windows.

It doesn't matter if she doesn't know where she is when she has no idea where she might go to find her way home.

Here she is, in the city of Peter, the city of Lenin, the city of Pushkin and Dostoevsky, of Pavlova and Nijinsky; the city of great culture and achievement that she read about with her mother on so many cold winter days and nights, and instead of thrilling to its sights she's saddened by hundreds of children scrounging for bottles in gutters, not to sell for pennies to spend at a fair, which is what Lena did at that age, but to make – what? Some kind of explosive they can hurl at the enemy? And the English words she heard only a few nights ago on her father's wireless radio return to her: *Molotov cocktail.*

Everyone is rallying to the cause, except Pytor it seems. A feeling of disappointment in him drops like a stone in the pit of her stomach. The peasant's pushcart. Its load. He's running away – but where? She yells at him, "What about my horses? You better not have sold them to a zoo or gypsies!"

He drops the pushcart poles, stops, and clamps both hands over his mouth, shaking his head so hard it might just fall off, silly man. She forgot she must hold to silence. She puts shushing fingers to her own lips, which causes him to drop his hands and slap his thighs, then pick up the poles and move on again.

She fights her returning feelings of frustration and panic and anger, wanting to pound the answers out of him, and wishing she knew the Russian words for why, where and how. She's only certain of one thing: she won't attempt an escape without Thor and her ponies.

Automobiles and cyclists and streetcars have disappeared. Once again, they struggle through a maze of street barricades, jungles of paving blocks and timber ferroconcrete, railroad iron, steel tubing – to halt tanks? They enter an enormous sewer conduit, the wooden wheels grumbling on cement, the cart bouncing on rough patches, and she holds onto the canvas rope so she won't fall onto the concrete.

Inside the sewer, light filters down from open manholes, like miniature searchlights, casting halos on the wet floor. Pytor runs through flushing water, ankle deep. Smell of mould, stronger stink of sewage. On either side, ammunition piled above the water line on platforms. Here and there, new boxes built into manholes and sewer openings for directing fire at – attacking Germans, their tanks? No Red Army troops or NKVD police, not even the People's Volunteers, not yet, but they're ready for street fighting, the Leningradski. Unable to see an end to the tunnel either way, she guesses that these barriers extend for many, many miles, and because they're so new they must be built by Leningradski now much farther down the line.

Wind rushes down from open manholes, like the breath of Wolf, and whistles through the drainpipes.

A voice rises, eerie and echoing. She feels a chill moving from the back of her thighs up her back to her neck, down both arms. But it's only Pytor – singing! – that *Katyuska* song again. Russians! They sing when they're drunk, when they're sad, when they're in love, and likely when they're angry. In the Ryss Garden in Visby the traders were so rowdy the toughest farm boy thought twice before picking a fight with them.

And here she is with a Russian thief, with no idea where he is taking her. "Stop!" she yells.

Pytor lifts his head, his face as red as the Soviet flag. He attempts a reassuring smile, and says, "Almost there."

She's furious with him for continuing to push the cart, but forgets her anger when rats scurry away from the jouncing cart, scuttle up the curve of the conduit. She hears a shriek, it slams against cement, echoes back, it's her own voice retreating: "*Where where where are you taking me me me?*"

She throws herself off the cart, falls on her hands and knees, scraping both on the cement. Never mind the pain, the spurts of blood. She reaches up, grasps the bottom rung of an iron ladder, and begins to climb up to the street, but strong hands on her ankles, then her waist, and she's pulled backwards, loses her balance – and falls – landing on top of Pytor.

They lie there in the muck, silent, the wind of traffic whistling above, rushing downward, like voices of ghosts. His arms hold her tight, then fall away. She rolls over, sits up, to discover Pytor has banged his head, his eyes rolled back, but his chest rises and falls, a rapid fluttering in his neck. Good, he's out cold. Now she can escape. But he may be seriously hurt, and she doesn't want the blood of even a horse thief on her conscience. She lifts his head – no blood oozing – and rests it on her lap, bending over him, unaware that she's crying, whispering, "Please don't die on me, I'm so sorry, I just want to go home, this is all so crazy, are you all right? Pytor, Pytor, talk to me. Say something, anything, just don't leave me." She feels his head, a lump rising at the back, he's hard-headed, swelling is good, it means the pressure isn't inward, and then she's kissing his forehead, his eyelids, cheekbones.

He opens his eyes. Reaches up, hands firmly on her neck, pulls her to him and kisses her, hard. His lips taste of chocolate. When she finally pulls away, he says in his bad Swedish, "You are big pest. Maybe worth it, maybe no, I don't know, *ja*, you are, Pony-girl."

She hauls back an arm, ready to slap his smug face, angry that her first serious kiss happened in a sewer and was given her by her captor, never mind if she does feel a strange pull towards him. Instead of giving him a well-deserved smack, she helps him sit up, and he rubs the back of his head, wincing. It's time to take charge. "Where can we get some ice to take down the swelling?" she says.

He uses the iron rung to get to his feet, steadies himself, still shaky.

"Your turn to ride," she says, pointing at the cart. "Up. Get up! I'll push you."

"Nyet! I no be carted and carried by woman."

"You're hurt. Do as I say." She stands with hands on hips, wagging a finger at him so he knows she means business. But he won't budge. "Have it your way," she says, and moves into position between poles of the axletree. She lifts them, they're lighter than they look, then pulls and pushes, rocking the cart, till it begins to move forward; and she's as good as a draft pony too, hauling Pytor's goods towards the light. Once, she looks back to make sure he's following, slowly but surely. She'll know when it's time to abandon him, when she can make her way home on her own with her horses – and his pushcart for disguise if need be.

They pass four more ladders leading to manholes overhead, and she guesses that means they've traversed as many city blocks. She's sweating, arms aching, blisters beginning to sting on her palms. She stops, removes her shawl and jacket, flings them on top of the load. Pytor eases between the cart and the cement wall, steps over the lowered poles, and picks them up, taking a position behind her; and together they push the cart out of the conduit near an old church with boarded windows and barracks that look ancient, with crumbling stone and mortar. The other end of the stony field opens onto a square surrounded by many market stalls, with a maze of alleys and lanes leading away from it, and beneath them the underworld they've just traversed to avoid street patrols.

"*Sennaya*," Pytor says, and Lena feels a thrill of recognition. Peace Market known as Haymarket before the revolution. Dostoevsky! The Brothers Karamazov lived here, in the Raspberry House between Spassky and Demidov lanes. For two hundred years it was the busiest shopping street of pre-Bolshevik Russia. She read about the pushcart and stall trade, the troikas and flower girls and women of the night. In the novel, the Poberti House was just one of many notorious dives, dens from which no one emerged alive. *Crime and Punishment* was full of petty thieves like Pytor, blackmailers, murderers and whores.

Money had no value and for bread anything was traded: a gold watch, a diamond ring, a fur coat or hat with earflaps. A woman's body. A man's life. Dostoevsky again. Surely, her imagination, fired by too many Russian novels, is about to run away with her.

It's all her mother's fault.

Carolina had been kept home from school as a child, but taught herself to read from her sisters' books she stole from their schoolbags and hid in the woodshed until her father found them and gave them back to Gusta and Hulda and Johanna, but it was the youngest sister, Johanna, who took pity on crack-brained Carolina and put them back in the overturned bucket till all the sisters were kept home from school to follow the reapers and gather the aftercrop in their leather aprons. Later, after Carolina married Gustaf, she was even more determined to prove she wasn't crack-brained. She devoured Lena's readers, and they learned together, mother and daughter. Carolina read almost every book in Visby's library, bought enough in the market to line three walls of shelves in her bedroom. She was always quoting one historian or another, reading passages from novelists Par Lägerkvist or Selma Lagerlöf aloud to Lena at night, boring guests at her table with trivia about Gustavus Adolphus or Napoleon's General Bernadotte and his first love Desirée who became king and queen of Sweden, or how many soldiers died of influenza in the trenches of the Great War. She consumed Russian novels like so many loaves of her good braided *vetebröd,* the details icing in the cracks. When she discovered an author she liked she'd read his entire works, fuming if there was one book in translation not available at the library, while Lena wondered why only men were published since it was the women in her family who were the storytellers, according to Carolina.

Soon, mother and daughter fought over who was the first to read a new book arriving from the mainland at the Visby Bibliotek, or a special order from a Stockholm bookstore, usually a birthday or Christmas gift from Gustaf, who didn't seem to notice that his woman was better read than he, and if he did, he wisely turned a blind eye and pulled his milking cap over his good eye. Then, when Lena read aloud to her mother, her father pretended to doze by the hearth, the occasional guffaw or derisive snort giving away his pleasure or dislike of something in the story.

Just wait until she gets home and can tell her mother how she saw the places described in the Russian novels. In Dostoevsky's slave market.

"I know where you're taking me," she says, dropping the poles. "You're not going to sell me!"

He just offers that small smile on one side of his long, wolfish face, and it's enough to make her flutter like a robin taking its first sunbath of the season in the fishpond Gustaf carved into the Gotland garden for Carolina. Lena swishes her gypsy skirts at him.

Pytor

Peace Market, Leningrad, June 24, 1941

PURGED OF PROSTITUTION AND THIEVERY by the Bolsheviks, the peasant market was closed after the revolution, but once again stalls have been erected, pushcart trade abounds, and greasy-faced vendors with steely eyes flash watches and Finnish knives in the linings of long astrakhan coats. Turbaned Persians and Armenians in long black and blue robes girdled by bright sashes. Tartars in workjackets. Dark-eyed Georgians and Turks in baggy pants. Tea vendors carry steaming samovars on their heads. Pigeons swoop down on dropped crumbs, scratch in the dirt. And oh, the women! Long, tight hobble skirts, with slits. Jackets with padded shoulders, left open to reveal ruffled blouses unbuttoned to show off their bosoms. They are the only women Pytor knows, and he's proud to have the Swedish pony-girl dressed just like them by his side. Red lips. Rouged cheeks. Flowers in upswept hair. They smoke boldly in public, something he never saw any woman do in his Lena's Visby; it seemed to be an island of respectable people. The market women here make eyes at Pytor, who winks or bows his head, then when they see Lena they lift their heads and tilt noses as high in the air as snobbish courtesans. When they pass by, Pytor's nose is assaulted by heavy odours of cheap vodka, Makhorka tobacco, stinky perfume that makes Lena sneeze, and he laughs. Saturday market or a fair with gypsies was never like this at her home, and didn't he see it often enough while seeking a way to steal the Gotlandruss.

He leads Lena among ordinary Leningradski – workers dressed like Maryushka, old women wrapped in shawls and carrying string shopping bags. Stalls full of Vologda lace, wooden toys, phonograph records, ribbons, stockings, sleds, gas masks, pine-board coffins, samovars, candles, caviar. Pictures and photographs of Lenin and Stalin. Blue fox, bear and tiger and wolf skins.

A thin woman who tries but fails to hide a balding head with a babushka scarf trades two dresses for a pound of sausage. On a counter, a loaf of bread with a price tag: 600 rubles. Jars of sour cabbage.

A Tatar boy with pus oozing from one eye has a dancing bear cub on a leash. Passersby applaud, but no one drops coins into his clay begging cup with it's English words: MONEY FOR HONEY. The boy is so thin his trousers are tied with a rope around his waist. He plunks down, cross-legged, on the dirty sawdust, and the bear ambles over to him, plops down, and lays its head in the boy's thin lap. The boy ruffles the fur, plays with its ears, then closes his eyes, head nodding. The bear paws the boy's shoulder, wanting more petting, then a bright pink tongue lashes out and swipes the boy's face, waking him up. Absent-mindedly, he kisses the bear's wet nose. Pytor drops a coin in his cup. "There you go, Vaslav."

Lena clasps her hands together, and Pytor is glad to see her so delighted, yet is also relieved that she is distracted and forgets that she's angry with him. He's sorry he had to take her away with the horses, but what could he do when he couldn't manage so many alone, and she kept getting in his way. Now, he wants to make it up to her, to please her.

In one stall, a crone pours molten sugar into greasy glasses, sifted through a cloth, then mixes in dirty flour to make some kind of candy or jelly that must taste vile. Flies abound, buzzing over and on the sugar. *"Mukha,"* Pytor says, and remembering that she's supposed to be mute, Lena whispers the word: "Fly." No one seems to have heard her poor pronunciation and realize that she doesn't belong here.

Young men rove in packs, bearing switchblades and barely concealed long-bladed Finnish knives. Many of them greet Pytor, but ogle Lena, which makes Lena sidle closer to Pytor. Wolf whistles. Happily, he wraps a protective arm around her shoulders, but scans the crowd, looking for the horse trader who outfitted the coal barge with oats. With so much packed in the cart, he isn't on a shopping trip, though he wants the NKVD patrolling the market to think he's a vendor and needs to trade his goods for food.

Pytor stops before a pastry stall, chats with a young woman with slanted eyes and a pigtail hanging over one shoulder. He calls her Lin though he doesn't know if that's her real name. He trades one of his ration cards for two meat pies, sliced fried onions in a square of greasy newspaper and two glasses of Ararat port wine. Two babushki huddle on a bench, tapestry bags between fat knees, and they shift to make room for him and Lena. They both have bunches of flowers tied with ribbons. Pytor leaves his pushcart behind the babushki bench.

"Haven't seen you around, Pytor Petrovich," says the smaller of the two women. "Buy a posy for your sweetheart? Only one ruble – or a bit of bread."

"I've been away," he says. "But like a bad kopeck I always turn up." He takes a clean, white handkerchief from his breast pocket, spreads it on Lena's knees, and she accepts the picnic lunch. He's worried about her getting sick again, but dares not utter a word about it lest she try to answer him. The meat pies make him remember eating at the Gotland market Swedish lamb patties fried in butter, with mint sauce. He hopes these don't make Lena homesick. She smiles at him, and he feels rewarded for his care of her, though she may have decided to be nice to him while looking for a chance to escape, which in turn makes him worry about how she would survive without him.

A bearded vendor in an astrakhan coat that's seen a better century holds up a cage full of canaries. "Good price. Very cheap. You like?"

"Not today, Igor." Pytor says. "Have you seen Ivan the horse trader around?"

Lena looks at him quizzically as if to say: Igor? Ivan? You know everyone!

"I hear he's got a new stud who keeps him in the saddle so long he can't get out of bed." The canary man leers, and Lena blushes, dropping her head over her meat patty. "See you around. Don't take any squirrel money." And tries to sell a bird to an old man with a humped back and neck so crooked his head almost touches one shoulder.

The wizened babushka with the red shawl leans forward so she can speak to Lena around her black-shawled companion. "They say the meat patties are made from ground human flesh, but not to worry, it's only dog or cat." She cackles. "Don't trade with anyone fat, with greasy face and crazy eyes."

Lena looks bewildered then ducks her head again over her food.

Pytor says to the grandmother, "She's deaf."

The plump babushka says, "It's only too true. During the Great War, some people ate ground human meat. I say we'll fare no better this time, but me, I'll die first."

"No use to talk to her, she's deaf and mute," Pytor yells. Then he whispers to Lena in Swedish: "You no listen." She returns a blank face, not faked, for she must read people here by a gesture, the hint of a smile at the corner of a mouth, a frown, a shrug. He wants to be able to talk to her, to hear what she's thinking and feeling, to be able to take away her fears of a land so strange to her.

He decides to teach her Russian, word by word every minute they are alone.

"Poor child." From her *sumka,* shopping bag, the babushka pulls a half-eaten Red October chocolate bar and offers it to Lena, who shakes her head, No thank you. The bag is full of books to trade for bread.

A shudder passes through the crowd, moving them like a wave rippling onto shore, then parting, many people scuttle away, darting behind stalls. On their bench, the babushki catch up their flowers and shopping bags, rock three times, pressing on their knees to help them rise, and hobble away, heads huddling together.

Pytor stands tall, booted feet wide apart, his shoulders squared, one hand in the pocket where he conceals his switchblade. He takes one sideways step so he partially hides Lena seated behind him. Just like every woman he's ever known in orphanage and brick factory, at state farms, on the streets, her curiosity is stronger than her fear of the unknown, and she peeks around him to see the horse trader wearing a fine blue fox hat, with earflaps turned up, a sheepskin coat, opened to show off Baltic amber pendants around his neck. Beautiful grey, high-top boots. He smacks a horse whip against a leathered thigh. This is the man who outfitted Pytor with boat and oats and hay, who expected they'd make a fortune trading the rare Gotlandruss.

Behind the man with beautiful boots swagger an entourage of young men ready *to move with the music,* commit a crime, whether it be *dennik,* a daytime theft, or *idti na shalynuyu,* unplanned theft. When Lena has learned enough Russian to talk with Pytor, he must try to explain to her the thieves' code first created in the Gulag that he learned in the Children's Brick Factory. In place of *govorit* (speaking) their language is *stukak* (knocking) because prisoners tapped on walls to talk to each other. They all wear tight leather breeches, colourful chemises, neckerchiefs, and military or trade-school caps tilted jauntily over their eyes. The tops of their soft boots are folded down, just like Pytor's, yet he doesn't consider himself one of them, though he owes Ivan plenty.

At first, the tough trader and streetwise Pytor greet each other with slaps on the shoulders, no handshake, because a deal has already been made – and broken because of the war. The trader shows off his gold teeth when he speaks and flashes a fake smile. "You owe me for the boat and feed. Pay up now!" He laughs like a horse neighing.

Pytor says, "If you want your share you'll have to keep to our arrangement, a deal is a deal. You pay me and I deliver the horses, five hundred rubles a head."

"We can grind them up for meat, who will know the difference when the belly growls." He shoves Pytor out of the way so he can have a good look at Lena. She drops her head, squeezes her hands together, as if praying that Pytor isn't bartering her.

"Nice trick."

"She's mine! She's not for sale or trade." Pytor steps closer to Lena, grips tighter the switchblade in his pocket.

"Every thing and every one has a price. Give me the girl and wipe out your debt." He speaks softly as if he doesn't want to frighten Lena – yet. With a gloved finger, the trader tilts her chin, forcing her head up and back as if she's a mare he wants to buy, and she looks wildly to Pytor for help. Before he can take more than two steps forward, she jerks her head down, and bites as hard as she can, her jaw springing open again, and the trader yanks his fingers free, revealing a row of teeth marks in the soft leather. The trader roars like an animal whose paw has been caught in a trap, but he hauls back his other arm and lands a backhanded blow to the side of her head that knocks her sideways onto the babushki bench. She crouches there, one hand on her cheek, a blow like that would make anyone see red and yellow stars, and tears well up in her eyes, but she seems too afraid to cry out.

"Teach your whore better manners."

"I'll teach you not to hit a woman." A red fury makes Pytor lower his voice, commanding, and he feels deadly calm, ready to kill Ivan for hurting Lena.

Hard-soled boots close in on the trader and Pytor. He hears the clicks of switchblades flicking open, the scrape of Finnish knives unsheathed. Pytor and the trader circle each other, the thieves-in-law cheering them on, the odds uneven and in favour of the heavier man, though Pytor is light-footed and quick; it's a hopeless situation, with the horse trader's boys there at his command.

PYTOR

"Musori!" the trader suddenly yells. "Scram!" And Pytor looks behind him to see the NKVD police patrol advancing upon them, not just looking for thieves with bread hidden under their coats. Just this morning, Pytor heard on his shortwave radio that the police search for deserters from the front, for troublemakers in bread lines, for people spreading rumours that the English or Americans are on they way to save the city, for panic-mongers and Old Believers spreading the word.

The thieves scatter, the horse trader clomping after them in his obscenely beautiful grey boots.

Quickly, Pytor kneels before Lena, and she sits up. "You hurt?" he says in Swedish. "You can run?"

Too late. The NKVD police patrol close in on them. A whistle shrill, a command, and the troop, brandishing guns and shooting wildly, take after Ivan the Horse Trader and his scattered gang of thieves, leaving two policemen striding towards Pytor and Lena.

"Quick, quick!" Pytor helps Lena scramble back onto the loaded peasant cart, then turns to face the policemen, one who looks too young to shave, the other heavy-set, with a moustache.

"Stop. Or I'll shoot." The youthful cop's hands shake. Maybe this is his first day on patrol.

Pytor says, "Good afternoon, thank you for saving me from those thieves. They tried to gyp me and would have beaten me blind if you hadn't come along."

"Papers!" demands the senior officer. His subordinate lowers his gun.

Pytor produces the leather folder containing his identification papers and Lena's. Will the policeman recognize a forgery?

"Name?"

"Pytor Petrovich Svetlov."

"Where do you live?"

"Leningrad."

"Why haven't you joined the People's Volunteers?"

"Comrade, I'm on my way to a recruiting station, but first I must sell my goods, you see? My wife will need a little *seichas* while I'm fighting for our country and great leader."

Pytor has drawn the policemen's attention to Lena, who cowers on top of the pushcart, likely wishing she could shrink or turn into a wisp of smoke and float away, over the sea, homeward. The junior officer struts around her, picking a boil on the back of his neck. His face is pimply.

"My wife, she is deaf mute, very sad it is."

With the butt of his gun, the first officer pokes at the canvas covering the cart here and there. "What have you got in there?"

"Just household goods," Pytor says. He unties the canvas at the rear of the cart, flips it back to reveal a makeshift *burzhuiki,* a pot-bellied stove, with rusted grille, surrounded by a pile of bricks. "Perhaps a little gift or two, for your kindness, for saving us from the thugs?" He digs out a leather-bound book. "Very rare. Signed by Pushkin himself." He reaches into the mound and finds a hand-carved bear, on hind legs. When trading, Pytor can always count on the fact that Russians love their Bear. He has never been able to think of himself as one of them, not when he was raised in the Children's Brick Factory.

The policemen scan the crowd to see who is watching, but vendors haggle with customers, business as usual. The patrol fire their guns at runaway thieves, some dropping dead on the cobblestones, others escaping into the conduit.

"Be off with you," the senior officer says, choosing the carving, while his junior pockets the book of poetry. "Don't let me catch you in this thieves' market again."

The pimple-faced recruit says, "Good luck at the front."

In the stony field, all but two *uzki* disappear into the sewer conduit, some of the patrol hot on their heels. The rest of the policemen nab the strays, shoot both in the head, and they thud to the ground. It all happens so fast no questions could possibly be asked of any of the thieves. They were simply there, caught, and killed.

Pytor mops his face and neck with his handkerchief. "Too close." He helps Lena on with her jacket, wraps the shawl around her shoulders, then rearranges the contents of the pushcart, creating a nest with rabbit-fur breeches, fox-fur hats. "Is better if you hide," he says in Swedish. And Lena looks only too glad to sink into the pile of furs, yet her face looks flushed, her arms reddening as if her veins are filling with liquid fire; he has felt it himself, the thrill of having escaped danger. She curls there, and Pytor hides her under the canvas, leaving a breathing hole at the back end where he laces together the ropes.

Soon, the pushcart is moving again, the din of the former Peace Market diminishes, replaced by the thunder of low-flying JU-88's and Heinkel bombers in command of the sky. Her jaw must throb, her knees must sting, and he wishes he could take her mind away from her pain and the memory of what just happened in the market by telling her to think of her *russ* grazing in a quiet meadow, of the twin colts curled for sleep against their mother's belly. How often he watched her in the moor before he made his move on her. If he hadn't been desperate for the money the horses would bring on a good market he might not have been able to carry out his plan, and he never planned to take her with him, it just happened when she fought so hard and he realized he needed her to look after the horses on the coal barge.

Far away, the racket of AA guns, the whine of falling bombs.

What's going to happen next?

Pytor sings, yes to Lena: *"Tepyer ya gorki sirotina* – Now I'm a bitter orphan! – *I vdrug vzmakhnul po vsyem, po tryom* – And suddenly he swept over all three horses." The only word she maybe can understand is: *troikoi*. But she's riding in a pushcart, not a troika. She must be exhausted. She falls asleep.

Though he knows from too much experience that too much has happened too fast to this Swedish girl, which may put her beyond feeling even fear now, he hopes that it's the last time he will expose her to danger in the Hunger Market.

Signe

River Neva and Lake Ladoga, June 27, 2004

ON THE FIFTH MORNING, The *Novikov Priboy* departs St. Petersburg. No families or friends of the tourists wave farewell on the dock. The ship's loudspeakers blare an unrecognizable naval air.

Signe sits in a deck chair, close to the entrance to the Panorama Bar. The going is smooth, the city built on Swedish prisoners' bones soon in the distance behind her. Here, the Neva has banks as steep as the North Saskatchewan's, sharply cut bays, with poplar and pine, like a gathering of northern people at a reunion. Along the shore, a few fishing boats, likely after salmon and sturgeon.

The young sun is warm on her face, and for a while she closes her eyes, lulled into a false comfort until she hears exclamations and shouts from the passengers leaning on the railings. She rises, but maintains a distance from the side of the boat and the water so far below the uppermost deck. She shades her eyes and looks away, into the distance. And there it is: Lake Ladoga, Europe's largest, known for its moody temperament, its quick change from great depths to shallow, rocky narrows. From Lena's stories, Signe knew it was big, but had not realized it was so expansive it would be impossible to see the far shore.

She has a little time to prepare for the ordeal of not being able to see land in any direction. She'll hide in her cabin.

Somewhere – out there – on a massive shield of ice – Signe took her first breath.

It wasn't just a family myth, but when he told the story of her birth her father's voice seemed to imply that she would have been a different person had she been born at home, maybe before a warm hearth or even in an antiseptic hospital.

Her throat constricts as if she's just plunged forward into an icy wind, and it hurts her lungs.

Now that she sees Ladoga, questions swoop down like seagulls looking for fish, but Lena and Maryushka and Pytor are no longer here to answer them. How long did it take Lena and the Gotlandruss – forty of them, each bearing food for the besieged city – to cross the Ice Road? They were attacked from the air by bombers. The ice appeared and thickened in different parts of the lake at different times, advancing in centrifugal rings from the banks to the centre, like growth rings of a great tree, perhaps the Tree of Life. Where the ice was thin and wouldn't support their weight, they lost ponies. Drivers. Yet again and again they crossed the Ice Road.

What made them do it?

It never before occurred to Signe to ask: Why would Lena risk her life and that of her unborn child?

Until now, it was just a story told late at night during a storm to make Signe forget about Mamma's Swedish gods of thunder and lightning, their battle for possession of her cowardly soul. Each winter, for five years, her mother and father took food into Leningrad and then loaded the empty sleighs and sledges with starving People of the Blockade and took them to country towns and collective farms. Now, Ladoga is made real, the sky and undulating water are as grey-brown as tarnished silver, their union pencilled on the horizon.

On the way from Leningrad back to the country island of Kizhi, with each crossing, how many evacuated people loaded on each sled or sledge, with a blanket roll, a kettle, candlestick? How many died before they reached the distant shore?

If you lost a horse, you lost the world, Lena said, and for her none so great a loss as Thor.

She was horse crazy.

She often led young Signe around the Livelong barnyard on an old Clydesdale, so wide her skinny legs stuck straight out the sides. Lena taught her never to stand behind a horse, ever. Her fear was a healthy respect. She must have been frightened during the siege, while crossing the ice. Signe wishes she had asked her how she overcame it. What made her so brave?

If I was born on the Lake, I could die on it.

Where the Neva meets Ladoga, a bottleneck and rapids. The riverboat picks up speed to match the current, it's like an airship encountering rough air, the ride bumpy. Signe shivers, but not from the cold. Deck chairs slide downhill and careen against the railing. She covers her mouth with shaking hands, and, afraid she'll throw up, she rushes to the railing. The wind tears at her eyes, at the ends of her shawl. It forces her to confront the memory that never really goes away; it's always rearing up, again and again, unrelenting, but she won't let it end until she arrives at the moment of no return, yet it has no end – ever.

She sees herself on the west shore of Lake Katepwa, a breeze whispering secrets in the poplar stand behind her cottage. She's reading Pushkin and revising her lecture notes for her class in Russian literature at the University of Regina, doubting her permissiveness in allowing the kids to take the boat out, insisting that Sasha not let her brother drive it, and above all, stay close to the shore.

They've rounded the bend, but will turn about at the dead end, and head back. It's a calm day, the algae thick and green on this side, but across the lake, at the Main Beach, it's clear enough to swim, and shrieking voices drift to her, like discordant sounds of an orchestra warming up for a Stravinsky ballet. And then she sees the red motorboat, in full throttle, speeding towards the opposite shore. She'll ground them for a month. Tapani must have bribed Sasha to let him drive. He's showing off, like a pilot doing a flyby, the boat arcing, weaving, crossing its own wake, its prow high. The lifeguard must be standing on his lookout, his whistle shrill (though it may be Signe who's on her feet, screaming). Bathers better scramble out of the water onto the shore! It's too far for her to see Sasha shaking Tapani, trying to shove him over, take control of the wheel. What has come over her boy? Then the boat has wings, it soars up, seems to fly straight towards the dock, a sharp turn in the air – how close is it to the end of the pier? – and then a crack, as if a gun has been fired, the end of the boat hits the dock, a slender body flung onto the rocks, an explosion, the gas tank. Fire and a roaring in Signe's ears. A din of noise that carries like the skirl of bagpipes over the lake, some of the screams her own, running for the car, it's too far around the south end of Katepwa, she must get there in time, but that's impossible.

The church bell announces vespers in the Anglican church. Sirens. Police and fire trucks from Fort Qu'appelle.

SIGNE

Over the lake, a fleet of pelicans head for the weirs, their sanctuary.

THE *NOVIKOV PRIBOY* FOUND ITS WAY safely through the bottleneck, it slows, the waters calm again. And the riverboat leaves the River Neva, heading out and into Lake Ladoga.

And Kostja creeps up behind Signe, on silent cat feet. "Don't worry," he says. "The riverboat captains say navigating is like driving small cart on stone-paved road. No riverboat has ever gone down."

The water is perfectly tranquil again. Signe stops shaking. She swallows hard, her stomach settling down.

"This is Road of Life," Kostja says. "It was called that during Second World War because the city's survival depended on food transports across the lake. One million people were evacuated. Still, over one million died of starvation. In summer, boats braved Luftwaffe bombs."

"I heard about it," is all Signe can say, the story of Thor told again and again, sometimes late at night, beside a campfire at Turtle Lake, or during an electric storm when she was afraid of lightning and thunder and Papa rushed the women outside to huddle in the cab of the ancient '46 Fargo he still used for hauling wood. He said, *You're sitting on rubber, a bad conductor of electricity,* and Signe didn't know what was worse, the crack of lightning like rockets exploding, or the din of thunder like bombs falling on faraway Russia where she was born. Lena and Maryushka were thankful they lived to tell about it, the war of all worlds, and the repeated crossing of the Ice Road.

Kostja sights a gull, bouncing on updrafts and scanning the wake for fish or leftovers tossed overboard by the cooks. Camera at the ready, he says, "I am having my second marriage."

He's too old to be starting a family.

"My first wife died." He says it as easily as pronouncing a day without touring, which is tomorrow. Before Signe can offer condolences, he rushes to the opposite railing, photographing the gull. Hold tight to silence. He will tell you what he wants you to know.

He must have sensed something in the way Signe sagged in her deck chair, rubbing at sore eyelids with fists clenched against the haunting memory of the boating accident. Sasha. Tapani.

When he takes a deck chair beside Signe, he says, "Buhd."

"Birrr-d."

"Bihd." Lips pursed. Of course, the "r" soft, he learned his English with the Brits when he took his PHD in England.

And it's like Thumper teaching Bambi how to say bird.

No, it's like kissing each other better, without touching.

Vozdushnyi Potselui, Lena and Pytor called them. Air kisses.

"Dusha v dushu," he says. Soul-to-soul.

She wants to invent a bird for him. It must take its colours from icons: red for beauty, the black of mystery and sorrow, white for the light of love.

Tak khorosho! How wonderful to hear a new song, Papa said, but that morning memory fails her again.

Slova dlya serdtsa. Words for the heart.

Slova dlya dushi. Words for the soul.

Tonight, the riverboat will cross Lake Ladoga while Signe sleeps.

In the morning, she will be on the opposite shore, perhaps on the other side of fear. Yes, she's finally learning to face it, no longer shrinking from it, and though this grief may never go away, she is determined not to let it control her anymore.

LENA

Tonight, instead of crying for her lost daughter, Signe sings: *Dusha v Dushu*.

Lena

Leningrad dock, June 27, 1941

LENA IS A STRONG SWIMMER, *and just now she's floating on her back, resting, while her ponies fan out in a wedge around her, their strong jaws cutting Vs though the sea, making waves that ripple and undulate towards the far shore.*

It's a long way, homeward to Gotland. She doesn't know how long she's been at sea, but the sun is high, its light glancing off the crest of waves, casting a sheen on wet hides. She rolls over, striking out again, but makes little headway, even the horses fight to keep their heads above water, short but powerful legs churning the water. Hot. The sun. Boiling the water. Dead herring. Chunks of dark rye bread like bobbing heads. Potatoes with eyes that blink. Red coral, shaped like fingerbones. Rockets on the horizon. Drone of flying tanks overhead. Wingless planes diving and surfacing, like humpback whales. On the far shore, a lighthouse launches into the sky, rises like a rocket firecracker at a fair. Mines explode, and she swims through fire. Smoke chokes her, stings her eyes, fills her nose. The horses shrill, buck in the water, red eyes rolling with fear. A table with a red telephone. A gilded throne, and on it Gensek, The Leader, the Ghenghis Khan of the Politburo. His body sags, moustaches droop. He doodles, colouring the eyes of drawn wolves red. The harder she swims, the weaker her arms, legs. All is slow motion. A beam of light slashes the sky. Leaflets falling, the ink indelible, the writing legible and in Cyrillic letters she's thrilled to be able to read: Beat the Jews. Beat the Communists. Surrender! Women and children, wear white to avoid bombs. *The ponies are now pulling red children's sleds. If she can reach Thor, he will carry her home. Not far. Pull harder. A runner within her grasp. She kicks and throws up her arms, leaping like a dolphin, and lands on the slippery sled. She rolls, floats on her back, panting. Phosphorous bombs exploding all around. A long parachute falling, not a Nazi pilot's, it's the new bomb, a magnetic naval mine. It explodes, flames turning into many russet horse hides, falling, falling on her. Heavy, she writhes, trying to throw them off. She cannot breathe. She sees herself rise up, stand tall, balancing with her arms, and Josif Vissarionovich Dzugashvili, called Koba by his friends, rides towards her on a cascading wave, lunges at her, his thick-knuckled peasant hands reaching for her throat.*

She screams, and wakes herself.

Opens her eyes.

PYTOR SHAKES HER AND YELLS in his poor Swedish. "Waking, wake. Only dream. Wake you up!"

She's buried in furs. Coats. Breeches. Those Russian hats. Pytor peels them away, lets her skin breathe. She's soaking wet with sweat. At home, she always sleeps with her feet sticking out of the feather *tika*. If she gets too hot she has a bad dream.

Pytor enfolds her in his arms, rocks her. "Shh, shh."

She pushes him away. Clambers out of the pushcart. They've reached the docks, the grain elevators. She looks both ways, then realizes that Pytor has moved the coal barge to a different wharf, farther down the Neva from where they first docked by a grove of spruce and pine.

She sees herself so suddenly alone, calling to a sailor,

"Where are you going?" Waving to the captain of a merchant ship. "Will you pass by Gotland? Could you take a letter?" No one hears her. The captain waves back.

Pytor says, "You. Make danger." He reaches into his pocket, takes out her fake identification papers and a wad of rubles tied with an elastic band, hands them to her, then abruptly turns on his heel, and pushes the cart up the gangplank, unbars the doors to the hold, shoves the cart inside, then closes the doors with a clank again. He takes the iron stairs to the helm. He pauses, turns. "You. Free. Go!" He lifts his cap, his face scrinched like a boy's when he's trying to be a man, and not cry when saying goodbye to someone he loves. "*Pak'a,*" he says, lifting one arm, the smallest of waves with his hand.

Lena doesn't know what to do now. Leave her horses, find an embassy of an Allied country, try to ask for work in exchange for passage on any passenger steamer heading west? The wad of rubles would likely be more than enough of a bribe for the captain of a Latvian or Estonian barge – but think of the danger: mines and bombs falling in the Gulf of Finland.

"Take me home." She points westward. "Gotland? *Dah,* we go."

"Sorry, no."

Of course, he'd be arrested the moment they arrived in Visby, charged with theft and kidnapping.

It's quite likely that Pytor has to flee the authorities since he's not among the *blokadniki,* the People's Volunteers, or a member of the Red Army. Worse, she has seen the pack of horse thieves out to skin his hide. He must be planning to head for the country, wait out the war, then when the evacuated animals are returned to the zoos sell Gotlandrussen and live comfortably forever after in a village house that isn't a sewer. Until then, maybe country folk will buy a horse or two for their fairs. It's all useless speculation. Didn't her father warn her never to try to out-guess a Russian, especially when trading in horses?

If she found her way back to Maryushka would she take her in, help her return home? No, Pytor's sister couldn't get rid of her fast enough, likely afraid of being accused of harbouring a spy.

In the Hunger Market, Lena saw the NKVD shoot first, without questions.

She's more afraid of being alone on the streets of Leningrad than staying with Pytor, who offers her some protection, at least.

"Pytor, Pytor," she calls, gesturing, "Come here. *S'pasibo?*" She says thank you instead of please. He takes the metal stairs two at a time.

"*Mor,*" she says. "*Far,*" she says, then tries to say father in Russian: *"Dadya?* They'll be crazy with worry, my mother and father." She mimes cranking a country telephone, an imaginary receiver held to her ear. "Telephone. If I could just call them and tell them I'm alive, not hurt."

"*Kom har,*" he says in poorly accented Swedish. He races back up the stairs to the wheelhouse, looking over his shoulder to make sure she's following him, looking as happily astonished as a child who has just been told that Kris Kringle brings Christmas presents.

Inside the wheelhouse: a string hammock and red blanket, a pot-bellied stove, a rickety captain's chair with a red star painted on its back, shelves made from orange crates that hold canned goods, sausages, and other non-perishable foodstuffs.

A small drop-leaf table for maps and charts, a wireless radio – and a telegraph!

Pytor hands her paper and pencil. "Put down. Message. I send ship-to-shore." He sweeps aside maps and charts to clear a space at the table, pulls the captain's chair for her as if he's a waiter at a restaurant.

While she thinks of a message to send to her father, Pytor pours fresh water in the seagull's tin can, which is wired to a cage Pytor must have acquired while Lena recovered at his sister's home. The bird has worked at the bandage with its beak, but failed to untie the knot. It should be changed. Pytor sprinkles grain into its feed tray. The bird flutters its good wing, screeches, then begins to peck at the seeds.

First she prints her father's name in capital letters: GUSTAF BJÖRNSSON. Then the address: BJÖRNSSON STUD FARM, LOJSTA, GOTLAND, SWEDEN, worried that it may take days for the Visby telegraph office to send the message to the farm with a boy on a bicycle. Then she hesitates over the actual message. Pytor likely can't read Swedish, yet he obviously trusts her not to send international police after him. If her father calls them, will the Stockholm police contact the NKVD? Would the Russians cooperate in a search for a kidnapper? What does a farmer's daughter from an isolated island know about international politics? It's all so much slop for a pigsty.

How badly does she want to go home? She feels a rush of excitement at the possibilities of more adventures awaiting her, once they've left the besieged city and stay away from the frontlines. If only Pytor would – or could – reveal his current plan for the horses. Unbidden feelings she's never felt before and cannot name creep up on her, turning her milk-white skin the colour of Pytor's Glory of Peace rose. Is it possible? Has she fallen in love – with danger? Surely not with this Nik-nik. "I'm not staying with you forever, you know. Just until it's safe to go home." How long can this war last?

If there's one thing she's learned about Pytor, it's that he trusts no one, apart from his sister, yet he's counting on her not to give him away now. She will teach him by not betraying his new-found trust in her.

She prints in large letters: DO NOT WORRY. AM SAFE AND WELL. RUSS ARE TOO. DO NOT TRY TO FIND ME. WILL RETURN HOME AS SOON AS POSSIBLE. YOUR LOVING DAUGHTER, LENA.

She has no idea how a ship-to-shore telegraph works, if translating Roman-letter Gutamål into Cyrillic is necessary, or even if Pytor is sending the message she wrote, but he seems to be taking it one letter at a time, the telegraph clicking its dots and dashes like a metronome; he frowns, pauses, scratches behind an ear, until he grins at her like a cat with feathers sticking out of its mouth. Her message has been sent.

"*Spas'iba,*" she says.

"*Pazh'alusta,*" he says. "*Nichiv'o.*" He opens the door to the wheelhouse, gesturing that she's free to leave, calling her *S'olnishka,* some kind of term of endearment, so he seems to be sorry to say good-bye.

"I'm hungry," she says. "What's for dinner, Nik-nik? Borscht?"

He doesn't answer, his head bent over a map, charting a course – maybe to grazing meadows and thinly populated villages – to wait out the war, which surely will not last longer than the white nights, after which darkness will fall with winter. He bites his bottom lip.

She could never leave her ponies behind.

Now, she must see to her Gotlandruss.

THE BAR ON THE DOOR to the hold isn't as heavy as it sounds when it closes shut. She lifts it, pushing with all her might, then heaves open the doors, leaving them ajar to let in fresh air and sunshine.

Thor greets her with a swing of his massive head, nudging her arms, wanting an apple or carrot. "Glad to see you I am too." His manger and the others are now full of straw, which makes the cleaning so much easier. Emptied feedbags have been replaced, there's enough oats to last the longest winter.

From now on, she will not be locked in the hold.

She rummages in the pushcart for Maryushka's string bag, and changes her clothes, dumping her sewage-stained and dusty skirt and stockings torn at the knees into the washtub. She wets what's left of her own petticoat and dabs it on the reddening scratches on her knees, wishing she had a tin of healing salve, sticking plaster. Without a mirror, she can't see how badly bruised her cheek is. It hurts only when she touches it. So leave it alone.

Then she feeds and waters her ponies. Lugging pails of oats and water, she promises them fresh air, sunshine and long romps in sweet clover – soon, yes soon. She sings while she works, *Gubben Noak,* an old drinking song about Noah leaving his ark, planting a vineyard, then getting drunk, and taking a bath.

The barge picks up speed, rocks, as if it's weaving through a watery mine field, though the Germans have not penetrated the Neva. She listens for the whine of bombs, explosions, AA guns, but hears only the hum of the motor, the cry of gulls following the wake in search of cast-off rubbish. She loses her balance, reaches for the railing of a manger, steadies herself, and tries to make her way toward the open doors. She's met with a blast of cold, wet air. Pytor didn't turn the boat around so they must be travelling upriver – downriver? – away from the city. Have they hit an early summer storm? The barge seems to be heading into waves, riding crests then plunging into troughs, the river as rough as a wintry sea. Best to ride it out; if she leaves the hold she might be washed overboard. She squats, hanging onto the railing, while Thor nickers to his mares, the foals cringe against their mother's heaving sides, other heads lift, eyes roll with fright. "It's all right," she says. "The captain knows these waters, the barge won't go down, it's nothing but a bit of rough water. Easy, take it easy."

And then, as suddenly as it began, it's over. The barge slows to normal speed, the water calm again.

Lena pulls herself up, rushes to the doors, up the outside stairs to the wheelhouse. Pytor says nothing, and she holds tight to silence lest he changes his mind and locks her in the hold again.

She feeds the wounded seagull bits of bread. It lets her finger its head and neck feathers. "You're getting better," she says. "Soon you'll fly away."

Then she goes back outside, taking the seagull in its new cage with her.

THE CITY IS EERILY SILENT behind them. No factory whistle, locomotive bell or church chime. Leningradski wait for another air-raid alarm. When she looks back she sees barrage balloons floating over spires and cupolas of the city.

They've just passed through rapids, around a great bend in the River Neva. From here, it's only thirty or forty miles of open country to the Finnish lines, if she remembers her geography correctly.

LENA

Here, the Russians have blown the bridges, and she can see soldiers spread over what must be six or seven miles of the north bank.

Close to the south shore where the river highway runs to Leningrad, an island and a fortress flying a red flag comes into view. "Shlisselburg," Pytor says, through the side window of the wheelhouse, and Lena remembers part of her own history. For a hundred years before Peter the Great, Oreshek, the ancient trade route from the land of the Varungians to the Black Sea, was held by the Swedes, and he who controlled Oreshek was in command of the flow of honey, spices, furs, slaves, gems, perfume, silks and flax to the Orient. After Peter wrested it back, he renamed it Shlisselburg, the Key City. Here, he incarcerated his wife, Yevdotiya. Here too, Nicholas I imprisoned six Decembrists for revolting in 1824 in the Senate Square. Pytor points out the marble plaque on the royal tower, but it's too far away to read. "Lenin's older brother," he says. "Shrine to martyr. No guns in fortress since Peter. Now they call it the Eternal Prison. No return from it." Pytor has the look of a sly and wary wolf. "In place like this I am born." His jaw knots again. He might as well be talking to himself. She wants to say how sorry she is, but doesn't know the words in Russian. Sometimes it's better to say nothing.

He says, "Ladoga Fleet," and points at a dozen or more sailors setting up cannon and machine guns. "Rifle-firing points and snipers' posts," he says. But Lena feels sorry for refugees on the wharf waiting for two tugboats heading towards them. A gunboat and cutters load women, children, wounded soldiers on stretchers. Lena doesn't need a general to tell her that if the Germans take this old Swedish fortress, the encirclement of Leningrad will be complete. Maybe she should have made a run for it when she had the chance.

Ahead, a lake without end. It must be Ladoga. Impossible to see the other side. "All night we cross," Pytor says.

On opposite shipping lanes, barges heaped with grain or vegetables: cabbages, turnips, carrots, and Lena cannot help but count – one to forty-nine – not enough to feed a city of so many million. Pytor's face is set, hard, and he still grinds his teeth, not speaking to Lena. Maybe he's worried about his sister finding enough to eat.

Then she sees the wreck of a munitions barge, the hull of another boat sinking near the shore. The coal barge yields to steamers packed with people fleeing the city. Like them, Lena has had no choice in her destination, but now she can no longer blame Pytor. She wants to be with him.

There is no night in this northland, just a greying sky, shadowing the city in blockade.

In its cage, the seagull sleeps, its good wing curved over its head.

Maryushka

Kirov Steelworks, September 8, 1941

THE KIROV STEELWORKS is so large it's a city within a city, with its many mills and foundries and plants. If it hadn't been for Irini, Maryushka's comrade in charge of the grenade works, Maryushka would have lost herself in the maze on her first day here.

It was called the Tula Cartridge Works then, its name changed to Kirov after the mysterious assassination of Leningrad's favourite son and leader who had opposed Stalin in the Politburo. "Our brass-rolling mill and copper foundry have supplied our army with ammunition since the time of Alexander the First," Irini explained to Maryushka. "In those days, brass and silver were scarce raw materials and were shipped from Germany." How ironic now. "Thanks to our Great Leader, the Man of Steel, we now produce bimetal for the first time in Russia. Isn't that wonderful!" Irini tilted her head and closed one eye.

"I didn't know his name means Man of Steel." Raised in an orphanage and then put to work in the Children's Brick Factory, Maryushka's education is lacking, compared to most

Soviet children, and she still feels inferior to her fellow workers like Irini.

Like most of the steelworkers, Maryushka lives in the Kolpino settlements and takes the streetcar to work every morning. Irini will get on at the third stop, where the statue of a factory worker, gun in hand, is dedicated to the Petrograd workers of the Revolution. Maryushka saves a seat for her by placing her Mosin-Nagant rifle, issued to every Kirov worker, on the wicker seat beside her.

The talk is always of the war. Worried about her husband, Mikhail, and leaning her head against the dirty window, Maryushka listens and doesn't listen to the rough and sometimes shrill voices around her.

— *How could our brave volunteers do that? Break and flee?*

— *They lost their weapons.*

— *A crime against the State!*

— *Yes, and they were shot by the NKVD police.*

— *Leave it to the army, not the police, I say.*

Posters everywhere: THE ENEMY IS AT THE GATES. No one, least of all Maryushka, understands why the Red Army retreats. The 23rd Army is lost in the dense forest and swamps only twenty miles from the city limits. Daily, more of the Popular Draft return on foot, in rags instead of uniforms, their hands raw, feet bruised and black with dirt and bloody bandages. The streetcar passes a defeated regiment, and a hush falls over the workers around her. Maryushka searches faces, but cannot find her husband. She can't get off the tram or she'll be late for work and suffer a reduction in her rations, yet she sees herself running from man to man, asking for news of Mikhail Davidovitch, but every person seems to shake his or her head sadly, *Sorry no.*

All this summer and fall, Maryushka has waited for a letter from her Mikhail, but none ever arrives, though she checks her apartment mailbox and slot at the Kirov factory each morning for the dreaded black-bordered official proclamation of death or notice of missing-in-action.

From daily reports issued to the Kirov workers, she knows only that he was sent with thirty thousand workers and students from universities to build fortifications and trenches, mine fields, gun emplacements and tank traps along the Luga Line, forty to seventy miles southwest of Leningrad.

The night before he left, Mikhail took her to a performance of *The Good Soldier* at the Radlov Theatre. The actors wore gas masks, and reduced her to tears. When they returned home, they tore each other's clothes away, their lovemaking desperate lest it be the last. She still hopes, in vain, for a child.

The next morning, Mikhail was among the 1st Kirov Division of Volunteers issued hand grenades and Molotov cocktails, picks, shovels, axes, hunting knives and guns from 1918. They were told to rearm themselves when their comrades fell in combat. Then, led by a red and gold banner presented by the remaining factory workers, they marched behind a band to Vitebsk freight station, where they boarded boxcars, headed for Batelsk, east of Lug. She later learned in the new military newspaper, *To Victory,* for the People's Volunteers, that they were attacked by German bombers. Her worst fear was dashed, for a while at least, when Mikhail was not listed among the dead.

The tram stops, and Maryushka cranes her neck, watching for Irini. There she is, third in line, her rifle over her shoulder, her dark hair tied up tight under her kerchief. She looks up, and Maryushka waves, but Irini doesn't smile, just nods abruptly as if accepting an order from Moscow she doesn't agree with; maybe she doesn't want to go to work, not just today, but ever. The skin under her large eyes is blotched with fatigue. Another night without sleep, keeping watch on the roof of her building, with pails of water ready to douse flames.

Maryushka places the rifle between her knees to make room for Irini, who plunks down on the hard wicker seat. "Good morning," Maryushka says.

"Is it?" Irini says. "You got a letter?"

"Not today."

"Maybe tomorrow."

The tram lurches forward, the overhead trolley sparking on its electric line like lights of fireflies falling but winking out before they hit the pavement.

Far off, fires burn on the other side of the city. Rainbows arch over the harbour. "Poor buggers," Irini says. She refers to the evacuees moved out of Tallin Harbour, twenty-three thousand people according to the news, in four convoys protected by gunboats, cutters and trawlers, headed for Kronstadt, the line of ships stretching for fifteen miles in the fog, while overhead German planes droned and anti-aircraft guns chattered ceaselessly. Sixteen warships sank. Ten thousand lives lost.

Suddenly, a familiar flash of light, and outside it's snowing leaflets again. The tram screeches to a stop, the driver opens the front doors, and rushes out to clear the tracks. This will take time the workers can't afford to lose, and they rumble out, grumbling and cursing the Nazis, to help the driver, a reluctant Irini and stoic Maryushka among them, their rifles slung over their shoulders.

Maryushka reads the first leaflet she picks up: THE BALTIC FLEET IS ENCIRCLED. This means new orders from Moscow at the Kirov today, another step-up in the production levels. The Man of Steel wants his experimental JS tanks to replace the monster KVs and he wants them NOW. He inspects every blueprint created by the Design Bureau, and has everyone quaking and kowtowing from the lowliest rivetter like Maryushka to the highest mucky-muck boss in the rolling mill.

"I don't know," Irini says. "Maybe the end of it all would be best for us."

Maryushka doesn't want to have this conversation again, not in public. Irini isn't pro-Nazi, not a follower of the mad Hitler, so much as she's weary of the arrests, the assassinations, of living with fear. Even when the skies are clear, she can't sleep, afraid of the Black Van, of footsteps on the stairs. If her grenade unit doesn't meet the production levels demanded by the Man of Steel she could be accused of sabotage, of being an economic *wrecker*. Her fingernails are bitten down to the quick.

"Look at this one," Irini says, "a warning." The leaflet reads: WAIT FOR THE FULL MOON. "That's tonight. Something terrible is about to happen!"

Maryushka places her hands over her friend's. "You're just tired," she says. "Let's go back inside."

"The Green Devils have taken Mga," Irini says. "The October Railroad to Moscow is cut." Her voice crackles like the sparks showering them from the streetcar's trolley. "How will we get food?" Her eyes are red-rimmed as if she's been weeping for weeks – and maybe she has, but hasn't dared open all her heart to her friend. Some things even the best of friends cannot talk about. Maryushka has never told Irini that her father was an officer in the White Russian army, that she was born the child of an enemy of the Soviet State.

"Don't worry," Maryushka says. "We'll take back Mga, you'll see."

The tracks are clear now, and the grim-faced workers file back onto the tram, a determined ring to their steps on the iron stairs.

Not far to go now, no stops left.

Maryushka doesn't know what to say to Irini. She leans against the window again. She closes her eyes to the sombre iron-working district, the flying streamers of smoke from the mills forming thick clouds above the city by day. At night the hundred feet high, towering colonnades of blast furnaces light the sky with flaring banners of flame. To the Nazi pilots, they must look like fires started by their own bombs. If the Kirov is destroyed, the war will be short-lived, and some like Irini bear no hope for Leningrad.

Maryushka will not be counted among the *frontoviki*, the disillusioned who complain of poor or inaccurate communiques from the Soviet Information Bureau, who apply for ration cards for dead relatives or imaginary people, who bribe house janitors to certify they live in empty apartments, not because she's afraid of the military tribunals – like Irini – but because she believes with all her heart in Zhukov's slogan: *Attack or die!* She doesn't believe the rumour that Stalin has now ordered his commanders: *Counterattack or be shot by a firing squad,* though Gerneral Rychagov of the Baltic District was sent back to Moscow and the scuttlebutt has it that he was shot, and everyone knows that the Lieutenant General of the Aviation Kopets committed suicide.

The streetcar stops at the gates to the Kirov, the workers tumble out, clutching their rifles, lunch buckets. They file through the security check, Maryushka showing her passbook to the guard, then punching in at the time clock.

Before they go their separate ways, Irini to the grenade factory, Maryushka to the tank assembly line, Maryushka touches Irini's arm. "Want to come for a late supper tonight? I've got a little pork to make *pelmeni,* if you can rustle up some sour cream." When Maryushka left the brick factory she didn't know how to cook anything, had never even tasted an egg, much less Siberian poached pastries shaped like a knot. Irini took her home and taught her how to make *okroshka,* that wonderful cold, summer soup.

Irini shrugs. "The curfew," she says. "I'd never make it home by ten."

Comrades jealous of Irini's position say she sleeps with Party bosses to get ahead, her latest lover is one of the Design boys from the Bureau, but young mothers are grateful to her for time off when their babies are sick or are given maternity leave. When Irini is flying and flaring she's higher than the smokestacks surrounding them, but since the war began she's been lower than the underground smelting pits.

"Well then," Maryushka says. "I'll see you tomorrow."

"Watch out for the full moon," Irini says, her large eyes dulled with a sadness Maryushka recognizes but hasn't felt herself since she married Mikhail. If only she could hear from him soon.

"Pay no mind to the propaganda," Maryushka says. "It's all a slag pile!" But Irini heads toward the grenade plant, back bent and head down as if she's carrying explosives, stepping carefully as if afraid of falling.

Maryushka makes her way, with hundreds of her comrades, through the steelwork compound. Long funereal coal sheds and slag piles surround the battery where iron is melted from ore. The furnaces rise from the sheds, inclined tracks delivering ore and fuel into the top of the hungry maws. The furnaces must be kept burning night and day, seven days a week; to let one go out would be a costly calamity, and production bosses' heads would roll.

She trudges on, passes the rolling mill that makes armour plate, wheels, axles and caterpillar treads. These massive rollers, these iron cauldrons look like giant frogs rearing on their haunches, growling, spitting and vomiting a blast of dazzling flame. Too many workers here suffer the black lung disease. The worker ahead of her turns into the mill, stops, hawking, and spits black catarrh. Maryushka places a gloved hand over her mouth and nose.

She's late, because of the leaflets and, afraid of suffering the indignity of a penalty, she takes a shortcut though the plants laid out in a square, which will save her ten minutes. She enters a long shed, a dusky cavern with open-hearth furnaces on either side. Through portholes she can see billows of seething steel. Just then the plug is removed and the dim vault of the building lights up with the fiery liquid steel streaming into the ladle, sparks showering like a million lights from hell. Filled, the ladle overflows, a bubbling white-hot cream that curls into black slag on the floor below it. She hurries past sweat-soaked workers mopping their fiery necks with bandanas. The furnaces roar, machinery screams.

At the end of the cavern, she yanks open the door, shortcutting through the blooming mill where a powerful roll squeezes heated ingots, flattening them into armour plate. Goggled men look like insects with huge red eyes. No one pays her any mind. And soon she's through the cooling mill that connects to the assembly plant where she works.

Quickly she checks her mail slot, holding her breath, but it's empty. For a moment, she sags with relief, then renewed hope lifts her and takes her into the women's locker room. She hangs her padded jacket on her peg, zips her overalls up to her neck, reties her babushka, knotting it on top of her head, so no hair can fall into her eyes, then puts on the heat-resistant helmet, the shield flipped up so she can see her way to the assembly line.

Here the moveable forts are being put together: lugs fitted into the right side of the front folding shield, which is then passed down the line so the next worker can mount the body of a periscope made of armoured glass; headlights installed on the front, a horn on the right side; then the red glass of the rear light mounted on the left side of the hull.

The Boss has removed his hard hat, and is mopping his fiery neck, bent over blueprints with the boys from Design. Good. He didn't see her arrive late, and maybe today he won't check the time sheet. Under the noise of welders and rivetters she catches snatches of their argument over gun cradles, the problem they must solve quickly or face the wrath of the Man of Steel.

— *He wants two gun turrets, not three, to make it lighter so it can go faster.*
— *The higher the speed the higher the rolling resistance.*
— *It can't be done. If we install an eighty-five millimetre gun we'll degrade the crew's work space.*
— *Get this, Comrade. He wants an anti-tank gun that can penetrate the German's Tiger's frontal armour from one thousand metres.*
— *Can't you make the hull bigger?*
— *The more powerful the gun the heavier the tank and loss of mobility.*
— *So we're back at the beginning.*

Maryushka has been assigned to the assembly line for turrets on the experimental tank begun in 1937. She relieves one of the workers on the night shift, only a few minutes late, and receives a black look from the tired comrade, who hands her the rivetting gun, then raises her shield. "I'm dead on my feet."

"The tram was stopped, we had to clear the tracks."

"It's always something, isn't it? Me. I'm done."

Maryushka doesn't even know the name of this worker, who is but one among the hundred Leningradski working in this plant alone. Irini is her only friend, the sole person Maryushka trusts, and this didn't come easily or lightly. The worker trudges off, likely to the public baths, then home to take her shift on the roof of her apartment, armed with her Mosin-Nagant rifle, watching for Panzers breaking through from the twelve mile approach to the city left unprotected when Novgorod fell to the Germans. Seven hundred years ago, at the mouth of the river, Alexander Yaroslavovich won the title of Alexander Nevsky when he led his knights from Novgorod against the Swedes led by Prince Birger whose plan was like Hitler's: to advance across the Neva, cross Lake Ladoga, then descend via the Volkhov River to attack Novgorod that was then the capital of Russia. On July 15, 1240, Nevsky routed the Swedes in Russia's most famous battle. If she could speak to Lena now, she'd say, Where is our new Nevsky?

Strange, how she holds the image of the tall Valkyrie-like figure of Pytor's love in her mind. She was jealous of the glow Lena brought to Pytor's face when she recovered from her stomach ailment, but now, facing her own mortality, she wants him to know a love like the one given to her by gentle Mikhail, its healing power. Most of all, she hopes Lena will replace her, Maryushka, and look after him, keep him out of trouble.

Maryushka lowers the protective shield and goes to work on a turret that rests on its armour plate through a bearing brace, the manual crank not yet fitted into it. She begins rivetting, the sound of the gun like that of a dentist's drill magnified ten times. It isn't a mindless job. All six sides of the turret's inclined walls must be rivetted before she can press the button to move the turret along in the line to the next worker who will install the backrest for the future commander; and she'll begin work on the next turret.

If she misses one rivet she, the daughter of a former, long-since-dead White Guard officer, will be accused of being a traitor to the war cause and sent back to the Gulag.

ALL MORNING SHE RIVETS, rivets, shifting her booted feet, until her arms ache from holding the heavy gun, the muscles on each side of her spine inflamed and sore, her kerchief soaked with sweat.

At noon, the assembly line mechanisms are shut down, and instead of the normal whistle, an announcement is made over the loudspeaker: all workers are to gather in the courtyard. No air-raid siren shrills. No one panics, everyone is used to official interruptions of their work. Mercifully, the Kirov hasn't been hit yet.

Maryushka leaves her shield and rivetting gun on its tripod stand, joins the line of workers filing outside; from the rolling mills and smelters and grenade and cartridge factories, her Leningradski comrades pour, like molten iron into the crucible of the square. There they mill, but come to attention when the Boss raises his loud-hailer:

"Our Great Leader has decreed that Leningrad shall keep four days' production of tanks – the KV 60-ton war dragons!"

Usually, they are shipped to Moscow. While the steel bodies, still unpainted, roll off the assembly line and out the opened double doors of the tank factory, the workers cheer Zhdanov their hero; everyone knows that Stalin would sacrifice Leningrad to save Moscow and expects their Party Leader Zhdanov to go down fighting street by street if the Germans break through their blockade. Maryushka is too tired to even care, much less cheer.

She's counting the hours until quitting time.

THAT EVENING, JUST AS MARYUSHKA is about to be relieved by the night shift, the factory whistle sounds the alert. All machinery stops. Air-raid sirens shrill. Maryushka quickly removes her helmet and shield and canvas gloves, then joins the workers rushing outside.

The night is foggy, filled with the sounds of cannon fire. German long-range artillery in Gosno must be shelling Vitesbsk freight station, Dalolin factory, Krasny Neftyanik plant, the Bolshevik factory, Hydroelectric Station No. 5. Smoke and long tongues of flame rise thousands of feet above the city. No rain clouds. Mushrooming black, greasy smoke casts a shadow over the land of workers.

"Badayev has been hit!" The voice is metallic, issued from a loud-hailer held by a Party boss. "Every worker is needed to put out the fire! Proceed to the front gates." The warehouses were built by a merchant named Rasherayev before World War I. Badayev's wooden buildings covering several acres in the southwest quarter of Leningrad store all the city's food!

Frightened workers rush through the gates. Those with trucks or cars hasten to the parking lots. Fire trucks and ambulances, their sirens screaming, head for Badayev, and Maryushka jumps on one of the running boards, not waiting for the streetcars.

The tower of smoke will make an easy marker for German planes when they return to bomb the city. Already the horizon is blood-red, criss-crossed by searchlights.

The streets, empty of pedestrians, are filled with a strange flickering red light, the smell of smoke.

Soon, the stench is so strong everyone ties their sweatbands or kerchiefs over their noses, and they move into billowing clouds that enter the mouth and sear the throat.

When she reaches the food warehouses, Maryushka leaps from the running board before the fire truck even careens to a halt.

Furious workers pass buckets of sand and water from hand to hand in a desperate and hopeless attempt to put out the fires.

She unties her kerchief, soaks it in a pail of water, then ties it over her nose and mouth again. Before a pyramid of sand dumped by city trucks, she grabs a pail and takes her place at the end of the line of firefighters.

"It's not right, it's just not right," the woman next to her yells. "Flour! Sugar! Meat! It should have been dispersed to the people!" It's her friend, Comrade Irina, in charge of the grenade section of the Kirov. Her face is sooty, hands blackened, already blistering and bleeding.

"It had to be hidden in secure buildings," Maryuskha says, scooping sand into another pail and handing it to Irina.

"You call THAT secure?" Windows blow out, glass shards reflecting red stars. Rafters collapse, crash to the ground.

By now, all of the city's firefighting apparatus has been brought to fight the Badayev fire, but it won't be enough to put out an inferno blazing over four acres.

Maryushka has shut down her emotions, all fear of and anger at the enemy numbed as if her heart is encased in a bucket of ice. Her arms ache, her palms sting with blisters. She should have gone back for her canvas gloves. Her kerchief steams and doesn't prevent the smell of burning meat, the acrid stench of carbonized sugar, the heavier smell of burning oil and flour. Bits of grain explode. Lard and butter sizzle, adding higher notes to the crescendo of crackling flames.

"You know how it happened, don't you?" Irini says.

"What are you talking about? Keep shovelling!" Maryushka throws another bucket of sand on the flames.

"It's the Nazi Rocketmen. They fire signals from rooftops to guide the bombers."

"Nonsense. Save your breath, your energy." The firemen are at their pumps, others ready with limp hoses.

Irini sets her pail down, hunches over, pressing on her knees, gasping for breath, a wild look in her red-rimmed eyes. "Former imperialists. Old intelligentsia. Kulaks!"

"Shut up and keep working!" The hoses writhe as water rushes through them, a firefighter quick to untangle one line too quickly let out, then arcs of water, like cascading fountains of light, and the workers cheer, but not Irini.

"Old White Guard officers. They offer bread and salt to the Germans." Irini bends, dips her bucket into the diminishing mound of sand, straightens and hurls it into the fire. Doesn't she know men like Maryushka's father were shot or sent to prison? How can any of them still be alive?

Maryushka refuses to let Irini communicate her fear to her. She doesn't listen to the workers when they feed on each other's terror at work. "False rumours," Maryushka says. "What the panic mongers see are just tracer bullets of AA guns firing from rooftops at German planes, and flares dropped by Nazi aircraft. No one is signalling to the enemy." Her shoulders ache, but she feels the rhythm now: bend, scoop, hurl, bend, scoop, straighten and toss, and again: bend.

"Are you calling me a liar?"

"Fight the fire. Not me." Sand blows back in her face, blinding her. She uses her scarf to wipe her stinging eyes, sweat from her brow, then reties it, squinting at Irini.

"Without food reserves, trains – we'll starve." Irini looks about to collapse in the ashes. She stares hard at the towering columns of fire, an empty bucket dangling from one hand. She drops it.

Maryushka says, "There's still the food barges and Lake Ladoga."

"The moon is falling," Irini says. What does she mean? The full moon is obscured by billowing clouds of smoke. Irini takes a few running steps, and dives headfirst into the flames – and disappears in thick smoke.

"Irini!" Maryushka yells, dashes forward, but is stopped by the wall of flames, the long scream from the other side of death.

Immediately, another worker takes Irini's place in the line. "Nothing you can do to save her. Keep shovelling!"

Maryushka picks up her pail, scoops sand into it, hurls it into the fire. Do it again. And again. Don't think about Irini, how she should have seen her despair sooner, might have saved her. Don't think about the possibility of Mikhail never coming home. Without Irini, she'll have no one. Pytor. Why hasn't he let her know where is is, that he's safe? Maybe he took the Swedish girl home. Wouldn't that be a mixed blessing.

She doesn't feel the ache in her arms and shoulders, in her back, the sting of broken blisters in her hands; she works mechanically, for the good of the great Soviet nation, though her hope of recovering even a morsel is faint. Tears for Irini streak down her sooty face.

Hours later, when the fires burn themselves out and the ashes cool, the workers sift and reclaim blackened, scorched sugar.

At least Irini won't starve as she feared. The loss of her only friend sinks in, deep as the scorched earth. Just as they were starting to know each other well, to dare to trust, Irini was taken from her. All Maryushka can cling to now is the hope that Mikhail will return.

She takes the tram home, Irini's seat next to her so empty. Exhausted, she drops her head, closes her eyes and imagines Mikhail at the stove, scooping chopped herbs into the steaming soup pot, the smell of good cabbage borscht a welcome and a lure. When she enters the apartment, he turns, and holds his arms open so she can rush into them.

She has nothing to look forward to after a quick supper of malt salvaged from closed breweries mixed with flour for bread as heavy as a cobblestone, watery soup with a little cabbage, a glass of tea, with a piece of candy made from sugar scorched black.

Every night, it's her duty to keep watch at the barricade in front of her apartment building, and during an air raid, put out rivers of fire on the roof with buckets of sand and water.

She can't remember when she last had a proper meal, a good night's sleep. The food she hoarded diminishes by the day.

By the time she reaches the workers' settlement the new day's light is weak, as grey as the ashes drifting and settling over the city.

WEARILY, AT HER CORNER, she steps down from the streetcar, looks up to find stone rubble and smoking support beams where once her apartment stood. Her training kicks in, all feeling forbidden, and she falls to her knees, her rifle at the ready, looking for German snipers in adjoining buildings. Seeing no one, she rises, slowly approaches the ferroconcrete barricade, skirts it, then picks her way down the *ulista,* avoiding huge craters, hunks of metal piping where bombs had smashed the water main and torrents of water gush like fountains at Peterhof palace.

She treads carefully, watching for German booby traps: whistling bombs, children's toys and fountain pens and cigarette lighters that explode when picked up.

A hand clutching a rag doll. She gags.

A leg still encased in a smoking brown boot, holes in the sole. She hunches over, losing the watery contents of her belly.

Straightening, she feels dizzy, and halts across what used to be a street from her apartment. From here she can only too clearly see rubble and blackened bricks and smouldering lumber in her courtyard. Lilacs bravely remain rooted in blackened soil, their autumn leaves scorched. Beneath them: an unexploded, delayed-action Erisman bomb, painted blue, speckled yellow like a giant egg, or no – like a huge dead bird, with spiky snout, a blunted end. Sappers in asbestos suits and goggles hunch around it with wire cutters and other tools in black boxes. Unable to move one step closer to the courtyard, she holds still as a statue in Catherine's park in the middle of what once was a gracious, elm-lined boulevard. Dare she look up at the only home she's ever known? She squares her shoulders, thrusts out her chin, then lifts her head.

The top floors are gone, the stairway still intact, but hanging like bones of a limb without a body. It's like looking at the open side of a dollhouse, everything left from this distance looks miniature. There, in the middle of the shell of the second storey, her living room/kitchen, the blue tiled stove, her extra pair of overalls still pegged to the clothesline above it; the table overturned and missing a leg; a huge crack in the wall, like a fault line in a mine, and she's certain the tiny and thin dark line is the nail on which hung her wedding photograph.

Shocked and stunned and still rooted, ankle-deep in rubble, she can only turn inward to memory, the only safe place left to her. Unable to see the images in the photograph, she sees it in her mind's eye, needing to remember how they looked together, not smiling for the factory cameraman, a glass of champagne in each hand, toasting each other. Because neither had family, the Party boss presented them with black bread sprinkled with salt, while the other workers cried, *"Gorko! Gorko!"* to sweeten the meal. She remembers his face, his wire-rim glasses slipping over his long nose, the look in his dark eyes as large and dreamy as a sleepwalker's. He had suffered the night blindness in the orphanage, and he insisted on wearing his glasses when they made love, so he could see her pleasured face, he said. She thought she'd never forget the way he brushed back his black hair so it curled over his ears, grew down to a V like the tail of a duck at the nape of his neck. Because his ears stuck out, the other orphans had called him Slonshenka, Little Elephant, and he pulled his *shapka* hat over them to flatten his ears to his head. Later, at work in the factory, after he was raised from grenade maker to welder he tied his elephant ears flat with a bandana that kept slipping when his forehead sweated, while he welded seams of tanks with a blowtorch.

Gone, the wall to the bedroom. Gone, the double bed where she once lay with Mikhail.

Even from down here, far from the skeleton stairwell, she can see through steel girders that once held floor and ceiling, clear to the smoking sky. One wall remains, and on it the toilet tank hangs crooked, its chain dangling, clanking against the sink.

Her tinned goods, the sacks of flour and cereal she hoarded, blown to bits.

She can't bear to look any longer, yet she's anchored in ashes of yesterday.

At her feet, a dented tin of tuna, which she grabs, and before another scrounger sees it, she shoves it into her overall pocket. Something coppery glints in the setting sunlight, and she lifts a twisted metal girder, and there: her samovar, its spout blown off, its belly dented from the fall onto concrete blocks, it's lid missing. She finds one red mitten and drops it into the samovar. A shoe. A pair of torn silk stockings tied together in a knot. Now she begins to dig with fervour, discarding anything too large to fit into the samovar, salvaging half a head of scorched cabbage, a blanket with holes, a singed fur hat, a bent spoon. Her back aches from bending, her blistered hands sore and chalky. A man's melton wool coat, with fox fur collar, what a find! Quickly, she puts it on, the sleeves too long, so she turns them back, making cuffs. The hem drags in the hot dust, and she realizes that her *valenki* boots are smoking, her toes and heels hot, the soles burning.

She backs up, and bumps into something soft and lumpy and large: an old woman she recognizes as Katia the seamstress from down the hall. She has collapsed in her rocking chair, one of the runners missing, so it tilts to one side; and when Maryushka touches her shoulder the woman falls over. Quickly, Maryushka bends, but withdraws her helping hands as if they've touched a hot stove. The shawled and eyeless head falls into the rubble, bounces off a cinderblock, rolls into the gutter.

And Maryushka turns to steel. She cannot utter a sound, her eyes blur, it must be the smoke, not tears.

She must flee, but where can she go?

Back to the factory. The Party looks after its workers.

Once again, she is homeless, but she isn't streetwise like her brother. Where is that *basmacki,* that anti-Soviet bandit, when she needs him?

She holds the samovar tight to her chest, and trudges back to the tram stop, treading on yellowing lilac leaves, the promise of an early winter.

Snow will soon cover this devastation.

She must believe that Leningradski will survive the war.

And then the indisputable knowledge washes over her and freezes her like an ice statue in Catherine's Park: Mikhail will never come home.

Signe

Mandrogi, June 2004

MANDROGI. THE NAME ALONE gives Signe shivers of recognition since Lena used to talk about the gypsies and their music that she loved there. Viewed from the dock, Mandrogi turns out to be a retreat from city life on the banks of the River Svir connecting Lake Ladoga to Lake Onega, though she doesn't see dachas anywhere. Signe follows the other tourists from the boat to a commercial tourist trap that consists of one new wooden building and a large tent where a picnic lunch is served, with local musicians serenading the tourists. There isn't much else to see, apart from a woodworking shop and a vodka museum – unless you're a birder. Or a romantic, younger than Signe and looking for a place to rendezvous: a mossy bed in muskeg country, up against a tree will do.

Kostja is eating at a table of birders. After a traditional Russian breakfast of porridge and blini, she's not hungry, and she leaves the tent, looking for adventure. Feeling far from old now, she wants a wild moonlight ride across the steppes in a troika right out of a Russian novel by Pasternak, the Chariot of Neptune pulled by three high-spirited grey Orlovs, the inside horse called The Furious, the outside The Flirt. Instead, she settles for a one-horse *drozhki,* a small, open cart, like the one her father used for hauling wood and going to town. This *drozhki* is painted blue, with apple-green motifs, leather seats. The *duga* is a wooden, yokelike arch extending from one shaft to another, so the horse's head looks like it's in a picture frame.

Without negotiating the fare, Signe climbs into the *drozhki,* driven by a young woman dressed in a red-embroidered, satin shirt, who immediately smacks the horse's rump with ribbons of leather; and they're off at a trot, the driver calling, "*Padi! Padi!*" to straggling birders, interrupting their sighting of a grebe flying straight towards Signe like a miniature Moose Jaw Snowbird out of formation in an air show.

Signe has no idea where the *drozhki* will take her, how long the ride, and she feels so transported into a new state of contentment – if not bliss – due to the lessening of her fears, she doesn't care if she misses the boat's departure.

She could be back home, on the homestead wrenched out of the bushland, picnicking on the shore of Turtle Lake, while Pytor goes out in his boat, looking for the Turtle Lake Monster – a hundred-pound jackfish he wants at least to see if not catch – and Lena spreads her skirts on a horse blanket, and begins again, her story:

In the forest of Lostja moor, once there was a herd of prehistoric horses that roamed freely. I was only a pony-girl, no older than you when I met a Russian poacher, Pytor Petrovich by name, and nothing was ever the same again.

This narrow path that takes her through alders and birches and pines could be the lane leading to her family's first log house near Livelong. Signe can see Lena in Canada carrying rocks in her apron for her flower garden, stopping to stoop and pick wild strawberries in the pasture, then chasing the cows home for milking. So often, Lena said: *Never will I forget Mandrogi, gypsy campfires, their music, such a romantic place it was, and so happy were we there.* Or no, perhaps it isn't so much her mother that Signe envisions as the first sighting of the old woman she wants to become – at peace.

When the cart turns away from the tourist area and passes a red dacha with latticework and a barn surrounded by a corral where horses gulp long draughts of water at a trough Signe swears she remembers a place she's never seen, and wonders if there's an equivalent in Russian to *déjà vue*. Here, she could retire, furnish the red dacha with her mother's red and black immigrant's trunk, a comfortable overstuffed, wartime chair, but find a bower of lindens for the Doukhobor bench and rough-hewn wooden chair she bought at an auction because they reminded her of Aunt Maryushka.

Her reverie is broken by the growl of a dog – and the word *borzoi* leaps into her head. Through the trees, she catches a glimpse of a wolf-hunter, its jaws clamped around the leather mitt of its trainer, and it's not a game they're playing. *It bites behind the ears and brings it down, the wolf.* And Signe is five again, warned often enough to leave well enough alone the borzoi squatting on its haunches at the kitchen door; Pytor's dog, more unpredictable than an Indian dog from the Thunderchild Reserve, waits for his master to finish his lunch and return to burning brush in the woods beyond the pasture. Kneeling, Signe says, *Stay and play with me.* The borzoi snarls, its eyes flash with a fear that she recognizes only now. The sudden snap of jaws, pain above her left eye and in her chin; she falls back, clutches her face, borzoi's claws clicking on the linoleum, the heavier thud of work boots, blood in her eye, she cannot see them, her mother and father. *Never to touch Papa's dog, I told you,* Lena says.

While Lena dabs at the wounds with cotton batting soaked in peroxide and applies gauze and tape, Papa holds Signe tight on his trembling knees, his crying the sound of sheep bleating when sheared. He doesn't want her face to be scarred like his – a long, jagged slash down his left cheek, the edges puckered like pinched pie crust – but this is no time for a story about a knife fight with a horse thief. Her cheek hurts too much, but she stops bawling.

The next morning, Papa's dog disappears – into the bush after a rabbit, Pytor says. The corners of his eyes and mouth turn down, that grim look a warning that nothing more may be said about his dog. She understands how he feels because she's half relieved that he's gone, but feels angry that he hurt her face. Not knowing what to do to make it better she refuses to eat her breakfast and when given permission by her mother to leave the table she tears down the slope to the barn where she chases the cats outside and over and under and around the woodpile until she's exhausted and the panting cats' tongues hang out of their pink mouths.

Only now does Signe realize that he must have shot it so it could never hurt his daughter again.

She was always afraid of dogs after that, and when she became a mother Signe never let her children have a canine pet, just cats – all named Pusskin by Tapani – and one gerbil that was eaten by Pusskin the Second.

Now, she fingers her forehead and then her jaw, the tooth-sized scars still there, like white but indelible tattoos. Papa was tattooed, a seagull on his shoulder, a wolf on his chest.

Signe stared at them while he shaved at the kitchen table, but she couldn't read the strange letters scrolled underneath the images, and was afraid to ask what they meant to him, much less why he had suffered ink injected under his skin. *They remind him of where he was born,* Aunt Maryushka said when Signe asked her.

On the so-called home stretch, the old horse plods along, and the Russian girl – who hasn't looked behind her once or tried to converse with Signe – smacks the swaying rump with a crop, the hide jumps and shivers, the horse picks up speed. "*Beregis! Beregis!*" And two waiters from the riverboat gangway, laughing. Again: the whip.

"I thought a Russian never hit a horse. You're supposed to talk to it." Just like Pytor, with apples and carrots secreted in his pockets, peppermints and toffee for Signe, and how, squealing, she climbed all over Papa, finding the treats in his shirt and overall pockets, even under his tractor cap. Candy was forbidden by Lena, who harped about sugar causing cavities, no money she had for dentists, and ninety miles to North Battleford was too far to go for toothache.

"Give it a carrot?" Signe says. The driver ignores Signe, maybe she doesn't understand English. The horse breaks into a trot not fast enough for the driver who applies the crop again, shouting something in Russian. Why the rush? So she can pick up another fare, or is the boat leaving without Signe?

No songbirds in the trees, the birders must still be infiltrating the woods, though in her inner eyes and ears Signe sees and hears a chickadee in the hollyhocks on the east side of her mother's house.

She has arrived at the end of a road that is not a road. They pass a new house and yard full of workhorses. The driver shouts, "*Hopp! Hopp!*" The horse takes a sharp right-hand turn: no sign of civilization, apart from the forks of another road that must lead back to the dock, the driver whipping again, and Signe cries out: "Ouch! That hurts." And amazingly, a clearing, and there is the museum and the birders heading for the boat; she has ridden in a circle.

The *drozhki* stops, the horse wheezes, tossing its head, and Signe gets out, pays the driver fifteen American dollars, much too much for such a short ride, only five minutes by her own watch.

She strolls towards the waiting boat, its five storeys looming high above the dock, its smokestacks seeming to reach for the sun. She feels as if she's returned home, the passage in two directions: one back to the Livelong past and the other forward to her paternal homeland.

Kostja waits for Signe on the dock, her first sighting of him since yesterday afternoon; he must have been birding again. His camera is slung around his neck, but he cradles it in his soft hands as if he's made a chair for a child. His unruly thatch of white hair looks like a robin's nest.

"You like horses," he says.

"It was just like riding in a cart from my childhood."

How can she tell him that this old gypsy camp quite possibly was the place of her conception? How does she know? A slip of the storyteller's tongue: *A fine place to make a baby, Mandrogi.* Lena.

Lena

Mandrogi, June 1941

THEY BEGIN WITH AIR KISSES while breakfasting on *kasha*, move to butterfly kisses over cabbage soup for lunch, then longer nipping and pecking after a particular supper of meat in aspic on the barge.

On this warm night, the barge is tied up against the bank of the river, hidden from a gypsy camp beneath overhanging foliage. On shore, caravans create a protective enclosure for half-naked children chasing scruffy dogs and scolding chickens. Mothers stir cauldrons over sparking fires, while swarthy men in tight pants and high boots play fiddles that break the hardest heart.

After their supper, Pytor is the first to bed down in the wheelhouse. Lena feeds and waters her ponies that are still in the hold since Pytor doesn't trust the gypsies not to steal them. She kisses Thor's nose and returns to her makeshift bed in the wheelhouse. Pytor is sound asleep in his hammock. She tiptoes to her hard bed before the cold stove, and curls into a light blanket. She tries to sleep on one side, then the other, flips over onto her back and stares at the swaying kerosene lamp. Finally, cold and homesick and unable to sleep, Lena crawls into the hammock beside Pytor. In his sleep, he folds her into his arms, one leg flung over her hips and just holds her, snoring into her ear. The barge undulates in its watery berth. The hammock swings. It's like being rocked to sleep in a cradle. The barge is tied up to a wharf at Mandrogi, and gypsy music from a nearby camp drifts through the open window, the violins weeping of betrayal and love lost. Her nose burrows into the hollow of his neck. His skin smells of woodsmoke from the stove, his breath of chocolate. The hammock sways, the gypsies sing, tambourines jangle, and Lena's heart drums in unison; she can barely breathe for the ache between her legs. They rock, she feels his staff rising, and she pulls him closer, arching her back. A small rocket explodes inside her, an involuntary mewling rises from her constricted throat, and she sees stars, yellow and blue the colour of the Swedish flag.

What has she done? She was asking for it, he could have taken advantage of her. Her mother told her never to sit on a boy's lap, she'd get a baby that way and be shamed before God and man. With the next swing of the hammock she tries to roll out, and is dumped on the floor, with a thump that wakens Pytor. He hangs over the edge, says in a sleepy voice, "What is happening?" then laughs like a loon.

Lena crawls back to her bed, rolls into her blankets, her back turned to him, to hide her shame. Silence. Only the lapping of waters against the hull, the sound of a gypsy dog yapping at a rabbit scurrying through the bush, or maybe even at the sleepy moon. Then Pytor laughs again, long guffaws. "Hush up!" she says.

But she does it again, this good Lutheran girl, creeps into his hammock, and stays night after night.

UNTIL SHE BEGINS TO WORRY about becoming an unwed mother, yet afraid to tell Pytor lest he abandon her; theirs is only a false paper marriage. Worse: she can never go home now, the shame would cause crack-brained Carolina to convulse with a Mother Fit from which she'd never recover. Her father and mother don't know exactly where she is, and cannot know that here the war is so far away the only signs of it are disturbing overflights of German bombers. German soldiers could advance this far any time, though there are no spoils of war, no armaments factories to be found nearby.

Most days, they just wander, a whole afternoon can vanish while fishing for the evening's supper cooked over an open fire. The ponies graze happily, never wandering very far from Lena, though Thor is moody now, and refuses wedges of apples Pytor cuts for him with his switchblade.

JUST NOW, FOR LENA AND PYTOR, summer has swept by too quickly. It's been an idyllic journey, traversing the River Svir joining lakes Ladoga to Onega. By not stopping nearby or ever going ashore, they avoid the larger villages she learns are called *derevnya,* with their ring of *izbas* that means log houses.

With Leningrad at least two days journey behind them by boat, many more on horseback by land, she's afraid to ask Pytor if he wants to go back to fetch his sister, his mood so black when they listen to the wireless.

With no one to talk to except Pytor, she's learning Russian fast; wanting to know the name of everything: *kasha, kholodets, derevo.* Everything she sees – the pine and poplar woods and fruit groves stretching away from the lakes and rivers, red dachas belonging to Party bosses, a mother bear and three cubs lumbering out of a stand of birch – is *tak korosho!* How wonderful!

How wonderful to lay a horse blanket in a grove of linden, feast on fried sturgeon, her own *hallonkråm* pudding laced with fresh wild raspberries, salted boiled eggs, pickled mushrooms, and *vetebröd* she bakes in Pytor's tin and nickel stove not as good as her mother's, but Pytor says it's *korosho,* and she licks the icing dribbling from his lips and chin.

Hidden in abandoned orchards or wooded dales, her Gotlandruss thrive on wild grass, apples and pears that Pytor picks by the bushel and stores in barrels of salt in the hold of the barge for winter. The foals are growing so fast they don't need to nurse any more. All the mares must be pregnant by Thor now since no kicking fights erupt among them.

The seagull's wing heals, it pecks at its bandages until one day they fall away, revealing new pin feathers. Pytor leaves the cage door open, daily the bird forays onto the deck, hops along the barge railing, exercising its bad wing – and finally flies away, with Lena shading her eyes against the brilliance of the sunlight until she can see it no more.

On hot summer nights, Pytor strings a canvas beneath four poplar trees, makes a bed of furs covered with a horse blanket, and they sleep naked under the stars, only their noses peeking out from the coverlet. Often, he builds a smudge to ward off mosquitoes.

SOON SHE MATCHES VERBS to nouns. *Stay at empty house on hillside. I no want to leave tomorrow. How long we get there?*

During long evenings, they listen to the news on the radio, which is always bad, yet containing a mixed message of hope for the Leningradski and fear of the war lasting so long she might never return home. Yet, how could she leave without Pytor?

Pytor reads *Eugene Onegin* to Lena, and once she stops trying to translate Pushkin's words into Swedish and allows her mind to dive and roll and swim into the language she begins to understand that Avoditia Istomina was a dark-eyed ballerina whose beauty and *soul-inspired flight* caused at least two duels

LENA

to be fought over her. *Istomina, thronged all around / by Naids, one foot on the ground / twirls the other slowly as she pleases / then suddenly she's off and there / she's up and flying through the air / the fluff before Aeolian breezes.*

They never camp in one place longer than two days, always on the move, finally charting a course north-northeast along the shores of Onega Lake to avoid Party bosses and NKVD patrols at Voznesenie where the River Svir joins Onega and the larger kremlin of Petrozavodsk on the northwest shore of the Lake. The German ring around Leningrad is at least a day's march away, yet overflights are a dazzling and grim reminder of Maryushka alone in the besieged city.

NOT FAR FROM THE ISLAND of Kizhi on Onega Lake, they find an abandoned dacha, half its roof gone, but there's a stove, a rough table and two chairs. While Pytor repairs the table legs, Lena sweeps and washes the floor so it will be clean for their bed of horse blankets.

Here, once again they let the ponies roam freely, but once out of the hold, Thor halts at the bottom of the portable gangplank, not so much standing guard while his mares and foals bound away to graze on the long grasses along the banks, as if to let Lena know something is troubling him, and he wants her attention. Yet, when she skip-hops happily down the plank, he swings away from her approach, lifts his tail and drops a load of horsebuns.

"Thor," she says. "What's the matter, boy?" She comes alongside of him, reaches out to push his forelock out of his eyes, but he sidles away from her. He stamps one foot impatiently.

"I know I haven't spent as much time with you lately," she says. "I'm sorry."

She takes a carrot from her apron pocket, but he curls his upper lip back in disdain. He snorts and swings his massive head up and down, the forelock bouncing with each nod. "I understand, really I do. How about a good brushing so you'll look handsome for me?" She takes the brush and curry comb from the pocket of Pytor's breeches she's wearing, and holds them out for him to sniff and smell his own scent. He lifts his forelegs and stomps them three times on the grass, then paws at a mossy stone, his lips vibrating while he blows. "All right, no brushing today." she says. "Maybe we could go for a ride." Thor loves to run, and he seems to know that no other *russ* can match him for speed and grace. He doesn't buck when she climbs onto his back and takes the mane in her hands, but he balks, refusing the command of her heels.

Lena purses her lips and makes kissing sounds that usually make Thor leap into a gallop. He drops his head, and kicks away the small boulder. "Let's go, Thor. No one can run like you." She strokes his neck. "I've missed you too, and I promise we'll explore the countryside every day, just you and I, no Pytor."

Thor stretches out his forelegs, pushing back, more like a stubborn mule than a thoroughbred forest horse.

"You big baby!" she says, smacking his rump, which causes him to jump, flinging her forward but not unseating her. She's never hit him in anger before, and she's instantly sorry. She dismounts, and begins by stroking his neck, cooing and telling him how strong he is, how faithful and true, and he's right to be disappointed and hurt that she has spent more hours with Pytor than with him. She never sleeps in the hold with him now. He shifts his feet, but lets her rub his twitching ears with one hand, while stroking his long nose with the other. Finally, he gives in and doesn't toss his head away when she kisses his nose.

LENA

Thor is munching the carrot when Pytor calls her to come and pick wild mushrooms he's found in a grove of poplar.

"Come, Thor," she says. "Let's go see what Pytor has for us." She starts off, and looks over her shoulder, only to see that Thor not only refuses to follow her, he is spitting out bits of carrot.

Males. What ever shall she do with them?

EVERY FEW DAYS, they listen to the news on the wireless.

On September 9, the Germans try to smash into Leningrad from the southwest through the suburbs of Krasnoye selo and Ligovo towards the Kirov factory, which is saved by the weakened Baltic Fleet. Bombs fall on the zoo, Betty the Elephant is killed, sables released into the streets, and that night Pytor howls like a dog in the Pavlov Institute, refusing all comfort from Lena. He must be worried sick about his sister. Or maybe he's despairing because he couldn't sell the horses, and now, if he sells even one he'll lose Lena, who would never forgive him.

Cross and grumpy all the next week, he complains that he prefers blini to her Swedish pancakes, the cream she whips has turned sour, he doesn't like it when she ties her braids on top of her head, it makes her look older than her years.

He sits alone in an apple grove for hours with the horses, brooding. Thor has all but stopped eating and keeps his distance from Pytor. She doesn't know what to do with either of them. She leaves Pytor alone to think on whatever is eating at his gut.

He never can last in one place long enough to settle down to a country rhythm Lena is used to and loves. This is the longest they've ever stayed in any village or abandoned farmstead.

Today, she's ready for him. She calls him into supper, the table set with candles and asters in a glass.

When he stomps in, and takes his seat by the Red Corner, she doesn't turn from the makeshift stove they brought with them. "Thinking, I am," she says. "War, it can't last, no?" She ladles cabbage borsht into his bowl.

"What happens tomorrow is no care for today," he says.

"Then why Gotlandruss?" Surely, he had big hopes, some kind of plan for the money he expected from their sale.

"Is no concern of yours."

"My horses they are!" she says in Swedish. She plunks the bowl before him, swipes stray hair from her flushed forehead, and stands with feet wide apart, her hands on her hips.

He dunks the end of a piece of rye bread hot from the oven into his soup, sucks it, then stuffs all of it into his mouth. He wolfs his food.

"Bad manners, you!" She clamps a hand over her mouth, instantly sorry. He's told her about the orphanage, one cup, one ladle for one hundred and forty *zornie,* never enough to eat.

"You don't like me, then go!" He sweeps the soup onto the floor, the bowl breaking into two pieces, jumps up, knocking his chair backwards.

Lena bends to pick up the pieces. She won't let him see he's made her cry. "You know I can't leave – it isn't safe."

He stomps to the door, then turns, and says, "I brought you here, and I'll take you back."

She straightens, thrusts out her chin. "You've never said you love me."

"I don't know what this is: love." He snorts.

"I'm sorry for you."

"What do you want from me?"

"I don't know. Together, I think. After the war. Where will we go? What do you want to do? Live in sewer again?"

He throws up his hands. "Start a horse farm!" he yells.

"Thinking I am about an aunt I have. In Canada. Maybe we go there when war is no more."

"Pack up, we leave in the morning."

And he's out the door, slamming it shut.

He didn't even tell her where they will go now. At least they should return to Leningrad to see if Maryushka has enough to eat, take her some food. Lena and Pytor, they are blessed with so much.

At the window, she watches him rounding up the ponies – they follow him now – and loading them back in the hold of the coal barge.

How long can this last?

She doesn't know where he will take her now.

The Island of Kizhi, October 1941

ON A CLEAR BRIGHT MORNING in the golden autumn, Lena and Pytor arrive at the wild and enchanted and unforgettable island of Kizhi on Lake Onega. Long before they dock in the small harbour, they see the massive silver church, its cupolas and spires reaching for the blue heavens. Abandoned by the Soviets, it stands alone on an apparently deserted island, a testament to Peter the Great's victory over the Swedes in the Northern War. Centuries ago, it must have been the centre of a thriving village.

Drawing closer to shore, Lena sees empty shells and scorched timbers where once *izbas* sheltered the families of farmers. Perhaps the land had been cleared of aspen to build the early dwellings, then too many summer storms – the deadly strike of lightning – had burned down the ancient log houses, leaving only the miracle of the untouched church.

They drop anchor. Pytor waves, drawing awestruck Lena's attention away from the spectacle of the sunlit Kizhi cathedral to a lone figure waiting for them on the shore. He looks like Moses, the classic Mujik, the Old Believer of Russian novels and folkore: long, white robes, a heavy cross around his neck, sandalled feet, wild tangled hair, a long beard. Arms lifted and spread wide as if he's Moses down from the Mount, he holds a shepherd's staff.

"Pytor Petrovich, g'dye tih, maya Pytor?" he cries, his voice ringing like a bell calling the faithful to his church.

"I'm here!" Pytor calls, lowering the gangplank, and rushing down it to receive the embrace of the – monk? – like the prodigal son returned.

Slowly, Lena follows, waiting to be acknowledged, while the two men kiss three times on both cheeks, slap each other's backs, their laughter rumbling like a gathering storm. The priest holds Pytor's face between his rough hands, turning his head this way and that, as if checking to see how well or sick he is, or maybe to determine that Pytor is real, not a vision.

"Who is this?" Black eyes fix on Lena, who is afraid of him. He might be mad, retreating from Soviet life, from the world, likely to fast and pray, which is against the law here.

Pytor presents Lena as if she's his wife or courtesan, actually taking her hand and bowing. "Lena," he says. "My wife, if you will be so good to bless us." Then he laughs, and it sounds like a wolfhound coughing up a ball of fur. "She's my Swedish pony-girl."

So that's why Pytor has brought her here. "What makes you think I want to marry the likes of you?" Pytor hasn't even asked her to marry him yet, and if he does she isn't sure she'll agree, though she feels bound to him tighter than the ropes stringing together her Gotlandrussen. "Pytor," she says. "I tell you. There is important. A something." No shotgun wedding for Gustaf Björnsson's daughter, but no returning home with a babe out of wedlock either. The shame would kill her mother. Lena doesn't want Pytor to think he has to marry her. "Talk," she says. "We must!"

"May I present Batyuska Viktor?" Pytor says.

The priest shakes his head, and his wild hair swirls over his displeased face. Why doesn't he like Lena? Because Pytor told him she's Swedish?

Pytor says, "Wait until you see what we have in the hold!" He races up the gangplank, unbars and opens the doors to the hold, while the priest shades his eyes against the glare of the sun.

Presently, Thor's head appears, he tosses it against the brilliant light, and when he sees Lena he trots smartly down the gangplank, his skitterish mares and their spindly-legged foals following, their unshod hoofs ringing, bone on metal. Thor halts, rubs his nose on Lena's hand, she finds an apple in her pocket, and he downs it in three quick bites, those large dark eyes softened as if he has forgiven Lena her neglect of him. Then he bounds away, the herd stretching their legs and loping along the shore, Frej and Freja stopping to lap up the water of Lake Onega. The mares begin to snatch at yellowing grass. After five months of wandering, the ponies are used to being taken into the hold of the coal barge, then set free in a strange place.

"Praise the Lord!" cries the wise man. "Come, come."

Pytor takes Lena's hand, and they follow the monk along a stony path scattered through scrub brush. A snake slithers in yellow grass. "Watch out," Pytor says. "Poisonous."

The silver cathedral looms before them, the light shading down to grey, the cupolas and spires casting shadows like long reaching fingers towards the Lake, and Lena suddenly realizes that it's made of weathered aspen, not silver. "Not a nail in it," Pytor says. "Built by Nestor, with only an axe. 'Such a thing there never has been before,' he said when he finished building the church."

"We going where?" Lena says, then returns to the comfort of her own language, "If you think that hermit is going to marry us right now, you're a *fubick!*" Lena learned the Scanian word from her mother, and doesn't know how to translate crazy fool into Russian.

Pytor stops, squinting against the fading sun. "*Davai?*" he says. "What is the matter now? You don't want to be my wife?"

Impossible man. "Are you asking me?"

"Is safer for you, maybe yes."

"That's not the right reason!" Exasperated, she shoves at his chest. "You, you Nik-nik! What makes you think I want to spend the rest of my life with a man who steals horses, who has no home, who can cook perfectly well but expects to be waited on like a czar, who –"

"I don't understand you. Speak Russian."

"Pytor, you don't have to marry me – for any reason."

"Noooo! I don't have to, you don't."

"Children. Do you want babies? You can't even support yourself – honestly."

"No, I can't." He may be a thief, but he isn't a liar.

"Pytor. Look. Me." He regards her, gravely. She smooths her chemise over her tight breeches. "Baby," she says.

The wise man has stopped, waiting, resting on his staff. "Glory be to God!" he says.

"When?" Pytor says.

"When did I get pregnant or when will it be born?" Lena says in Swedish. She counts on her fingers, July plus nine months, would make it March. "After the snow?" she says, not knowing the Russian word for spring. "It doesn't mean you have to marry me," she says in Swedish.

And then, he swoops her up, and staggering, carries her to the doors of the cathedral. "You weigh more than a ton now," he says, then grunts. The orthodox priest heaves the doors open, and once inside, Pytor sets down Lena, who loses her breath and cannot speak she's so filled with awe. Light filters through the arched windows, dust motes sparkle like the souls of stars falling to the earth. The floor has been freshly swept and washed, but no pews. Apparently, Russians stand before their Lord. An ornately carved box is suspended between arched beams, and she suspects that priests must have once preached to the peasants from there. A wall of icons, the story of Jesus carved in wood, a railing between it and the people who used to worship here.

The priest begins the mass, it's all in Russian, and she understands more than the words, silently praying for the forgiveness of her sins: for falling for a bandit, even if he is a good one, for crawling into his hammock before taking their vows, for shaming that good man, her father, for being impatient and unkind and resentful of her crack-brained mother. The litany of the mass, of her sins in thought and word and deed before God and man, seems to take forever. The priest kneels before the altar, rises and rings his bell, crosses himself, raises his arms, praying in Russian.

She kneels beside Pytor and he places a hand lightly on her neck.

The eyes of the icons watch them.

She hears the cooing of unseen doves nesting high above them, perhaps in a belfry or under the arching rafters. The light deepens, night beginning to fall, a promise of winter, the days of darkness. Her knees hurt, but she dare not rise until she feels forgiven.

A shadow falls, and she looks up at the priest, who holds a silver chalice, the blood of Jesus and the host together, to be taken with an ornately carved wooden spoon. In her home Lutheran church, the host is given to each person, and Lena's feeling of guilt is compounded when the priest serves Pytor but not her, likely because he assumes that she hasn't been baptized into the orthodox church.

Batyuska Viktor kisses his cross. He takes Lena's elbow, and she rises. He places her hand in Pytor's. "Yes," Pytor says, and the priest looks to Lena, so she says, "*Ai noid u lust u kyed u frust.*" Pytor and the priest cannot know it's an old Gotland saying: I promise to love you in lust and cold and frost.

With an impish smile, Pytor just happens to find two pewter wedding bands in his pocket. He had planned this marriage all along!

Then the Blessing, and they are man and wife.

No witnesses to the ceremony, only a priest left over from imperialist days.

No announcement to a congregation.

No organ playing the recessional hymn.

No bells ringing.

No feast.

Not even a proper bridal bed waiting for them.

The holy man disappears behind the wall of icons. "Wait," Pytor says.

And Batyuska Viktor returns, bearing yellow-brown paper

that looks like birchbark, edges ragged as if cut by rusted pinking shears, scorched. It's a certificate of marriage. With a fountain pen dipped into an inkwell, he prints Pytor's name in Cyrillic, then looks at Lena.

"Lena Ivanovna," she says, but signs her name: Lena Maria Björnsson. Sometimes, it's hard to know who she is: Gustaf's and Carolina's daughter, the Swedish pony-girl, or Pytor's deaf-mute woman. Soon she'll be somebody's mother.

Tonight, Pytor will send a telegram to her parents, advising them of their marriage. How can Lena explain to him how badly it hurts – right here in the middle of her chest and throat – that her mother wasn't at her only daughter's wedding? It feels like she swallowed a knife and it's cutting up her insides, trying to work its way out of her heart. The first news from Russia about Lena's whereabouts since they left Leningrad will likely explode in poor Carolina's head like a dozen grenades. Better Lena had died than be joined in an unholy matrimony with a man who lives in a communist land, never mind that at least for now she seems to be safe. Lena can just hear her mother wail. What ever has Carolina done to deserve this? It was no small rebellion on Lena's part, but it's not as if she ran away and eloped against her parents' wishes, though when they receive the news they might think that, and Lena won't be there to defend her actions or ask their forgiveness. She swallows hard, lifts her chin, and squares her shoulders. *Never shall I be sorry for what I have done this day.*

She takes her new husband's arm, and they leave the church that shines like silver in the falling light.

PYTOR HAS ONE MORE SURPRISE for Lena: an *izba,* a real house to call home until the war is over and she and Pytor can find a permanent place to live, maybe even in Gotland, for all she knows.

It may have been a manse, or log house belonging to a well-to-do kulak, as large as any merchant's home in Visby, but made from antiquity, hidden amid a grove of apple, pear and cherry trees she hadn't been able to see from the shore.

Latticework, intricately engraved with birds of the forest. An upper balcony supported by massive columns.

On the edge of the lake, close to the Kizhi Church, its stairs to the verandah have been repaired and washed down this very day. There, the priest leaves the bride and groom, swinging his staff and marching away to a barn with sagging roof.

Inside: a large room, with an enormous tiled stove, a sleeping platform with a straw-filled mattress and shabby blankets that will need washing. Kindling in a rusted bucket, aspen logs neatly piled before the oven. Pytor immediately begins to build a fire, for the chill of autumn is upon them.

The only other furniture in the room is an old loom beside the Red Corner, which holds an icon and a cross, like a small altar. Lena takes a step toward it, and Pytor warns, "For men, only."

"Sorry," she says, and immediately regrets saying it. Marrying Pytor doesn't make him the boss of her.

Once the kindling is crackling, Pytor builds a small pyramid of dry aspen, and with a whoosh, his fire leaps. He closes the iron door. Then, abruptly leaves the house. She watches him loping off to the boat, likely to fetch his pushcart, foodstuffs.

Though the house seems to welcome her, with its sturdy beams and sheltering walls, she hasn't been married long enough to feel as if she's the mistress of the house the way her mother charges about the Gotland farmhouse, bossing her husband about, which he seems to enjoy, beaming at her while he removes his manure-caked boots and leaves them on a special mat by the door, then scrubs his face and grimy hands in the washbasin before seating himself at his woman's table.

What will they have for their wedding supper? No smorgasbörd, for sure. Still, there's fresh salmon from yesterday's catch, dill and condensed milk to make a cream sauce. Too late to make *vetebröd*. No cupboard or even makeshift shelves, and wondering where the holy man stores his food, she decides to explore. To the right of the stove, five or six steps lead to a kind of attic or storage shed, a surprise since she expected a bedroom. The room is larger than the one she just left, maybe it was once a byre for a cow or two, to shelter them from fierce winter wind off the Onega. A boat and oars, large enough to hold a family, but wanting repairs. Halters and harnesses. Sickles and scythes. A forge. Anvils and hammers. An overturned cart, one wheel missing. No one has dusted or swept for decades. She sneezes. Pigeon poop everywhere.

To the left, double doors on rusted hinges. She pushes them open carefully, afraid one will collapse and fall on her, but it hangs precariously from the upper bracket and doesn't crash. A sloping ramp made of cobblestones almost hidden by weeds leads down to what once must have been the barnyard. At the bottom she looks back, and realizes she's just left a loft.

Here, a slant roof with rotting shingles covers a mound of dirt. A root cellar! The door is warped, but swings open easily, and she smells oil, the work of the hermit. It's dark inside, so she leaves the door open to let in light, expecting smell of mould, wet earth. Instead, the scent of spring potatoes. She makes her way to the back of the cellar, turns so the light from the door enables her to look around at the hermit's preparations for winter. Why would the hermit store so much? Where are all the people of his congregation? Is he awaiting their return, this mad man hidden away from the warring world?

Birchbark baskets full of asparagus, beets, cabbages, mushrooms of every size and colour, that she could pickle if she had jars. Wild strawberries and raspberries and black currants for jam. From the rafters hang hams and sturgeon, curing. Bushels of salted apples and pears. Finding an empty birchbark basket, she begins to gather food for her wedding supper.

Eggs stored in watery ashes, and she dips a finger into the mush, tastes it: lime and olive oil. But the most astonishing thing of all is a skin bag that she guesses is a calf's stomach containing cheese. She didn't see any cows. Or a garden. Maybe this island isn't as deserted as she first thought, maybe there's a collective farm or a village on the far side, hidden by aspen woods.

She hears Pytor calling her: "Lena, Lena, *g'dye tih, maya* Lena!"

She ducks out of the root cellar. "I'm coming!"

She finds Pytor unloading the pushcart: furs to cover their bed on the stove, copper pots and pans, the bricks from the potbellied *burzhuika* to make shelves, his bag of books, an icon of the Madonna and Child, two dufflebags stuffed with their market clothes, his and hers. A battered violin case wrapped in a mothy rabbit skin and tied with a red belt.

When he sees her carrying the basket of fresh fruit and vegetables, he allows a smile brimming over like cream leaking from a butter churn. "We stay here? You like it here?"

"Yes, I like very much." It will do just fine until the war is over and she can take her husband home to Gotland. She wants her mother with her when the child is born. Surely, an armistice will be declared soon. It's almost winter.

But now, she must feed them all, this new family.

LENA

THAT NIGHT, WHILE THEY FEAST on cabbage soup, fried sturgeon with almond and mushroom sauce, steamed asparagus and beets, and chocolate pudding made from the last of Pytor's Red October candy bars, they don't listen to the news on the wireless, not wanting to dampen their spirits, though Pytor says, "I wish Maryushka could have been here, even if she doesn't believe in God."

"My family," Lena says. When she receives the telegram, Carolina will weep because she wasn't at her only daughter's wedding, and Gustaf will grump, and say, *Just be glad she's safe,* then study the map of Russia in his atlas, trying to guess where in Russia his Lena might be hiding, where bombs might not be falling.

"I hope she's getting enough to eat, Maryushka," Lena says. "We have so much, I feel guilty."

From a clay jug, Pytor pours another cup of *samogon,* the peasant moonshine Father Viktor had brought them earlier. "I"m sorry," he says.

"For what?"

"When we go back to Leningrad I buy you a proper gold ring." He looks impish, one eyebrow raised, that half-smile on one side of his face.

"My grandfather was a wood carver," Lena says. "He moulded pewter into rings, gave my grandmother one shaped like a flower. My mother still has it. Our pewter rings are perfectly fitting." In Russian, she says, "I love ring."

"This, for you." From that endless pocket of surprises, Pytor takes a silver ring set with Baltic amber the colour of the setting sun. "Very good," he says. "Bugs in the stone." He removes the pewter band and slides the amber one on her ring finger, but it's too big, so she puts it on her middle finger.

Then Pytor frees the violin from its case, its frets set with mother-of-pearl. He begins to apply resin to the bow. "I only know one song," he says. "*Katyuska*. I play for you, then you learn too, yes?"

"When war is over," she says. "To Gotland we go, yes!"

Carefully, he sets aside the violin. "You incorrigible – woman!" He tackles her, knocking her onto her back. She won't let him kiss her.

"I mean it, Nik-nik. You want? First say we go to Sweden."

"I'll take you anywhere, but first give with the kiss."

ON OCTOBER 14, THE TEMPERATURE drops, it's too cold for Lena to take her morning sauna then swim in the lake, and just before noon: the first snow. Soon, when the lake freezes, barges and ships bearing grain and food will no longer be seen on Onega Lake, heading for Ladoga and Leningrad, the city of frost.

Pytor is worried about Maryushka, berates her memory because she refused to escape with him.

Lena fusses over the ponies, taking care to brush Thor and braid his mane and forelock. The mares are well along, heavy with foal. This November the spring-born foals won't have to be separated from the mares since there is no one to sell them to. Their hooves are growing long, and she has no tools to trim them, never mind that for centuries they roamed the moor without aid of any man.

News on the wireless is very bad: The line to Mga has been cut, severing all ties with Moscow so no food can be brought from there to the besieged city. The German troops have encircled Leningrad with their tiger tanks, and have cut off roads to the east too, starving out the Leningradski. Lena understands enough Russian now to gather the basic information: long food lines and empty grocery store shelves.

Lena and Pytor look at each other and say her name in the same breath: "Maryushka."

He smacks his palms together and says, "My sister is stupid foolish woman. Never could I tell her anything."

Maryushka

Leningrad, Winter 1942

THE GERMANS HAVE KNOCKED OUT the water system, sewage pipes are frozen, electricity has been cut, and now Maryushka, weakened from lack of food, pours the last of her water into a basin. She hasn't had a proper bath in weeks.

It's too cold to undress. She reaches under the man's coat she found in the rubble outside her first apartment – this bombed-out building her fifth residence in more weeks than she wants to remember. With numb fingers, she unbuttons her quilted jacket, unzips her coveralls, rolls up her undershirt. She dips a washcloth into the water, wishing she had a good bar of soft soap, wrings out the cloth then reaches under her clothing again to wash her armpits, lifting the folds of skin where once her breasts bloomed fully. She swipes the blue petals between her legs. Quickly, she rearranges her clothing and buttons up the man's coat.

Then she boils the wash water in a saucepan to purify it, huddled on the only chair she hasn't burned in the stove, listening to the wireless news of the fall of Kiev, and of the striking of the old *October Revolution,* fire in its forecastle, but how it continued to pound Ligovo from the sea canal until it was towed into Kronstadt for repairs.

She longs for *shashkik* in Kars style, Georgian soup, toasted almonds, Kievsky cutlets, pirogi pies.

When the water boils she rises, her knees stiff as an old woman's. She reaches up to the cupboard above the stove, lifts down a canister, and opens it: the flour was made from pine sawdust, and it reeks of malt and mould. Not enough to make more than two blini. Yesterday, the grocer had announced that only twenty days supply of flour is left for the entire city. Quickly, she pours a little water from the samovar into a cup, adds two spoons of *kasha,* stirs two bits of bread into it, then eases onto her chair again. She mustn't eat too quickly or the sudden fatigue will overtake her. With the rest of the water she makes a glass of weak tea sweetened with scorched sugar.

While eating – just a bit at a time – she scans the pages of *Leningradskaya Pravda: We will be cold – but we will survive; we will be hungry – but we will tighten our belts; it will be hard – but we will hold out; we will hold on – until we win.* The weather forecast warns of lower temperatures, but not cold enough to thicken the ice on Lake Ladoga and allow passage of food transport trucks. The second chain of encirclement around Leningrad tightens, an article reads, with the Germans close to Gostinopolye, the base for Ladoga supplies under artillery fire, the supply chief and his helper killed when the warehouse caught fire. Maryushka feels numb – inside and out – only wanting to be warm again. She saves the newspaper for tonight's brief fire – unless she can find wood, or burn the legs from her kitchen table.

Then, on the wireless, the voice Leningradski wait to hear every day. Pavlov, whom the people call The Food Dictator, announces that he has tons of potatoes and vegetables harvested before the fields froze outside the city. While he speaks, trucks are delivering the food to grocery stores in specified areas.

She must hasten to the nearest grocery before the lines are too long, before the food is all gone.

And water. All water pipes are frozen and her samovar is empty again. After she gets her rations, she'll draw water from the Neva. Better take a bucket along.

Then, still bundled in the man's coat and a newer black shawl she'd traded for a heel of bread, she leaves the apartment for the dark winter day.

SIX HOURS LATER, she's still huddled in line beneath a shop sign swinging in the cold wind, while snow whirls around her so strongly she can barely see the woman in front of her.

The scuttlebutt from Moscow is shocking today, and Maryushka doesn't know if she believes it, though it races like fire down the line, and Maryushka can't see the speakers for snow; it's a secret whispered by ghosts:

— *Did you hear what happened in the Kremlin?*
— *Thousands of bureaucrats!*
— *Tried to flee the capital toward the rear.*
— *Workers' detachments intercepted them.*
— *They pushed their automobiles into the canal.*

When it's her turn she hands the grocer her passbook, without looking up at him, so he won't see the fear in her face. She holds open her string bag, with hands so blotched and swollen they look frostbitten, and he deposits in it her monthly ration of one third of a loaf of bread, one pound of meat she's sure is horse, a pound of cereal, three-quarters of a pound of flower-seed oil, a little salt.

"But the news this morning —"

"I'm sorry about the vegetables," he says, gruffly. "The trucks broke down and they froze, or so say the bosses." Party bosses always snatch the best and the most for themselves.

Mustering her courage, she lies: "I have a child needing milk. Will you take these?" She unties her scarf and removes the red amber earrings Mikhail gave her as a wedding gift. The grocer pockets them, then gives her a packet of powdered milk.

"That's the last of it," he says.

She doesn't want to worry about next month's rations. Food supplies shipped by boat and barge across Lake Ladoga were stopped by ice on November 15, the worst fear of the *blokadniki* realized when the last shipments were sunk by Nazi planes. Until the ice is thick enough to bear the weight of trucks no food will reach the city.

For the first time, she understands her brother, how he lives from day to day, with no thought of tomorrow. She wishes she had but one of his forged ration cards. She'll forgive him anything and everything if only he would return to her.

"Closing time!" The grocer pulls the blind down on the window.

Maryushka wonders if the grocer held back food for his own family, and she wouldn't blame him if he did.

She hides the string bag of groceries inside her coat, for fear of someone snatching it from her. She picks up her bucket, and leaves the shop, but is pushed aside by a shawled woman frantic to get inside before the grocer locks the door. Maryushka falls, her right shoulder hitting the snow banked hard against a fence, but she doesn't let go of the bucket.

The woman bangs on the closed door. "Let me in! Let me in!"

Maryushka's shoulder feels as if it was hit with a sledge hammer. She's afraid to move, but pushes against the fence, the board loose, it cracks as if it was hit by a bullet. Quickly, she's hauled to her feet and shoved out of the way, while the rest of the *blokadniki* silently tear at the boards to take home for firewood. They're destroying Soviet property. She sways, clutching her coat, its concealed contents.

Carefully, she puts one foot forward, then the other, feeling her way, dimly aware of heavily bundled bodies skulking past her, hurrying home to light fires that won't last the night.

The wind has let up, and snow falls like miniature angel wings from a sky mercifully empty of bombers.

Slowly, she makes her way towards the Neva River to join other bundled women hauling buckets of water from steaming holes chopped in the ice.

Soon, her feet are numb in her felt boots, one mittened hand shoved deep in the pocket of her greatcoat, the pail dangling from her crooked elbow, her other hand cradling the bag of food under her coat as if it were a child in her womb, a small comfort.

She clenches her teeth against the pain in her shoulder. No use to go to a hospital. They don't put plaster casts on shoulders. She knows what to do when she gets home: tear a sheet and bind her arm tight to her body, make a sling for her arm. Because the telephone lines have been cut, she can't call in to work tomorrow and ask for sick leave. If she shows up at the Kirov, the Boss will send her to the infirmary. She'll need pain killers, if there are any that haven't been sent to the front.

The hunger pangs are gone now, replaced by a heavy feeling, as if she's carrying lead weights in her belly, her pockets, boots. She sees what's left of her body, as if from a great and high distance, this small, haggard woman picking her way towards the river, so old and frail, as if decades have been stolen from her, leaving her withered and spare long before her time. The pail hung on the elbow of her good arm bangs against her scrawny thigh.

Near at hand, children in the yard of a boarding school run by the State tear down the remains of a wooden house for firewood. For weeks, she has watched them working, pale-faced girls using bloodied fingers with torn nails, though older boys have brought axes to chop planks and boards into kindling and hammers to attack nails and brads; theirs is an angry, desperate act. A teacher whose face is hidden between folds of a tattered shawl hands out jars of what looks like soup – or maybe cereal – but most children pocket them, the day students likely wanting to take them home to their families at the end of the day. A sad reminder that she has no family, other than a woebegone brother who has gone missing, with no word from him in almost six months. No children for this Little Mary, her periods stopped three months ago, which frightened her until she learned from her comrade workers that they didn't miss the curse as much as they longed for a good bowl of borscht.

Enormous craters scar the streets of her passage. Streetcars wait for spring, for electricity to return, some blasted and lying on their sides, cables dead and dangling like antennae of giant ants. She treads with care, circuiting private telephone cables that hang like twisted skeleton bones, disconnected from their poles, the lines cut because Stalin doesn't trust the Leningradski, but once each day he allows loudspeakers on every lampstand to blare announcements and promises of victory from the Kremlin.

Snowbanks have become huge barriers, and she struggles between them; it's like making her way through a white tunnel without light to show its end. These streets haven't been cleared of snow, the workers too weak now to lift a shovel. Here and there, her galoshes break through the ice crust and she sinks to her knees, then crawls forward until the snow is frozen deep enough to withstand her weight again. All along, abandoned cars and trucks look forlorn and lost in this Stalin-forsaken city.

Dogs have disappeared from the streets. Cats.

She takes a shortcut through the park where Peter's sandbagged statue bears the inscription: TO DEFEND THE FLEET AND ITS BASE TO THE LAST OF LIFE AND STRENGTH IS THE HIGHEST DUTY. The planks at the base are missing and a sign left: *He's not cold and we will be warm.* Giant maple trees shudder and drop glistening loads of frost.

She folds her shawl around her face, breathing into it so the warmth floats back onto her frostbitten face. She peers out, stepping carefully, slowly. A sparrow, frozen on the wing, drops to the ground. Before Maryushka can reach it, a boy with a slingshot, grabs it up, hides it under his jacket, and scampers down an alley. Another boy armed with a stick chases a bold rat around an empty trashcan. He looks too much like Pytor, with bowed legs, the buckles on his rubber boots jangling. "Go home!" she calls. Foolish child. Does his mother know where he is, how he's scrounging for food? The loudspeakers have warned against children being kidnapped on the streets. Rumours abound that sausage is made of human flesh, but Maryushka believes they are spread by panicmongers, enemies of the State. It is true that women eat their lipstick and mix face powder into ersatz flour for bread. She's tried it herself, never mind the taste, it was edible.

She feels frost melting on her eyelids, and swipes water away with her only red mitten, causing her skin to burn.

Finally, an idling truck bearing corpses from the Hermitage spins its wheels, then lurches forward, and grumbles away, down the boulevard to its last destination. Maryushka continues on her way, used to the cold now, but the pain in her shoulders is intensified by their involuntary hunch against the rising wind.

She hopes Leningrad won't be hit by another storm, not today. The snow arrived early this year, the workers learned why the word consumption was prefaced by the word galloping when it tore through the Kirov, laying off too many grenade makers. Now, grippe lays low the youngest workers who receive the smallest rations. Everyone suffers puffy eyes, the first sign of dystrophy caused by bread made of chaff, plaster sweepings, and wallpaper paste.

She ploughs through the snow, climbs over drifts, plunging back onto the street, scaling mounds of corpses buried beneath, her breath frozen before it leaves her mouth, her throat burning. A milkman's wagon lies overturned on its side, its horse attacked by toothless babushki with butcher knives and grim-faced, wild-eyed young mothers, some of them workers she knows, slaughtering haunches with bread knives. The melting snow runs red.

Then she sees them, the red and yellow sleds of children. Everywhere: on the broad Nevsky boulevard, sleds move towards hospitals and cemeteries. Pulled by the black-faced living fulfilling their duty to the dead, some bear coffins of unpainted wood, others pails of water, many bundles of wood for cold stoves. Corpses swathed in rugs, sheets, towels, curtains. Smell of yellow snow. Stench of turpentine from a passing truck full of bodies bound for the cemetery.

Ahead, a woman of undeterminable age collapses beside a children's sled she was pulling towards the cemetery where a mountain of corpses covered with snow awaits burial in a common grave being dug by two men in shabby fur coats and hats. No longer shocked by such a sight – she's seen cremations in open squares, long trenched graves dynamited by sappers at a dozen other cemeteries, even outside the Kirov factory.

By the time Maryushka reaches the fallen woman and bends to see if she can help her to her feet, the woman stares at something only she can see, her eyes sightless to this grim, grey world. Maryushka unties the red shawl around the woman's head, rolls her over, wincing with pain, pulls the shawl free, then wraps it around her own shoulders. On the sled, a small corpse shrouded in a dirty sheet embroidered with the initials of the dead child. Maryushka is too weak to lift and add the mother's body to the frozen mound on the sleigh. She puts her bucket on top of the corpse, picks up the tump rope, shrugs the straps around her good shoulder, and pulls the sled forward, over hummocks of snow towards the cemetery. The pain in her unburdened shoulder is excruciating, but she pushes on, with a determination born in the Gulag and fostered in the brick factory.

At the entrance to the cemetery, a Party boss in an astrakhan coat and blue fox hat demands three days bread ration or three hundred rubles for a coffin and a grave. She won't waste her strength on anger. Ignoring him, Maryushka leaves the body of the unknown dead child, but keeps the sleigh, and pulls it back the way she came, heading for the Neva with her bucket.

She stumbles down the slippery, granite steps leading down to the river, her worn felt boots slipping on spilled water, the sleigh sliding easily and bouncing behind her, the bucket rattling. She steps around and over corpses of women who slipped and fell and never got up. They are held by the silence of the city.

The bucket brigade stretches on Gorokhovaya. Without an ice pick and with no strength left to dig a new hole in the ice, Maryushka waits her turn in a long line of silent and shabbily dressed women, huddling. Some of the women wear woollen masks, with peepholes cut out for their eyes. Just as the poet Olga Berggolts said on the radio this morning: *Tears of Leningradski are frozen.*

After what feels like three days instead of three hours, she reaches the hole dug in the ice, and fills her pail, the ache in her shoulder constant now, but if it was broken she wouldn't be able to move it at all. If it's just bruised it should heal in a week.

Then, she struggles back the way she came, homeward.

ON THE WAY HOME, she comes upon a downed picket fence before a small house without a roof. What a find! Looking about her, afraid a mob will descend upon her to steal the wood and she won't have the strength to fight them off, she stealthily piles on the sled as many pickets as it will hold, as she can pull, given her stiffening shoulder and the extra weight of the full bucket of water. Before she can set off, she leans against the sled, resting her aching back and shoulder, her legs trembling with fatigue. She breathes through the ends of the red shawl, the little heat it offers easing the pain in her throat.

It's dark and beastly cold when she reaches her gloomy flat on Bolshoi Prospekt on the Petrograd side of the Neva. She's lucky to have found it, the bombing having caused such a shortage of housing, but there's always a worker who can help if his palm is crossed with bread or a forged ration card,

She finds a message in her mailbox left by an Old Believer or Molokan: *Only God can save Leningrad. Pray to Him.* Maryushka crumbles it up to add to her kindling, the need for warmth her only care, apart from the searing pain of hunger, yet the old anger returns with the reminder of the loss of her mother's faith when praying yielded little heat in the state orphanage known as the Children's Brick Factory.

She opens the door, lifts the pail of water from the sled, favouring her bad shoulder, sets it inside, sloshing icy water, then drags the sled in after her. The cold entrance to the building smells of wet wool.

It takes two trips to lug the water pail and sled up one flight of stairs, and the second time she nearly collapses on the landing, resting there, gulping for breath, her throat and nose burning. Her shoulder feels as if someone is drilling hot rivets into it.

Rising, she's so dizzy the floor tilts, the walls fold into themselves, threatening to cave in and crash down on her weaving head. In the dark, she gropes along the wall, feeling for the doorjamb, the frame, knob, not sure if she's on the left or right side of the hallway. She feels a brass knob, like a frozen apple. Turns it. Shoves, the door yields, and she enters her rooms, no use to fumble for a light switch. She keeps a candle and matches on a ledge beside the door, but her patting and groping hand, numb with cold, cannot find them. Slowly she feels her way into the room, her breath coming easier now, but her knees buckle.

When her eyes adjust to the dark she sees a potbellied stove laced with ice suspended on bricks, its grille frosted. No samovar. She realizes she's in the wrong room. She thinks she hears the mewling of a cat, sees white breath, not her own. On a rug before the stove lies a woman holding a bundled baby, its fists punching the cold air.

Maryushka kneels beside the mother: frozen hands locked in the death grip around her child. Maryushka has never seen this woman before; she must be just another homeless worker, like Maryushka, wandering from apartment to apartment, bombed-out house to bombed-out house, looking for shelter, scraps of food, a blanket. The crack of breaking fingerbones, "I'm sorry," and she frees the bundle, holding it on her lap. Blue lips, eyes that seem to glow darkly, tears frozen on parchmentlike cheeks. "Hush, hush, Ladushka, what is your name?" She raises her knees, rocking the child from side to side. "Ladybug, Ladybug, where have you been?" The baby stops crying, the knuckle of her forefinger stuck in its mouth, gumming it, sucking. "What ever will I do with you?"

She takes the baby out of the flat to her own room, just across the hall.

WHEN SHE LAYS THE CHILD on her bed pulled close to the stove, it begins to scream bloody murder. "Yes, yes, I know," Maryushka says. "You're hungry. First I must make us a little fire." She crumples the message from her mailbox and the daily newspaper and shoves them into the belly of the stove, adding kindling. Her numb hands shake, the fingers aching with cold, and it takes three strikes before the match is lit and the paper catches fire. She breathes on the flames, and when the blaze is strong enough she adds her last few sticks of wood. Remembering the sleigh and the water, she hastens to the hallway to drag them inside, slopping ice water on the frosted floor, the needs of the baby giving her a new energy, or perhaps she's reaching into reserves she didn't know she had; after filling the samovar, almost screaming with pain, she drags her mattress even closer to the stove. She leaves a pile of pickets near the stove to dry out for tomorrow's fire.

When she feels it's warm enough to risk uncovering the child, she peels away two tattered blankets, a dirty nightdress, and removes a sopping flannelette towel. A girl. "You must have a name, Ladybug. What shall I call you, Lybachka, Little Love? For now, Lyba will do." She pours a little warm water into a bowl, wets a cloth and cleans the baby, who does not kick her matchstick legs or wave her snowchild arms. Her thin bottom is raw, and Maryushka dabs gently, but the baby shrieks. Quickly, she takes a near-empty box of baking powder from her cupboard, sprinkles its dregs on the rash, and the baby quiets, sucking her knuckle again. She uses a towel for a diaper, then wraps the baby in its blankets. Clean and warmed, Lyba dozes while Maryushka cooks her ration of cereal, separates it into two bowls, adds powdered milk, stirring until it's mush.

Lyba coughs. Her nose is running, her skin blue-grey but cool, no sign of fever.

At first, Lyba doesn't take to the spoon, wanting to suck it, and Maryushka wets her little finger and rubs it on the baby's lips. Lyba licks it off, then opens her mouth, and Maryushka spoons a little onto her tongue. "That's a good girl, a little more, eat nicely for Aunt Maryushka." Lyba regards her with dark eyes, as large and slanted as a Tatar's. She coughs up yellow phlegm. Maryushka wipes the baby's chin and running nose.

Then Maryushka rocks the baby to sleep, singing Pytor's Ladybug song, wondering where he is and if he's getting enough to eat.

At the back of her cupboard she finds just enough dry mustard in a forgotten tin to mix with water for a very small plaster and spreads it between the folds of a flannel cloth, then finds half a teaspoon of oil to smear on Lyba's thin chest, tucks the plaster between her blue skin and nightdress. "There," she says. "That will loosen the phlegm." She decides to waken Lyba in four hours and feed her the rest of the milk.

Beside the fire, she removes her coat and underclothes, wincing when she pulls her bad arm out of its sleeve. There, on her arm, just where it curves into her shoulder, a bruise the size of an apple, the colour of one rotting. With a knife, she scrapes ice from the pickets into a cloth, folds it, then tears the end of a sheet to make a bandage to hold the icepack to her arm. Using her teeth to pull one end taut, she manages to tie a knot in the ends. She nearly screams putting on her clothes again. Soon, the pain is numbed by snow turning to icy water.

In the morning, she'll lug the dead body down the stairs and leave it at the gate of the courtyard for the death trucks to pick up, see what she can salvage from the empty apartment across the hall, some books or sticks of furniture to feed the hungry stove. The dead woman's ration card; she'll need it to buy cereal and milk for Lyba.

She will take the baby to work with her. No one will ask if the child is hers, or how she'd hidden her pregnancy, not even if Lyba is a foundling. Even honest workers raid empty apartments, looking for a heel of bread, a crust of mouldy cheese. They steal gas masks from the shoulders of bodies found under stairs, coats and boots from the dead in freezing rooms, in rockers before cold stoves. They will understand who Lyba is, baby bottles will be found, towels to make diapers.

Maybe tomorrow the news from the fronts will be good, or the ice on Lake Ladoga will be thick enough for army trucks to transport evacuees, and bring food to Leningrad.

Lying beside the child she already thinks of as her own, she covers them both with blankets, curving her good arm around the baby. "We're going to be fine, you and I," she says. "It was supposed to be better for you than for the likes of me – and it will, I promise. Once this bloody war ends."

Now she has Lyba to care for, someone else besides her miserable self to worry about, just like the time of the Gulag where Pytor was born, and during the long dark winters in the Factory For Making Angels.

"*Bayushki bayu,*" she croons.

Signe

BECAUSE ONLY MARYUSHKA HAD MEMORIES of the women's prison where Pytor was born, she was the only one who could tell Signe that part of the Svetlov story and only after they had left Russia.

She must have felt a great need to impart them to Signe since it was a great effort on her part to explain Signe's gruff father, why he rarely spoke to Signe, and when he did it usually was an order: "Get dressed, Lazy! Fill the woodbox for your mother."

While picking wild strawberries in the Livelong pasture, Maryushka told Signe that she was the best thing that ever happened to Pytor, that when he called her Lybachka or Lybatsa it meant My Little Love, that when she was born he had asked Lena not to give her a Russian name because he was fed up with everything Soviet. Yet, her middle name, Elizavita, was in memory of his mother.

Signe plunked down on the grassy bank of the Turtle River among willows and hucked berries into the murky water. None of Maryushka's stories helped her understand her father, though Maryushka said she didn't want Signe to turn against Pytor and run off to the city without saying goodbye.

The way Maryushka told it, Pytor's daughter baffled him, and he had left it to Lena to raise her. Signe wanted a father who helped her with her homework, who would tell her she was beautiful in her confirmation dress, who would explain why the cute boy who sat behind her at Patchgrove School hit her over the head with his lunch pail – instead of chastising Signe for teasing the boy.

According to Aunt Maryushka, Pytor just didn't know what to say to Signe. He hid behind his newspaper. He went to town without her, wouldn't let her ride the Indian ponies in the circuit fairs, and never allowed her to attend the dances at the Turtle Lake pavilion. Maryushka said she understood his fear, but Signe only saw him as mean and unreasonable.

Signe was headstrong and tough – too much like Pytor, everyone said. Maryushka said maybe he saw himself in his daughter – and whenever Maryushka tried to tell Signe stories from the old country to help her understand Pytor, Signe would say she didn't care what happened in Russia, it was now that was important, so dump it in the slop pail and get on with it. She discovered the love of learning from her bookish mother, and planned – not secretly – to head for the city and university, and never look back. But Maryushka was afraid that one day her brother would die, without Signe knowing how much he loved her.

So Maryushka had started, very early on, frightening Signe with stories, with an unspoken theme: This is what happened to Pytor to make him the man he is today, nothing can change that, and all you can do is love him.

She did this for Pytor, but mostly for Signe who was, she said, the daughter she never had herself and made up for her disappointment at not having a child of her own.

SIGNE

Seating herself beside Signe on the riverbank, spreading her skirts, and helping herself to strawberries in Signe's pail, she told Signe that the siege of Leningrad wasn't the whole story, and whenever the years before the war crept up on Maryushka like thieves in the night, she said she felt like she was drifting away like smoke from their fires burning in ashcans in Leningrad. She also told Signe that there was too much she just couldn't tell anyone, not even Signe, her Dushenka. Who in peaceful Canada would believe her? Who would understand what it was like never to have a full belly – not ever in your life – just because you were born in a prison camp, the child of enemies of the State?

"Imagine having no memory of a home, not even knowing your own father."

"That's easy," Signe said. "Mamma tells me I'm a Björnsson, Papa says I'm a Svetlov. I don't want to be Russian if it means taking after him!"

Maryushka told Signe that every Russian – forever – had a given name, a patronymic name, and a family name. But Pytor only ever knew that his mother's name was Elizavita and that his father was an officer in the White Army who fought under Admiral Kolchak – because Elizavita told Maryushka and she told Pytor – and that his father had been awarded St. George's Cross by the czar himself.

After the Civil War of 1918, Pytor's father was among the new criminals, a class enemy who had opposed the Revolution.

Signe said: "I don't care about your dumb revolution! We live in Canada! Not Russia. Just forget it!"

"This is your story too, Dushkenka, my smart girl. Be still, and listen, and upsidedown cake we make when we go back to your mamma's kitchen."

"Not if you eat all the strawberries."

"Now I forget where I was in Story. Let me think."

"The Revolution that happened before you were born." Signe forgot to pretend she wasn't interested in the family history.

So Aunt Maryushka told Signe that after an attempt on his life, Lenin's policy of Red Terror began, with the *Prikaz* (decree): *Give them a taste of the workers' lot!* The Svetlov family home and lands had been confiscated, and Signe's grandfather and grandmother were sentenced to eight years in prison, first in the basement of Smolny Institute when the regular prisons were bursting with enemies of the People, then to an enforced exile in the first Kontslager, a concentration camp that became known as SLON, a northern Camp of Special Significance, its ironic name taken from *slon,* which means elephant.

"Makes no sense to me," Signe said. "Elephants in Russia."

"Tell that to Stalin. He sent all White Army officers to Solovetsky, the first camp of the Gulag. In the spring of 1924, prisoners arrived daily at the west docks. I was there, with my mother."

Maryushka

Solovetsky, April 1924

BEYOND THEM, the far expanse of the White Sea. To the north: Sekirka, and the hilltop church with its punishment cells in the basement. The original fifteenth century monastery now the prison house.

MARYUSHKA

Here, Maryushka and her mother are separated from Maryushka's father. Five years old and held in her pregnant mother's arms, she waves from the prison ship, while her father marches with other men to the monastery, then is seen no more and never again.

Then Maryushka and her mother are transported in an old Swedish cargo ship to the women's punishment camps at Anza Island in the north. On board, everything frightens her: holes in the floor for toilets; grillwork and steel netting for walls; a small stove that smokes; nothing but frozen bread, salted fish and one cup of rank water thrown down by guards who often take women into a separate cage and force them down, humping on top of them, while the other women bang tin cups together, pray and shout as if they're deranged. Maryushka cries and clings to her mother.

Against the cold wind from the sea, amid the scream of the seagulls, Maryushka and her mother are marched from the dock at Anza to the camp. The line halts under a sign: THROUGH LABOUR, FREEDOM!

Three barracks for the women and children, the guards housed in an old church. The camp commander, Chekist Vanka Potapov, welcomes the arrivals by bragging that he has killed four hundred people with his own hands. "You whores are so lucky," he says. "In Solovetsky, prisoners are left naked in bell towers, their hands and feet tied behind their backs. They are marched two kilometres to the baths, unclothed in freezing weather, and when the guards shout, 'Dolphin,' they are forced to jump off the bridge. And you think you're hard done by because you will have to cut down a few trees."

His words make the women cry out for their husbands, the children bawl for their fathers, and he strikes full on the face one woman before him who falls on her knees and begs for mercy.

Maryushka's mother picks her up and holds her tight. She whispers, "Stay away from that man."

On the way to the barracks, they are shown the only brick building in the camp, with its own gates and armed sentry posts: *Shtrafnye Izolyhaheri* or SHIZO, the punishment isolator for those who refuse to work for the Soviet State, who commit a camp crime, who might try to escape, or practise their religion. The *monashki* are women who pray and sing hymns and are stripped and beaten for that crime.

Then to the baths, where Maryushka watches her mother and the others forced to take off their clothes under the full gaze of leering male guards, then given camp uniforms: long underwear, a black tunic, quilted pants, an outer padded jacket, a felt hat with earflaps, rubber boots, mittens, short padded coats, stockings that ride to the knees and birchbark shoes.

No clothes for the children, who squat on the cold floor, sucking thumbs, mewling. Maryushka waits for her mother to catch her up and take her somewhere safe where the porridge is hot, the milk fresh. Instead, she must watch doctors poking at other mothers' milk-swollen breasts, peer down their throats. A guard grips her mother's neck, bending her over, so a doctor can stick fat, gloved fingers up her bum. Too afraid to scream, Maryushka stuffs her mouth with the collar of her coat.

When the camp barbers begin to shave the mothers' heads, the children bawl, and when the dirty floor is buried in hair of every colour under the Russian sun it's their turn, and mothers hold them down, promise them treats they can't produce, threaten them with a good smack on the behind if they don't stop screaming.

MARYUSHKA

Maryushka is too frightened even to squeak, and her small hands shake in the grip of her mother's, while a gap-toothed barber shaves off her own hair as short and bristly as the winter hide of a horse. "Don't cry, Dushenka, my little dove. See, my head doesn't hurt. It just looks bad." When she turns her head abruptly to look at the yowling boy in the next chair, the razor nicks her head behind her ear, and the barber she cannot see behind her, gives her a dirty rag to press against it to stop the bleeding, while he shaves the other side of her head. Clumps of dirty red hair fall onto her shoulders, into her lap, onto the floor. Her mother steals a lock and conceals it between her bosoms.

Then they're taken to the barracks. After the dark city prison, at first the cell seems luxurious to Maryushka. The window is open, no bars. Along the walls, beds made of broad wooden planks actually have sheets as well as blankets, far better than *sploshnye narif,* the bunks of the city prison.

Quickly, Maryushka and her mother learn their new names. They are *zeks:* prisoners of the Gulag.

The *starosta* is a half-blind, prison elder suffering from scurvy, who keeps the cell clean, marches the inmates to the toilets, hands out food, and resolves fights among the women. She gives Maryushka and her mother a wooden bowl of spoiled cabbage and potato borsht, slimy with fat, and herring heads not fit for pig slops. Then, Maryushka is put to sleep on a mattress made of wood shavings and rags that stinks of mildew. Her mother sits beside her, trying and failing to shoo flies away from Maryushka's face, singing "Ladushki, Ladushki where have you been?"

The last thing she sees before she fades away into dreamland is a kerosene lamp smoking above her head.

Bedbugs falling from the ceiling.

SHE'S AWAKENED BY THE SHRILLING of many children, and discovers the cause: mothers have gone to work.

She is herded, with the other children in her cell, to the children's day camp.

In every wooden crib, babies scream, while one old woman gobbles porridge from an iron pot in the middle of the table. Maryushka creeps about the room, peering at the other children, some of them listless and leaning against the cold wall. One girl clutches a carved wooden doll. All the children have sores on their lips, blue skin, shadows under their eyes. The screams of babies soon turns into the cooing of sick pigeons.

A boy pees blood in a bucket, his buttocks black and red and yellow with bruises. Maryushka plunks down in a corner, wraps her thin arms around her bony legs, trying to keep warm. She watches the old woman. When she has had her fill, she scoops slop into a wooden bowl, and shuffles towards the naked boy, shoves him down, then squats before him, pushing a spoon to his tightly closed lips, opening a sore that leaks blood. He swings his head away from the nurse, refusing to eat. She straddles him, holds his nose, and when he opens his mouth for air she forces the mush into it. He gags and the porridge spurts onto her dirty dress. She hauls off and whacks him on the head. Still, he refuses the food, weakly turning his face towards the wall. His hands scrabble in the dirt floor, his toes twitch.

"I'll eat it!" Maryushka says. "Leave him alone."

The nurse ducks her head as if Maryushka had struck it, and she looks around, her mouth open in a haggish grin, revealing rotting teeth. "Come here, *Garnoedy*," she says,

MARYUSHKA

"Shit-eater!" Maryushka obeys. "If you want food, you'll do what I tell you, *Pomoechniki,* Slop-swiller! Hold his head."

"Why doesn't he want to eat?"

"Do as you are told, *Zek!*"

While Maryuskha holds the boy's head, the nurse forces a tube down this throat, then pours the gruel into it. "Why I do this, I don't know. He's a *dokhodyagi.*" A reacher, a goner.

When she heaves her body off the boy's and scuttles away to the next child, he lies there, sweating from the exertion, and Maryushka helps him climb into his bunk, where he curls on his side and sticks his finger down his throat, instantly puking up bile and blood with the mush.

Maryushka rubs his back, and doesn't know what to say, then just lies down beside him and tries to keep him warm. She chants: *"Ladushki, Ladushki, gde byli u babushki,"* listening to older children greedily gobbling down their meagre breakfast.

Then mothers burst into the cell, Maryushka's not among them since she's not yet nursing a baby.

Every four hours, *mamki,* the mothers with babies, are given a fifteen minute break from their labour to feed their infants, who had cried themselves back to sleep and have to be wakened, then listlessly seem to suck, while their mothers coo and some sing, and all fret that there's never enough time, their milk is drying up, Lord help them. They wear white masks over their mouths.

Then the guards pull the mothers away from babies who howl hungrily again, no end to their pain and anger.

No use trying to play with the other children. Even the older ones cannot speak yet, and utter a few unconnected words, or howl, mimic each other, blows their only way of communicating their fear and anger. Most just lie all day on their cots.

In her corner, Maryushka pulls loose threads from rags for mending, a task she learned in the city prison.

She waits for her mother to return from work.

THAT FIRST NIGHT, Maryushka's mother, wearing a wreath of grass and birchbark to protect her bald head from mosquitoes, brings her a pocketful of wild mushrooms and berries, and a heel of bread she says was left from her lunch, though Maryushka knows it means her mother didn't have enough to eat. She doesn't like *khvoya,* the pine needle brew, but gulps it down to please her mother. Having never known good food or a full stomach, she has little interest in what is given her; eating just something that has to be done, as quickly as possible, never mind the taste.

That night, she falls asleep, listening to the strange chanting of the boy's mother: "*Kyrie eleison, Christe eleison.*" She seems to be sewing.

THE NEXT MORNING, the woman has a strange, faraway look in her eyes, as if she's gone blind to this world. Her son is shrouded in old towels she'd sewn together.

The guards arrive and carry the bundle outside. Maryushka runs to the window and watches them open the door to a shed and throw the corpse inside. Maryushka dashes back to the middle of the day room. There, Dezhurnaya, the old woman who cleans the barracks says she told them about the religious singing. A few minutes later, the boy's mother doesn't protest when the guards return, strip her, drag her out to the centre hall, with the rest of the mothers and their children following them, Maryushka clinging to her own mother's rough hand.

MARYUSHKA

Before the morning assembly of women workers, the camp commander, Vanka Potapov, calls the boy's mother a *monashki,* then beats her himself before the guards haul her to the dreaded *Shtrafnye Izolyhateri* or SHIZO, the punishment isolator.

A short while later, after the mothers are marched to the forest to cut wood, Maryushka watches from the open window, while guards lug many corpses from the shed and pile them on carts. One smaller body might be the boy's, and she hopes that wherever he is now – maybe in her mother's heaven – he's getting good food – and likes it so much he eats it all up. She has no idea what good food is, just that it's not the slop she's given.

NKVD officers smash each head with a pickaxe or stab emaciated bodies with a *szompol,* a wire with a sharpened point.

Maryushka presses her small fists against the dirty pane, scrubbing circles. Someday she will leave this bad place, find her family home and uncover her father's sword – maybe in an attic or turret or basement coal bin – and then, even if it takes forever, she will hunt down these men with no respect for the dead and kill them in their sleep. The point of entry for her avenging sword will be that soft spot on the side of the head, between the corner of the eye and the ear, where the guards' hair is shorn. She will shove the sword deep into the brain so it passes behind the eyes and comes out on the other side.

Maryushka wants to but dares not leave the prison to look in the forest for her mother to make sure she's safe, not hurt by men with *szompols.* So many trees to fell, logs for the mill, only their bark to burn in the prisoners' stove, roots and pine needles to boil for brew to ward off scurvy. Don't think about fleshless bones and the death carts, rags from corpses for mending thread.

She does vow to remember forever the boy and his last act of defiance, his refusal to eat his only way to exercise free will.

Now, there are only bones to read, and wings in the winter light, carrying souls of the dead.

TODAY, THE CAMP HAS BEEN HIT by the worst *purgai* of the season, and the wind howls a death chant around the barracks. Snow blocks the doors, and without enough wood allowed indoors to keep the stove going all day and all night, icicles hang from the rafters, water freezes in the buckets.

Before she sets off for work in the dark of morning, Elizavita tells Maryushka that the storm is only Grandfather Frost's wild hair, and not to worry so much.

She looks like a snow woman, with a great, round belly, twigs for legs and arms.

All that day, Maryushka watches for the women returning to the barracks, for the lights of their lanterns. The sun won't appear until spring.

That evening, Elizavita doesn't return from work, and one of the few kind camp nurses tells Maryushka that Elizavita has been taken to the maternity hospital so she won't worry about her mother. She helps Maryushka sneak into the ward, and hides her behind the potbellied stove. Then she leaves the ward, promising to be back soon. Maryushka can stay where she is if she's quiet and doesn't disturb the new mothers.

Here, new mothers wearing white caps and masks nurse their newborn. Four nurses, with skin as grey as Caucasian bees, buzz around a woman in a corner who thrashes and hollers for her husband, she wants to see him before she dies, while one nurse slaps her face and tells her to put her mind to the work she has to do now. This only makes the woman madder – and frightens Maryushka.

When the nurses leave the cell for supper, Maryushka finds her mother in a corner, bent over, clutching her belly, and scurrying in a circle like a dog Maryushka vaguely remembers tamping down blankets in a basket before it went to sleep. "It makes it go faster," she says. Then she straightens and says it won't be long before Maryushka has a new brother or sister, she was in labour all day, and her water has broken. "Here we go!" she says, and lies down on an iron cot spread with *Solovetskie Ostrova,* the Gulag newspaper she uses to teach Maryushka how to read. She grabs the edges of the mattress and grips them until her fists turn white. It must hurt worse than a beating.

"Nurse! Nurse!" Maryushka yells.

"They'll be back when they're good and ready," Elizavita says. Her face turns purple, her bony chin digs into her thin chest, and she grunts as if she has to go to the bathroom badly and has nothing to pass, but poop as thin and watery as gruel slides from her. Her knees are raised, separated, and blood trickles onto the newspapers. She inhales deeply, then takes short, shallow breaths. Maryushka shivers, so cold in the hospital cell, the logs chinked with frost, and someone has stuck a pillow in the window to keep out the wind. But Elizavita sweats as if it's the hottest day of summer. Her lips are cracked and chafed. "Water," she says. "Wet a cloth."

"You're doing well, just keep taking deep breaths between, pant when you're bearing down." The speaker is a woman in the next cot, who seems to be too weak to get up and help.

"I've done this before," Elizavita says. "But I was younger and stronger then." Maryushka wrings out a rag in melting snow she found in a basin and swabs her mother's wind-beaten face. Her neck is as wrinkled as a plucked chicken's in the cookhouse for guards. Elizavita bears down again, longer and harder, till a blue vein pulsing in her neck looks as if it will burst. No time for her to rest between contractions now, and Maryushka fears her mother will stop breathing, until she says: "Catch it!" A blue head with matted mossy fuzz emerges – and seems to be stuck. Elizavita pushes again, and a wizened thing slides onto the bloody newspapers. It has two small mushrooms and a rootstem like a withered parsnip between its legs.

"It's a freak!" Maryushka says, though she has known the difference between boys and girls since she was three.

With a great heave, Elizavita manages to sit up, grasp the baby by its ankles and hang it upside down, smacking it twice on its thin buttocks. "A boy, your father will be so proud."

The boy parts its blue lips, takes his first breath, and yowls like a cat whose tail has just been stepped on.

"Now, we have to cut the cord," Elizavita says. "Whatever will we use?" The nurses keep all knives and scissors locked away from zeks.

"Your teeth, idiot," says the woman who made such a fuss earlier. She seems to suffer no pain now.

"Psst!" The nursing mother in the next bed has somehow concealed a pair of scissors in her bedclothes, and she reaches over and hands them to Maryushka. "Be sure and give them back."

Elizavita cuts the cord, then ties the short end into a knot. The other end dangles out of her vagina. "I've a bit more work to do," she says, lying back on the cot. She tells Maryushka to wash the boy and wrap it in a tattered towel she will find on shelf beneath a wooden table next to her bed.

Maryushka wrings out another rag, tries to warm it between her hands, then gingerly begins to clean the baby, whose skin is turning bright pink, especially his wrinkled face, he's so mad about something, maybe about being slapped, about being cold, or maybe he doesn't like the light from the kerosene lamp shining in his blurry eyes. "I'm your sister," she says. "And from now on you have to do what I say. Be good and stop your stupid crying."

When the baby is clean and dry, but still yowling, she wraps it in a towel that has been boiled but has old birthing stains on it. Her mother grunts again, and afraid another baby is coming out, Maryushka watches her mother pass the cord and a huge, flat piece of rubbery flesh that stinks like a slop pail. "Wrap it in the newspaper," Elizavita says, "and bury it outside in the snow. We don't want it in our soup tomorrow morning." The other women laugh, though it sounds more like crying to Maryushka. "Now give me my baby, he must be hungry."

Maryushka lays the bundle in her mother's arm, wraps the bloody afterbirth in the newspapers, then hastens outside where, buffeted by Grandfather Frost's fierce breath, she digs a hole in a snowbank, stuffs the package into it, then brushes snow on top of it, hoping no hung-over guard or greasy-faced cook will notice the small mound in the morning. Her hands burn with cold.

When she returns, blowing on her fists, she finds her mother struggling to feed the baby. "Help me," she says. "When he opens his mouth push his head towards the nipple." She tickles his cheek with one finger, and he twists his mouth, the lips parting enough for Elizavita to drip a liquid that looks like mucus into his mouth, then ease her pointy nipple into it, while flattening her breast with her other hand so his nose is clear and he can breathe. This time he latches on, and begins to suck, little greedy guts.

"His name is Pytor Petrovich after your father," Elizavita says. She has strung a small silver cross around his neck, tied with a blue velvet ribbon, and now she carefully tucks the blanket-towel around his neck to hide it. Maryushka didn't know her mother had a cross, can't imagine where she had hidden it, and now is terrified the children's nurse or a guard at the baths will discover it and send her mother to the Judas Hole in the isolator. As if reading her mind, Elizavita says, "He will need it for protection. I'll be so careful no one will ever find out my boy is a Christian."

That night, Elizavita tells Maryushka a story about the olden days, one she must promise to remember and tell Pytor when he's old enough to understand it. "Not so very long ago," Elizavita says, "when a child was born, a cross was placed around his neck, which the person wore until the day he crossed over into God's heaven. But there is another custom, one which began very long ago, so long ago it was the time of Yaroslav the Wise. When a boy turned seven, three locks of his hair were cut and put in an amulet that he wore to the end of his days. He was taken to the courtyard on which his mother had laid a carpet. His father and and godfather bowed to the boy, and then his father lifted him onto a very fine horse, and led him back to the threshold of the house. There he was given many gifts, and cake was crumbled over his head."

"What a waste of good food!" Maryushka says.

"Oh, it was for good luck," Elizavita says.

"I don't believe in luck." Wishing her father would escape from whatever prison he's been thrown in and come for Maryushka and her mother doesn't ever bring him to her. It isn't luck that gives her a pair of multicoloured mittens, it's her own ability to steal bits of wool from corpses before the

MARYUSHKA

guards throw them in the shed, and then separate the threads, tie them together and wind them into a ball for her mother, who uses sharpened twigs for knitting needles.

"When your brother turns seven, if I'm not there, I want you to cut three locks of his hair, bind it and put it around his neck so he will grow into a strong man like your father." Before frightened Maryushka can protest that her mother must never die, Elizavita grips her wrist so hard it hurts. "Promise me!"

FOR THE NEXT TWO YEARS, Maryushka looks after her brother every waking moment, giving him a rag soaked in her own mug of milk to suck on while their mother works in the greenhouse, changing his ragged towel diapers, bouncing him on her hip to shush him, singing the song her mother had sung to her in the city prison:

Ladushki, ladushki, gde byei	*Ladybug, ladybug, where have you been?*
U babushki	*By Babushki.*
Chto eli kashku?	*What have you eaten, porridge?*
Chto pili brazhku?	*What did you drink, homemade beer?*
Chastooshka!	*Just old mush for babies!*

AND THEN, ONE MORNING, before Elizavita leaves for the greenhouse, the half-blind *starosta* elder orders the women to take all children two years old and older to the assembly in the courtyard, where they are to await further orders.

"What does it mean?" Maryushka asks her mother.

"I don't know, Lyubatsa, My Little Love."

Hoisting Pytor onto her hip, she takes Maryushka's hand with her free one, and they follow the other mothers outside.

There, two NKVD officers and enough policemen to fell a forest await the women and their children. Silently, grimly, the women form their lines, shushing fussing toddlers on their hips.

The rooks have returned, swooping down to their nests in the bare branches of poplar struggling to greet the spring. The earth is muddy but warming beneath her bare feet, and Maryushka squishes her toes, then sneezes, which makes her mother squeeze her hand. She licks snot from her nose.

The Bigshot, Vanka Potapov, is making a speech about the Leader. A shiver passes through the crowd of women, and Maryushka can feel her mother's legs trembling so much she's afraid Elizavita will fall down. Something bad is about to happen, and Maryushka lifts her head, and listens.

"Under his Five Year Plan, our great Leader decrees that children of Soviet enemies must be taken away from their mothers at age two in order to free women for work and increase production in the Gulag."

The woman in front of Maryushka falls to her knees, praying.

"They will be taken to the Children's Brick Factory where they will learn a trade and become good Soviet citizens who will make you proud. "

"Not the orphanage!" From somewhere far behind Maryushka.

"It's the Factory for Making Angels!" A woman in the front line.

"Over my dead body!" Another mother crouches, holding tight her child, and rolling into a ball, the bones of her spine in sharp relief down the back of her gingham dress. The girl's bare and bony legs stick out like the mother has sprouted new limbs from her sides. Is she trying to smother her child? Death better than losing her baby?

A whistle blows, shrill as the screams from the women. The NKVD police descend upon them, with billy clubs as if a riot has broken out, the din of protests scaring the rooks who flutter up from the trees in a whoosh of black rain, shaking the branches as if by a sudden wind.

Maryuhska cannot breathe, her face pressed into her mother's belly, the feel of her thin arm tight around her head giving little comfort. Pytor is screaming. The rough bark of male voices, the thud of clubs, children crying, mother's calling their children's names. Suddenly, Elizavita pries Maryushka's hands from her thighs, shoves her behind her, all of her shaking like the thin trees, but she stands tall, her shoulder blades almost touching under her dress; she's so emaciated Maryushka could count the jutting bones of her spine. Elizavita's voice is low, erupting from her empty belly like a growl. "You'll have to kill me before I let you take my children."

Maryushka can't see the face of the large man who strikes down her mother, the blow to her head knocking her sideways, but she doesn't let go of Pytor. She lies there, in the mud, blood from her ear pooling, trickling into her footprint. Maryushka falls upon her mother, trying to protect her from further blows with her own small body, but rough hands pull her up by the shoulders. She kicks, legs working as if she's running in the air. She can't see the policeman carrying her to the black van. She flails her arms, trying to smack the heavy body behind her, swings her head so violently to one side it hurts her neck, trying to bite one of the leather hands gripping her shoulders.

On either side, other uniformed men carry away screaming

children, one carries two boys the same age as Pytor by the neck like squirming puppies.

Behind, the sky is filled with the wind of weeping mothers. She calls her mother's name.

Where is Pytor? The last time she saw him he was lying beneath her mother.

Through the opened gates, the back doors of the waiting black van gape like the opened jaws of a hungry and angry animal disturbed while devouring its prey. She's thrown inside, and lands on the mud-spattered metal floor. The benches on either side are filled with cowering children, none of them Pytor. Already, the van reeks with urine and shit.

The doors bang shut, a bar clangs into place, someone hits the door, a signal to move out.

And the truth slams home: she will never see her mother again.

The vans take the children to a transport ship that will take them from Anza Island to Leningrad.

ON BOARD THE TRANSPORT SHIP, most of the children are seasick and can't hold down the meagre rations of bread and milk, pickled herring. Maryushka searches for Pytor and finds him squatting in a corner of the hold, bashing a stone against the sweating wall. He isn't seasick, and she feeds him her rations, sings him to sleep, vowing never to let him out of her sight again.

When they reach the mainland they're met by more black vans, and this time Maryushka carries her brother with her. Twice each day, the vans stop and the children relieve themselves in hard ruts of the road, squat in ditches to eat their rations while NKVD with guns guard them from bandits, though why anyone would want to steal such a raggle-tagged bunch of *zornies* is beyond Maryushka.

When they arrive at Leningrad's Brick Factory for Children they are sullen and exhausted from lack of sound sleep, awakened by every backfire of a truck, new sounds of motorcars passing them. Maryushka promises Pytor a warm bath, porridge with brown sugar, maybe some raisins in rice pudding, a clean bed with sheets and blankets, a down-filled pillow. Surely, the Leader doesn't expect a two-year-old to make bricks.

Now, she has no idea where they are in Leningrad, since there were no windows in the black van that brought them here. The Children's Brick Factory has its own guardhouse, gates, barbed wire and huts with peeling paint, no lamps.

With the others from her van, Maryushka, carrying Pytor on her hip, is herded into a receiving room. Here a woman in a brown uniform, with hair sprouting on her upper lip, tells them, in a loud voice, that they are children of Enemies of the State. "You will forget your parents!" she shouts.

Another woman at a scarred table munches a green apple, the first Maryushka has ever seen. On the table: a pile of ragged papers, a small black tin that maybe holds boot polish for the guards.

Names are called through a loud-hailer held by the hairy woman, and each child steps forward; lines form, dark-eyed children with sties on their eyelids and thick curly hair are separated from the bald children from the Gulag. These are gypsy children, arrested for the crime of nomadism, whatever that means. In another shorter, straggling line are children of White Army officers and dispossessed *pomeshiki* and kulaks who died in the Gulag – Maryushka and Pytor among them – and the crimes of their fathers and mothers announced.

"...stole leftover grain" to feed their families, no doubt. "...stole five apples, a crime against State property." When Maryushka's and Pytor's names are called, the crime of their father is the worst of all: treason! Maryushka holds her head high, her chin thrust out, while Pytor sucks a knuckle, his head on her shoulder.

While the children scratch itchy legs with one bare foot, or hide their faces behind dirty hands with shame, or bite the insides of sunken cheeks so they won't cry, the tinny voice rattles on about their new life before them. "If you break bars on the windows, climb over the walls and try to escape, you will be caught and severely beaten." Unlike the Gulag, those who attempt escape will not be shot, or so they are told, but Maryushka doesn't believe it. They want the children to run away so they can get rid of them once and for all.

Then names are called again, and one by one the children are to report to the apple woman. It takes a long time to register children with no home, no parents, and the children squat on the floor, some fall asleep. When Maryushka's name is finally called, she hoists Pytor onto her hip again, and minces forward to the table, carefully.

"Hold out your right hand, palm down." Maryushka is afraid she will be strapped or her fingers broken with a club. The loud-hailer woman grabs her hand, twists her fingers and presses the tips, one by one, starting with her thumb, onto the black pad in the tin, then touches them onto a paper, leaving her fingerprints like a signature on the paper. "Other hand!" Maryushka has to shift Pytor onto her other hip to free her left hand.

Fingerprinting Pytor isn't so easy. When the bossy woman reaches to take his hand, he swats her on the nose. "Let me do it," Maryushka says. "He'll be good for me." She holds him on her hip, head forward, shushing him and telling him it doesn't hurt. "Look at the mark your finger makes. Isn't it nice?" Pytor smacks the paper and smudges it, and the irritated apple woman gives him a green look, crumples the paper, and gives Maryushka another. This time, Pytor slaps the paper with both hands. He's yanked out of her arms by the loud-hailer woman, who holds him upside down by his feet. The apple woman stand up, twists his left arm around his back, then roughly fingerprints his right hand. Pytor screams, his face turning red, then he holds his breath, and it turns blue. Maryushka rubs his bald head. "Don't cry. Be good and it'll be over faster, and then maybe we'll get something good to eat."

When it's done and her brother is thrust back into her arms, they are given red star caps. No bath. No clean clothes. She returns to her place in line, rocking Pytor, bouncing him, but he won't stop yowling. He rubs snot from his nose onto her shoulder.

Finally, they are led out of the large receiving room to the compound, down a gravel path that hurts her bare feet, though the skin around her heels and the bottoms of her toes are calloused and toughened from walking rocky paths on the island of Anza.

The gypsy children are split from the group and led into the first hut, the children of kulaks along with Maryushka and Pytor into the second.

The doors are shut, locked, and the new arrivals huddle together in shock, not knowing what to do now.

THE HUT IS OVERCROWDED, filthy, ariot with one hundred and forty wild *zornie*. A few children sleep on the dirty floor, without sheets blankets or pillowcases. Older boys play cards with torn-up pictures of Stalin.

"This is worse than Anza," Maryushka says.

"You will not criticize!" The speaker is the loud-hailer woman. Where did she come from? She yanks Maryushka forward, shoves her to the centre of the room. "You will be an example to those new here." She points at a stool. "Stand on it!"

Maryushka sits her brother on the floor. "Don't move." She steps up, finds her balance, then looks for her brother to make sure he hasn't crawled away.

Pytor squats on the filthy floor in a wet diaper and whines in a guttural prelanguage of his own for his sister to feed him, pick him up and play *Ladushki,* bouncing him on her lap. "I'm here," she calls to him, and Pytor looks up, toddles forward, halts, then sits before the stool.

"You will look at our Leader!"

She faces a portrait of Stalin on the opposite wall. She feels as if the teacher with wavy hair is trying to hypnotize her. "I feel dizzy," she says. "I'm hungry." She receives a smack on her bare legs.

"Repeat after me. I will forget my mother."

"I will *never* forget my mother."

Her buttocks are struck with the ruler. She flinches but doesn't cry out, the teacher hits her again, and she feels a welt rises on her skinny thigh. She almost falls from the stool, but finds her balance again, determined not to give in, the teacher can beat her black and blue, but she'll never forget Elizavita. She repeats her name in her head – *Elizavita, Elizavita, Elizavita* – until it becomes a silent chant, a promise.

"Repeat after me. I will forget my father." Whack, and another bruise. Maryushka bites her lip so hard it spurts blood.

"I have forgotten my father." This alone is true. "Father," she whispers, calling someone who can never rescue her.

Finally, she is allowed to step down from the chair, and she plunks down beside her brother.

"Father?" he says. Pytor doesn't know this word: *father*. He understands almost everything Maryushka says — "Eat for Mama, Sleep for sister, Don't cry" — but he can barely talk, a fist in a cheek, or a punch in the belly far more effective for a boy who has, at age two, learned never to trust anyone, other than Maryushka who gives him food, comfort in the dark when invisible dust eats away his baby fat.

In a far corner, naked toddlers squat on the dirt floor, shivering and picking at their toes, waiting their turn for the bath in a tin tub, while two nurses pour cold water over a screaming girl-child. Pytor is so thin he looks like he's reading his bones: purple blotches around his knee. They must be itchy. He scratches, and Maryushka stops his hand. "You'll only make it hurt more," she says. He plays with the skin, loose and wrinkly. Dry. A boil oozes yellow gunk. He pokes it until it bursts, redly.

A long-armed boy climbs the barred window like a monkey, bangs on the glass with a tin cup, while other boys hurl at him bad names Maryushka knows better than anything else: *Garnoedy, Pomoechniki, Dokhodyagi.* The monkey has stolen the only cup, and if he doesn't give it back, the gang of older boys will turn him into a *fitili*, a wick they will blow out.

Pytor squeezes the stone he always holds in his hand, until it drips blood.

"Stop!" Maryushka says. She holds his hand in both of hers.

The monkey throws down the cup, boys and a few girls set upon it like maggots on carrion, and a fight breaks out, until a guard scoops up the cup, and the pack slinks away to their corners to plot anew their escape.

The monkey clambers down, hooking blue toes around the wire, then scampers over to Maryushka and Pytor. He beat his scrawny chest. "I am the son of a kulak!" he says.

"Kulak," Pytor says, and pats his own bony chest.

"You don't know what the word means," Maryushka says. "You are a Svetlov, like me, like our mamma and papa."

"Svetlov," he says.

"Yessss," hisses the son of a kulak. "He's one of us!"

"He is not!" Maryushka says.

It doesn't matter what the teacher asks Pytor after that – "Who was your father? Are you satisfied he was an enemy of the People? What is the name of our Great Leader?" – Pytor always and only answers, "Svetlov."

But Maryushka soon knows what the teachers want to hear: "I have forgotten my father. He was an enemy of the People."

"And your mother, a traitor to the State!"

"I will forget my mother, an enemy of the People."

Now, Maryushka feeds Pytor salty cabbage soup from the ladle since it's his turn. He wants to know why she said that, about Mama, but Maryushka doesn't answer.

Later, when he lays his confused and sleepy head on her thin chest, she bends over him, and whispers in his ear: "God will remember their names."

Maryushka holds Pytor tight and sings him to sleep, *"Da, gotovyas v boi spasny pomni mat svayu* – When preparing for the dangerous fight – *spi, mlydayenets, moi prekrasny* – please remember your mother. *Bayushki bayu."*

MARYUSHKA

MARYUSHKA SWIFTLY LEARNS obedience to Bloody Sunday, the drill for marching on hammer-and-sickle flag days. She learns obedience to the Soviet Law of, the root of, the number to the nth degree. But Pytor's only obedience to numbers is measured by cups of milk that can be taken away when he says, "Svetlov," or crumbs of stale bread that may be added by stealing them from a weaker child under the rule of stick or the stone he always holds in his fist.

Pytor is a sleepwalker, one of the upright dead, with the face of someone gone from himself.

At first, Maryushka wakens when cold air replaces the small body keeping her warm like a little pot-bellied stove, thinks her brother creeps about the other children looking for a bit of bread or a piece of turnip to steal. In the tattered chemise that serves as a nightgown, with its unravelling hem trailing in the dirt, he looks like a ghost weaving through the uneven rows, passing a hand over a head without touching, bending to peer into a face with blue lips, or one shadowed under the eyes. He seems to question each child, and when she wraps her worker's coat tightly around herself to ward off the cold and tiptoes after him, she hears him say, "Elizavita?" Not Mamma. And she understands: he looks for the woman whose name he must never forget, no longer trusting the remembering completely to the God of that mother.

Abruptly, he wafts away, like grey smoke, only halted by the door of the hut, where a guard dozes on a metal chair. He raises his arms and presses them against the wall, but she stops him before he bangs his head, and taking him by the hand, leads him back to their sleeping.

"*Sleep, good boy, my beautiful, bayushki bayu,*" she sings softly, "*quietly the moon is looking into your cradle.*" Just as in the Cossack lullaby, *The time will come, then he will learn the pugnacious life.* "*Bayushki bayu.*" Until then, Sleep well. "*Bayushki bayu.*"

BY AGE SEVEN, he can talk, though rarely speaks.

He grabs at the cup, and learns how to fight back, not to let anyone hit or stab him. By now, his hair has grown long and shaggy to his shoulders, thick and stiff with dirt, like the coat of a wintering wolf.

In the middle of the night before his Name Day, while he sleeps, Maryushka takes the switchblade he hides in his boot, and cuts three strands of hair from the back, hoping he won't notice his hair is thinner – he hardly ever combs it anyway. By the light of the moon, she braids the tresses into a ribbon to hold the cross around his neck, only sorry that she has no horse, no father or godfather to bless him with cake crumbled onto his sleeping head. One day, perhaps? Such a foolish hope. No, she did it because she had promised her mother.

In the morning, he sits up, instinctively reaches behind his head for the missing hair. The wretch is such a light sleeper.

"What have you done to my head?"

"Only what mother told me to do – on your Name Day. It's so you'll grow up strong like our father. I made a rope to hold your cross."

Pytor pulls the cross from under his chemise.

"Careful so no one sees it!" Maryushka warns.

"No one else has one," he says.

"That makes you special. But mind you keep it hidden." He doesn't bathe and no one cares enough to give him a change of clothes so the cross won't be discovered if he's careful with it.

Pytor tucks the cross on its braided hair-rope back into his shirt. "Thank you," he says.

"If you get caught, I had nothing to do with it."

"Am I supposed to say a prayer?"

"How would I know? Do whatever you want, but say it to yourself."

"I'm thankful I have you for a sister."

Maryushka rumples his yellow hair.

PYTOR REFUSES TO WORK at the brick factory, and bears mutely his punishment time of four hours each morning standing on the stool. He refuses to attend school, to sing Stalinist songs, and spends the remaining four hours of the day again on the punishment stool.

He will not talk, though his legs are bowed, bruised beyond his sister's belief. Nothing she ever says about *tufta*, the Russian way of swindling the boss, or reminding him of the Gulag sayings – *Man is wolf to man* and *They pretend to love us, and we pretend to work* – will change him since they seem to hold no meaning for him.

At age ten, he fully finds his voice, but learns to lie.

"The cigarette butts were on the ground near the guardhouse."

"I don't know where the vodka came from."

"I didn't steal nothin'."

He's a constant embarrassment to Maryushka, and she often resents him, lectures him on behaving and telling the teachers what they want to hear, and though he promises to try, the rebellion seems to be bored into his very marrow. Once he finally learns how to read, after hours spent with Maryushka puzzling out the letters that join to make words, he devours any book he can get his hands on, and at first Maryushka believes he buries himself in Lenin's *Communist Manifesto* so the teachers will leave him alone, until she discovers he pastes pages of stolen novels like *War and Peace* into the book and she understands it's not so much a love of literature as a way of disappearing: stories take him somewhere else, away from the orphanage to a place that may not be entirely better, but is always different from the children's factory.

MARYUSHKA IS FIFTEEN, has earned merit badges for good behaviour, a Young Pioneers striped apron. She is one year away from graduating to permanent work in a factory and deeply in love with Mikhail Davidovitch, a grenade maker, as hardy as the Russian thistle choking out lesser weeds in the courtyard of the brick factory; they plan to marry, once released, and hope they will both be given work in the Tula Cartridge Factory, rooms in a collective flat nearby – and maybe, somehow, take Pytor with them. But, Maryushka is beside herself with worry over her brother, no longer able to protect him from the hooligans, the *maloletki* who make slaves and hostages and prostitutes of the younger boys, gamble with cards, trash the dining room, attack guards with shovels and bricks stolen from the factory – and escape to the streets and sewers of Leningrad.

Pytor seems to fear nothing and no one now. He's brazen, insolent with the caregivers and teachers. His posture, the sneer on his lips, the cock of his head speak louder than words: *Try and make me.* His character was forged by the Soviet hammer, and won't change – not even when love for his sister softens his iron heart. A youth of sharp contrasts, lacking in self-confidence, with a strong belief in the inevitability of poverty and death, he harbours an uncontrollable disrespect for authority, sees everything in terms of army colours of reds and whites, and as far as Maryushka can see, he is motivated only by the need to fill his belly.

Before he leaves the orphanage forever, Pytor doesn't say goodbye to his sister.

Outside, in the darkest of winter nights, he pauses by the wire wall. "You can die today," he says. "I'll die tomorrow." Another saying from the Gulag.

"Take care," she says, hoping he has a chance outside the brick factory. If he gets caught he'll be beaten – or maybe he'll get so hungry out there, alone in the city, he'll just come back on his own, and take the punishment, then settle down to work, making bricks.

She gives him a leg up, he pauses on the top, a small salute, then swings his leg over, and jumps.

And he is gone, over the wall.

Signe

Yaroslav, June 2004

THE SMALL KREMLIN OF YAROSLAV was left untouched first by the Soviets, who didn't destroy its churches, and then the Germans, which was another miracle. In the green-cupolad Church of St. Elijah the Prophet, they lean, Kostja and Signe, shoulder-to-shoulder, engulfed by frescoes painted in 1680 by Kostroma artists, the entire interior of galleries, vaults, piers, portals and even window sills a blanketing tapestry of the life of Jesus.

Kostja whispers: "The eyes of the icons follow you everywhere; you don't watch icons, they watch you. The icon makers captured the soul through the eyes." That explains Kostja's eye-to-eye, iconoclastic artistry: the hypnotic gaze of his wolf wary among the denuded forest of birch and beech; his brown bear eating the remains of a *tur* and lifting its head to growl a warning to the cameraman; his raptorial black vulture as remote as Mt. Elbrus, the highest peak in Russia. "Always the eyes," Kostja says, "the eyes turn on you." A true Russian son of the soil, he trusts no man. In him, the wilderness abides. And that's what brought them together.

He translates an inscription on an icon: *I will pour the Good Word out of my heart.*

As if the saints are unhappy looking down on the tourists, as if they have returned to life, their voices, instruments of God, strike like lightning and seem to fill the church with fire, first in a low thrumming, the beginning of thunder, then one singular lifting, followed by a falling, like a cascade of waterfalls. Kostja turns Signe by her shoulders so she sees: in the corner of the apse below the panel depicting the Angel appearing to Mary, a Yaroslavian tenor, a bass and a baritone – very ordinary Russians in black shirts and red ties. They sing *a capella.* Suddenly, amid a throng of birders and American peasants, her spirit lifts and she allows it to be filled with song.

She imagines a gilded pleasure boat lined with velvet and covered with silk canopies. The boatman wears livery, a cherry-red uniform, with embroidered jacket and feathered hat. *Russ.* He looks like Kostja, and he sings only to her. When the trio stops singing, a wing-swept hush that has fallen over the crowd is broken by a burst of applause. Signe's eyes blur, and she tastes salt.

She says, "What were they singing?" Only to find that Kostja has disappeared, likely rushing out to look for Masha, the orphaned brown bear that lives in the Saviour Transfiguration Monastery. He said he wanted to photograph it, and just now he must think that the light is just right for capturing the soul with his camera's eye. Never mind, only too soon she will find herself in a continuous state of missing Konstantin the Constant. After decades of drought brought about by grief and the refusal to listen to any music that might remind her of her losses, music has re-entered her half-Russian soul and it's more than she could ever articulate to anyone, never to Kostja, a stoic northlander, too much like Pytor Petrovitch Svetlov. Joy is a new word in her vocabulary, in any language.

How will she be able to say goodbye to Kostja? If only she knew the words and the tune to *Long Life To You* sung by an Orthodox church choir after a concert. At home, when her father put a record on his antique gramophone and wound it up, she hadn't paid attention, wanting to go outside to the stoop and dress kittens in doll clothes, and was scolded by Pytor.

If Signe could return to that time, what could she say to put it all right? I'm sorry. I have seen your land, listened to its songs, and I am freed by your music, its passion your pain.

All along, Signe has followed what she believes is the same route taken by her mother during her escape from the seige of Leningrad. Often, she remembers again the story Lena told her while her Swedish Frost Giant breathed on the birch and poplar and the wind froze his breath and made icicles on the Livelong immigrants' log house.

It was the one story Signe couldn't hear too many times because it ended with her.

It was already too late to save everyone left alive in the city, Lena said, *but we had to try, and we had the horses.*

Lena

Lake Ladoga, Winter 1942

FOR LENA AND PYTOR, the journey back to Leningrad begins at the edge of Lake Ladoga, when, from a safe distance, they watch engineers testing the ice with a light horse.

"How thick does it have to get?" Lena says.

"I don't know," Pytor says. "I'm guessing that four inches might support a horse without a load, seven inches a horse pulling a sledge with a ton of freight." He scratches his head through his woolly hat. "I'd say a truck needs at least eight inches of very solid ice." Because the ice didn't even begin to form in the Shlisselburg Gulf before late November, Pytor says it won't be until early January until it's strong enough for any transport.

The engineers dip their measuring sticks into the water, shaking their heads, or waving their arms since the level of water rises with the wind.

Lena and Pytor look at each other. "Let's talk to them," she says.

"*Nyet!* Time to go."

"The ponies, Pytor. We could do it."

"Too dangerous."

"No harm in talking." Lena rises from the snowbank, in full view of the engineers, and strides towards them, with Pytor chasing her.

He catches up quickly and scurries in a circle around her, flapping his arms and smacking his hands against his fur breeches. "Are you mad? You speak so poorly, they'll think you're German."

"Then you do the talking." She marches on, leading with her belly.

"What do you want to know?"

"Just what's going on, if we can help."

"They'll think we're spies!" He grabs her arm, whirls her around, and she leans her forehead against his, cap to frosted cap.

"Think of Maryushka," she says.

The engineers have seen them. "Don't say a word!" Pytor warns. He raises an arm in greeting. "Good morning, comrades."

The engineers look at each other. The larger of the two lifts his goggles and shoves them back on his fur hat. His padded jacket and furs give the false impression that he's the size of a bear, with hungry, blackberry eyes that glow in the sunlight glancing off snow.

"This is my wife, Lena Svetlova," Pytor says. "She's deaf and mute."

"Alexander Popoff," the older one says. "My son, Kolya." The younger Popoff is a smaller replica of his father, but his nose is longer, eyes closer together, and he frowns so hard he looks cross-eyed.

"Will the road open soon?" Pytor says. "I have a sister in Leningrad."

Alexander nods, understanding.

Lena removes her mitten and holds out her hand for the horse to smell, wishing she could ask its name. The horse tosses its head, but doesn't shy, lowering it again to let Lena stroke its nose. It snuffles, rime ringing its nostrils. Its long lashes are frosted.

"She's good with horses, my wife," Pytor says. "How long will a crossing take?" Lena rewards him with a wide, encouraging smile.

Alexander says, "The projected route from the lake edge here —" he points northwest behind them – "will run twenty to thirty miles, linked at the Leningrad end of the lake to the old railroad branch. The line connects five Leningrad depots."

"Don't give him false hope," Kolya says.

It's all Lena can do to keep silent. The horse bobs its massive head up and down, matching the rhythm of her stroking its long nose, as if agreeing with Kolya.

"Ah," Pytor says. "The fall of Tikhvin. I heard on the radio."

Kolya stamps his feet. "A new land road must be built to Ladoga to run from Novay Ladoga through the many villages from Karpino Aborye. If finished in fifteen days, this road could deliver two thousand tons a day." He speaks slowly, as if that will help Pytor understand the seriousness of the situation.

Lena is dying to get into the conversation, but dare not speak. How many tons of food could her ponies carry to Leningrad while the city waits for truck transport? It might make a difference of many lives saved. She wants to hitch Thor to a sleigh so badly tears spring to her eyes, and she wipes them away with her fur-lined glove.

"I know that stretch," Pytor says. By now, so does Lena, though they traversed it by boat during the summer. The route extends for two hundred and twenty miles along the old Yaroslav tract of ancient forest, tamarack swamps, cranberry or Klukva bogs, lakes surrounded by dense timber and uninhabited wilderness.

On the radio this morning, The Food Dictator warned that he has food to last only two more days.

No one says it, but Lena understands: Build the road or die.

"Nice talking with you," Pytor says. "Come, Lena!"

They leave the engineers measuring the ice. It barely supports their own weight, and the horse's back hoofs break the crust. It would hold Thor, but maybe not a sleigh loaded with food.

All the way back to Onega, Pytor broods, and Lena works up an argument to try and convince him that fate brought her and her ponies to Russia.

TWO WEEKS LATER, at home in their *izba* on the island of Kizhi, Lena has still not been able to get Pytor to agree to take the horses to Ladoga.

"You would risk our baby?" he says.

"Perfectly healthy, I am. Walking does me good." The mares, heavy with foal, need exercise too.

How did they come to the need to make this decision, to these desperate hours? They read between the spoken lines of the wireless radio announcer. Every day, rations are reduced. In the city, bodies pile up in courtyards, parks, at the gates to cemeteries.

Yet, it can't be a moment of enlightenment for Pytor, no sudden surge of altruism or a first pang of a social conscience that will make him agree to her plan to use the horses to take food to starving Leningradski. No load of food will ever be enough to save more than a few hundred souls.

Lena says, "All *blokadniki* are dying of starvation."

And paling, Pytor says, "Maryushka may already be gone."

He turns on a heel and leaves their *izba* to round up her Gotlandruss, all forty of them, except Frej and Freja born in the spring of the year.

Father Viktor says, "I will call the people together."

All that day, and half of the next, they make plans, pack warm clothing and non-perishable food, and load it all on the backs of Thor and his mares.

WHEN THEY SET OUT, Father Viktor leads the way, with Lena and Thor at the head of the long line of ponies. Pytor brings up the rear.

Not trusting the strength and depth of the ice on Lake Onega, they skirt the eastern shore, and run short of forage for the horses when they reached Vytegra, but Pytor is afraid of NKVD patrols, and they avoid the small kremlin there. They lose another day, but push on to Voznesenie, without sleep, the warmth of a fire, a hot drink.

A wide crevasse and open water near the entrance to the canal forces them to travel south before angling northwest again, the ponies tiring, even without loaded sleds to pull.

Not once does Lena give in to the first pangs of hunger, the numbness spreading from her toes to ankles; call it folly or insanity, the holy man promises sleighs and sledges, food depots all along the River Svir. Pytor didn't call her a stubborn Swede for nothing.

THEY JOURNEY FROM VILLAGE to village, on the far side of Lake Onega, across that immense expanse of ice.

Father Viktor waves his staff, not only calling upon God to save the Leningradski, but all people of Russland to feed the hungry, may the old saints and God preserve them.

At first, the people avoid them, and Lena guesses that they are afraid to be seen listening to – much less talking to – a priest. But babushki, who must remember how it was before Lenin and the Bolsheviks, fall to their knees, crossing themselves. One crone, blind in one eye, calls out, "A wise one always comes with help for people in time of trouble."

Soon, Lena hears the word *help* pass from one to the other over a glass of kvass in small taverns, beside stoves in *izbas,* in safe corners of barns that smell sweetly of hay.

– *What can we do to help?*
– *The ice won't hold the lightest horse, much less a sledge.*
– *How many bushels of wheat could we muster?*
– *It won't be enough, but it will help.*

All along the River Svir, when they arrive at Voznesenic, Podporozhie, Mandrogi and Lodeynoe Polie, supply depots spring up, with collective farmers and townspeople and villagers bringing whatever they can spare: a bushel of wheat, a crate of frozen chickens, apple boxes full of frozen salmon and sturgeon, baskets loaded with jars of pickled cabbages, herring, beets; blankets and fur coats and hats. Lena's belly is so large now she chooses from the pile of clothing a man's rabbit-lined breeches, a heavy snow jacket, and blue-fox hat with flaps tied tightly over her ears.

Lena and Pytor and Father Viktor wait for the road to open, but still the ice won't hold even the lightest horse belonging to engineers, all hide and bones, so weak it couldn't pull an empty sleigh. On the shore of River Svir joining Onega with Ladoga, they wait, watching engineers testing the depth of the ice. The front hooves of their thinnest horse crack the permafrost, the sound enough to break the stoutest heart.

"But it will hold Thor," Lena says, leading him onto the ice, with the mares obediently following.

AND THEN, THEY'RE HIGH-STEPPING across a field of snow at the south end of Lake Onega, and the voices of the people coming to meet them drift like snow driven by a strong wind, sharp and clear:

— *A mirage?*
— *A miracle!*
— *Prehistoric — so fat.*
— *Look at — cropped manes — long tails, such thick necks. Maybe they're our Tarpans come back to life?*
— *Trucks won't get through —*
— *Thick and heavy bellies. Bloated from starvation? Oh, with foal!*

LENA

The people laugh and cheer and hug each other. Lena waves to them.

A clutch of babushki wagging their heads and clucking their tongues, pointing at Lena tells her that they're tsk-tsking over her big belly, shaming her with a look or a pointing finger for going out in public.

Lena wants to stop and tell them all that they've come such a long way already, from Kizhi high in the northeast, and no stopping them now. Ahead, Father Viktor asks them to find feed for the horses. "Who will volunteer as drivers?"

ONCE AGAIN, WOMEN BRING them cottonseed cakes for the journey across the ice.

A day is lost while sleds and sleighs and sledges are found, harnesses and even cleats for unshod hooves, pincers for trimming thick nails.

Lena's forest horses don't like the wooden yoke fitting over their shoulders and framing their heads. At first they balk, duck their heads and pull backwards. After a long summer and autumn of being free of the bit they toss heads, resisting, but soon adjust to the foreign ways, with Lena talking them into it with soothing words, stroking their thick necks, and offering rewards of dried apples for good behaviour.

When the sleds and sledges are piled high, the Gotlandrussen refuse to respond to their Russian drivers' orders, and Lena makes the rounds again, teaching the drivers to make kissing sounds instead of yelling *Padi, Husha, Juch!* to get them going, *Snabbre, snabbre* instead of *Beregis, Beregis* to make them go faster. And finally *Ptro!* when they want them to stop. "If you use force they'll balk and refuse to move," she says. "Speak nicely."

A weak sun is rising when they finally set off, with the promise of only a few hours of daylight. Ahead, the sky is white, a snowstorm brewing near Podporozhie, the first rest stop, where there is hope for bread and tea with sugar, oats or hay for the horses.

Lena leads Thor, breaking trail across slushy ice. The only sounds are the clicking of cleated hooves and the cracking of ice, fissures streaking away from the trail like bony fingers scratching on a chalkboard of snow. The blankets and feedbags, covered with hoarfrost, look as if they've been flour-dusted, and Thor's thick lashes are white, his nostrils rimed. He blows a misty breath.

Behind them, the column of ponies pulling sleds stretches for a mile, with large spaces left between each; if one horse breaks through the ice, the one following should have time to stop and halt the line.

Pytor pulls up the rear, so far behind her Lena cannot even signal to him.

So far so good. She plods along, beside sure-footed, faithful Thor, his bobbing head and steady gait setting the pace, not too fast to wear out the mares, they're making good time, if the weather holds. From time to time, she feels her belly rippling, the baby turning, nudging her onward with a foot or fist.

Three rest stops, new drivers replace the tired at Podporozhie, more sacks of flour and food concentrates loaded at Mandrogi, each pony limited to a few hundred pounds. Hardtack, sugar, macaroni and cottonseed cakes are given the drivers at Lodeynoe Polie. They share the cakes with the ponies.

AT THE LAST MAKESHIFT DEPOT before Lake Ladoga, in an ice hut Lena and Pytor gulp glasses of steaming tea with sugar.

LENA

Two engineers in white coveralls, their goggles shoved back on their fur hats, take stools, wanting to talk. They introduce themselves as Alexander and Kolya, father and son.

"We have met before," Pytor says.

Kolya says, "Your wife, the one good with horses." He laughs. "Why didn't you tell us about your ponies then?"

Pytor shrugs. "The idea hadn't struck him yet," Lena says.

"I thought you couldn't speak," Kolya says. His crossed eyes look even more pronounced by their expression of surprise.

"She's wary of strangers," Pytor says, casting a furious now-you've-done-it look at Lena.

"There's been trouble since the November thaw," Alexander says. He removes his fur-lined gloves and warms thin hands over the grille. "We lost forty trucks in seven days. Sank to the bottom of the lake. Are you sure you know what you're up against? The road is shelled and strafed by Nazis."

Kolya nods. "Kilometre No. 9 is the most dangerous point. Cracks in the ice."

"We'll be careful," Pytor says, gulping his tea. "What about the forest road?"

"It finally opened on December 6, but it's so narrow two trucks cannot pass, and a haul from the railhead to the Leningrad side of the lake will take ten to twenty days," Kolya says. "Trucks would need two weeks to make the round trip from Zaborye to Novaya Ladoga, only able to cover twenty-five miles each day."

"Abandoned," Alexander says. "In three days, three hundred and fifty trucks got stuck in drifts or ran off the shoulders of the road."

Kolya says, "Our brave soldiers fight in bogs, waterlogged peat fields, in the forests and marshes between Mga and Tikhvin.

You'll never get through by land, and if you do the railway is cut both ways – south to Moscow, northwest to Leningrad."

"Then we cross the Lake," Pytor says.

"I'd advise against it," Kolya says. "Wait till the first aid stations and repair depots are set up. Once our troops retake Mga the railway will reopen. Till then, supplies are pouring into Tikhvin and are being loaded onto trucks heading north to Ladoga."

"We don't have trucks to break down," Pytor says, "just ponies, very light ones." He casts a meaningful glance at Lena, who rolls the hot mug between her palms.

The baby turns, its head or bottom bulging in her left side. She feels the need to pass her water again, though she just went in the outhouse. The pressure of the baby on her bladder makes her feel like she has to go too often, especially now she's so close to delivery. She can't tell Pytor that she fears the problem of relieving themselves once they're on the ice. It's faster and easier for men, who don't have to drop their breeches and bare their bottoms to the danger of frostbite; and while they pee they can hold their dinks in their hands to keep them from freezing.

"No worry," she says. "Russ get through, to be sure."

"Look, you're nice kids," Alexander says, " but you really don't know what you're in for. We've got nineteen thousand workers just waiting for the ice to thicken, GAZ AA trucks and three ton ZIS-5s that can speed across the ice at forty miles per hour. Once we get going we can make two trips a day."

"It'll take forever to cross with your little horses," Kolya says.

"It's dangerous," Alexander says. "Give it up. We can slaughter the horses for meat."

The shock makes Lena drop her mug, and tea splashes her fur-lined boots. "Over my dead body!" she shouts in Swedish. "You'll have to cut me up for meat pies first. Pytor, let's go!"

LENA

Kolya looks at her with suspicion. "She's not a German, is she?"

Pytor forces a laugh. "Swedish, but she's far from neutral. She's on our side."

It's the first patriotic thing Lena has ever heard Pytor say.

When she rises, she presses her hands against her back, then smooths the front of her jacket, noticing how low the baby rides now. That's what's causing so much pressure on her bladder. Kicking high, under her breastbone, this child is never still, what a promise of a holy terror to come, just like his father. And yes, she's sure it's a boy, Gustaf, already named for her father, though Pytor says he doesn't care if it's a boy or girl, as long as the child is healthy.

"At least wait until the storm passes," Kolya says. "It's insanity to start out now."

"Every hour costs lives," Lena says, shifting from one foot to another.

"I won't try to stop you," Alexander says, shaking hands with Pytor. He gives Lena a map, points out and with a red pencil circles the symbols of landmarks she and Pytor must follow to their destination: Finland Station outside Leningrad.

"God speed," Kolya says, whispering, his black eyes darting, likely afraid a Party boss will hear him. "If you must go, be sure to mark your trail with the red flags, one every one hundred metres. Keep to one trail, so you don't go in circles or get lost. Once the storm passes and the ice is thick enough we'll send out snow-clearing detachments at the other end. Closer to Leningrad."

"Thank you," Pytor says. Why does he bow to authority when he hates it?

"Maybe we meet up during *next* crossing," Lena says. She won't shake hands with people who eat horsemeat.

And Lena and Pytor and their caravan of hardy but easily handled forest horses set off across Lake Ladoga, The Road of Life.

A FEW HOURS LATER, where the River Svir flows out of Ladoga Lake, they slosh through to firmer ice, but plod into a white wall of snow, the easy going now behind them and ahead a vast wasteland of ice and wind. Lena wraps her red scarf around her forehead, nose and mouth, leaving her eyes protected by snow goggles given to her by the engineers.

Snow quickly covers cracks in the ice, hides watery crevasses that could swallow a pony.

She can see nothing through the whirling snow, but counts one hundred steps before staking the first red flag, causing the ice to crack, and after four the new trail behind them disappears in whorls that look like icing on braided lifebread. The convoy is long, sleds and sledges lurch and tilt, their runners scarring the ice, but the heroic *russ* plod on, their tails slicing the wind, the rhythm of their movement a song of ice cutting a tunnel through a wasteland of wind and blowing snow.

The cold air stabs the lungs, though Lena breathes through her scarf. Snow settles on her fur hat and shoulders. Flakes melt on her eyebrows. Icicles hang from her fur breeches. She's up to her ankles in snow, feet sliding on wet ice beneath, and she slams headlong into a drift, backs up, halting Thor; and the column stops.

She approaches the hummock, swiping at the wall of snow, for a moment thinking they've hit a hut buried there, but she sees her own face shining back at her, like a ghost's, then rubs away more snow, only to discover the hump of a fender. She kicks at rubber, causing a small landslide, and there: an overturned truck. Having somehow drifted through the river of snow too far off the projected route, they're too close to the shore road now.

    Best to wait out the storm. She digs under the frozen canvas on Thor's sledge and lifts out a kerosene lamp. Unable to strike a match, she removes her fur mitten, crouches down beside the sledge, uses her scarf to create a small tent out of the wind, and within the hollow she's able to strike the wooden match, light the lamp and replace the glass. Then rising, she waves it twice, a signal for a rest stop.

    The drivers huddle beside the sleighs and sleds, beating their fur-lined mittens together, holding them under their armpits. Impossible to build even the smallest of fires to melt snow for tea. She eats half a cottonseed cake, feeds the other half to Thor. He gathers the cake with his lips, so careful not to nip her fingers with his teeth, the rubbery lips tickling her skin. When he's done she kisses his soft nose. His nostrils are rimed with frost.

    The wind is dying. Snow lifts, still sifting onto her head and shoulders, onto Thor's frosted head and blanket. He shifts his feet, then hunkers down beside her, waiting out the storm. His body emanates heat through the blanket covering his back, such a comfort to her. Yet, she's afraid of falling asleep, and beats her shoulders to keep awake. The baby is stilled.

    Po dolinam I po vzgoryam. A voice in the winter wilderness, like the howl of a wolf, but it's the wise one, singing a hymn or a marching song, *shla diviziya fpyeryot,* it's all Russian to Lena, *shtoby z boyem vzyat primorye.* The drivers pick up the tune, the words, *Byeloi Armiyi aplot,* their voices a chain of command to the elements, *shtoby z boyem vzyat primorye,* rising and falling, stronger than the wind and blasting snow, *Byeloi Armiyi aplot.*

Byeloi means white, *armiyi* is army. They must be singing a song from their Civil War. Lena remembers her "Everyday Song." *One doesn't know where one has come from / or where one is going / One must kick oneself in the ass and get up and keep on going.* Through the deluge of freezing wind, the thrum of male basso rises so strongly the sound vibrates in her chest like strings of a cello, the higher trumpeting of tenors, *Etikh lyet nye smolknit slava / nye pamerknit nikaga,* enough to make her cry. They're singing something about glory, about *partizanskiye* – partisans! – and stormy nights like this one, about an end to something. Saints call upon saints to still the wind, stop the snow, get them through to the harbour at Shlisselburg.

Thor struggles to his feet, his pawing hooves test the ice that is much firmer now the temperature has dropped so low. He turns his head as if asking, Well, are you ready to go on?

Lena swings the lantern over her head, a signal to the drivers.

The sun is long gone, darkness covers the wasteland, the wind dying, thinning clouds scudding across a wafer moon. It stops snowing.

Lena stakes another red flag into the ice, releasing a sliver of water. The stake sinks only three to four inches, and Lena worries about the thickness of the ice. Only a hundred metres to the next, don't think about how far to Shlisselburg, if they can make it to Leningrad, just another hundred metres to plant the next flag, then the next, two, and then three, keep going, one more.

She's stopped by the sight of a wind-tattered red flag now hanging limply on its stake. They've been moving in a circle. Fear and disappointment and the feeling she's failing in her mission almost brings her to her knees. She bends over Thor and wraps her arms around his neck, burying her face for a moment in that bristly but soft spot between his ears. He stamps his front hooves as if impatient with her: don't be so hard on yourself, get a move on, Girl!

But she isn't sure which direction to take now, checks her compass, the stars in the sky, looking for the Bear. And then she hears them, the Heinkels and JA 88s, they're swooping landward towards Leningrad, like flying dinosaurs. Too late she douses the lamp, they've seen the convoy of ponies. Bullets strafe, exploding snow. Thor rears, then bucks, shrilling. Lena ducks beside the sledge, covering her head, her belly tight against her knees, baby kicking hard as if in fury, the ice beneath her vibrating, her breath lost. Some of the mares break the line, taking off for cover that isn't there. With a terrifying crack, the ice splits, and a crevasse opens up and swallows them. The screams of terrified – or hit? – ponies, drivers. Racket of flying guns, ice exploding, a shower of flame, snow.

Then the sound of retreating planes, the moaning of horses and men, quickly overtaken by a silence deeper than the Ladoga, the silence of being alone on the ice.

It's broken by Thor's whinnying, calling his mares back from the edge of darkness.

Lena pulls her heavy body up, and bending her knees, wants only to wrap her arms around Thor's neck again and seek comfort there, but she must see how much damage has been done to the sledges, how many horses left.

Blood on the snow, pooling, spreading from under overturned sleds. She makes her way along the column, the second driver, a boy of sixteen or seventeen, lies dead in the snow, but the mare, Daisy, blows, scratching one hoof on the ice as if hoping to uncover grass.

The next driver is alive, a farmer from Mandrogi, but his legs are caught under his overturned sled, a ton of provisions.

Three drivers appear out of the dark, crouch against the sled, counting "One, two, three, LIFT!" and free the Mandrogi man's crushed legs. His face is whiter than the ice he lies upon. The other drivers carefully lift him on top of the sled, he roars with pain, then passes out, mercifully.

Pytor lumbers through the drifting snow, catches Lena in his arms. "You are fine? The baby?"

"*Dah, dah,* help the others, we must. How many lost?"

"Five men, three horses. What do we do?"

"No leave sleds! Food we take to Leningrad."

Lena doesn't know if Thor and the mares can manage the extra loads, but she directs the surviving drivers to hitch the five driverless sleds, one extra to five of the strongest ponies.

And they set off again, this time without the lantern to light the way.

Follow the stars.

HOUR AFTER HOUR, staking red waymarker after red waymarker, they trudge on, until the moon slides behind clouds, and the black night begins to shade into charcoal grey, then lift to the colour of pewter. Ahead, lights winking out like dying stars. "Shlisselburg!" Lena cries. But all of Russia is in blackout, it couldn't have been town lights.

The mares are exhausted, the line almost at a standstill. Lena calls a halt at the next waymarker, lets them rest, miming to the drivers that they must feed the ponies the last of their cottonseed cakes to give them enough strength to make it to the Gulf, praying they won't find open water there.

The driver with broken legs died in Father Viktor's arms during the night, and Pytor orders the driver of the second sled to leave the body beside the red flag. One load is lightened.

He offers hope to another with bloodied bandages trailing under his fox fur hat. "Not far to go now. Just hold on another few miles." What a change Maryushka would see in her brother now. What a good man he is, and didn't Lena first see it the day of the wounded seagull?

Lena rests against Thor's sledge, hands shoved into her rabbit breeches, fingers exploring pains under her belly. It hurts to touch on the left side, she must have pulled a muscle. She breathes a little easier. It can't be contractions, the pain is unceasing, oh Dear Lord, it's much too soon, she's only at the end of her seventh month. Pytor squats down before her. "Can you go on? Better you should ride on sleigh."

She hauls herself upright, and the pain leaves her. "*Nyet, nyet,* fine I am." She cannot add her weight to Thor's load, he's straining with every step. "Let's go!" The baby isn't moving now.

After she stakes four more red flags, she sees the light flashing, a rhythm to its blinking, then whiteout again. Eyes fixed on that horizon, she leads Thor and the caravan towards it. The light is larger this time, clearly alternating green and white before it dies again. Then a tower or spire takes shape in the far sky, a grey rampart the same shade as the lightening horizon. Yes, the fortress of Shlisselburg, the lights a signal, someone taking a risk since the airborne Nazis might see it instead of Lena, but someone knows they're coming, someone is watching out for them, dear God in Heaven.

Lena leaves the head of the line, trudging through the snow to Pytor, and tells him she will pull up the rear, in case they are stopped by an NKVD patrol.

She's seized with cramps beneath her belly again, but lumbers on, cradling the unborn child in her arms. Then the pangs cease. Just a false alarm. Yes, didn't her own mother tell her about her own days and days of false labour before Lena was born?

They leave the stretch the Leningrad engineers called Ladoga Road of Life stretching into white infinity, like the steppes. They skirt the watchtower still held by the Red Army. It's in full view now, the Soviet flag unfurled over the fortress, two old cannon mounted on the wall, its sights useless and facing the waterfront. Nazi troops set up posts so close Lena can see them forcing fur-hatted men and shawled women to dig trenches and dugouts at gunpoint. Four workers hang from crossbeams. If she can see them, they surely will soon sight her caravan of ponies. She must make a decision and fast: try to hide the ponies in frost-burdened groves of spruce and pine – or run! But there is Father Viktor, striding towards the Germans, who don't see him until he's almost upon them.

Not knowing if he can speak German and unable to imagine what he might say to distract the enemy from the ponies or persuade them to allow her caravan safe passage, she can do nothing except trust him and pray he won't be shot. Clasping Thor's halter, she says, "Now, my brave pony, let's go!" Making kissing sounds, she starts running, and Thor leaps into a trot, his whinny to his mares low as if he's aware of the danger. They race for the grove, crashing though the underbrush, leaping and bounding in snow up to the pony's knees, her calves; the only sound the crackling of ice, the swoosh of snow falling from laden branches; and she runs till her breath hurts in her chest, then keeps on going, praying the sound of forty times four hooves won't alert the German guards talking to Father Viktor, the slide of many runners muffled by a newly broken trail through snow now packed hard, thick with a layer of frost.

Once out of the woods, she allows Thor to slow the pace, but dare not halt the caravan, though she walks backwards for a moment, relieved to see Father Viktor far back, pulling up the rear now. She waves at Pytor but can't shout to him. Even from this distance, she can see his face breaking up, his mouth open in a silent cry, not so much of pain that comes with loss but the struggle to help Father Viktor hold to the pace. Whatever he said to the Germans worked, but Father Viktor can barely stay on his feet, even with Pytor holding him up; they look like one man split into two, like the first of paper dollies cut by a child from a grandmother's doily.

They dare not stop and rest, not yet. The running has caused a cramp in her left side, just under her belly. It comes and goes, surely just a stitch that will cease when she rests and catches her breath.

"How are you, Thor?" He's blowing, his steps measured and laboured, but his ears twitch forward as if to say, Keep on going.

THE APPROACH TO SHLISSELBURG is as difficult as the crossing of Lake Ladoga's south end; it's fraught with the danger of running into abandoned trucks, AA batteries in shelters made of ice blocks. They tunnel through walls of snow left by graders. Every kilometre, they're stopped by a traffic officer in a white camouflage cape, directing them forward with red and white flags. Every kilometre, the pain in her underside hits her again, but only lasts a few minutes, it's nothing she cannot bear. Once they reach the next rest stop she'll be fine.

She looks back and sees that Father Viktor keeps pace with Pytor on his own now.

They pass more ice block shelters, wood and barrels of gasoline piled before them. At lesser intervals, repair shops for trucks, camouflaged AA posts, more broken-down trucks half buried in snow.

They finally reach an evacuation office in run-down barracks, where a long line of bedraggled people wait to give their documents to three Russian officials in fur hats.

— *There's no place to stay the night!*
— *It's at least twenty below zero! We'll freeze.*
— *Hush, they're giving out food coupons.*
— *Food? What food?*
— *Dry rations. Hardtack, pea soup, hot cereal.*
— *You must be dreaming.*

A woman holding a large, child-size object bundled in a white chenille bedspread screams when officials wrench it away from her. Lena cradles her round and protruding belly.

When they see the fat ponies, a hush falls over the mob, and Lena is afraid they'll rush them. Long-bladed skinning knives appear, but two NKVD patrolmen take over, rifles raised. She hears Pytor say something about horses bearing food for *blokadniki,* and they are allowed to pass, though dark looks are cast their way. A tremor passes through the crowd of emaciated people and the word: *cannibals.* Lena's belly is round, her cheeks plump, windburned. The guards escort the caravan away from the barracks: it's too dangerous for the ponies amid hundreds of starving people.

Lena is afraid that she and Pytor and Father Viktor and the forty Russian drivers cannot go on without food and rest. Quickly smoothing the map drawn by the engineers for her, she realizes that there are rapids to portage before reaching the Finland Freight Station at Leningrad, the designated collection point for food arriving from Ladoga lake area.

On the other side of Shlisselburg, the guards leave the

caravan of ponies, wishing Pytor good luck. He trots forward and takes the lead now, but Lena can't drop back without Thor. She takes his halter, turns his head, and leads him alongside the caravan. At first, the mares want to swing around and follow him, but he trumpets to them as if ordering them to follow Pytor. They stall, but Pytor has learned well to show them affection, bits of cake an offering to Daisy, who takes the lead, trotting smartly with head held high, and the rest follow her, though they swing their heads at Thor quizzically.

THE NIGHT IS CLEAR, CRISP. Lena leaves the staking of flags to Pytor, glad he's far ahead and can't see her cringing against the cramps, every half kilometre now.

She doesn't know how long it will take to trek around the rapids. She's hypnotized by the sight of foaming water, steam rising from the undulating fall, beards of frozen moss clinging to rocks, icicles strung from pine like the Swedish Frost Giant's decorations for Christmas. She trudges on beside Thor, as if she's a sleepwalker, teeth clenched against pain recurring like a bad dream, almost oblivious to the ache in her back, her feet numb, hands curled inside her mittens. Shoulders hunched she drives herself forward, keep moving, there's food to be delivered, rest soon, a good sleep and she'll be fine. The baby.

ON THE SMOKY, FOGGY MORNING of the next day, the weak sun breaks through thick snowclouds when the convoy reaches the outskirts of Leningrad, its spires and towers and onion domes miniature and seeming to float above low-lying clouds; the stark whiteness scrabbled with grey more like an artist's rendering of landscape without figures than a real picture of the skyline. It shimmers like a mirage. In the distance, Lena sees German soldiers wintering in dugouts and permanent trenches. She wishes she was leading an army that might attack the Nazis and take away all their food. The smoke of many small fires filters the frosty air. Pushkin village, the backbone of the city's defence lies fractured, with its great parks and Catherine and Alexander palaces and villas shrouded with rubble and snow. How often she had pondered this very scene conveyed in all seasons in encyclopedias and school text books and even travel magazines in the Ryss Garden in Visby, wishing, oh with great longing, that she could travel the world and see such grand sights. And now, there they are, in ruins. It's enough to make her weep, but best to delay feelings of sadness to a time when the release of food to people and settling them onto evacuation sleighs will cause the bad feeling to be alleviated by one of relief, if not joy.

To the west, the barricaded road leads to the unmistakable and grand Peterhof Palace. She wishes she had seen the famous tiers of fountains when she was in the city last spring, before it was bombed. Now, command posts have been built from pine and spruce, and Lena longs for a stove hot to the touch, a proper bed with down-filled duvet. Hidden from their view by thin birch thickets and underbrush, she can see the Red Marines in their black wool capes and steel helmets, waiting for the next battle – or are they snipers?

Peterhof Palace, once described as the rival of Versailles in every history book in the Visby Bibliotek, now a mere shell of once grand apartments and banqueting halls, only its arches and chimneys and marble stairways to the gardens still a monument to the past; all guarded by two sentinel Red Army soldiers mounted on shaggy horses, their gilded sabres glinting in the new sun. With astonished eyes and gaping mouths, they stare at the caravan of ponies as if they see ghosts emerging from the mists of the past. It makes Lena feel proud of her small horses. Ahead, Pytor waves his arms while explaining their mission to a guard on horseback, then races to the end of the line to tell Lena that the statue of Samson that once overlooked the great fountains cascading down to the sea is gone. "It must have been shipped off to Germany," he says, then kicks a mound of rubble. "Thieving Krauts!"

"Keep moving!" Lena says, though she understands that he fusses over something so trivial as a marble statue, unable to bear the thought of starving people, one of them his sister and only living relative. When Lena's mother awakens from a Mother Fit so severe she might have swallowed her tongue and died, Carolina fusses about a front tooth chipped from grinding during the spastic episode.

"Go on," Lena says, and Pytor returns to the front of the caravan.

South of Peterhof, shore batteries shower shells on the enemy Lena cannot see.

From here, all of Leningrad's skyline is visible and she checks the landmarks against the symbols on the engineers' map: coal docks where once Pytor's barge was anchored; twin towers of Forel Hospital; the chimneys of the Kirov iron works where Maryushka is, hopefully, still making tanks; cupolas of churches; the Admiralty spire; all within sight of German guns. For the first time since she left Leningrad, Lena feels truly threatened by this war, and doubts the wisdom of exposing her unborn child to it. Still, she must go on and try to find Maryushka.

Here, they follow train tracks. No locomotives. No boxcars that might have been laden with foodstuffs. Silently and grimly, they strain forward, the ponies pulling hard now, even Lena afraid of what must surely lie ahead: the grand city of Peter bereft of hope, for God seems to have forgotten its name too. Lena prays it isn't too late for food. The train of ponies moves slowly towards bombed-out ruins.

Finland Freight Station is surrounded by AA guns that obviously failed to protect it from bombs that smashed into the yards, hurling trains from the rails. Coaches and freight cars now lie on their sides in smoking rubble among switches, sidings and damaged terminals. The station is still strewn with corpses of women and children. Bomb craters. Twisted metal.

Here is where Lenin returned from Switzerland on April 16, 1917 and spoke to the revolutionaries from an armoured car. Now, the bust of the first Bolshevik is covered with ashes, a broken vase and plastic flowers strewn at its base. An ill omen for the Bolsheviks if the Germans win this war. All the greater reason for Lena to take her husband and his sister – and her child – home to neutral Sweden.

They find the remains of a first aid station, half its roof caved in, a sign hanging upside down from an arch. Lena sinks to her knees on the ice, holding her belly against pain that won't go away, the sudden flooding into her rabbit-skin breeches.

"It's too soon, too soon."

Signe
Uglich, June 11, 2004

ONE LAST STOP IN UGLICH before Moscow where Kostja will leave the tour and go home to his family, three days before Signe returns to Canada. She doesn't want to see Moscow without him. She envies him his healthy children. How lucky they are to have Kostja, her only Russian friend.

Last night, he invited Signe to his home outside Moscow to meet his family after the tour ends on Sunday, but her flight will have left that morning. So, he promised to take her to see the small kremlin of Uglich today.

The Church of St. Dimitri-on-the-blood, built in 1692, after the canonization of the tsarevitch, looks like a red-and-blue cake made especially for Dimitri's Angel Day (birthday), with its ornate windows, cornices, series of pilasters and star-studded cupolas. Kostja explains: "The architecture is old style – *kerem*. White, in Russian, means soul. The stars on the blue domes mean that the soul of the child is in heaven." *Sasha, too.* Here, the young tsarevitch, Dimitri, son of Ivan the Terrible, was exiled by his father, then assassinated by Boris Gudinov on May 15, 1591, though a tribunal ruled that the seven-year-old died during an epileptic seizure while playing with a knife.

It might have happened yesterday. Kostja is one of the Faithful. "The kremlin of Uglich is not in the present; it all lives in the past," he says. "Never mind the doubting Thomas historians, the bell ringer saw it happen, it all was the will of God."

"Do you believe everything that happens is His will?" Why would He take Sasha from Signe, leave Tapani eternally young – and simple-minded? Signe's prayers for healing were never answered, but here she has found something she cannot name within herself that goes beyond grief and fear and even joy. It's like turning a corner and meeting – yourself.

"Noooo. He gave us free will. Too easy to blame God for the evil of men, yes?" Hitler. Stalin.

"Yes, you're right, my wise friend."

Kostja captures the brilliance of the church at different angles while the light is still good enough for taking photographs. He believes in the hereafter. Signe is too moved to tell him that she doesn't believe in the Sunday School version of heaven. Hell is on earth, man-made. Because of Sasha, the girl who will never grow up, who had known first love, who believed she would someday become an archeologist and unearth the Lost City of Atlantis, Signe believes her departed soul simply returned to another dimension, a place of the unity of spirit, an infinity beyond the limits of human understanding. Signe never erected a tombstone. Sashenka is not in the grave. Now, she decides to return to Sasha's resting place and build around it a white picket fence like the ones she erected around her parents' graves, and fill the spot with tiger lilies and, because her fear has vanished in this country, with the national flower of Russia – whatever it turns out to be – she'll ask Kostja.

SIGNE

This morning, the *Novikov Priboy* stopped beside a lock in the Upper River Svir, and Signe rushed with the other tourists to the uppermost deck to watch the riverboat pass through it. The day began with an overcast sky, with shadows against the red Russian sun. A break in the clouds, like the parting of curtains allowed a light within a light that permits the passage of the Soviet eras into a different renaissance here. Light returns to this land, slanting in shafts of praise to the enduring Russian soul that is now free. Kostja told her then that tomorrow – June 12 – is Independence Day, and that once again the pre-Soviet, red and white and blue striped flag flies over the Kremlin. It all holds a promise for the unborn child of Kostja – if only he could see it. "A new child will be born," he said, "into the cradle of sadness we call Earth." Without knowing about Signe's daughter, he said he will name his child Sasha or Sashenka, short for Alexandra. Of course Signe was moved, but silently and unafraid, she watched the lock in the Upper Svir River fill with water to allow the passage of the riverboat.

In Russia, apparently it's nothing for a woman to cry. Now, Kostja simply puts an arm around her shoulders. In this small clearing, on the shores of the Volga, beneath linden trees, he asks Signe to pay attention to the songs of three different birds: the complaint of the crow, the higher lyrical call of a lark, and the fluting of another she cannot name, but may be a nightingale.

Just then, church bells call the devout to service. "Forty-on-forty, we call this," Kostja says. "In Moscow, there are six hundred and forty bell towers full of gold, their ringing enough to fill the whole sky, as we say. You will hear them, yes."

Before an old pre-Soviet building, a trio of bedraggled locals play oompahpah songs, and Kostja halts, not to listen to the music, but to show Signe: on a grassy knoll, mother and father grebes teach their young how to fetch twigs and fallen feathers for their nest. "Look! Look!" he says. "They are – how you say? – tutoring."

And suddenly, a sun shower. Kostja opens his umbrella, although Signe wears a hooded slicker and doesn't need it, and they stroll, arm in arm, looking for another church. "We call this mushroom rain," he says. Mushrooms sprouting under the spruce. Maryushka said it was a bad omen, too many, a sign of many deaths. Though she pickled them for winter, she never ate a morsel; they reminded her of the Siege.

Then they move on, aimlessly wandering, he taking her hand when they reach a curb, and a block further on, to step over a puddle in the gutter. She's not used to his old-world, courtly European manners, but give her a chance and she'll grow accustomed, yes.

All too soon, it's over, the mushroom rain, and two babushki in heavy winter coats and kerchiefs come between Signe and Kostja, the kind of thing Lena and Maryushka would do if they were here and knew that Kostja is married, with another child on the way. These grandmothers offer bunches of violets, cowslips and forget-me-nots, likely from their gardens. Kostja brushes by them, starting off ahead, but unzipping her camera bag, Signe finds an American dollar, gives it to the smallest babushka most like Maryushka, with fat, ruddy cheeks, in exchange for the bouquet tied with a blue ribbon. Kostja watches, a quizzical look on his face, like a cat overseeing a family of robins testing the temperature of a bird bath.

Suddenly, the women rush Signe, almost knocking her off her feet, shouting in Russian and shaking the flowers in her astonished face. She lifts high the camera bag to show them it only contains the camera. "*Izvin'iti.* I'm sorry, I'd buy all your flowers, but that's all I have, just one dollar. I didn't bring my purse." The Intrav staff had warned the tourists to beware of pickpocketing gypsies – not of grandmothers.

And Kostja is there, speaking softly in Russian but very quickly and pleasantly, there are too many consonants in the words; Signe can't know what makes the women lower their arms and back away from her.

Signe gives him the forget-me-nots. He sniffs them, probably thinking of his young botanist wife.

The linden and beech shake off raindrops. They turn back, towards the dock, passing pre-revolution, single-family dwellings, maybe still owned by workers in the Uglich watch factory. One painted red with white latticework captures Signe's fancy, and she photographs it. She could never abide apartment living in the cities crammed with millions of people, but here – don't even think about it. She must go home to Tapani.

There's still enough good light for more photographs, if Signe doesn't mind, and Kostja leaves Signe dockside, ducking through the underbrush to take a short cut back to Dimitri's monumental church. "*Spasibo,*" she says, understanding his obsession with birds, but wishing he wouldn't rush away, leaving her in the returning rain.

She enters the park, with its tourist kiosks as far as the eye can see, ends up at the entrance to the small kremlin. Beneath the temporary shelter of a giant aspen, a solitary woman in the rain sings her heart out, like a robin announcing the dawn of spring after a long siege of winter.

With the Rybinski Reservoir and Rivers Sheksna and Kovzha and Lakes Onega and Ladoga far behind, the *Novikov*

Priboy will leave the River Volga, enter the Moscow Canal, and head for Kostja's home.

Perhaps it would be best if Signe just slips her moorings and steals away in the night.

Ah, but she can't wait for dinner on the boat, hoping Kostja will sit with her, instead of with the crew. She's starving. The thought stops her cold. How easily the words slide into her mind, how much she takes for granted. She can't ever truly know what it was like during the Seige, how it must have felt to starve to death.

Maryushka

Leningrad, Winter 1941

SHE'S ALWAYS BEEN MOTIVATED by the need to be seen working, but she hasn't been able to rise from her bed on the floor for days. How many? She's lost count since Lyba died.

The foundling simply refused to eat, turning her head away from the bottle or spoon, lips pursed. She was hot to the touch, and swabbing with cold cloths couldn't bring down the fever. Coughing racked her bony chest, but the mustard plasters wouldn't break up the pleghm that gurgled in her throat. She was too weak to fight it, and didn't even cry. For hours, Maryushka just held her, crooning, trying to talk her into living. "Don't give up, Dushenka. Some day we'll always be warm, we will feast on blini with caviar stacked to the ceiling." All night, every night, Maryushka held her inside her heavy coat and under their blanket, for the first time praying to God not to take her Little Sun.

Finally, one morning, Lyba just didn't wake up when Maryushka turned back the edge of the blanket, and took away Maryushka's last hope of surviving the siege. The bundle was cold, yellow-blue the face of the child, like an old porcelain doll's.

She no longer can bear to look at her gaunt face in a mirror. Her own skin on arms and hands is lead-grey, the colour of a Caucasian bee, which makes her think of honey, sweet and sticky, spread over buttered bread, good bread, made with wholewheat flour, not wood cellulose. Her legs have wasted to the size of pickets, though her ankles have swelled beyond recognition. Her neck has thickened with fluid. Her breasts are gone, only shrivelled nipples left. No muscle in her arms, just skin loose and as wrinkled as a plucked chicken's. Her bowels have stopped moving, she passes water rarely now, as if her body preserves it. She smells so foul she keeps her nose sticking out of the blanket.

Her larder is empty, save one teaspoon of cereal, enough water in the samovar to pour into a cup and heat over a wick in a pool of oil. She hasn't the strength to sit up and make her last small meal. It will only make her want to sleep, sleep and never wake up. She must stay awake, but has nothing and no one to live for, not even Pytor who has his Lena now, be thankful for that much – if he's still alive.

The stove is cold. She has burned all her furniture, the last of the pickets, the books she found in the flat across the hall.

Stairs are too hard to climb now. If she did find wood, she wouldn't have the strength to chop it for kindling. Her *burzhuki* stove has a chimney with a vent through the *fortochka* window, she's always been afraid of fires, so much creosote building up in the pipe, and she's too weak to take it down and scrape it clean.

She wishes she could listen to the news, but she traded her wireless for a half loaf of bread – was it a week ago? Before Lyba left her, yes.

Ponies from Gotland. The voice is loud and metallic, not God's, not even Pytor's. It's coming from the loudspeaker outside, of course, it's been silent for weeks and weeks, with no electricity. Static. Silence. Then: *food supplies being distributed in Petrograd.* The voice breaks off and she listens hard, but no news about what kind of food or any change in rations allotted per person.

She begins to drift, certain she's losing her mind as well as her body, the shape of a snout on the ceiling, an arched neck, a horse head, ears pricked up, and there is Lena astride a pony the size of a big dog, her long legs hanging down on either side of it's rotund belly, with Pytor in his silly red star cap, leading the horse by a long leash.

The last time she waited in a food line, she was attacked by a street urchin wearing a red star cap. At first, he made her think of Pytor, and she wasn't afraid, too many children whose parents had died lived in cellars of bombed houses and stole food from shops, even when beaten. He held a pen knife to her throat, wrenched her purse and ration card from her hand, everyone else in line shrinking back with fear, before the grocer lumbered out to the street, waving a butcher knife. He couldn't run fast enough to catch the wretch. He saw it happen, but he wouldn't give her her ration of bread, not without her card. It was impossible to get a new card due to fraudulent losses reported by those trying to get extra rations.

MARYUSHKA

No use to go to the cafeteria at the Kirov, the factory now a frigid morgue where her comrades steal coal from the foundry and huddle around stoves.

She stares at the shifting shapes on the ceiling, she hasn't gone mad, isn't seeing things; the weak sun has cast shadows from the leafless trunk and branches of the oak tree outside, so large no one in her district has had the strength to chop it down for firewood.

The crackling voice on the speaker outside her building sounds like a machine gun, this time warning of criminals bearing military rifles, revolvers. Citizens are to report landlords who steal ration cards from the dead. Parents must keep children off the streets. Many are missing. Food crimes are listed: three men shot for stealing loaves of bread; five men shot for stealing flour from a truck; two women shot for profiteering on the black market. It must have been the Hungry Market. Pytor's place.

She now wants to think of her brother as a noble bandit. When she heard a worker's story told at the factory it alleviated her fear for Pytor. It wasn't a wild rumour, it was true. One of the youngest workers, a girl named Vera, told the hushed women huddled by the stove that she had been attacked by a gang from the Hunger Market on her way home from work the night before. They forced her to give them her fur coat, overalls, felt boots. She crouched there, naked and freezing, listening to the crunch of boots on the snow, the bandits leaving, when she felt someone fold a leather jacket around her shoulders. She ran home, and this morning when she put the jacket on to go to work, she found a loaf of bread in the pocket. Yes, that was something Pytor would do, take away with one hand, give with the other.

She wills him to return to the city. If he's here, Pytor would go to her bombed-out apartment, then head for the Kirov works, trying to find where she lives now – if she's alive at all. She's moved from one empty or abandoned flat to another so many times – will anyone know where to find her? Pytor wouldn't give up in despair – but where would he go?

Maryushka swings her withered legs to the side of the mattress, with her hands pushes herself up to a sitting position, the effort turning the dusky room into a dark cavern. She waits for the dizzy spell to pass, then stares at her shrivelled feet. Will they hold her? She pulls her boots over her socks, then reaches for the cold stove, pulls herself up, sees stars as if she's fallen on the ice and banged her head.

She lights the wick with her last match. Holds the spoon over it, until the frozen cereal melts, then eats it slowly, a nip and a lick at a time, to make it last longer. Then she pours the last of her water into a cup, heats it too over the sputtering wick, and downs it. Immediately, she feels the terrible need to collapse on her makeshift bed again, fall into a blessed sleep, but with a will born in the city prison and fostered in the Brick Factory for Children, she forces one foot to move, then the other, still using the stove for support, then gropes for and feels her way along the wall to the door.

She knows where to find Pytor.

The Hungry Market.

She reaches for the doorknob, but her knees won't hold her, they buckle, and she falls to the frosted floor.

Using her elbows, she crawls back to her mattress where she lies, listening for a light step on the stairs outside, for Pytor to find her before it's too late.

Pytor

Ice Road, January 21, 1942

OUTSIDE THE CITY, ON A SHEET OF ICE LAYERED with soft, new-fallen snow, Lena drops the babe as easily as a mare her foal. She is surrounded by drivers, each one offering unwanted advice to Pytor:

— *Make a blanket tent for her to keep out the cold.*
— *Give her a shot of vodka, it'll slow her down.*
— *Someone find a doctor, get her to a hospital.*

When it slides into her breeches Pytor is terrified the babe will suffocate, then freeze when he peels away the rabbit skins. The baby is underweight, far from full term as Lena calls it, but it has both arms and legs, no hair or eyelashes or eyebrows. It mewls like a newborn kitten, its eyes large and unseeing.

Two NKVD guards hear Pytor shouting, Lena shrieking, and duck out of the hut. The drivers shrink back and take up positions beside their sleds and sledges, guarding the ponies with their alpenstocks. Pytor won't let the police touch his child or his wife. He clears the baby's nose with his thumb, then tucks the blue girl inside Lena's heavy jacket so she won't freeze while he shrugs out of his own camouflage cape and coat and chemise. He shakes with cold when he takes the babe from protesting Lena again, telling her to hush up. Her Russian spoken with a Swedish accent is dreadful and might give her away.

"Your tattoos," she says, and he keeps his back to the police so they won't see his chest with its wolf, his shoulder with the seagull, and know he was a *zornie,* a street kid born of enemies of the State.

He puts his cross around the baby's neck, wraps her in the chemise, and gives her back to her mother. Then Lena starts grunting again, and he has to dig into her breeches to pull out the rubbery mass of flesh, cut the cord with his switchblade, and throw the afterbirth to the emaciated police dogs, who fight with a frenzy over the raw meat. He feels the heat of frostbite when he quickly pulls on his clothes, then turns to face the NKVD.

When they demand to see his papers, Pytor wants to put out the eyes of the policemen with his switchblade, but his survival instincts kick in, and he begs them to let him take his deaf-mute wife into the city and to a hospital before the baby dies, before his wife bleeds to death. Then he points to the caravan. "I need your help. You must protect my ponies. In two days time, we go back across the ice, this time with as many evacuees as the sledges will hold. We will bring more food to the city until the ice can hold trucks." Then he shouts, "DO YOU UNDERSTAND?"

Finally, they understand. Because he doesn't fully trust the NKVD not to slaughter the horses for food, he bribes them with two bottles of vodka, a basket of frozen sturgeon, and a bushel of cereal from Thor's sledge.

Before he leaves with Lena and the baby, he tells the drivers to build a barricade with rubble from the bombed-out station

PYTOR

to blockade the ponies against starving citizens, Red Army deserters and bands of thieves from the Hunger Market. He puts the *kolkhoznik,* a farmer from the collective at Voznesenie, in charge and tells him, "If the cops make one wrong move, kill them."

Then he takes Lena and their baby towards the city limits, looking for a doctor.

IT'S SURPRISINGLY EASY to enter the city, the route from Lake Ladoga the only way in or out of the blockade. Though he cannot see them, the Red Army is perilously close to the Germans encircling the city, and that knowledge gleaned from many recent broadcasts on his wireless makes his skin creep, as if ants crawl up his spine and around his neck. Added to his constant fear for Maryushka, who is somewhere oh so far from here, is the new anxiety for the mother of his child. He feels as if he has the strength of three horses that should be pulling this sleigh.

And with this new-found, residual energy he didn't know he had, Pytor pulls the troika laden with furs. He doesn't dare harness three horses to the sleigh for fear of being attacked by starving Leningradski. The runners slide easily, smoothly on the ice. Beneath the furs huddle Lena and the newborn, a girl she has named Signe – what kind of a name is that for a Russian child? *A strong one,* Lena had said when she first held her to her breast. If they make it back to Kizhi, Pytor will have the baby christened Elizavita after his mother, Pytronova to indicate she is his daughter, Svetlovna the family name. This child is Daughter of Light, a first ray of hope for Pytor.

"*Russen? Russen?*" Lena calls.

And Pytor calls back, "Yes, yes, they're safe."

He really doesn't care about horses right now. He has to find a doctor.

When he finds what may be the remains of a road, he enters the city. These streets are empty of people.

No automobiles or trucks or trams.

No smoke drifting straight up from chimneys.

He trudges on and on, until icy ruts beneath his *valenki* tell him he's entered an avenue leading straight to the twin towers of Fortel Hospital.

THE IRON GATES OF THE HOSPITAL are closed, bodies of people who made it this far strewn about, some frozen to the iron pickets, hands in a death grip around the rungs. Behind the fence, the hospital looks as if it's just being built, for only iron girders still stand and one concrete wall, the windows of the shells of the towers like unseeing eyes of the dead.

He swings his head to look back at Lena in the sleigh. She says in Swedish: "She's sucking! I think she's angry because milk hasn't come in yet, but she's sucking and kneading my breast."

"Speak Russian or don't talk at all," he says. She always lapses into Swedish when she's excited or afraid. Even though there's no one on the street, he's afraid she'll be overheard by an NKVD patrol and mistaken for a German or a foreign sympathizer.

Pytor trudges on, trying to remember where he will find another hospital, but street signs are gone, so many buildings and houses, the roads and sidewalks not cleared of snow. If he could find the Kirov he'd find Maryushka's apartment. Fear for her, for Lena and his child, spurs him on, his breath steaming before him.

PYTOR

Just when he thinks he should beat a retreat, return to the Finland Station, he recognizes Leo Tolstoy Square by the statue of the great author. The gate to Erisman hospital and the wooden fence gone, likely stolen for fuel. The building still stands, though one wing has disappeared. Mountains of frozen corpses dusted with snow. On the top of a bloody snowdrift lies the head of a girl with blonde braids, the face gnawed away, likely by hungry rats, the eyes hollow and staring. Quickly he glances back at Lena, afraid she has seen the sight too, but she has her head ducked over the babe, crooning a lullaby. He'll have to teach her his ladybug song.

The entrance is strewn with corpses. He wants to carry Lena up the stairs, but she pushes his arms away. She flings back the furs covering her and the child, but lets him take her arm when she clambers out of the sleigh. "I'm fine," she says, but hunches over, and he takes her elbow, steering her up the stairway, one foot at a time.

Inside: corpses in corridors, reception rooms.

THE HALLS ARE CRAMMED with people lying on the floor, on gurneys, with sick people waiting to see a doctor, for an empty bed in an overly crowded ward. Moans. One man with one blue eye and one brown eye laughs and cries at the same time, slapping his head. On benches, people sob or stare into space. Pytor gags against the stench of urine and shit emanating from stained rags and shabby clothes.

Most people are too wrought up, too ill with dysentery or typhus, to notice Pytor and Lena, how their cheeks are round and flushed with health, their clothes don't hang from their bodies like scarecrows. One scrawny child with a face black from starvation and bald patches on his blue skull yells,

"Cannibals!" His mother pulls him onto her knees, shrinks from the sight of people with meat on their bones.

Afraid of being mobbed or attacked by many with crazed eyes, Pytor doesn't know where to go, what to do, but sees a woman wearing a bloody white jacket. A stethoscope hangs from her neck. She bends over a babushka with blood running down her left cheek, and stanches it with a towel. "You need stitches," the doctor says. "Press it, firmly."

"I can't see, I can't see," cries the babushka. "My house fell down and hit me."

"Wait here." She's about to turn into a door with no glass in its window, no lettering, when Pytor catches her arm.

"Please help," he says. "My wife has just delivered a baby." He points at Lena leaning against the peeling wall for support.

The doctor swipes at stringy hair that looks like it hasn't seen soap or even a brush for days. "You'll have to wait your turn."

Pytor throws up his arms. "So many dying, but one child maybe you can save."

"So it can starve?"

"I have food," Pytor says.

The doctor frowns, looks over Pytor's shoulder as if seeking a policeman or a Party boss. "Where did you get it?"

"Here and there, in the country. We've come over the Ice Road, with forty horses loaded, not enough for everyone, but it will help."

"Do you have any bread?"

Pytor has come prepared, and he swings his dufflebag over his shoulder, digs in it and pulls out a loaf of bread wrapped in a red cloth. He offers it to the doctor. She gives it to the babushka, who breaks down, sobs between chest-wracking coughs, thanking the doctor, the strange healthy man, the

Good Lord, and all the saints. She shares it with the children of other patients, breaking it into pieces and passing it down the row of benches.

"Come with me."

Pytor helps Lena shuffle into the doctor's office. The windows are blacked out, but enough light from a candle reveals a scarred oak desk piled with yellowing files, a cabinet with broken glass, a skeleton dangling from a coat rack in a corner. No examination table. Anything that can serve as a bed has likely been taken to the wards. The doctor gestures for Lena to take the metal chair before the desk.

"Baby first," Lena says, in passable Russian. She opens her jacket, and places the bundled baby on her lap.

The doctor kneels. "Let's have a look at you." Lena unwraps Signe, and the doctor gasps, though she's likely seen much worse: missing limbs and sightless eyes of wounded men and women from the front. "How many months?"

"Seven?" Pytor says, answering for Lena, afraid she'll reveal her foreign origins. "Maybe eight isn't so bad, she's got all her parts."

"She should be in an incubator," the doctor says, "but our power plant was knocked out, no electricity for two months." She tucks the ends of her stethoscope into her ears, breathes on the metal to warm it, then places it on the baby's thin chest. She listens, her fatigue-lined face as cold and unrevealing as her instrument. Signe yowls. Finally, the doctor hangs the stethoscope around her neck again, straightens, and leans on her desk. "Her heart is good, lungs a little small." She folds her hands, regarding the candle. "The little ones catch up fast, but these days, with no food –" Her voice trails away, like smoke from a fire snuffed out by snow.

"Isn't there anything you can do?"

"You can try Statsionari, the convalescent centre just opened in the Astoria Hotel. You'll find a little better food there, but it's reserved for scientists, the intelligentsia." She looks at Pytor's red star cap, raises one black eyebrow.

"I have money," he says.

"It's not worth the ink and paper it was printed on, food the only currency now."

"Not a problem. But my wife?" Pytor says. "There was a lot of blood. She's very weak."

"I'll have to ask you to leave the room," the doctor says. Does she want to interrogate Lena? "I need to examine her."

"Oh." Women's business, of course. With his red star cap folded between his frost-burned hands, Pytor leaves the room, only to pace outside, avoiding resentful looks cast his way by waiting patients. They hate him because he's not starving, because he bribed his way in and got to see the doctor, while they have been waiting for days, too many doctors ordered to the front. He needn't be afraid of them. No one has his strength. He feels sorry for them.

When Lena finally emerges from the room she's beaming, all cleaned up, her bloody rabbit breeches gone, replaced by white ski pants and jacket likely left by a mortally wounded patient from the front who no longer needs them. The baby is wrapped in clean blankets and Lena's own red shawl. The doctor has also given Lena towels, a bottle of disinfectant with a skull and crossbones on its label. "What did she say?" Pytor says.

"You are good midwife," Lena says. "Careful I must be not to get – how do you say? – infection. I'm health is good. So much fat she never see since war started." She struggles to find more Russian words to soothe Pytor's fears. "Milk, she come in two more days, and Signe, she get fat like her mama. Keep her warm, we must, and prayers we say, yes."

"Why the poison?"

Lena laughs. "For my bath."

Pytor has a vision of a sauna, hot water steaming, the smell of perfumed soap, oil of the linden. Where in all of Leningrad can he find wood to heat stones? Public baths long since closed.

"How soon can you travel?"

Signe fusses, and Lena holds her up to her shoulder, patting her back, but Pytor thinks Lena is avoiding his question because she cannot lie to him. They must save as many people as the sleds and sledges will bear, evacuate them across Ladoga, then return with more food.

When they leave the hospital, they find a small scoundrel, a gypsy boy with a tasselled cap racing away with one of the fur robes. "Let him go," Lena says, climbing into the troika.

Pytor tucks the remaining furs around Lena and the baby, hiding his bag of food under Lena's feet, noticing her boots are stained with blood.

Now he must find Maryushka, take her out of this city of death.

PYTOR DIDN'T PLAN ON RETURNING to the Hungry Market, but it's on the way to Maryushka's flat, and once there, he decides to trade a bit of bread for a new pair of boots for Lena. She will need them on the return trip across Lake Ladoga.

Before he even enters the marketplace, he's accosted by a short, rotund man with fat and greasy cheeks, a waxed moustache like Hitler's. He's wearing a karakul coat and wolfskin hat, earflaps turned up, new leather boots. He fingers his moustache, his shifty eyes taking in Lena, the high colour of her skin, her plump cheeks. Lena pulls the fur robe higher, careful so Signe can breathe but not be seen.

"Got any food to trade? What would you like, a samovar as good a new, a Chippendale chair for your woman?"

"A new pair of boots for my wife," Pytor says. "Fur-lined if you have them."

"Come with me." The fat little man leads Pytor away from the square, down a winding alley to a brick house that once belonged to a merchant but has seen more prosperous days. He stops before the red door with a wreath of ribbons hanging from a bell. He pulls on the silky rope, and the bell clangs. They wait, ringing footsteps are heard, like a Cossack's spurs clanking on a wooden boardwalk in an exile village. The door swings open, and the head of another greasy-faced man appears beneath a red stocking cap, the kind Scrooge might have worn in Dickens' novel. His black eyes glint in the weak sun. 'Oh good, a living one," he says, and receives a knock on the side of his head from the fat man, causing the tassel on his cap to swing in his crossed eyes.

"Don't listen to him," the trader says. "Good bargains upstairs."

"I'll be right back," Pytor calls to Lena.

"I don't need boots," she says.

"Quick as a wink," Pytor says, and follows the two men inside, leaving open the red door in case he needs to beat a fast retreat. Then up a steep staircase to the second floor, his left hand closed over the switchblade in his pocket.

At the top of the stairs, the taller man with the tasselled nightcap opens another door, steps inside, followed by Pytor, who, suddenly colder than he was outside, waits until his eyes adjust to the dim, darkly red light. Heavy draperies shut out the sunlight, and he doesn't know where the light is coming from – there is no stove in the cavernous room – but it casts an eerie glow on strange shapes hanging from hooks on rods that extend from one wall to another. A foul smell, like that found in an unclean butcher shop when meat has gone bad in summer. Bear carcasses? Then he sees a human hand, too small to belong to anyone except a child, fingers closed in a death grip. He staggers back.

"Get him!" shouts the tallest man with the red cap.

Pytor whips out his switchblade, slicing a long red line across the greasy forehead. He turns and runs, taking the stairs two at a time, the first man who lured him here as hot on his heels as his short, fat legs will allow, but panting.

Pytor slams the door in the fat man's face, hears the hard smack and imagines a broken nose. "Police!" he yells, though none are in sight, and sure enough the doors remain closed, the cannibals don't appear.

He runs to Lena as fast as he can, never has he been so glad to see her. She says, "What happened? Are you fine?"

Without frightening Lena by telling her about the human abattoir or explaining how close their escape, he picks up the axle-tree of the sleigh and pulls as hard as he can, away from the Dostoevsky alleyways, no longer a Peace Market. His legs and even arms feel like jelly. He trembles and shakes, he might have been killed, and he shudders to think what might have happened to Lena and – oh dear God in his dead mother's heaven – to his newborn child. Though he placed the cross belonging to that mother around small Signe's neck, he believes he feels its imprint, cold and heavy beneath his fur-lined clothing. Perhaps it protected him, his family. He sees no one. He hears no voice, not a whisper in the cold, crystal-thick air. Yet, he feels as though someone – out there on that frozen expanse of ice – cared enough about him to save his humbled Russian self so he can look after those he loves now more than that wretched life that was spared. His throat aches so badly he can hardly breathe, and he tucks his chin inside his fur-lined collar so every breath puffs back warmly, blurring his eyes. He vows never to tell anyone about the cannibals of Hungry Market.

What just happened will likely bring bad dreams forever after, and he now feels as if he's wading through deep water instead of snow, skeleton hands like the one he saw hanging from a hook writhing and falling and digging their way down from a sea above, reaching for him. Skulls. Jaws snapping.

But something else has happened to Pytor Petrovich Svetlov.

His thoughts scramble over each other like *zornie* children after grain scattered from a freight car. Yes, with an ironclad will, he will go back onto the Ice Road, with as many evacuees as the sleds will hold, then continue carting food from the country to the Leningradski long after the trucks are moving steadily along sixty routes covering a thousand miles, the Road of Life the final way out of this war-ravaged country.

The final escape will have to be through Finland. Others have done it.

Lena has an aunt in Canada who used to write to Lena and her mother often when Lena lived in Gotland. She told him about her so often all along the river system, at every turning, because she was afraid of her parents' rejection of him and said emigration might be the answer for them. Lena said that her aunt described Canada as a country that accepts people of every tongue. The land is not unlike Russia, with rivers and lakes and poplar and spruce in the north and great expanses of treeless land for growing wheat in the south. There's farmland for the willing worker – or for someone like Pytor who's eager to learn how to till and harvest all that golden grain.

Lena must post a letter to this aunt, and another, as many as necessary to plan their emigration to a land where people are not driven to eat each other, where a man can earn an honest living. He doesn't know what he might do there, perhaps farm or even raise horses, though they could never take the Gotlandruss with them. How sorry Lena will be to leave them behind with her father, a studhorseman and staunch Lutheran who surely would never accept a poacher into his family, never mind a Russian thief.

"Where are we going now?" Lena calls.

He shouts, "KANADA!" He feels as if he's known this decision would come to them ever since Kizhi when she first mentioned the land across the Bering Strait, but first he must find a way to reach that safety. Finland is the only way out now.

WHEN HE REACHES MARYUSHKA'S street, he finds it empty of people, and at first he believes he was so lost in himself he made a wrong turning, but no, there is the courtyard with its stand of lilacs, bare birdberry branches bent under wet snow. Her apartment lies in snow-covered ruins.

Undaunted, he heads for the Kirov steelworks to see if she is there.

He won't leave Russia without her, if he has to hog-tie her and carry her kicking and squealing onto his coal barge.

Already, Pytor and Lena have lost a day, searching for Maryushka from bombed-out rooms to abandoned apartments.

AFTER HOURS OF PULLING THE SLEIGH down empty street after empty street, of searching through five abandoned apartments, and talking to Kirov workers and even some Party bosses, they finally find her lying on a mattress before a cold stove, even more emaciated than the girl he remembers in the Children's Brick Factory. Only a wick in a saucer bereft of oil. Cupboards bare of rations. No wood to build a fire; she had burned her table, bedstead, chairs, books.

He kneels before her, and takes hold of both her blue, clawlike hands. He tucks them under his chin, for a bit of warmth. He feels as if he's floundering in a cold lake, about to sink for the third time, his entire life with Maryushka floating before his eyes.

"You've come," she says. "I waited." She can't finish the sentence, but Pytor understands that she had held on until she could say goodbye to him.

Lena kneels across from him, their infant held out like an offering of hope to Maryushka. He releases his sister's hands so Lena can place their bundled newborn in Mayushka's arms. "Look," she says, "her name is Signe."

Having just been nursed, the baby sleeps, but she burps, then her tiny tongue darts out and licks her upper lip. Maryushka stares at the child as if she sees a ghost. "Lyba," she says.

Pytor is pleased that she's recalling the term of endearment meant for a small, well-loved one. But Maryushka is so gaunt her nose protrudes like a crone's. Her skin is blue, with red blotches, a sure sign of impending death that he saw too often among the derelicts living beneath the city streets. She can't leave him now! Food. He has more than a morsel of bread left in his pocket, even more hidden in Thor's saddlebag, but it's a reason to live that he must give his sister – and fast!

PYTOR

Pytor says, "Your niece needs you to sing the Ladybug song." He's always been used to pretending that danger may be kept outside, that exhaustion and starvation is normal. Seeming to share his thoughts, Lena gives his sister a small bite of a cottonseed cake, as if she isn't worn out from the long trek and hasn't just given birth.

With Signe holding tight to her own little finger, Maryushka says, "I had a baby – for a little while. Her name was Lyba." She tries to sing the Cossack lullaby, but loses her voice in tears after two lines: "*Stanu skazyvat ya skazki* – I will tell you fairy tales – *pyesenki spayu* – and sing you little songs."

Maryushka protests weakly when Pytor lifts her and carries her down the stairs to his sleigh, complaining that he never listened to her so why should she listen to him now, which gives him hope for her survival. She lets him bundle her in furs beside Lena and the baby.

Then he sets off for Finland Station, where the ponies wait under NKVD guard. This time the sleds and sledges will transport as many people as they can bear across the Road of Life that is Ladoga.

IN THE MIDDLE OF A FROZEN FIELD of mangled iron and frosted rubble, Finland Station is full of bedraggled evacuees, who must have heard about the caravan of ponies over the loudspeakers on every corner lamp standard. A long line of emaciated people has formed before three NKVD officers checking documents and issuing coupons for rations to be had in what's left of the cafeteria.

Pytor stops between the depot and the holding pen for the ponies. He's catching his breath, and is stunned to see Lena step down from the troika. He reaches out to her, and she shuffles to him. "Hold baby," she says. "I see Thor." He folds the bundle into his arms, cradling it, lifting the edge of the shawl to make sure the baby is breathing underneath it. Her soft breath mists in the air, and he carefully folds the end over her head again. He lifts his head to speak to Lena, but she is leaning on the top of an iron railway track that creates a rung of sorts for the makeshift enclosure, her arms around the neck of that horse of hers on the other side of the barricade, its massive head on her shoulder, while she strokes its neck. The pony's large eyes bulge, it's long-lashed lids closing down; Thor looks smitten, delirious, even his ears drooping with some kind of equinine love. Pytor doesn't have to hear Lena's voice to know she's talking to that small studhorse as if he's human, showering him with terms of endearment that Pytor has heard many times before but doesn't have to translate because of the silly tone of voice she uses, like a peasant in the first blush of romance. Lifting his child and holding her close to his shoulder and neck, he rocks, feeling jealous of – a horse! No one has ever petted Pytor Petrovich Svetlov! He's a fearless man of the sewers, and he'd never tolerate such nonsense. Nevertheless, this child born too soon will need all her mother's attention. Best to nip this in the bud. "Lena! Lena!" he calls. "Come here! Now! Right now. Do you hear me?"

She does hear him, and she turns her head, her face so glowing with affection for that miniature stud she could provide light for a whole neighbourhood in this wintering city deprived of sunlight and electricity.

Signe starts to yowl, like a basket of newborn kittens after their mother goes mousing, and Pytor is glad of it. "Your baby is hungry!" he yells.

PYTOR

What is Lena doing now? Kissing – a horse's nose!

"HUNGRY!" he yells. "YOUR DAUGHTER."

And too slowly to suit Pytor, Lena makes her way back to him. Thor tosses his head, and nickers, then swings around and trots back to his mares. Lena turns and calls to him, "I won't be long. We'll be leaving again soon."

When she reaches Pytor, he thrusts the bundled and squawking baby into her arms, and shoves Lena's shoulder. "Go feed her."

Lena throws him a look of bewilderment, but treads carefully on sheer ice into the station.

Now, Pytor must see to securing space on a sled or a sleigh for his sister.

THE NKVD OFFICER IN CHARGE of guarding Lena's ponies says, "You need a ticket for your sister. Papers, please!"

Still in the sleigh, Maryushka looks stricken, her pupils so black in eyes far too big for her caved-in face. He must get her ticket then have her join Lena in the makeshift evacuation depot where there's a little food and some warmth beside stoves. She looks frightened, "You haven't got them?"

"A *bashmacki,* he stole them."

"You'll have to give up that seat and give it to someone else," the guard says.

"She can ride in the sleigh with my wife and baby," Pytor says.

"That'll be an extra loaf of bread." He pokes Pytor's ribs, then rubs his fingers together.

Pytor clutches the switchblade he carries in his pocket, but manages to keep it concealed, clenching his teeth. Begrudgingly, he takes his last loaf of bread out of his dufflebag and hands it over to the policeman. Maybe he has children too.

"Look, I'm sorry about the ticket," the officer says, swiping at his Stalinlike moustache, "but I'm under orders. You'll have to go to Smolny Institute."

If it wasn't for Pytor there would be no sleds and sledges, if not for Lena no ponies to pull them. He isn't even sure how many are left, his only concern was Lena and the safe delivery of their child.

"It's all right, Pytor." Maryushka says. "You go." She climbs out of the sleigh, and he catches her before she falls on the ice.

Pytor carries his sister into the crowded station and sits her on a blanket beside Lena who is nursing the baby. Lena rises, and says, "Food I'll get for Maryushka." She disappears into the makeshift food station among a throng of emaciated people holding out rings and books and fur hats to tough but brittle-looking NKVD policewomen guarding cauldrons of watery soup.

Someone touches Pytor's shoulder, and he's afraid he might go berserk and hit the person for no reason other than fear and frustration, but it's one of the sledge drivers, a pudgy, ruddy-faced man from Uglich. "Trouble," he says. "Some bloody black market operator wants to buy a horse."

Pytor follows him outside, dodging among hopeful but starving people, to the supply sledges loaded with food held back for the return trip across the ice.

THERE, IN THE MAKESHIFT ENCLOSURE, now roped well away from the station, the shaggy ponies rest for the trip back to the country. Only their heads may be seen over the barricade of charred wooden beams, train tracks, concrete blocks and bricks.

Pytor asks the Uglich driver, "What about the forty tons we brought?"

"Some drivers did bargain with profiteers, but it was loaded onto trucks and taken to grocery shops." The worker from the Uglich watch factory first arrived at a depot with pocket and wrist watches sewn into the lining of his jacket, ready to trade them for food. Pytor isn't sure he can rely on him, though he was patient enough with Daisy, and even shared cottonseed cakes with her.

"You hope," Pytor says. He doesn't trust anyone.

"There's the troublemaker," the watchmaker says.

It's Ivan the horse trader, still moving with the music, this one *idti na shalymuyu,* unplanned theft. He doesn't have his gang of thieves with him. Pytor hasn't seen him since he tried to buy Lena in the Hungry Market. He must have fallen on hard times, his beautiful grey boots replaced by ordinary *valenki* down at the heels, his sheepskin coat stained with grease.

"You'll have to bargain with him," the driver says to Ivan, backing away. "They're his wife's horses."

Turning on a heel, Ivan sees Pytor and his now-thin face lights up with recognition. "Just the man I want to see," Ivan says. He slaps Pytor on the back. "You still owe me for the boat."

"I'll bring it back in the spring."

"Let me see, if I remember correctly there was also grain, enough oats to feed a whole district porridge for a year." The trader rocks back on his heels, and crosses his arms over his chest. "I'd say five horses and your debt is clear."

"Can't do it," Pytor says. "I need the ponies to evacuate a lot of starving people."

"So you keep your horses. How many sledges of food do you think they're worth?"

"Give me more time – say until the end of summer. I'll fill the hold of the barge with grain from the country and deliver it –"

"Leningradski, they need food NOW. A lot of meat pies I can make with ground horse."

"Look past the end of your nose," Pytor says.

"I"m looking at starving people who will pay for horsemeat."

"Without the horses they'll die walking across the ice," Pytor says, knowing such an appeal to Ivan's better instincts is useless. He has no social conscience as defined by the Party, yet Pytor feels for these starving people who have been ravaged by war. He also has never forgotten how Ivan hit Lena. His hands clench into fists.

Ivan smacks his horse whip against his leather coat.

"Take one step toward those horses and I'll kill you," Pytor says.

The blow across his face is delivered so quickly, so sharply, Pytor reels, loses his balance, falls to one knee, and clutches his face against the pain. His hand comes away bloody. When he looks up, the trader seems to have vanished, but no, there he is: in the middle of the compound going after Thor. The pony rears, shrilling, and the trader cracks his whip over Thor's head. He won't spoil a hide that will sell for bread. Thor's whinny alerts the drivers guarding the ponies, all hardy country boys, who begin to close in on Ivan.

"He's mine!" Pytor says. Blinking blood from his right eye, he rises, and leaps over the ropes into the horse compound, draws his switchblade. "So we fight." Ivan is taller than Pytor, but older – maybe well into his fifties, his muscles gone flabby. They circle, two wolves moving in, the winner will take the kill.

PYTOR

The whip snakes out, zinging, but Pytor ducks. He lunges, the trader steps aside so the knife misses him by a hair.

"If the NKVD see you they'll shoot you both," the Uglich driver warns, keeping a safe distance from the whirling whip.

"This has been a long time coming," Pytor says. "He's a thief without honour."

"You little fucker." The whip lashes out again, Pytor dodging to the right, his instincts sharp as his switchblade. This time, his knife passes under the trader's armpit, and before Pytor can lurch backwards, Ivan has him in his grip, one arm around his neck, the arm and hand holding the switchblade twisted behind his back; and they're locked in a wrestling hold, the bear hug crushing the breath out of Pytor. Then Pytor hears a gunshot, the sound breaks in his ears, and seems to crack the very air as if it were made of ice. The trader slumps, releasing Pytor, who gasps, and then Pytor lets Ivan fall to the ground, his head banging on snow packed down hard by unshod hoofs. Blood pours from a ragged hole in the trader's back, just between his shoulder bones, the sheepskin surrounding it burned black and smoking.

The NKVD officer in charge of the station stands with feet wide apart on the other side of the ropes, holding a smoking gun.

"Thanks," Pytor says, but feels his first double-edged prick of conscience, of guilt. Now he can't ever honour his debt, even if it was owed to a thief.

The man from Uglich in charge of the ponies says, "Better see to your face, Pytor. It's bleeding."

IN THE FIRST AID STATION, Pytor finds Lena leaning against a scarred wall, holding Maryushka and feeding her bits of dry

Red Army rations provided by the NKVD, the real bosses of the army. "Not too much or you'll get sick," Lena says, spooning into Maryushka's gaping mouth a few spoons of concentrated pea soup and dried cranberries washed down with her first half glass of tea in more days than Pytor wants to think possible. When she sees Pytor's bleeding face Lena picks up the bundle beside her and gives the baby to Maryushka to hold, jumps up and rushes to him.

"What happened?" She lowers her voice so she doesn't waken the dishevelled evacuees rolled up and sleeping in blankets on the floor all around them.

"Remember Ivan the terrible horse trader?"

"Sit down. Let me have a look at it." He's barely aware of blood oozing and trickling down his jaw.

Obediently, he takes her place on the bench, tilts his head back and to the side so she can dab at the long slash that runs, by the feel of it, from his right ear to the corner of his mouth; his whole cheek hurts. "Not too deep," she says. "How do you feel?"

"Will I lose my beauty?"

She doesn't laugh at his joke. The wound must be bad. "Dizzy? Weak?"

"Just tired."

In the baby's bundle, she finds one of the clean towels the doctor gave her, and presses it against his face. "Here, hold it, while I see if I can find something – salve, gauze and sticking tape."

Holding the towel against his face, he closes his eyes, listening to Maryushka cooing, the baby burping, she must have just been nursed. Colour returns slowly to his sister's cheeks, though they remain sunken, her eyes hollow. She has no eyebrows or eyelashes. He's only dimly aware of the snuffling and snoring and coughing of emaciated and sleeping people waiting for tomorrow when they hope to leave the besieged city of Leningrad – perhaps forever.

Shortly, Lena returns. "Some first aid station," she says. "But these will have to do." A roll of bandage that looks like it was made from rags. She's holding her own bottle with the skull and crossbones on the label. Bending over him, she pours a liquid the colour of rust onto a cotton ball. "Drop towel," she says. Her Russian still suffers a Swedish beating.

"Will it hurt?" he says.

"Two babies I don't need," she says. She dabs at the cut on his cheek. Only the pressure hurts, his skin bruised as well as slashed.

"I'm glad I can't see myself," he says. "I don't like the sight of blood."

"Hush, almost I am done." She folds a long strip of bandage, places it on his face, then taking his hand, puts his fingertips on the top of the bandage. "Hold."

She bites off two ends of some kind of tape, and sticks the bandage into place at the corner of his mouth. "Letting go," and she tapes the top.

"I need a drink," he says, but there's only a hot mug of weak tea to be found, and he gulps it down, quickly. "I must see to Maryushka's ticket. I won't be long."

"Tell police you are boss of horses! You say who goes, not – how do you say? – functionaries?"

"Everyone must have a ticket," he says. "No special cases."

"Out in cold you go! No!" Lena pulls his cap over his ears, his jacket hood over his head, tying it tight at the neck. "Keep face warm."

Pytor kisses his Lena, then, kneeling, touches the baby's cheek and sleeping Maryushka's forehead with his fingertips.

At the door, he pauses and looks back at his family, Lena the only person who is bright-eyed, her cheeks flushed with health. And bursting with a new feeling he cannot name because it feels good and hurts at the same time, he's gone into the cold again.

It's a long way to Smolny Institute in the city.

THE ICE ROAD IS NOW OPEN, it's the morning of January 21st, 1942, a day Pytor doesn't ever want to forget, not just because this morning his daughter was born. Evacuation tickets are available at Smolny Institute, and Pytor, jaw hanging slack against the pain in his right cheek and nursing patches of red and white frostbite on his hands, blows on his fists, rubs his hands together, then pulls on his mittens, and tucks his hands under his armpits. He stamps his feet, and waits in line for three hours to buy, beg or bribe a bureaucrat for a ticket for his sister.

Finally, over a loudspeaker, the announcement: *Instead of fifty, only twenty-five buses will depart for evacuation points along the Lake.* Shouts and moans and curses and prayers to God erupt from the crowd.

He doesn't need a thermometer to tell him it's 30 degrees below zero. The ice will hold the heaviest truck now.

Thousands of evacuees setting out on their own without a guide are doomed. He notices infants wrapped in towels and shawls.

When it's his turn at the grilled window the functionary says, "Name!" It's never a question, always an order.

"I want to buy a ticket for my wife from Finland Station," Pytor says. "I was told I could get one here." Without identification papers and Maryushka's ration book he hasn't a hope of getting a ticket for her; he presents Lena's forged papers. He won't leave his sister behind.

"Only tickets for buses here. If you're leaving from the Finland Station you'll have to buy your ticket there. Next!"

"You don't know how lucky you are that there are bars between us," Pytor says.

"Next!"

"You heard the man," says a voice behind him. He turns to find a young mother, holding a boy far too old to be held, his long legs wrapped around her waist nothing more than bones shoved into potato sacks wrapped tight and tied with string.

"I'm sorry," Pytor says, and he doesn't mean for holding up her turn in line.

The voice from the loudspeaker continues to rattle: *Evacuation on foot is not permitted.* The route will be patrolled by NKVD guards, who may be bribed with cigarettes or vodka. Nothing ever changes, yet today he is no longer the careless streetwise urchin bent on survival at any cost.

The bus drivers demand bread or flour from the starving evacuees who hand them their tickets.

Pytor watches the first buses leave, smoke drifting straight up from tin chimneys of *burzhuiki* stoves thrust through the roofs. He wants to kill someone – a Nazi, Hitler, especially Stalin for abandoning the Leningradski – but he clenches his fists in his canvas mittens. It hurts his jaws to grind his teeth, and his anger diminishes, melted by the need to hasten back to Finland station in time for his own departure for the Ice Road.

He doesn't know if his women can withstand the trek across the ice again. But to stay here means immediate death for wasted Maryushka. Signe is premature and must be taken to the country where Lena will get enough food to keep her milk from drying up.

Once again, he sets off for Finland Station.

There's a long Ice Road ahead of him.

Lena

The Ice Road, January 22, 1942

THIS TIME, WITH BABY SIGNE AND MARYUSHKA, Lena rides on the first sledge pulled by Thor.

The NKVD officer who took Pytor's bread and sent him on a goose chase to Smolny Institute looked sheepish and turned his back when Pytor lifted Maryushka onto the sledge. He was hungry too. Lena thinks that forgiveness must be new and strange to Pytor, but probably a good feeling he can't yet imagine keeping for his own.

They follow the waymarkers, red flags Lena staked in the ice only three days ago. Since then, the ice has thickened to the needed depth to hold an endless column of trucks. Graders clear the rough surface, widen the narrow Ladoga Road that extends into white infinity, leaving high walls of snow, so the small caravan tunnels its way, passing truck repair shops, AA batteries in ice-block shelters, wood stacked outside, barrels of gasoline.

Amazingly, it's so much easier going this time, not just because Lena rides on a sledge with her sister-in-law and other evacuees bundled in furs. Every kilometre, traffic officers in white camouflage capes, direct them forward, waving white flags for Go, red for Halt.

From time to time, they must pull over, or stop, to allow food supply trucks heading for Leningrad to pass them. The drivers, who must have heard about the heroic ponies but still can't believe their eyes, wave or shout from side windows, cheering them on through snow beginning to flurry, the wind rising and breathing across the drifts created by graders.

When they reach the western shore, Lena is blinded by headlights sweeping over snow and ice. So little room to pass, the road so narrow here, and roadside they find the first overturned car, its passengers who had set out on foot, dead only a few yards from it. "Poor souls," Lena says to Maryushka, who might have been one of them. Maryushka snuggles deeper into her furs, only her sharp nose sticking out, rimed with frost. Lena worries that Maryushka may be too weak to survive the crossing.

Once on the Ice Road, Leningrad far behind them, they discover first aid stations being built at frequent intervals where Pytor allows rest stops. He likely loathes the necessity, but he must make the rounds, stopping at each of the sleds and asking, "Have you any dead? Throw them out!" Two or three corpses left behind every kilometre lighten the loads, the ponies paying no-never-mind, they're used to the dead and dying now, no longer rearing or rolling red eyes, ears pricked in fear, nostrils flared at the smell of death.

At the first rest stop, Pytor brings Maryushka a small bowl of hot cereal, her second cup of tea, Lena insisting she not gobble it, eat slowly, slowly. Lena's milk has come in early, and proudly she nurses Signe in front of the male drivers, villagers and farmers, who, not used to seeing a breast bared in public, avert their eyes only after Lena places her shawl over Signe's head to keep her warm.

Before they clamber back onto the sled and sledges, the haggardly thin evacuees bow before Pytor, kiss his hand, as if he's a czar returned, a lord of the Lake. He drops his head, flushing to the roots of his wild matted hair. "I am proud of you," Maryushka says.

Across the ice by moonlight. The night bitterly cold, yet they hit a patch of open water, slosh around it on ice with an inch of water lying on top of it. Thor plods, his cleats clicking when they encounter clear ice, his head tossing. A convoy of lorries swings into view before them, lurching and motors grumbling, black smoke spiralling from exhaust pipes; they drive without lights for fear of Luftwaffe bombers.

Pytor looks back quickly, checking on his wife and baby and his sister. Their breath steams whitely in the dark. Lena gives him a small wave: *yes, we're fine*. He tugs on Thor's reins, "*Hopp! Hopp!* Make way for the truck, Boy." Thor never likes to be told where to go, and he pulls left instead of right, his left front and back hoofs slipping, he's down, on his side, sliding towards a crevice opening as if struck by strafing bullets. The sledge tilts, like a boat listing, its runner scraping the ice, throwing the evacuees onto the ice away from the hole. Lena and the baby tumble off the sledge in a bundle of rolling furs, narrowly missed by the lorry, followed by Maryushka who lands on top of them. It happened so fast Lena didn't see it coming, the accident, and she holds Signe tight, lying still and stunned for a moment. Maryushka groans.

The trucks rumble past, blocking Pytor's way, the space between them and the overturned sledge too narrow to allow him to reach Lena, who has the baby bundled inside her heavy jacket, and is shoving Maryushka. "No!" Pytor yells. "Open water!" Lena pulls Maryushka back on top of her, holding on for dear life. She's so emaciated Lena barely feels her weight, her shrivelled face puckered next to Signe's. The baby whimpers, nuzzling under Lena's chin.

The other pony drivers hang back, helpless, afraid to approach lest their added weight widens the hole in the ice. Women evacuees thrown into the snow farther back begin to sob, the old pray; they've come this far, dear Lord let them make it to safety, to food and a fire. The last of the trucks stops, careening to a halt, dangerously close to the crevice, to the floundering pony, shrilling in the dark.

Lena's pony slides into the hole, the empty sledge skidding after him but stopping on the edge of the huge crevice. His front hoofs scrabble on slippery ice, but unable to find footing, he can't heave his heavy body out of the freezing water, the reins taut and tugging, the sledge slowly sliding towards the open water. Thor's eyes roll, redly, long teeth bared, ears flattened; he thrashes. Lena feels his panic rushing through her own body like an electric shock.

The driver of the lorry jumps out of his truck. "Help!" Pytor yells. "Take the back of the runners and pull, I'll push from the front." But it's no use, though they shove and haul with all their strength, they can't budge the sledge. There isn't time to unhitch some of the mares and use them to pull Thor out of the freezing water.

Lena is desperate to help Thor. "Roll off," she says to Maryushka, "away from the hole. Be careful!"

Maryushka is sitting up now, looking like she's just awakened from a good dream to discover herself in the middle of a waking nightmare. Lena checks Signe to make sure she's still breathing, wisps of the baby's breath wafting whitely to meet her own.

From its sheath, Pytor pulls his Finnish skinning knife, slashes the leather trailing on the ice, and the sledge stops sliding. Lena shouts, "Don't cut! He'll sink!" But the sledge and pony are too heavy to pull back onto the newly created Ice Road.

He quickly ties the reins attached to the *duga* around Thor's thick neck to the front fender of the idling army truck. "Back up," he yells at the driver, who steps backwards, then climbs into the cab. Then Pytor inches as close to the hole as he dares, reaching for the yoke.

"Be careful!" Lena shouts. She helps Maryushka to her unsteady feet. "Can you hold the baby?" She takes Signe out from under her jacket and tucks her inside the man's greatcoat that Maryushka wears, then drops to her knees, and crawls to the edge of the hole beside Pytor.

"Come to me," she says to Thor. His front hooves scratch the ice, his back legs bunching, but he's can't heave himself out of the icy water that rises and sloshes in a widening pool, in the reflection of the winter moon.

The truck motor grinds, the wheels spin, digging into the ice. The driver sticks his head out of the window. "Can't do it!" he yells. The truck might break through the ice, widen the hole, and Lena and Pytor will fall into the freezing water.

They stretch their arms but can't reach the yoke or even the ragged reins slapping the jagged edge, the pony screaming now.

"Try again, that's it, come to me, Thor."

"You're too close, you'll fall in too," Pytor says. "Back away!"

Weak and freezing, Thor loses his grip, front hoofs sliding, he sinks, submerges, then rises again, only his head out of the

LENA

water, great black eyes glowing in the dark. Each time he goes down, he pulls the sledge closer to the edge of the gaping hole, creating a small bank of snow. Fissures widen with a heart-wrenching crack.

Maryushka rocks the baby, crooning.

"Please, dear God," Lena whispers. "No. Not my Thor. Don't take him." The pony sinks again, then rises, only his blunt snout surfacing, blowing steamy breath, his last. The third time he doesn't rise again. She watches black bubbles rising and bursting, praying that Thor will leap out of the ice water and fly onto the shelf that holds her safe. There is a long, black moment. When Thor doesn't resurface, only then does Lena curl on the ice, weeping. With her mittens she frantically swipes at the snow, clearing a patch, as if on a frosted window. Beneath the ice, the body of her horse drifts, its tiger-striped back bumping against the ice crust.

Pytor thanks the lorry driver for stopping, for trying to help. The man is almost as emaciated as the people Lena and Pytor transport to safety, even his moustache thinning, his face sallow in the moonlight. "We lost half our convoy to the bloody Nazis," he says. "Watch out for burning trucks, melting ice." They slap each other's shoulders, and the driver leaves them, wishing them good luck.

With the truck gone, Pytor lifts Lena to her feet. She beats her fists against Pytor's chest. "Why did you cut him free?"

"There was nothing else to do."

"You beast! Beast! Beast!" He folds her arms and fists and holds her so tight she finally loses her breath and the last of her energy; she slumps against him, and he lifts her and struggles to a sledge, settles her between baskets of frozen fish, and covers her with furs. He rearranges boxes, piling one on top of the other, sacrificing some to make more room. Then he fetches and carries Maryushka and the baby, and tucks them in beside Lena who feels numb now, inside and out.

They lose another half hour while the farmers from Mandrogi redistribute Thor's load of evacuees to other sleds, righting the sledge. Pytor heats water over a kerosene stove to make tea that Lena refuses till he reminds her she has a child who needs her milk, drink, drink for Signe Elizavita Svetlovna.

Then Pytor settles weeping Lena and bawling Signe and grimly silent Maryushka on the sledge again, allowing the six weakest evacuees from Leningrad to ride in the troika pulled by three horses.

They push on, Pytor straining against the weight of the sledge bearing his wife and sister and daughter bundled in furs, the silence of the wasteland of ice heavy upon them.

Finally, Maryushka says, "It was only a horse. Be thankful it wasn't your baby."

Lena wants to yell at her sister-in-law that Thor wasn't just a horse – not ever! She says, "He was my horse. He once saved my life and I failed to save his."

She lays her head against the bundle in her arms, and closes her eyes, refusing to talk to her sister-in-law though she can almost hear her mother saying to her: *No good will come of that.* Thor was ten years old, with white hairs like pin feathers around his nose, his eyes rheumy, but he was still strong, and oh, so faithful.

Maryushka falls asleep, and snuffles and snorts, the sounds irritating Lena's raw nerves. She feels hollow, empty of her own past, without Thor. Yet, her breasts replenish themselves, the pain a reminder of her new responsibility for another person who will never know a special forest horse named Thor. Lena vows to be faithful to his memory by telling her daughter Thor stories when she's older, surely in a time of peace and plenty.

THREE MORE REST STOPS, and they smell burning rubber and gasoline and grain, the sweet smell of scorched sugar and sizzling fat, before they come upon a wrecked convoy, trucks overturned like turtles on their backs, twisted metal frames, scorched shreds of canvas, fenders with jagged bullet holes. Dead drivers hang out of windows, lie half buried under trucks, scattered on bloody drifts.

The drivers boil water for tea on glowing ashes. The evacuees dig in ruins, scrape blackened sugar, and find crates of concentrated pea soup that were flung wide and landed in the snow. They pry off the lids, and drop the packets in tin cups, scoop up fried cereal to make *kasha,* with powdered milk dissolved in hot water.

Watching them, Lena lets Pytor rock her and Signe. He tells her to be thankful it was only a horse, not the baby, but she was there when Thor breeched, sliding onto wet moss, and she rubbed him down, helped him find first footing, taught him to pull a pony cart, not to shy on the road to Visby when a motorcar rumbled towards them.

"He took me to school every day – and home again." Home is Gotland. And then the home-longing overtakes her, and nothing Pytor can say or do will take it away, not even his brand new promises to return when this blasted war ends.

She pushes him away, changes the baby's towel diaper, her hands shaking with cold, then tucking the bundle back inside her jacket, she rises. "Let's go," she says. "These people we mustn't fail."

WHEN THEY REACH THE FAR SHORE, the evacuees from Leningrad tumble off the sleds, fall to their knees, some crying, until they hear voices raised in song, and see lights of lanterns waved by villagers on the embankment. Then country folk in heavy fur-collared coats and sheepskin *valenki* boots come running, they weep at the sight of ponies high-stepping across the ice, bearing the first survivors from Leningrad. Women wrapped in red shawls carry between them steaming vats of cabbage borsht, the aroma strong enough to bring strong-willed men to their knees.

It's only the first round trip across the Ice Road, though Lena can't imagine or guess how many there will be before either the Allies or the Axis wins and this war ends.

EACH TRIP, EACH WINTER OF THE SIEGE, more ponies are lost, the twins Frej and Freja in a storm, Daisy lugging the load of fodder, falling through the ice at an unexpected patch of open water, and six more, stolen by NKVD guards, slaughtered and sold to black market profiteers for twelve cases of vodka. The tally mounts, but with sixty truck routes covering a thousand miles, rations are soon increased in the city, and one million people are saved from the Wolf, another million taken across the Ice Road.

No one knows how many months or years of blockade lie ahead. Lena and Pytor and Maryushka will carve out one winter at a time, each one a day that never ends.

Signe

The Island of Kizhi, June 2004

IF THERE IS AN OLD BELIEVER IN ALL OF RUSSIA, surely Signe will find him on Kizhi. Here, Lena and Pytor hid from NKVD patrols looking for foreigners. Maybe, Signe will meet a holy man like the Father Viktor of Lena's ice story.

Far ahead, Kostja leads the birders towards The Church of the Transfiguration. Built in 1714 by Peter the Great to commemorate the defeat of the Swedes in the Northern War, it rises on the flatland, like a mirage in wood, its twenty-two cupolas and aspen shingles shimmering like silver through the waning mist. The tourists step aside or kneel on the footpath, and their digital cameras blink like fireflies. The local guide tells the story of Nestor, who built the massive summer church without nails, using only one tool, an axe, then he hurled it into Lake Onega, proclaiming, *"Ne brylo net, I ne budet takoi,"* and Signe feels the truth of Nestor's words: *There never was, nor will there ever be again such a thing.*

Yes, Signe has been here before. Then, with a child's faith, she believed the church was made from silver; she saw how it caught the light and held it, so it shone even when the sun went to bed.

The Kizhi guide says, "During the Time of Troubles, the Russian settlers here were at the mercy of Swedes." During the Second World War, for five years, Signe's parents were at the mercy of Nazi bombers, the Wolf at the gates of Leningrad, but here they found refuge. Now, the island is at the mercy of American tourists, who are warned against smoking on the island. A motley bunch, men in sweat-stained Tilley hats and women toting bulging carry-on bags over drooping shoulders, they step carefully on the path, heads down, watching for poisonous snakes in the grass.

This is what she came to see: Old Russia. Ahead and closer now, the Kizhi ensemble of church, chapel, bell tower, peasant house and barn, windmill and bathhouse is an original song in wood calling her home.

Signe, say good morning to the trees.

The first stop: a Russian settlers' ornately decorated log house likely far beyond the dreams of her immigrant mother in Canada. Maybe Lena and Pytor found shelter in an *izba* here. There was a house belonging to a hermit in their story. Signe can't know if she was told about it so often she pictured it as if it were her own memory, or if she really did live in it for her first five years. Oh yes, she has seen this house before! Or one just like it, perhaps. How can she be sure? She was only five years old when she left for Canada.

Something makes her look up: on the balcony, Kostja leans over the corner balustrade and at first she assumes he takes a photo of her because he lowers the camera for a moment and smiles at her. Then he squints again, raises the camera, and photographs the small but ancient graveyard stretching away between house and church. Her view of it and the sea behind it is so much better she wonders why he doesn't photograph it from below, something to do with perspective perhaps.

So unlike the Livelong graveyard surrounded by blue spruce that shelter her parents' graves, this Russian place of the dead is defined by wooden crosses and markers that look like troika yokes. Graves. Signe doesn't want to think about it, but cannot prevent herself from seeing Sasha's grave in Regina, the white picket fence enclosing a riot of wild tiger lilies. She doesn't want to think about her son, how nothing she can say to him will convince him that it was an accident, that he didn't kill his sister. He can't even ride a bus now, go to a café for a milkshake, he's so afraid everyone who sees the purple side of his face with its missing ear will know he was reckless and wild, a show-off who thought only of himself, how he wanted to impress the girls in their bikinis on the beach.

The field of yellow flowers stretches beyond the house like the prairie towards an infinity better said in Russian: *prostor.* And Signe sees her five-year-old self beyond the horizon: the wild Livelong child tearing barefoot, down the grassy hill to the Turtle River, her mouth and white Sunday dress berry-stained, hair ribbons unravelling and flying like banners of freedom.

Still angry at being taken across a vast ocean from her home in Kizhi to yet another place empty of people, she acts up in Canada, and is now in trouble for laughing when Aunt Maryushka farted, for not changing into her overalls after Sunday School, for gobbling down strawberries meant for her mother's upside-down-cake, for forgetting to gather birchbark kindling for the stove. She crawls through the barbed wire fence, ripping her best skirt. Scolding crows flutter up from the bush. In the field, she leaps from boulder to boulder, the sky turning above, a song rumbling in her belly, then rising to her throat; she sings madly, the tune of her own making, arms lifted to the expanding sky. There is no known language for the song of rocks. She imitates the gurgle of water rushing clear and smooth over the beaver dam and burbling over stones.

Her word for wolf is the lonely call it makes in the night. She sings to the herefords, a lowing, mimes the chewing of their cud. Workhorses lift their heads from a saltlick, and she nickers so they will know her name: Signe.

Tomorrow she will be kept indoors, this untameable child, harder to catch than a cat refusing to come out from under a granary. She will eat more garden peas than she will shell, knock her father's icons from the Red Corner with the flyswatter, count chickadees in the hollyhocks outside the kitchen window and spill the vinegar instead of cleaning the glass, until her mother won't be able to stand her any longer and will send Signe outside with a pail of slops to feed the chickens.

Signe wants to catch that child, but no, best to let her run freely unafraid again.

She hasn't been home to Livelong since Lena died, the farm rented out on a sharecrop basis to a family that lives in town, and now she wonders if a holiday in the homeplace might help her son. A picnic by the river, yes. But gone the house, granaries, barns.

The last time she drove out to the northern Saskatchewan farm only the spruce-lined lane remained, Lena's weed-choked garden, a hole full of rocks and rubbish where once the farmhouse faced the road, the well with its pump. New aluminum silos replaced the old granaries Pytor built. Tractors and a combine housed in a quonset hut big enough for a festival of ghosts. Turned on its side, the old caboose, only peeling patches left of its red paint. She opened the side door, and out flew a land gull, and with it the memory smacking her in the face of a squab she had found there, one wing broken, and how she fed it milk with an eye dropper and bits of bread, until one morning when she returned to the caboose she found it stone dead. She ran, crying, to her papa. Pytor wiped her tears with the handkerchief he always carried in his overall pocket. He made a last resting place for the bird in a cigar box lined with cotton batting, then buried it beside the river. A multi-patched, red star cap folded between his work-thickened hands, he said a prayer in Russian she couldn't understand, except for one word: *ptitsa*. Bird.

For her birthday, he gave her a canary in a yellow, wooden cage he made himself, with leaf-scrolls painted green.

Lost in the wilderness of northern Saskatchewan, Signe hasn't been listening to the guide, who announces that it's time to go inside the Russian farmhouse.

IN GROUPS OF TEN, the tourists enter the main room that once served as kitchen, living and sleeping room. Signe can imagine Lena here, learning how to make blini and borsht for her Pytor.

Immediately drawn to the immense Russian stove, the sleeping platform Lena had told her about, Signe fails to imagine how an entire family could sleep in tiers, even the trundle bed sliding out from the bottom near the women's corner. When she grew too big for a cradle, perhaps she slept on such a bed. She tries to photograph it, but birders keep getting in her way.

Waiting for them to leave the room and enter the guest bedroom, she remembers sleeping beneath a window and a man's heavy hand brushing her hair away from her brow. Sometimes, calloused palms caught her cheeks between them and roughly rubbed them till they burned, and her eyes swam with angry tears. Her mother and father were gone, and she was terrified they would be swallowed by the Frost Giant who had covered the windows with ice so thick even her own breath wouldn't melt a circle clear enough for her to see if Lena and Pytor and the ponies were returning across the lake. In the guest room, her aunt lay weak and wheezing, and there was nothing to do but huddle by the tiled stove. Her rag dolls, Erica and Yonny Yonson, lay listless in her lap.

Kizhi, Winter 1946

AND THERE HE IS, the ugly man who cooks her borscht but can't coax or force her to eat it. He's long in the face, the black beard pulling down his cheeks and smothering lips as red as pickled beets. He's whittling again, the chips flying up and scattering at his booted feet. He blows on the wood, holds it up to the light, then grunts, and taking the carving with him, he disappears into the byre. Good.

In the other room, Auntie moans in her sleep, likely dreaming again of ladybugs crawling across the high ceiling beams and cascading down the logs onto her bed. Sometimes, she even sings the ladybug song in her sleep, though sing isn't really the right word, it's more like a high call of the first rook when the last of the snow leaves the island and the birds return from wherever they go in winter. Maybe they follow the Swedish ponies trekking across the frozen lakes with food from the big man's root cellars. He doesn't know what to do with Signe, how to get her to stop crying in her sleep, to try just a little of his good soup, maybe skate on the lake when the weather clears. She won't talk to him, not because she hates him so much as – well, he isn't her father. Signe doesn't understand why her mother has to leave her every winter, why doesn't the man with ropes holding up his horse-blanket dress go instead, and if he doesn't want to get caught by the police he should cut off his long beard and hair and wear ordinary clothes like her father, a blousy shirt and pants tucked into warm boots. Oh yes, Signe could tell the people she lives with a thing or two, if she felt like it.

She picks up Erica and Yonny Yohnson, and knocks their woolly heads together, but plops them unceremoniously in their wooden doll's cradle when the big man tromps back into the kitchen. He bangs the doors behind him. He's carrying a wooden box, but she pays him no mind. He sets the box on the table beside the window, then takes bread wrapped in cheesecloth from the larder and slices two pieces. Then, from the bucket of icewater he takes a jug of milk and pours it into two glasses usually meant for tea. Seating himself on the bench at the table with his back to Signe, his big shoulders block her view of the table, not that she really wants to see what he's going to do with the box.

Without turning around to look at her, he says, "Girl, I want to show you something."

"I'm not hungry," she says. She crosses her arms and hits her sides with her elbows. So there. Try and make me.

He lifts the box and shakes it. Something in it rattles. "Not food." he says.

She stands on tiptoes, but can't see over his massive head, although it's ducked over the box. She inches closer, and suddenly his whole body whirls and one large and long arm circles her waist and lifts her and plunks her down on his hard knee. He grips her so tightly it's hard to breathe. "Now sit you still and watch." He lets go, and just as she tries to jump up, he paws her shoulder and shoves her down again.

"You can't make me." she says.

"Just look," he says. He slices the bread into long fingers. "This one," he says, "is your mamma, and she's so thirsty, but there's no milk on the ice." He takes another thin piece of bread and says, "This one is your papa, but no tea for him."

Signe knows that one-for-mamma and one-for-papa trick to get babies to eat their mush. "I'm not a suckie baby!" she says.

"This is the lake." He spills and spreads sugar on the oilcloth. "And here is the milk they need to keep strong." He pours milk into a saucer. Then he dances the breadcrusts towards it, but the wind of his breath knocks them down into the sweet snow. "What shall we do to help them cross the ice?"

"Ponies!" she cries, in spite of herself.

And out of the wooden box march four ponies, each carved in a different running position. The old man takes the Mamma bread and sits her on one of the ponies, then "gallumph gallupmph, across the ice we go, but oh no! Wind is too much and down we go." The Mamma bread falls into the lake, and he rolls her onto her feet, she's all covered with sugary flakes. The pony lies on its side, but brave Mamma bread tippytoes up to the saucer and leans forward and takes a long drink, and then along comes a giant with bulging black eyes and a beard down to his knees and he's got long sharp teeth and he bites off the head of the mama bread.

"I'll save you!" Signe cries. And she puts the Papa bread on the second pony that's rearing on its hind legs, and off they gallop, but the pony slips on the ice-sugar and falls, and she rolls the bread in the flakes and marches it up to the milk and dunks it head-first, then takes a big bite, the milk sweetened by the sacrifice of her father to save the people.

SIGNE

And so the ice game goes on, winter day after winter day, until Christmas when Auntie is in charge of ponies made of gingerbread and the giant girl named Signe eats only the ears and tails while watching out the window for Father Christmas to bring safely home her mother and father, who must be nice and fat because of all the sugar bread she ate and milk she drank for them.

And then, one morning through the windows there's a new spot, and another, and then many, and soon they take the shape of ears and flying hooves, and the sound of runners scraping ice comes just before the nickering and snorts and calls of high-stepping ponies headed for barn and mangers full of sweet hay. They number more than the ponies in the wooden box that kept Lena and Pytor safe from the Frost Giant's breath.

NOW, IN FRONT OF THOSE WINDOWS overlooking Lake Onega, a weaver's loom and a spinning wheel to fill the idle days of Lent when flax took on its magic powers. And there, at the pinewood table, a woman appears, wearing the traditional headdress decorated lavishly with pearls from mussels found in Lake Onega, and tendrils escape from the cap as fragile as seaweed, as grey as ashes. Peasant blouse, skirt and red jumper. She embroiders a pillowcase with red thread. *Upset with you, I am,* she says. *I never see you anymore.* She lifts her head to reveal the triangular face, bow-shaped lips and gap-toothed smile of Signe's Aunt Maryushka, called Little Mary even when she was old because, Lena said, she never grew for want of food.

"Auntie, I didn't know you were here, or I would have come sooner."

No excuse. It's your mamma's doing, that hothead. She's still angry with me for eating her flowers. She got stuck with the poacher, my bas-macki brother, you know.

"I'm sorry. I promise to see you often."

Every Sunday for dinner. Bring your mother, no excuses.

"Auntie, it's not my fault."

Signe, never would you allow yourself —

"— to enjoy much in life."

Too much you love to suffer. Too much Russian in you. And whose fault is that?

"You don't know what happened to me!"

I know enough. You were born on the Ice. You are survivor!

Why didn't she tell Signe that before, so she would understand?

"Auntie, I've been weeping all across your land — for joy." Signe hears an echo of her aunt's voice in her own.

Yes, it is so good you crrry. CRY, *Golubchik, my dove, Dushenka, my little soul.* CRY!

Khudaya. The word *thin* equates with *bad* in old Russian. Signe remembers Maryushka as fat, never satisfied; she couldn't ever consume enough food, but now Maryushka is almost emaciated, her skin pale and transparent as parchment. She wears an amulet necklace. According to the myths Signe learned at her elders' knees, amber was formed from the tears of people weeping over the tombs of fallen heroes. It fails to hide Maryushka's collarbones, brittle as egg shells. If Signe took her in an embrace she would crumble into dust. Is this what Signe will look like when she's old?

"My mother — Lena — is she here too?"

Mmmm, yes and no. Your mamma, she went to sleep. Wait and watch for her, with lighted torch at night. You, Dushenka, wait by window for your mamma, I fix soup. Lena, she bent so low she did washing for Swedish navy, a Martha, that one, better to be a Mary like me and bathe feet of Jesus. But I want to know about this birding man. Be wary of Rusalki, *the water spirits who take their pleasure by luring young men and tickling them to death until they drown.*

"Oh, he's just a friend."

Too much like my brother he is, no? All clammed up, feeling words but refusing them.

"He's a scientist, a birdwatcher."

He should see instead mermaids combing their hair on the footbridge near boathouse, if he wants good fortune in work. You, Dushenka, draw a bath, with herbs and kvass from fermented bread and within one year you will be married again, but not to this man. Remember, it takes three horses or one Russian woman to turn mill post.

"What is that supposed to mean?"

Be off with you! To Church of Lazarus for healing. You can't miss it; it looks like big boat. Russian Lazarus, he was assassinated, but Great Light blinded his killers. Bell-ringer never died.

Signe's Aunt Maryushka was raised as a Soviet and forced to reject all traces of her aristocratic ancestry as well as the faith of her mother, yet once free to roam the Canadian bush and pastures the soul of a peasant emerged, and with it the wisdom of those who lived and loved this land.

Wait! Do not forget Radonitsa!

"I don't know what that means."

For shame! That is why we must return to the place of our ancestors. Everything is forgotten in New Land. On Remembrance Day, you take food to graveyards for departed ones and provisions you give to the poor, you must do this. Promise!

Remembering how her mother and aunt took Swedish lifebread and Russian blini to Pytor's grave in Livelong, and even poured coffee from a thermos on the soil around the tiger lilies, Signe says: "I promise. For Sasha, I will do this."

Maryushka disappears, leaving her embroidery on top of the table. Into the border of the pillowcase she has worked *Dushenka* among petals fallen from the stems of snowdrops. It means: My Little Soul.

So much Aunt Maryushka tried to teach Signe when she was alive, and now Signe must stare at the hard face of her own regret at not having listened to her, never mind the folly of youth. She needs an Old Believer, not her father.

Through the front windows, Signe sees Kostja entering the Russian bathhouse on the river bank.

THE SAUNA LOOKS LIKE ANY OLD OUTBUILDING on a northern Saskatchewan farm, but unlike the small barns and henhouses, the bathhouse's aspen walls still haven't weathered badly, though it must be as old as the farmhouse. Both have been restored so well they look newly built.

Inside, the air is steamy, and she hesitates at the door connecting a small dressing room and the steam room. The window is still clear enough for her to see the crystalline stones and rocks piled to create a stove without a chimney. On the bathing platform, Kostja, his loins wrapped in a towel, throws a bucket of water on the rocks, and steam explodes in his face. To heat the rocks he must have been in the sauna the whole time she was in the farmhouse.

A pretty girl is not afraid when a man sees her in the bath, but an ugly girl is frightened to death. Is same with man, I say. Go away, Aunt Maryushka!

None of the Intrav or local guides said anything about whether or not anyone on the tour could have a Russian steam bath – or even swim in the lake. The island is a heritage site, and Signe is surprised that Kostja took this risk, this liberty, unless he has obtained permission to take a bath after the tourists and birds have left this part of the tour and gone on to the souvenir kiosks.

"Come in or go out," he says. "You are letting in cold air."

Signe steps inside, and closes the door, not sure of Russian etiquette, if women are allowed when men are in the *banya*, though surely families bathe together. "I thought you'd be birding."

"The Americans, they're kissing the walls of Lazarus' church, trying to make better their teeth. I think maybe they get splinters in their gums."

"I don't believe you."

"They make fun, but is true place of miracles. A Russian knows this."

What if a person is only half Russian? Is only one half of the truth then revealed to her? Suddenly Russian rises to her throat: *parit'saya,* and she says, "*S lyokim parom!* Well, I'll leave you to your *banya*," but she looks about for a place to sit, without getting her clothes wet. The bench is sopping, so she just leans against the doorframe. If he invites her to join him she just might shuck her clothes like a cocoon.

"Oil of the linden. Is good for the skin." He slathers his chest. Sweat drips down his long, aristocratic nose. Should she offer to oil his back? Or beat him with a birch broom? Is that what a good Russian woman would do? If his wife is a botanist, their apartment must be filled with a profusion of greenery, a hothouse of flowers: ivy, heliotrope in windows, jasmine jardinieres on landings, camellia bushes in corners, orchids around lamps

"Are you real? I mean, Russia is getting to me. I'm beginning to see things. I think it's time to go home." Or take a vow of chastity. Well, as Aunt Maryushka used to say when visiting her Finnish neighbours: nothing like a jump in winter waters to cool one's ardour. Aunt Maryushka made it very clear that Finns call it sauna, but the correct Russian word is *banya*.

Kostja brushes past her, emanating heat, his skin smelling richly of linseed and soap. Through the door, she follows, and he's crashing among willows, charging onto the dock, with a whoop he dives into the cold waters of Lake Onega. A spray of water, like one of the fountains at Petrodvorets, the Summer Palace, and he emerges, arms raised in a salute, shaking water from his fly-away hair. He rolls in the water, like a Siberian seal.

At the farm, during those long ago summers, Mamma took Signe to the Turtle River, its bottom muddy, and there she learned to dog paddle, while her elders floated on their backs away from the beaver dam, their long hair fanning in the water, golden skin glistening in the young light.

THEY HAUNT THE WOODS on her father's Livelong farm, the women in her family who have gone before her.

They take after their horses, though they galumph like the cows they chase home for milking, heads down, rumps swaying, this wife and sister and daughter of a horse thief.

They head for the Turtle River. Signe picks strawberries as wild and red as her hair. Named for the valkyrie who carried slain warriors to Valhalla, so strong at sixteen, she can lift in each arm a stook as heavy and tall as a man. As sleek and skitterish as a racehorse at the starting gate, she high-steps through pine and poplar shivering towards the water.

Signe finally got out, and fled to the city. She jumped the

gate and ran as fast as Kajsa Maja, the runaway racer Lena named after a gypsy queen who once could be heard singing in the Hangman's House at the North Gate of Visby, her home city in Gotland.

Small Maryushka gathers in her apron birchbark and wood chips, bluebells like *skogsstjärna* Lena transplanted on her husband's grave, the woodflowers of her homeland.

Every morning, Lena bridled the mare, hitching to the child's sleigh the skitterish Kajsa Maja to carry Signe down the railway tracks to Patchgrove School built by Outlanders so their children wouldn't speak broken English.

Never step behind a stalled horse and get kicked in the head, the women warn, that's how the horseman, Pytor, finally met his Maker.

The women shuck their ginghams and sunhats, as easily as peeling silk from corn husks. Naked in the muddy-green water, their hair let down and streaming like manes, their rippling bodies gleam in haloed light.

They remain etched forever in northern light falling over the rainbow bridge linking their Livelong woods to Kizhi's.

SIGNE'S HEART ISN'T RACING, she's not sweating, or feeling nauseated. Maybe it isn't the water she fears so much as the fear itself, what it does to her. Wait now, get a firmer grip on this. When she lost her children – one to death, the other to an illness even the doctors don't fully understand – she felt as if she'd lost all control.

How she envies Kostja, floating freely on his back. Logic fails her, but she feels somehow – loosened from her old self. But not enough to race into the water and romp with Kostja.

Hovering above him, a very small red and black bird. He

whistles, and the bird – maybe a vermillion flycatcher? – seems to answer, its song like laughter, the notes ascending then descending before it flies away.

But: another missed opportunity?

He is constant, loyal to his wife, and that's only part of his attraction.

Signe doesn't know much about his daily life here. She imagines his woman bellied up to the stove in a communal kitchen left over from Soviet times. He likely doesn't wash his own socks, make his own soup.

If she hustles, she'll have time to find a gift for Tapani in the tourist kiosk. Maybe a fur hat he'll never wear, unless it's big enough to fit over the helmet that stops him from banging his head on the floor or walls. In Moscow, she'll look for a three-stringed balalaika for him.

Without a farewell, since he's so absorbed in splashing about in the water, Signe turns away, but stops, trying to decide which way to go to find the tourist kiosk. And she hears the hoofbeats first, like the muffled sound of the four o'clock train crossing the trestle near Patchgrove School when heard through a downy pillow. In summer, it always awakened her from her afternoon nap, and she imagined its wheels wrapped in rags so it wouldn't disturb her mother and aunt. Viewed from the bottom of the garden or from the swimming hole near the beaver dam, the train seemed to float above the poplar and spruce. But it isn't the Livelong train she sees through the mists of the imagined past or even through the flying spray cast up by hooves galumphing along the shore of Lake Onega. Surely, it's a mirage, as wavering and dappled with sunlight as any oasis seen through eyes of a desert traveller. Foaming nostrils. Tossing heads. The bunch and ripple of muscle. The thud of bone on a weed-strewn shore, the hooves unshod. And here they come, straight for Signe, the smallest horses in anyone's world, east or west, so close now she can see the lead stallion's dorsal stripes, the tiger colouration of Thor, how he calls his mares to follow him. Of course, none of this can be real, it's the ghost of her mother's favourite horse come in search of her, to give her comfort, and she almost fails to step back, out of his way, as he dashes past her, his head tossing in recognition she only imagines, the nickering meant for those who follow him, not Signe. Jumping back, her feet sink in the soft shore, water filling her shoes, and she almost loses her balance, dropping her shoulderbag, but catching its straps before it hits the water. Bits of sod and spray and weeds flying up, the ponies flash by, veering and winding in and out of the shallow shore. It's a joyous romp and gallop, but not without purpose if only Signe knew their destination, their quest. Not so many, less than a dozen, but they're Tarpans for certain, perhaps descendants of Thor that hid in the woods or were deliberately left by Lena and Pytor, for a reason that escapes Signe. She has lost her breath. And the last one, as golden as a palomino but so many hands shorter, the mane and tail albino white. Such huge, bulging eyes. She's young, spindle-legged, but so spirited she swings her head, and then leaps like an Arab taught to dance, and she's coming straight on, right towards Signe, who has never looked any horse in the eye before, having always approached the Livelong nags from the side before mounting them, and suddenly she's less afraid that this horse won't stop but will charge right into her and hit her in belly and chest and flip her high into the air and over her head than she is of the fierce recognition. This Gotlandruss knows who Signe is, she's claiming her for her own, and if she had arms she'd throw them around Signe's neck. Clutching her bag to her chest, Signe backs up just as the pony halts before her, snuffling. She tosses her head, lips curled back, and nickers. Barely aware of the pain in her throat, how hard it is to breathe, Signe stammers: "Sorry. If only. An apple. I don't have – anything – to give you." And this makes her eyes well up, and she tastes salt, her chest caving in and knees buckling; she sinks into the water, it's cold enough to make her shiver, goosebumps erupting on the backs of her arms. It's just deep enough to cover her legs and soak her shoes, the small waves lapping against her thighs. The horse snorts, tosses her beautiful head, and bounds away, looking back only once, as if calling the others and telling them they missed an important moment in the isolation of their island lives.

And there is Kostja, lifting her by her armpits, wanting to know if she's fine. "You want to swim? Put on bathing costume. At least take off clothes."

"I would scare the horses." she says, laughing and crying at the same time.

He plunks her down on the shore. "Watch out! Do not sit on horse plops."

"Thor's descendants," she says. "Could be." In Lena's story, the mares had been covered by Odin, and if it takes eleven months for gestation the first foals would have been born in May.

"What is doing?" Kostja says.

Every winter after that, more forest horses were lost when they crossed the Ice, but Thor would have sired some ponies born each spring, and maybe some strayed or were deliberately left behind with Father Victor. If only Lena were still alive to tell Signe if those disappearing ponies are Russian Tarpans or real Gotlandrussen.

SIGNE

"You are fine." This time, it isn't a question. "Nice and wet. You should go in *banya* first, then water, not water then *banya*." He tries to make the joke. But Signe realizes that her clothes are sopping and lake water dribbles down the sides of her cheeks.

And she bawls, long and hard, howling for Sasha and Tapani, but unthreatened by the waters lapping at her sopping shoes. "I had nothing," she says. "Not even a cookie crumb from lunch."

"Horses don't look so hungry," he says, squatting beside her. He picks a long grass, chews on it, squinting against the light haloed against the spires of Nestor's silver church. Then he says something in Russian she doesn't fully understand: "*Vsego samogo khoroshego*." Without translating she hears the words: wish and beautiful. To her, he's saying something more than *all the best,* in a less formal way, and she recognizes it's something he would say to his family or closest friend. He says something else about a red – no, beautiful – experience, and ends with: "*Obnimayu*." It means hugs. With her father it was always a warning: *Bear is coming to get you!*

Kostja swings around behind her, takes her in his arms, and holds her tight until she lets the tension flow out of her limbs and sags against him, her left cheek on his smooth shoulder. He places his sopping head on her right cheek, lake water dribbles onto her forehead and merges with the tears running down the side of her face. Her wet shoes reach only just past his knees. They could be riding double, slowly homeward after a Sunday picnic at the lake. He shivers from cold, but she doesn't want him to let go of her.

Further down the shore, the small herd of prehistoric horses bounds away, their tails and unshod hooves flashing as silver as the spire on the Kizhi church.

"Real, they were so real," Signe says.

"Not to be afraid," Kostja says.

"I wasn't afraid of the horses," she says, glad he cannot see her crimson face. Yet, she casts her head aside and folds her hands across her mouth.

He says, "I think it is not so much water that frightens you." He's shaking now, and needs his clothes, a hot drink beside a fire, but his concern is only for her. "When you face it, the thing you fear most, it disappears like fast horses, yes. And then you are free too."

"First I see my Russian aunt who isn't there, then horses from my mother's past."

"Too much you struggle," he says, "but I see you are better now, in this place of healing, it happens sometimes. Is good, no?"

"I have been here before," she says. "I lived here the first five years of my life."

"Is good, very good for you, but not so good if you catch cold and can't enjoy rest of trip with American peasants." He lets his arms fall, she's loathe to be released, but when he rises she takes his offered hand and lets him lift her to her feet. Steady now.

"I must find a gift for my son," she says. "Maybe a miniature horse, if such a thing is to be found here. Sadly, he's not too old in his head for such a plaything."

"I be seeing you," Kostja says, "*P'aka,*" and he leaves her to find her own way back to the ship. Once she looks back: he's racing back to the Russian *banya* for his clothes.

She didn't find a *staret,* but then, she didn't really look, expecting one to jump out of the water – or walk on it straight for her.

Never mind, the trip is not over yet.

SIGNE

She steps carefully around steaming horse buns beset with swarming flies. Her shoes squeak.

ON THE WAY TO THE KIOSK, Signe hears the fluting call of the vermillion flycatcher, from the highest branch of a linden. A hidden light dapples the leaves. *Say good morning to the trees.*

She turns off the path, makes her way across cropped grass to the field of yellow flowers facing the lake. The light turns the aspen church into silver.

She has been here before!

Signe, say good morning to the bird. Dobre outre, ptitsa.

The flycatcher lifts off, calling again.

Petals and seeds brush against her drying skirt, burrs stick to her wet shoes and socks. The wind from the lake is chilly, waves white-crested. Gulls patrol, looking for fish. Butterflies flit and hover over yellow flowers.

Signe, say good morning to the butterfly. Dobre outre, babochka!

Signe plucks a yellow flower, just holds it in steady hands, gazing at the broad expanse of the lake, the light haloed over the church.

Again, Signe sees the child. She's riding on her father's shoulders, so high she can touch a leaf, saying, *Birches, to you good morning.* She kisses the leaf. She likes so much leaves and flowers and starts to pay attention to butterflies, their sun-shiny flittering. Every morning is like this, her father's hands tight on her ankles, *Hang on tight, Lybatsa. Can you make that sound, like frogs,* kva-kva, kva? *Dobre outre, Lyagushka! Good morning, Frog!* Until all the bright world sings, the silver aspen, its shining leaves wet with kisses from the night, the grumpy frogs wanting to sleep in but awakened by birds, their song of morning for this daughter of Pytor Svetlov, daughter of light.

THIS LAST MORNING IN MOSCOW, Kostja strides down the corridor on the second deck, causing a stir among birders shopping for last gifts in the reception area. The way he swaggers, he might be a red Cossack or one of the Chevaliers Gardes in white, with a red cape, high jackboots and a silver helmet surrounded by a shining double eagle. He finds Signe before the window of the *Priboy*'s gift shop. He stands, feet planted wide apart, hands on hips, as if blocking her escape out the portal to the deck.

Signe fingers the scarlike lines radiating from his left eye. "It looks like you were clawed by a cougar."

"Just from the sun."

"But you have lines only around one eye."

"From squinting into the camera."

Like Kostja, on this voyage Signe built a lookout platform, his eyes her binoculars.

She will take home a twig, a feather, a scrap of paper and create a nest of words in a letter to him that he will never understand.

"I don't really know you. I only understand you from watching and listening, from what I see and absorb about you from your land." Signe can't look at him now; she drops her head, folds her hands. "I only take home a part of your culture, your language, a particle of your land, its enormity." She takes a deep breath, unsure of the wisdom of telling him how she really feels about him. "Kostja, you are my first and only Russian friend. I will never see you again. When I get home I will hear news of your country – and wonder how you are."

"Oh I will write and tell you I am fine."

"Tell me a lie now." That everything will be *korosho,* not just when she arrives home, but forever after.

"For you I will tell really big lies." He spreads his hands. "Sometimes I write and write and get carried away and cannot stop." He shakes his head, and a tuft of hair falls on his forehead. She wants to smooth his brow. Heat rises in his face; he's as scarlet as a red tanager. Slowly, they've been moving towards the stairs.

"You are in terrible danger," she says.

His face lights up, as if clouds across the steppes have cleared away, enabling a glorious new sun to be seen, finally, after too many days of winter darkness. "What shall we do about it?"

"Run!"

"I haven't signed my book for you." He backs down the stairs.

"I'll get it. What cabin are you in?"

"There." Right beside the gift kiosk.

"I'll be right back."

WITHIN MINUTES, SHE TAPS ON HIS DOOR. He opens it, offers her a glass of wine, without ceremony and almost perfunctorily, as if it's just a matter of being a polite host. What could have happened in the last ten minutes or less to dissolve or change the feeling erupting between them?

She says, "No, thank you." She perches on his bunk, intending to leave quickly.

He's almost packed, his laptop closed in its case, his dufflebag gapes open, and something makes him take from it a photograph and hand it to her. "My wife."

"She looks like a little girl!" The botanist squats over a potted tomato, one elbow on a knee, squinting up as if annoyed at being disturbed or distracted from her work. Her reddish hair, much darker than Signe's, is done up in many pookie-tails, short and stiff as whisk brooms. She doesn't look very happy. But the photograph remind Signe that she is no longer young, and therefore, likely not attractive to any man even if he is her own age.

"She has two children, five and seven. Soon we have – how do you say? – a herd! My first wife, she died four years ago."

"How long have you been married to – the second?" Why won't he tell Signe her name?

"A year and a half." And now, a baby, in just a week or two born into his Cradle of Sadness.

Frantically, he shoves a book on Japanese birds into his duffle bag, a stray sock he finds in front of the gaping cupboard door, the returned photograph. There's enough time before they dock in Moscow for him to finish his packing. What is making him so anxious? Surely, he's not afraid of his new Canadian friend.

Now. Now would be a good time to tell him about Sasha, how she will never stop missing her. She could tell him about Tapani, his illness another kind of loss, how she will always wish for something better for him, but no longer misdirect her fear onto water. But she no longer needs to talk about it – to anyone. She doesn't need to look for a *staret* since she found the memory of Father Viktor at Kizhi. This morning she sang her father's favourite song in the shower: *Ostsvetali yabloni I grushi, uplyli tumani nad rkoi* – apple and pear trees have lost their blossoms, the river mists have vanished – *Ukhadyila z byergega Katyusha, unasyila pyseenku damoi* – Katyushka left the river bank and took her little song back home.

Signe was born on the Ice. It means she's a survivor, but it took a trip to Lake Ladoga and the island of Kizhi on Lake Onega to learn the truth of it.

SIGNE

"Experience has bred in us that there is a limit to what the human can understand – or change," he says, rising. "Always we must accept the tragic as well as joy." He's not just referring to the death of his first wife. Russians talk in universals, not specifics. Signe learned that from Pytor, who couldn't unlock his own pain and show it to her. How afraid he must have been for his pony-girl giving birth on the Ice. He was a *zornie* transported from Russia to a different land and culture, but still steeling himself against his fear and anger at the political powers that made him an orphan of that state – but surely not at his daughter, Signe.

"I must go." The buses are waiting to take the tourists to the Moscow circus, the last event of the tour. Signe lifts her arms, circles them around his neck, just holding him because not everything must be said. This is about comforting only, the strength of the spirit Lena found here – and in Lena and Pytor and Maryushka – anything else as superficial as the song of fake gypsies.

And then Signe understands: the love of this land has so filled her half-Russian soul, she sought someone else to guide her and give it expression for her. Instead of a holy fool she found Kostja. She will remember him birding among the linden and beech, photographing the sparkling, vibrant cupolas and domes in Uglich, the latticework peasant house in Kizhi – and suffer *the home-longing*.

For the first time, she wonders if she has never recovered from being uprooted from the land of her birth. Just like her father before her.

THE FLYING CRANES HAVE RETURNED to Moscow's Sparrows Hill. They bring their own light, their flight the greatest sighting. Beneath the dome of a sanctuary refound, their calling an

orchestration of fallen soldiers who turned into white cranes and flew away.
Searchlights turn their feathers, faces blue.
With each release, flight becomes a joining of palms chalked white, a flip in the air, every bird wings back to its perch.
This last flight a hymn to the rescue of fallen soldiers.
Five Cranes spin, spectres hung under the temple dome, the last pulleyed up and up, to the top of the sky.
Another release, the last bird-becoming-human again falls, dives headfirst towards the net, a somersault, he lands on blue feet, winged arms raised so peace may prevail in Russia.
Now Signe can return home.

HOME AGAIN. In the bird sanctuary Signe photographs the solitary swan to send to her first and only Russian friend, Kostja. She wants him to understand why she felt so at home in his country, why she now suffers what her mother called *the home-longing*.

But she will never be able to articulate – in words or photos – what happened to her in his northland. The journey she had imagined – meeting an Old Believer – was not the same as the real trip to Russia where she stood on the verge of Ladoga and was not transformed so much as changed, little by little, from a frightened bird with clipped wings to one hopping from stone to rock to stone across Canadian Lake Katepwa without losing balance and toppling into brackish algae-clogged water.

The sanctuary, a part of man-made Wascana Lake, is sheltered by hand-planted elm, cottonwood, birch and pine, also indigenous to the shores of Lake Ladoga, the Neva and Volga rivers, her newly found place of belonging. The page-wire fence, with its wrought-iron turnstile, keeps out unwanted nocturnal visitors, not the birds who could escape it easily.

A yellow school bus deposits a horde of young invaders, and the birds retreat to the middle of their pools where children cannot reach them. Clutching plastic bread bags, the screaming kids descend on the birds, the boys hucking bits of broken bread. "I hit one!" hollers a redhead. The girls crouch on the wooden deck, wanting the birds to eat out of their hands, their calling and cooing ignored by the feathered, well-fed population of the park.

Signe retreats, crossing the footbridge connecting ponds, and is nearly trampled by five hissing boys chasing a wobbling goose missing one wing. It hobbles to the edge of the bridge, then leaps into the water, and swims frantically to join the mallards, while the regal swan patrols the perimeter. Disdainfully bypassing blobs of bread tossed at it, it feeds on water insects skimming the murky surface.

Her Swedish/Russian blood boils with the memory of a siege not her own, and, like Lena and Pytor and Maryushka before her, she sits on a wooden bench to outwit, outwait, outlast the invaders.

Poplars shiver at the sight of a shattered peace, as a northern wind rises – so unusually cold for the end of June – and she buttons her polar-fleece cardigan. The fleet of mallards hold their line in the middle of the pond, flanked by two sentinel geese. On the opposite embankment, white ducks feed on new tendrils of grass struggling to thrive on prairie gumbo packed down hard by rain and pummelling feet. This earth needs topsoil, peat moss, a sun shower. She doesn't understand why the birds don't fly away – maybe as far as the steppes.

In that clear blue sky, a few scattered clouds look like spirits of birds looking down at the plight of their descendants, with sad eyes and drooping, elongated necks.

This is what Signe's father's Russia – and Kostja, the birdman – did to her: turned her into a cockeyed birder.

Where are the finches, siskins, thrushes and chiff-chaffs of that northern land now her own? Oh where is Kostja's blue throat, the sight of which thrilled the birders on their last day in Russia?

The ducks crane their necks, as if hoping the school bus will depart soon. The swan preens, picking at bird lice, then rises in the water, like a ballerina on points, shaking water from its feathers. The willows lean towards the water as if protecting the swan hiding now in shadow. Crouching, Signe focuses her camera, trying out the eye-to-eye technique so evident in the photographs Kostja took during the St. Petersburg-Moscow tour and emailed her this morning.

What is she doing here now? Surrounded by goose shit, shivering on a splintered bench, watching a bedraggled swan bereft of a mate or signets, Signe looks up, and in that vast prairie sky she sees a Russian church, its cupolas and domes shrouded in snow, and stretching forever beyond it, the frozen steppes, an empty troika pulled by three white horses. In the foreground, a figure, impossible to tell if it's the spirit of a man or woman, but within a single breath, it kneels, taking a photograph of a night. White.

Time to head home to make Tapani's lunch. He acted up a little when Signe returned, pouting and refusing to speak to her. When Signe asked him if he had composed any new songs, he looked stricken, and dashed outside, patrolling the back yard, head cocked in a listening attitude, as if hearing music in the rustle of the elms. Later, wearing his grandfather Pytor's cross on a new chain she'd brought him from Moscow, he began to compose a new song of loss.

Now, in the parking lot near the Centre of the Arts, Signe unlocks her Land Rover, climbs into the driver's seat, but doesn't turn the ignition. She leans back, for one last look at the sanctuary. Above the shelter belt, wind-torn clouds re-invent a great white bird, driven out of the blue, its long beak and crested crown like a stork's. Spirit Feathers, like the Russian Firebird's falling to earth, the sight enough to make Signe believe in the legend told to her by Maryushka, how the honest peasant girl she was named for turned into the bird of many colours and her feathers covered the earth. Wing bones vibrate like strings of a cello, their music in the wind. A hole in its breast diminishes with each wind-breath, until it closes; healed.

It's impossible to see where the land ends and the ice begins, where the ice yields to sky until spectres appear on the horizon, then lighten and enlarge themselves like crystals shaping into starflakes, the silhouettes white and heaving large, frost and snow puff up from high-stepping, fast-flying hoofs. White on white, their breaths steaming. The first sound the scrape and swish of runners on ice, the shout of the trailbreaker, *faster faster, we're almost home*. And here they come, the ponies of Gotland! Through the shimmering mirage: blankets of snow, frosted manes. Slivers of ice clinging to shanks and dorsal stripes. They brave bullets from diving Heinkels, strain against the weight of sledges and troikas. They bear the first survivors from Leningrad, cadaver-thin. And somewhere bells ring, enough to fill the whole white sky.

Then the great wind-borne wings swoop down, touch tip-to-tip, as if they would capture Signe, lift her, and carry her back to Russia where she was born on the Ice.

Acknowledgements

While researching my second novel, *The Last Echo,* I discovered the descendants of the prehistoric horse, the Gotlandrussen, and gave one blue forest horse named Lara a cameo appearance, but I never forgot them. It was only when I learned that engineers tested the ice on Lake Ladoga with a light horse that I knew I must invent the story of a heroic trek across the Ice Road.

Before anyone else, I wish to thank my husband, Ron, for taking me to Russia, where I found Lena's and Pytor's and Maryushka's story, then to Gotland to see the Lojsta moor and the forest horses numbering two thousand today. I will also never forget the kindness of the caretaker who answered my questions with patience, our driver who taught me key phrases in Gutamål, and Nils, the furniture maker from Gotenburg who became my long-lost brother.

Dr. Konstantin Mikhailov of Moscow, my first Russian friend, gave me far more than my first lessons in Russian. From him I gleaned the spirit of that great and long-suffering nation. The Russian songs used here were given to me by him. The Swedish references I learned at my grandmother's and mother's knee while they sang me to sleep in my Livelong home.

I'm forever grateful to Sandra Birdsell for her encouragement, her sharp insights and fresh approach to story, alerting me to the changes my characters go through from the moment they embark on their journeys to their closure.

Britt Holmstrom, originally from my own grandmother's stomping ground of Malmo, keeps me from veering on the trail of the Scanian dialect and led me to the Gutamål.

I also wish to thank the Bees – Annette Bower, Shelley Banks, Leeann Monique, James Twettwer, Linda Biasotto and Anne Larko – for their monthly encouragment and keen criticism of much of this novel.

Before the novel, many paragraphs began as prose-poems, all of which were critiqued by the Poets' Combine: Gary Hyland, Robert Currie, Judith Krause, Bruce Rice and Paul Wilson.

I have stolen the name but not the character of Signe from my only aunt, a woman as strong as the valkyrie she was named for, who took me swimming in the Turtle River, and gave me other memories of her love to cherish.

Finally, my deepest gratitude to Jack Hodgins, the bird on my shoulder, whose guidance and patience and depth of understanding reflects back to me on every page.

Thanks to the Saskatchewan Writers Guild and Weyerhauser of Prince Albert for offering the John V. Hicks Long Manuscript Award in 2005.

An excerpt from the last chapter, entitled "Bird Santuary" was published in *Regina Secret Spaces: Love and Lore of Local Geography:* Beug, Lorne; Campbell, Anne; Mah, Jeannie, editors. Regina; Canadian Plains Research Centre. 2006.

Among the many sources of research for this novel, I wish to acknowledge: *The 900 Days: The Siege of Leningrad,* Harrison Salisbury, Harper & Row, 1971; *GULAG: A History,* Anne Applebaurm, Anchor House, 2003; *Land of the Firebird: The Beauty of Old Russia,* Suzanne Massie, Heart Tree Press, 1980; and *Ice Road,* Gillian Slovo, Little Brown, 2004.

About the Author

Byrna Barclay is the award-winning author of novels, short story collections and a playscript. *The Forest Horses* was the recipient of the John V. Hicks manuscript award. Her story collection *Crosswinds* received the Saskatchewan Fiction Award, while *Girl at the Window* was a finalist for the same award. Her first novel, *Summer of the Hungry Pup* received the Saskatchewan First Novel Award, while "Speak Under Covers" was named a most distinguished story by *Best American Short Stories*. Her drama *Room With Five Walls* received the City of Regina Award.

Byrna Barclay received the Saskatchewan Order of Merit in 2005. She lives in Regina.

 **Mixed Sources**
Cert no. SW-COC-001271
© 1996 FSC

 **ENVIRONMENTAL BENEFITS STATEMENT**

Coteau Books saved the following resources by printing the pages of this book on chlorine free paper made with 100% post-consumer waste.

TREES	WATER	SOLID WASTE	GREENHOUSE GASES
21 FULLY GROWN	9,809 GALLONS	596 POUNDS	2,037 POUNDS

 Calculations based on research by Environmental Defense and the Paper Task Force. Manufactured at Friesens Corporation